I0784593

Marah Ellis Ryan

The Treasure Trail

OK Publishing 2021

Marah Ellis Ryan
The Treasure Trail

The Story of the Land of Gold and Sunshine

Published by
MUSAICUM
Books

- Advanced Digital Solutions & High-Quality book Formatting -

musaicumbooks@okpublishing.info

2021 OK Publishing

ISBN 978-80-272-7583-0

Contents

CHAPTER I KIT AND THE GIRL OF THE LARK CALL — 11

CHAPTER II THE RED GOLD LEGEND — 17

CHAPTER III A VERIFIED PROPHECY OF SEÑORITA BILLIE — 32

CHAPTER IV IN THE ADOBE OF PEDRO VIJIL — 37

CHAPTER V AN "ADIOS" —- AND AFTER — 40

CHAPTER VI A DEAD MAN UNDER THE COTTONWOODS — 47

CHAPTER VII IN THE PROVINCE OF ALTAR — 54

CHAPTER VIII THE SLAVE TRAIL — 61

CHAPTER IX A MEETING AT YAQUI WELL — 65

CHAPTER X A MEXICAN EAGLET — 70

CHAPTER XI GLOOM OF BILLIE — 77

CHAPTER XII COVERING THE TRAIL — 79

CHAPTER XIII A WOMAN OF EMERALD EYES — 87

CHAPTER XIV THE HAWK OF THE SIERRAS — 99

CHAPTER XV THE "JUDAS" PRAYER AT MESA BLANCA — 104

CHAPTER XVI THE SECRET OF SOLEDAD CHAPEL — 114

CHAPTER XVII THE STORY OF DOÑA JOCASTA — 126

CHAPTER XVIII RAMON ROTIL DECIDES — 131

CHAPTER XIX THE RETURN OF TULA — 142

CHAPTER XX EAGLE AND SERPENT — 149

CHAPTER XXI EACH TO HIS OWN — 155

CHAPTER I
KIT AND THE GIRL OF THE LARK CALL

In the shade of Pedro Vijil's little brown adobe on the Granados rancho, a horseman squatted to repair a broken cinch with strips of rawhide, while his horse —- a strong dappled roan with a smutty face —- stood near, the rawhide bridle over his head and the quirt trailing the ground.

The horseman's frame of mind was evidently not of the sweetest, for to Vijil he had expressed himself in forcible Mexican —- which is supposed to be Spanish and often isn't —- condemning the luck by which the cinch had gone bad at the wrong time, and as he tinkered he sang softly an old southern ditty:

> Oh —- oh! I'm a good old rebel,
> Now that's just what I am!
>
> For I won't be reconstructed
> And I don't care a damn!

He varied this musical gem occasionally by whistling the air as he punched holes and wove the rawhide thongs in and out through the spliced leather.

Once he halted in the midst of a strain and lifted his head, listening. Something like an echo of his own notes sounded very close, a mere shadow of a whistle.

Directly over his head was a window, unglazed and wooden barred. A fat brown olla, dripping moisture, almost filled the deep window sill, but the interior was all in shadow. Its one door was closed. The Vijil family was scattered around in the open, most of them under the *ramada*, and after a frowning moment of mystification the young fellow resumed his task, but in silence.

Then, after a still minute, more than the whisper of a whistle came to him —- the subdued sweet call of a meadow lark. It was so sweet it might have been mate to any he had heard on the range that morning.

Only an instant he hesitated, then with equal care he gave the duplicate call, and held his breath to listen —- not a sound came back.

"We've gone loco, Pardner," he observed to the smutty-faced roan moving near him. "That jolt from the bay outlaw this morning has jingled my brain pans —- we don't hear birds call us —- we only think we do."

If he had even looked at Pardner he might have been given a sign, for the roan had lifted its head and was staring into the shadows back of the sweating olla.

"Hi, you caballero!"

The words were too clear to be mistaken, the "caballero" stared across to the only people in sight. There was Pedro Vijil sharpening an axe, while Merced, his wife, turned the creaking grindstone for him. The young olive branches of the Vijil family were having fun with a horned toad under the *ramada* where gourd vines twisted about an ancient grape, and red peppers hung in a gorgeous splash of color. Between that and the blue haze of the far mountains there was no sign of humanity to account for such cheery youthful Americanism as the tone suggested.

"Hi, yourself!" he retorted, "whose ghost are you?"

There was a giggle from the barred window of the adobe.

"I don't dare say because I am not respectable just now," replied the voice. "I fell in the ditch and have nothing on but the Sunday shirt of Pedro. I am the funniest looking thing! wish I dared ride home in it to shock them all silly."

"Why not?" he asked, and again the girlish laugh gave him an odd thrill of comradeship.

"A good enough reason; they'd take Pat from me, and say he wasn't safe to ride —- but he is! My tumble was my own fault for letting them put on that fool English saddle. Never again for me!"

"They are all right for old folks and a pacing pony," he observed, and again he heard the bubbling laugh.

"Well, Pat is not a pacing pony, not by a long shot; and I'm not old folks —- yet!" Then after a little silence, "Haven't you any curiosity?"

"I reckon there's none allowed me on this count," he replied without lifting his head, "between the wooden bars and Pedro's shirt you certainly put the fences up on me."

"I'm a damsel in distress waiting for a rescuing knight with a white banner and a milk-white steed —- " went on the laughing voice in stilted declamation.

"Sorry, friend, but my cayuse is a roan, and I never carried a white flag yet. You pick the wrong colors."

Whereupon he began the chanting of a war song, with an eye stealthily on the barred window.

> Hurrah! Hurrah! For southern rights, hurrah!
> Hurrah for the bonnie blue flag
> That bears the single star!

"Oh! *I* know that!" the voice was now a hail of recognition. "Cap Pike always sings that when he's a little 'how-came-ye-so' —- and *you're* a Johnny Reb!"

"Um! twice removed," assented the man by the wall, "and you are a raiding Yank who has been landed in one of our fortresses with only one shirt to her back, and that one borrowed."

He had a momentary vision of two laughing gray eyes beside the olla, and the girl behind the bars laughed until Merced let the grindstone halt while she cast a glance towards the house as if in doubt as to whether three feet of adobe wall and stout bars could serve instead of a dueña to foolish young Americans who chattered according to their foolishness.

There was an interval of silence, and then the girlish voice called again.

"Hi, Johnny Reb!"

"Same to you, Miss Yank."

"Aren't you the new Americano from California, for the La Partida rancho?"

"Even so, O wise one of the borrowed garment." The laugh came to him again.

"Why don't you ask how I know?" she demanded.

"It is borne in upon me that you are a witch of the desert, or the ghost of a dream, that you see through the adobe wall, and my equally thick skull. Far be it for me to doubt that the gift of second sight is yours, O seventh daughter of a seventh daughter!"

"No such thing! I'm the only one!" came the quick retort, and the young chap in the shade of the adobe shook with silent mirth.

"I see you laughing, Mr. Johnny Reb, you think you caught me that time. But you just halt and listen to me, I've a hunch and I'm going to prophesy."

"I knew you had the gift of second sight!"

"Maybe you won't believe me, but the hunch is that you —- won't —- hold —- the job on these ranches!"

"What!" and he turned square around facing the window, then laughed. "That's the way you mean to get even for the 'seventh daughter' guess is it? You think I can't handle horses?"

"Nix," was the inelegant reply, "I know you can, for I saw you handle that bay outlaw they ran in on you this morning: seven years old and no wrangler in Pima could ride him. Old Cap Pike said it was a damn shame to put you up against that sun-fisher as an introduction to Granados."

"Oh! Pike did, did he? Nice and sympathetic of Pike. I reckon he's the old-time ranger I heard about out at the Junction, reading a red-fire riot to some native sons who were not keen for the cactus trail of the Villistas. That old captain must be a live wire, but he thinks I can't stick?"

"No-o, that wasn't Cap Pike, that was my own hunch. Say, are you married?"

"O señorita! this is so sudden!" he spoke in shy reproof, twisting his neckerchief in mock embarrassment, and again Merced looked toward the house because of peals of laughter there.

"You are certainly funny when you do that," she said after her laughter had quieted down to giggles, "but I wasn't joking, honest Indian I wasn't! But how did you come to strike Granados?"

"Me? Well, I ranged over from California to sell a patch of ground I owned in Yuma. Then I hiked over to Nogales on a little *pasear* and offered to pack a gun and wear a uniform for this Mexican squabble, and the powers that be turned me down because one of my eyes could see farther than the other —- that's no joke —- it's a calamity! I spent all the *dinero* I had recovering from the shock, and about the time I was getting my sympathetic friends sobered up, Singleton, of Granados, saw us trying out some raw cavalry stock, and bid for my valuable services and I rode over. Any other little detail you'd like to know?"

"N-no, only needed to know it wasn't Conrad the manager hired you, and I asked if you were married because married men need the work more than single strays. Adolf Conrad got rid of two good American men lately, and fetches over Mexicans from away down Hermosillo way."

"'Cause why?" asked the man who had ceased pretense of mending the saddle, and was standing with back against the adobe.

"'Cause I don't know," came petulant response. "I only had the hunch when I saw you tame that outlaw in the corral. If he pulls wires to lose *you*, I'll stop guessing; I'll know!"

"Very interesting, señorita," agreed the stranger reflectively. "But if I have a good job, I can't see how it will give me aid or comfort to know that you've acquired knowledge, and stopped guessing. When's your time up behind the bars?"

"Whenever my clothes get dry enough to fool the dear home folks."

"You must be a joy to the bosom of your family," he observed, "also a blessing."

He heard again the girlish laughter and concluded she could not be over sixteen. There was silence for a space while only the creak of the grindstone cut the stillness. Whoever she was, she had given him a brief illuminating vision of the tactics of Conrad, the manager for the ranches of Granados and La Partida, the latter being the Sonora end of the old Spanish land grant. Even a girl had noted that the rough work had been turned over to a new American from the first circle of the *rodeo*. He stood there staring out across the sage green to the far purple hills of the Green Springs range.

"You've fixed that cinch, what you waiting for?" asked the voice at last, and the young fellow straightened up and lifted the saddle.

"That's so," he acknowledged. "But as you whistled to me and the call seemed friendly, it was up to me to halt for orders —- from the lady in distress."

Again he heard the soft laughter and the voice.

"Glad you liked the friendly call, Johnny Reb," she confessed. "That's my call. If ever you hear it where there are no larks, you'll know who it is."

"Sure," he agreed, yanking at the cinch, "and I'll come a lopin' with the bonnie blue flag, to give aid and succor to the enemy."

"You will not!" she retorted. "You'll just whistle back friendly, and be chums. I think my clothes are dry now, and you'd better travel. If you meet anyone looking for a stray maverick, you haven't seen me."

"Just as you say. *Adios!*"

After he had mounted and passed along the corral to the road, he turned in the saddle and looked back. He could see no one in the window of the bars, but there came to him clear and sweet the field bugle of the meadow lark.

He answered it, lifted his sombrero and rode soberly towards the Granados corrals, three miles across the valley. Queer little trick she must be. American girls did not usually ride abroad alone along the border, and certainly did not chum with the Mexicans to the extent of borrowing shirts. Then as he lifted the bridle and Pardner broke into a lope, he noted an elderly horseman jogging along across trail on a little mule. Each eyed the other appraisingly.

"Hello, Bub!" hailed the older man. "My name's Pike, and you're the new man from California, hey? Glad to meet you. Hear your name's Rhodes."

"I reckon you heard right," agreed the young chap. "K. Rhodes at your service, sir."

"Hello! K? K? Does that K stand for Kit?"

"Center shot for you," assented the other.

"From Tennessee?"

"Now you're a sort of family historian, I reckon, Mr. Pike," suggested K. Rhodes. "What's the excitement?"

"Why you young plantation stray!" and the older man reached for his hand and made use of it pump-handle fashion with a sort of sputtering glee. "Great guns, boy! there was just one K. Rhodes a-top of God's green earth and we were pardners here in Crook's day. Hurrah for us! Are you cousin, son, or nephew?"

"My grandfather was with Crook."

"Sure! I knew it soon as I laid eyes on you and heard your name; that was in the corral with the outlaw Conrad had driven in for you to work, it wa'n't a square deal to a white man. I was cussin' mad."

"So I heard," and the blue eyes of the other smiled at the memory of the girl's glib repetition of his discourse. "What's the great idea? Aside from the fact that he belongs to the white dove, anti-military bunch of sisters, Singleton seems quite white, a nice chap."

"Yeh, but he's noways wise at that. He sort of married into the horse game here, wasn't bred to it. Just knows enough to not try to run it solo. Now this Dolf Conrad does know horses and the horse market, and Granados rancho. He's shipped more cavalry stock to France than any other outfit in this region. Yes, Conrad knows the business end of the game, but even at that he might not assay as high grade ore. He is mixed up with them too-proud-to-fight clique organized by old maids of both sexes, and to show that he is above all prejudice, political or otherwise, he sure is corraling an extra lot of Mex help this year. I've *companeros* I'd go through hell for, but Conrad's breed —— well, enough said, Bub, but they're different!" Mr. Pike bit off a chew of black plug, and shook his head ruminatively.

Rhodes looked the old man over as they rode along side by side. He was lean, wiry and probably sixty-five. His hair, worn long, gave him the look of the old-time ranger. He carried no *reata* and did not look like a ranchman. He had the southern intonation, and his eyes were wonderfully young for the almost snowy hair.

"Belong in the valley, Captain?"

"Belong? Me belong anywhere? Not yet, son," and he smiled at his own fancy. "Not but what it's a good enough corner when a man reaches the settlin' down age. I drift back every so often. This ranch was Fred Bernard's, and him and me flocked together for quite a spell. Singleton married Bernard's widow —— she's dead now these seven years. I just drift back every so often to keep track of Bernard's kid, Billie."

"I see. Glad to have met you, Captain. Hope we can ride together often enough for me to hear about the old Apache days. This land has fetched out three generations of us, so it surely has some pull! My father came at the end of his race, but I've come in time to grow up with the country."

Captain Pike looked at him and chuckled. K. Rhodes was about twenty-three, tall, almost boyish in figure, but his shoulders and hands suggested strength, and his mouth had little dents of humor at the corners to mitigate the squareness of jaw and the heavy dark brows. His black lashes made the deep blue of his eyes look purple. Young he was, but with a stature and self-reliant manner as witness of the fact that he was fairly grown up already.

"Where'd you learn horses, Bub?"

"Tennessee stock farm, and southern California ranges. Then this neck of the woods seemed calling me, and I trailed over to look after a bit of land in Yuma. I wasted some time trying to break into the army, but they found some eye defect that I don't know anything about —— and don't more than half believe! I had some dandy prospecting plans after that, but there was no jingling in my pockets —— no outfit money, so I hailed Singleton as an angel monoplaned down with the ducats. Yes sir, I had all the dream survey made for a try at some gold trails down here, going to take it up where the rest of the family quit."

"You mean that, boy?" The old man halted his mule, and spat out the tobacco, staring at Rhodes in eager anticipation.

"I sure do. Reckon I've inherited the fever, and can't settle down to any other thing until I've had one try at it. Did do a little placer working in the San Jacinto."

"And you're broke?" Mr. Pike's voice betrayed a keen joy in the prospect.

"Flat," stated K. Rhodes, eyeing the old gentleman suspiciously, "my horse, saddle, field glass, and gun are the only belongings in sight."

"Ki-yi!" chirruped his new acquaintance gleefully, "I knew when I got out of the blankets this morning I was to have good luck of some sort, had a 'hunch.' You can bet on me, Bub; you've struck the right rail, and I'm your friend, your desert *companero*!"

"Yes, you sound real nice and friendly," agreed K. Rhodes. "So glad I'm flat broke that you're having hysterics over it. Typical southern hospitality. Hearty welcome to our city, and so forth, and so forth!"

The old man grinned at him appreciatively. "Lord boy! —- I reckon I've been waiting around for you about ten year, though I didn't know what your name would be when you come, and it couldn't be a better one! We'll outfit first for the Three Hills of Gold in the desert, and if luck is against us there we'll strike down into Sonora to have a try after the red gold of El Alisal. I've covered some of that ground, but never had a pardner who would stick. They'd beat it because of either the Mexicans or the Indians, but *you* —- say boy! It's the greatest game in the world and we'll go to it!"

His young eyes sparkled in his weathered desert face, and more than ten years were cast aside in his enthusiasm. K. Rhodes looked at him askance.

"If I did not have a key to your sane and calm outlining of prospects for the future, I might suspect loco weed or some other dope," he observed. "But the fact is you must have known that my grandfather in his day went on the trail of the Three Hills of Gold, and left about a dozen different plans on paper for future trips."

"Know it? Why boy, I went in with him!" shrilled Captain Pike. "Know it? Why, we crawled out half starved, and dried out as a couple of last year's gourds. We dug roots and were chewing our own boot tops when the Indians found us. Sure, I know it. He went East to raise money for a bigger outfit, but never got back —- died there."

"Yes, then my father gathered up all the plans and specifications and came out with a friend about fifteen years ago," added Rhodes. "They never got anywhere, but he sort of worked the fever off, bought some land and hit the trail back home. So I've been fairly well fed up on your sort of dope, Captain, and when I've mended that gone feeling in my pocketbook I may 'call' you on the gold trail proposition. Even if you're bluffing there'll be no come back; I can listen to a lot of 'lost mine' vagaries. It sounds like home sweet home to me!"

"Bluff nothing! we'll start next week."

"No we won't, I've got a job and made a promise, got to help clean up the work here for the winter. Promised to take the next load of horses East."

"That's a new one," observed his new friend. "Conrad himself has always gone East with the horses, or sent Brehmen, his secretary. But never mind, Bub, the eastern trip won't take long. I'll be devilin' around getting our outfit and when the chance comes —- us for the Three Hills of Gold!"

"It listens well," agreed K. Rhodes, "cheeriest little *pasear* I've struck in the county. We'll have some great old powwows, even if we don't make a cent, and some day you'll tell me about the mental kinks in the makeup of our Prussian friend, Conrad. He sounds interesting to me."

Captain Pike uttered a profane and lurid word or two concerning Mr. Conrad, and stated he'd be glad when Billie was of age. Singleton, and therefore Conrad, would only have the management up to that time. Billie would know horses if nothing else, and —- Then he interrupted himself and stared back the way he had come.

"I'm a forgetful old fool!" he stated with conviction. "I meandered out to take a look around for her, and I didn't like the looks of that little dab of a saddle Conrad had put on Pat. You didn't see anything of her, did you?"

"What does she look like?"

"A slip of a girl who rides like an Indian, rides a black horse."

"No, I've seen no one," said the young chap truthfully enough. "But who did you say your girl was?"

"You'll find out if you hold your job long enough for her to be of age," said Pike darkly. "She'll be your boss instead of Conrad. It's Billie Bernard, the owner of Granados and La Partida."

"Billie?"

"Miss Wilfreda, if you like it better."

But K. Rhodes said he didn't. Billie seemed to fit the sort of girl who would garb herself in Pedro's shirt and whistle at him through the bars of the little window.

CHAPTER II
THE RED GOLD LEGEND

It took less than a week for Kit Rhodes to conclude that the girl behind the bars had a true inspiration regarding his own position on her ranches. There was no open hostility to him, yet it was evident that difficulties were cleverly put in his way.

Not by Philip Singleton, the colorless, kindly disposed gentleman of Pike's description. But by various intangible methods, he was made to feel an outsider by the manager, Conrad, and his more confidential Mexican assistants. They were punctiliously polite, too polite for a horse-ranch outfit. Yet again and again a group of them fell silent when he joined them, and as his work was with the horse herds of La Partida, that part of the great grant which spread over the border into Sonora, he was often camped fifty miles south of the hacienda of Granados, and saw no more of either the old prospector, or the tantalizing girl of the voice and the whistle.

Conrad, however, motored down two or three times concerning horses for eastern shipment, but Rhodes, the new range capitan, puzzled considerably over those flying visits, for, after the long drive through sand and alkali, the attention he gave either herds or outfit was negligible. In fact he scarcely touched at the camp, yet always did some trifling official act coming or going to make record that he had been there.

The Mexicans called him El Aoura, the buzzard, because no man could tell when he would swoop over even the farthest range of La Partida to catch them napping. Yet there was some sort of curious bond between them for there were times when Conrad came north as from a long southern trail, yet the Mexicans were as dumb men if it was referred to.

He was a compactly built, fair man of less than forty, with thin reddish brown hair, brows slanting downward from the base of the nose, and a profile of that curious Teuton type reminiscent of a supercilious hound if one could imagine such an animal with milk-blue eyes and a yellow mustache with spiky turned-up ends.

But Rhodes did not permit any antipathy he might feel towards the man to interfere with his own duties, and he went stolidly about the range work as if in utter forgetfulness of the dark prophecy of the girl.

If he was to lose his new job he did not mean that it should be from inattention, and nothing was too trifling for his notice. He would do the work of a range boss twelve hours out of the day, and then put in extra time on a night ride to the *cantina* at the south wells of La Partida.

But as the work moved north and the consignment of horses for France made practically complete, old Cap Pike rode down to Granados corrals, and after contemplation of the various activities of Rhodes, climbed up on the corral fence beside him, where the latter was checking off the accepted animals.

"You're a cheerful idiot for work, Bub," agreed the old man, "but what the devil do you gain by doing so much of the other fellow's job? Pancho Martinez wasn't sick as he played off on you; you're green to these Mexican tricks."

"Sure, I'm the original Green from Greenburg," assented his new *companero*. "Pancho was only more than usually drunk last night, while I was fresh as a daisy and eager to enlarge my geographic knowledge, also my linguistics, Hi! Pedro! not the sorrel mare! Cut her out!"

"Linguistics?" repeated Pike impatiently.

"Yeh, nice little woman in the cantina at La Partida wells. I am a willing pupil at Spanish love songs, and we get along fine. I am already a howling success at *La Paloma, La Golondrina,* and a few other sentimental birds."

"Oh, you are, are you?" queried Pike. "Well, take a warning. You'll get a knife in your back from her man one of these fine nights, and the song will be *Adios, adios amores* for you!"

"Nothing doing, Cap! We play *malilla* for the drinks, and I work it so that he beats me two out of three. I'm so easy I'm not worth watching. Women don't fancy fools, so I'm safe."

"Well, I'll be 'strafed' by the Dutch!" Pike stared at the young fellow, frowning in perplexity. "You sure have me puzzled, Bub. Are you a hopeless dunce by training or nature?"

"Natural product," grinned K. Rhodes cheerfully. "Beauty unadorned. Say Cap, tell me something. What is the attraction for friend Conrad south of La Partida? I seem to run against a stone wall when I try to feel out the natives on that point. Now just what lies south, and whose territory?"

The old man looked at him with a new keenness.

"For your sort of an idiot you've blundered on a big interrogation point," he observed. "Did you meet him down there?"

"No, only heard his voice in the night. It's not very easy to mistake that velvety blood-puddin' voice of his, and a team went down to meet him. He seems to go down by another route, railroad I reckon, and comes in by the south ranch. Now just what is south?"

"The ranches of Soledad grant join La Partida, or aim to. There are no maps, and no one here knows how far down over the border the Partida leagues do reach. Soledad was an old mission site, and a fortified hacienda back in the days of Juarez. Its owner was convicted of treason during Diaz' reign, executed, and the ranches confiscated. It is now in the hands of a Federal politician who is safer in Hermosillo. The revolutionists are thick even among the pacificos up here, but the Federals have the most ammunition, and the gods of war are with the guns."

"Sure; and who is the Federal politician? No, not that colt, Marcito!"

"Perez, Don José Perez," stated Pike, giving no heed to corral interpolations. "He claims more leagues than have ever been reckoned or surveyed, took in several Indian rancherias last year when the natives were rounded up and shipped to Yucatan."

"What?"

"Oh, he is in that slave trade good and plenty! They say he is sore on the Yaquis because he lost a lot of money on a boat load that committed suicide as they were sailing from Guaymas."

"A boat load of suicides! Now a couple of dozen would sound reasonable, but a boat load —- —"

"But it happened to every Indian on the boat, and the boat was full! No one knows how the poor devils decided it, but it was their only escape from slavery, and they went over the side like a school of fish. Men, women, and children from the desert who couldn't swim a stroke! Talk about nerve —- there wasn't one weakling in that whole outfit, not one! Perez was wild. It lost him sixty dollars a head, American."

"And that's the neighbor friend Conrad takes a run down south to see occasionally?"

"Who says so, Bub?"

The two looked at each other, eyes questioning.

"Look here, son," said Pike, after a little, "I'll hit any trail with you barring Mexican politics. They all sell each other out as regular as the seasons swing around, and the man north of the line who gets tangled is sure to be victim if he stays in long enough."

"Oh, I don't know! We have a statesman or two who flirted with Sonora and came out ahead."

"I said if he stayed in," reminded Pike. "Sure we have crooks galore who drift across, play a cut-throat game and skip back to cover. The border is lined with them on both sides. And Conrad —- —"

"But Conrad isn't in politics."

"N-no. There's no evidence that he is, but his Mexican friends are. There are men on the Granados now who used to be down on Soledad, and they are the men who make the trips with him to the lower ranch."

"Tomas Herrara and Chico Domingo?"

"I reckon you've sized them up, but remember, Kit, I don't cross over with you for any political game, and I don't know a thing!"

"All right, Captain, but don't raise too loud a howl if I fancy a *pasear* occasionally to improve my Spanish."

The old man grumbled direful and profane prophecies as to things likely to happen to students of Spanish love songs in Sonora, and then sat with his head on one side studying Kit ruminatively as he made his notes of the selected stock.

"Ye know Bub, it mightn't be so bad at that, if you called a halt in time, for one of the lost mine trails calls for Spanish and plenty of it. I've got a working knowledge, but the farther you travel into Sonora the less American you will hear, and that lost mine of the old padres is down there along the ranges of Soledad somewhere."

"Which one of the fifty-seven varieties have you elected to uncover first?" queried Rhodes. "The last time you were confidential about mines I thought the 'Three Hills of Gold' were mentioned by you."

"Sure it was, but since you are on the Sonora end of the ranch, and since you are picking up your ears to learn Sonoran trails, it might be a good time to follow your luck. Say, I'll bet that every herder who drifts into the *cantina* at La Partida has heard of the red gold of El Alisal. The Yaquis used to know where it was before so many of them were killed off; reckon it's lost good and plenty now, but nothing is hid forever and it's waiting there for some man with the luck."

"We're willing," grinned Kit. "You are a great little old dreamer, Captain. And there is a fair chance I may range down there. I met a chap named Whitely from over toward the Painted Hills north of Altar. Ranch manager, sort of friendly."

"Sure, Tom Whitely has some stock in a ranch over there —- the Mesa Blanca ranch —- it joins Soledad on the west. I've always aimed to range that way, but the lost mine is closer than the eastern sierras —- must be! The trail of the early padres was farther east, and the mine could not well be far from the trail, not more than a day's journey by mule or burro, and that's about twenty miles. You see Bub, it was found by a padre who wandered off the trail on the way to a little branch mission, or *visita*, as they call it, and it was where trees grew, for a big alisal tree —- sycamore you know —- was near the outcrop of that red gold. Well, that *visita* was where the padres only visited the heathen for baptism and such things; no church was built there! That's what tangles the trail for anyone trying to find traces after a hundred years."

"I reckon it would," agreed Rhodes. "Think what a hundred years of cactus, sand, and occasional *temblors* can do to a desert, to say nothing of the playful zephyrs. Why, Cap, the winds could lift a good-sized range of hills and fill the baby rivers with it in that time, for the winds of the desert have a way with them!"

A boy rode out of the whirls of dust, and climbed up on the corral fence where Rhodes was finishing tally of the horses selected for shipment. He was the slender, handsome son of Tomas Herrara of whom they had been speaking.

"It is a letter," he said, taking a folded paper from his hat. "The Señor Conrad is having the telegraph, and the cars are to be ready for Granados."

"Right you are, Juanito," agreed Rhodes. "Tell Señor Conrad I will reach Granados for supper, and that all the stock is in."

The lad whirled away again, riding joyously north, and Rhodes, after giving final directions to the vaqueros, turned his roan in the same direction.

"Can't ride back with you, Cap, for I'm taking a little *pasear* around past Herrara's rancheria. I want to take a look at that bunch of colts and size up the water there. I've a hunch they had better be headed up the other valley to the Green Springs tank till rains come."

Captain Pike jogged off alone after some audible and highly colored remarks concerning range bosses who assumed the power of the Almighty to be everywhere the same day. Yet as he watched the younger man disappear over the gray-green range he smiled tolerantly for, after all, that sort of a hustler was the right sort of partner for a prospecting trip.

The late afternoon was a golden haze under a metal blue sky; afar to the east, sharp edges of the mountains cut purple zig-zags into the salmon pink of the horizon. The rolling waves of the ranges were bathed in a sea of rest, and now and then a bird on the mesquite along an arroya, or resting on branch of flaring occotilla would give out the foreboding call of the long shadows, for the heart of the day had come and gone, and the cooler air was waking the hidden things from siesta.

Kit Rhodes kept the roan at a steady lope along the cattle trail, drinking in the refreshing sweetness of the lonely ranges after hours of dust and heat and the trampling horse herds of the corrals. Occasionally he broke into songs of the ranges, love songs, death laments, and curious sentimental ditties of love and wars of old England as still crooned in the cabins of southern mountains.

> *I had not long been married,*
> *A happy, happy bride!*
>
> *When a handsome trooper captain*
> *Stepped up to our bedside,*
>
> *"Rise up! rise up! young man," he said,*
> *"And go along with me,*
>
> *In the low, low lands of Holland*
> *To fight for liberty."*

The ancient song of the sad bride whose lover proved false in the "low, low lands of Holland" trailed lugubriously along the arroya in a totally irrelevant way, for the singer was not at all sad. He was gaily alert, keen-eyed and watchful, keeping time to the long lope with that dubious versification.

"And they're at it again pretty close to the 'low, low lands of Holland,' Pardner," he confided to the horse. "And when you and I make a stake you'll go on pasture, I'll hit the breeze for Canada or some other seaport, and get one whack at the Boche brown rat on my own if official America is too proud to fight, for

> Oh-h! oh-h! Oh-h!
> In the low, low lands of Holland,
> My love was false to me!"

Then, after long stretches of sand dunes, mesquite thickets, occasional wide cañons where *zacatan* meadows rippled like waves of the sea in the desert air, he swung his horse around a low hill and came in sight of the little adobe of Herrara, a place of straggly enclosures of stakes and wattles, with the corral at the back.

Another rider came over the hill beyond the corral, on a black horse skimming the earth. Rhodes stared and whistled softly as the black without swerving planted its feet and slid down the declivity by the water tank, and then, jumping the fence below, sped to the little *ramada* before the adobe where its rider slid to the ground amid a deal of barking of dogs and scattering of children.

And although Kit had never seen the rider before, he had no difficulty as to recognition, and on a sudden impulse he whistled the meadow-lark call loudly enough to reach her ears.

She halted at the door, a bundle in her hand, and surveyed the landscape, but failed to see him because he at that moment was back of a clump of towering prickly pear. And she passed on into the shadows of the adobe.

"That's the disadvantage of being too perfect, Pardner," he confided to the roan, "she thinks we are a pair of birds."

He turned at the corner of the corral and rode around it which took him back of the house and out of range from the door, but the dogs set up a ki-yi-ing, and a flock of youngsters scuttled to the corner of the adobe, and stared as children of the far ranges are prone to stare at the passing of a traveler from the longed-for highways of the world.

The barking of the dogs and scampering of the children evidently got on the nerves of the black horse left standing at the vine-covered *ramada*, for after a puppy had barked joyously at his heels he leaped aside, and once turned around kept on going, trotting around the corral after the roan.

Rhodes saw it but continued on his way, knowing he could pick it up on his return, as the Ojo Verde tank was less than a mile away. A boy under the *ramada* gave one quick look and then fled, a flash of brown and a red flapping end of a sash, up the cañoncita where the home spring was shadowed by a large mesquite tree.

At first Rhodes turned in the saddle with the idea of assisting in the catching of the black if that was the thing desired, but it evidently was not.

"Now what has that *muchacho* on his mind that he makes that sort of get-away after nothing and no pursuer in sight? Pardner, I reckon we'll squander a valuable minute or two and gather in that black."

He galloped back, caught the wanderer but kept right on without pause to the trickle of water under the flat wide-spreading tree —- it was a solitaire, being king of its own domain and the only shade, except the vine-covered *ramada*, for a mile.

The startled boy made a movement as if to run again as Kit rode up, then halted, fear and fateful resignation changing the childish face to sullenness.

"*Buenas tardes*, Narcisco."

"*Buenas tardes*, señor," gulped the boy.

"I turned back to catch the horse of the señorita for you," observed Rhodes. "It is best you tie him when you lead him back, but first give him water. Thirst is perhaps the cause he is restless."

"Yes señor," agreed the lad. "At once I will do that." But he held the horse and did not move from his tracks, and then Rhodes noticed that on the flat rock behind him was a grain sack thrown over something, a brown bottle had rolled a little below it, and the end of a hammer protruded from under the sacking.

Ordinarily Rhodes would have given no heed to any simple ranch utensils gathered under the shadow where work was more endurable, but the fear in the face of the boy fascinated him.

"Think I'll give Pardner a drink while I am about it," he decided, and dismounted carelessly. "Got a cup that I can take my share first?"

Narcisco had no cup, only shook his head and swallowed as if the attempt at words was beyond him.

"Well, there is a bottle if it is clean," and Rhodes strode awkwardly towards it, but his spur caught in the loose mesh of the sacking, and in loosening it he twisted it off the rock.

Narcisco gasped audibly, and Rhodes laughed. He had uncovered a couple of dozen empty whiskey bottles, and a tin pan with some broken glass.

"What you trying to start up here in the cañon, Buddy?" he asked. "Playing saloon-keeper with only the gophers for customers?"

He selected a corked bottle evidently clean, rinsed and drank from it.

"Yes —- señor —- I am here playing —- that is all," affirmed Narcisco. "At the house Tia Mariana puts us out because there is a new *niño* —- my mother and the new one sleep —- and there is no place to make a noise."

"Oh," commented Rhodes, "well, let the black have a little water, and lead him out of the way of mine. This gully isn't wide enough to turn around in."

Obediently the boy led the black to the sunken barrel catching seepage from the barrel under the drip. Rhodes tossed the sack back to the flat rock and noted an old canvas water bottle beside the heap, it was half full of something —- not water, for it was uncorked and the mouth of it a-glitter with shimmering particles like diamond dust, and the same powder was over a white spot on the rock —- the lad evidently was playing miller and pounding broken glass into a semblance of meal.

"Funny stunt, that!" he pondered, and, smiling, watched the frightened boy. "Herrara certainly is doing a bit of collecting *vino* to have a stock of bottles that size, and the poor kid's nothing else to play with."

He mounted and rode on, leaving Narcisco to lead the black to his mistress. He could not get out of his mind the fright in the eyes of the boy. Was Herrara a brute to his family, and had Narcisco taken to flight to hide his simple playthings under the mistaken idea that the horseman was his father returned early from the ranges?

That was the only solution Rhodes could find to the problem, though he milled it around in his mind quite a bit. Unless the boy was curiously weak-minded and frightened at the face of a stranger it was the only explanation he could find, yet the boys of Herrara had always struck him as rather bright. In fact Conrad had promoted Juanito to the position of special messenger; he could ride like the wind and never forget a word.

The shadows lengthened as he circled the little cañon of the Ojo Verde and noted the water dripping from the full tanks, ideal for the colt range for three months. He took note that Herrara was not neglecting anything, despite that collection of bottles. There was no wastage and the pipes connecting the tanks were in good condition.

He rode back, care free and content, through the fragrant valley. The cool air was following the lowering sun, and a thin mauve veil was drifting along the hills of mystery in the south; he sang as he rode and then checked the song to listen to the flutelike call of a lark. His lips curved in a smile as he heard it, and with it came the thought of the girl and the barred window of Vijil's adobe.

She permeated the life of Granados just as the soft veil enwrapped the far hills, and she had seemed almost as far away if not so mysterious. Not once had he crossed her trail, and he heard she was no longer permitted to ride south of the line. The vaqueros commented on this variously according to their own point of view. Some of the Mexicans resented it, and in one way or another her name was mentioned whenever problems of the future were discussed. Singleton was regarded as temporary, and Conrad was a salaried business manager. But on a day to come, the señorita, as her mother's daughter, would be their mistress, and the older men with families showed content at the thought.

Rhodes never could think of her as the chatelaine of those wide ranges. She was to him the "meadow-lark child" of jests and laughter, heard and remembered but not seen. She was the haunting music of youth meeting him at the gateway of a new land which is yet so old!

Some such vagrant thought drifted through his mind as the sweet calls of the drowsy birds cut the warm silence, now from some graceful palo verde along a barranca and again from the slender pedestal of an occotilla.

"Lucky you, for you get an answer!" he thought whimsically. "Amble along, Pardner, or the night witches get us!"

And then he circled a little at the north of the cañon, and the black horse, champing and fidgeting, was held there across the trail by its rider.

"We are seeing things in broad daylight, Pardner, and there ain't no such animal," decided Rhodes, but Pardner whinnied, and the girl threw up her hand.

"This time I am a highwayman, the far-famed terror of the ranges!" she called.

"Sure!" he conceded. "I've been thinking quite a while that your term must be about up."

She laughed at that, and came alongside.

"Didn't you suppose I might have my time shortened for good behavior?" she asked. "You never even ride our way to see."

"Me? Why, child, I'm so busy absorbing *kultur* from your scientific manager that my spare moments for damsels in distress are none too plenty. You sent out nary a call, and how expect the lowest of your serfs to hang around?"

"Serf? That's good!" she said skeptically. "And say, you must love Conrad about as much as Cap Pike does."

"And that?"

"Is like a rattlesnake."

"Don't know that rattlesnake would be my first choice of comparison," remarked Rhodes. "Back in Tennessee we have a variety beside which the rattlesnake is a gentleman; a rattlesnake does his best to give warning of intention, but the copperhead never does."

"Copperhead! that's funny, for you know Conrad's hair is just about the color of copper, dusty copper, faded copper —- copper with tin filings sifted through."

"Don't strain yourself," laughed Rhodes. "That beautiful blondness makes him mighty attractive to our Mexican cousins."

"They can have my share," decided the girl. "I could worry along without him quite awhile. He manages to get rid of all the likeable range men *muy pronto*."

Rhodes laughed until she stared at him frowningly, and then the delicious color swept over her face.

"Oh, *you!*" she said, and Rhodes thought of sweet peas, and pink roses in old southern gardens as her lips strove to be straight, yet curved deliciously. No one had mentioned to him how pretty she was; he had thought of her as a browned tom-boy, but instead she was a shell-pink bud on a slender stem, and wonder of wonders —- she rode a side-saddle in Arizona!

She noticed him looking at it.

"Are you going to laugh at that, too?" she demanded.

"Why no, it hadn't occurred to me. It sort of looks like home to me —- our southern girls use them."

She turned to him with a quick birdlike movement, her gray eyes softened and trusting.

"It was my mother's saddle, a wedding present from the vaqueros of our ranches when she married my father. I am only beginning to use it, and not so sure of myself as with the one I learned on."

"Oh, I don't know," he observed. "You certainly looked sure when you jumped that fence at Herrara's."

She glanced at him quickly, curious, and then smiling.

"And it was you, not the meadow lark! You are too clever!"

"And you didn't answer, just turned your back on the lonely ranger," he stated dolefully, but she laughed.

"This doesn't look it, waiting to go home with you," she retorted. "Cap Pike has been telling me about you until I feel as if I had known you forever. He says you are his family now, so of course that makes Granados different for you."

"Why, yes. I've been in sight of Granados as much as twice since I struck this neck of the woods. Your manager seems to think my valuable services are indispensable at the southern side of this little world."

"So that's the reason? I didn't know," she said slowly. "One would have to be a seventh son of a seventh son to understand his queer ways. But you are going along home today, for I am a damsel in distress and need to be escorted."

"You don't look distressed, and I've an idea you could run away from your escort if you took a notion," he returned. "But it is my lucky day that I had a hunch for this cañon trail and the Green Springs, and I am happy to tag along."

They had reached Herrara's corral and Rhodes glanced up the little gulch to the well. The flat rock there was stripped of the odd collection, and Narcisco stood at the corner of the adobe watching them somberly.

"*Buenos tardes!*" called the girl. "Take care of the *niño* as the very treasure of your heart!"

"Sure!" agreed the lad, "*Adios*, señorita."

"Why the special guard over the treasure?" asked Rhodes as their horses fell into the long easy lope side by side. "The house seems full and running over, and *niñitas* to spare."

"There are never any to spare," she reminded him, "and this one is doubly precious for it is named for me —- together its saint and its two grandmothers! Benicia promised me long ago that whether it was a boy or a girl it would be Billie Bernard Herrara. I was just taking the extra clothes I had Tia Luz make for him —- and he is a little black-eyed darling! Soon as he is weaned I'm going to adopt him; I always did want a piccaninny for my own."

Rhodes guided his horse carefully around a barranca edge, honeycombed by gophers, and then let his eyes rest again on the lustrous confiding eyes, and the rose-leaf lips.

Afterward he told himself that was the moment he began to be bewitched by Billie Bernard.

But what he really said was —- "Shoo, child, you're only a piccaninny yourself!" and they both laughed.

It was quite wonderful how old Captain Pike had managed to serve as a family foundation for their knowledge of each other. There was not a doubt or a barrier between them, they were "home folks" riding from different ways and meeting in the desert, and silently claiming kindred.

The shadows grew long and long under the sun of the old Mexic land, and the high heavens blazed above in yellows and pinks fading into veiled blues and far misty lavenders in the hollows of the hills.

The girl drew a great breath of sheer delight as she waved her hands towards the fire flame in the west where the desert was a trail of golden glory.

"Oh, I am glad —- glad I got away!" she said in a hushed half-awed voice. "It never —- never could be like this twice and we are seeing it! Look at the moon!"

The white circle in the east was showing through a net of softest purple and the beauty of it caused them to halt.

"Oh, it makes me want to sing, or to say my prayers, or —- to cry!" she said, and she blinked tears from her eyes and smiled at him. "I reckon the colors would look the same from the veranda, but all this makes it seem different," and her gesture took in the wide ranges.

"Sure it does," he agreed. "One wants to yell, 'Hurrah for God!' when a combination like this is spread before the poor meek and lowly of the earth. It is a great stage setting, and makes us humans seem rather inadequate. Why, we can't even find the right words for it."

"It makes me feel that I just want to ride on and on, and on through it, no matter which way I was headed."

"Well, take it from me, señorita, you are headed the right way," he observed. "Going north is safe, but the blue ranges of the south are walls of danger. The old border line is a good landmark to tie to."

"Um!" she agreed, "but all the fascinating things and the witchy things, and the mysterious things are down there over the border. I never get real joy riding north."

"Perhaps because it is not forbidden, Miss Eve."

Then they laughed again and lifted the bridles, and the horses broke into a steady lope, neck and neck, as the afterglow made the earth radiant and the young faces reflected the glory of it.

"What was that you said about getting away?" he queried. "Did you break jail?"

"Just about. Papa Singleton hid my cross-saddle thinking I would not go far on this one. They have put a ban on my riding south, but I just had to see my Billie Bernard Herrara."

"And you ran away?"

"N-no. We sneaked away mighty slow and still till we got a mile or two out, and then we certainly burned the wind. Didn't we, Pat?"

"Well, as range boss of this end of the ranch I reckon I have to herd you home, and tell them to put up the fences," said Rhodes.

"Yes, you will!" she retorted in derision of this highly improbable suggestion.

"Surest thing you know! Singleton has good reasons for restricting your little pleasure rides to Granados. Just suppose El Gavilan, the Hawk, should cross your trail in Sonora, take a fancy to Pat —- for Pat is some *caballo*! —- and gather you in as camp cook?"

"Camp cook?"

"Why, yes; you can cook, can't you? All girls should know how to cook."

"What if I do? I have cooked on the camp trips with Cap Pike, but that doesn't say I'll ever cook for that wild rebel, Ramon Rotil. Are you trying to frighten me off the ranges?"

"No, only stating the case," replied Rhodes lighting a cigarette and observing her while appearing not to. "Quite a few of the girls in the revolution camps are as young as you, and many of them are not doing camp work by their own choice."

"But I —- " she began indignantly.

"Oh yes, in time you would be ransomed, and for a few minutes you might think it romantic —- the 'Bandit Bride,' the 'Rebel Queen,' the 'Girl Guerrilla,' and all that sort of dope, —- but believe me, child, by the time the ransom was paid you would be sure that north of the line was the garden spot of the earth and heaven enough for you, if you could only see it again!"

She gave him one sulky resentful look and dug her heel into Pat. He leaped a length ahead of the roan and started running.

"You can pretend you are El Gavilan after a lark, and see how near you will get!" she called derisively and leaned forward urging the black to his best.

"You glorified gray-eyed lark!" he cried. "Gather her in, Pardner!"

But he rode wide to the side instead of at the heels of Pat and thus they rode neck and neck joyously while he laughed at her intent to leave him behind.

The corrals and long hay ricks of Granados were now in sight, backed by the avenue of palms and streaks of green where the irrigation ditches led water to the outlying fields and orchards.

"El Gavilan!" she called laughingly. "Beat him, Pat, —- beat him to the home gate!"

Then out of a fork of the road to the left, an automobile swept to them from a little valley, one man was driving like the wind and another waved and shouted. Rhodes' eyes assured him that the shouting man was Philip Singleton, and he rode closer to the girl, grasped her bridle, and slowed down his own horse as well as hers.

"You'll hate me some more for this," he stated as she tried to jerk loose and failed, "but that yelping windmill is your fond guardian, and he probably thinks I am trying to kidnap you."

She halted at that, laughing and breathless, and waved her hand to the occupants of the car.

"I can be good as an angel now that I have had my day!" she said. "Hello folks! What's the excitement?"

The slender man whom Rhodes had termed the yelping windmill, removed his goggles, and glared, hopelessly distressed at the flushed, half-laughing girl.

"Billie —- Wilfreda!"

"Now, now, Papa Singleton! Don't swear, and don't ever get frightened because I am out of sight." Then she cast one withering glance at Rhodes, adding, —- "and if you engage range bosses like this one no one on Granados will ever get out of sight!"

"The entire house force has been searching for you over two hours. Where have you been?"

"Oh, come along home to supper, and don't fuss," she suggested. "Just because you hid my other saddle I went on a little *pasear* of my own, and I met up with this roan on my way home."

Rhodes grinned at the way she eliminated the rider of the roan horse, but the driver of the machine was not deceived by the apparent slight. He had seen that half defiant smile of comradeship, and his tone was not nice.

"It is not good business to waste time and men in this way," he stated flatly. "It would be better that word is left with the right ones when you go over the border to amuse yourself in Sonora."

The smile went out of the eyes of the girl, and she held her head very erect.

"You and Mr. Rhodes appear to agree perfectly, Mr. Conrad," she remarked. "He was trying to show me how little chance I would stand against El Gavilan or even the Yaqui slave traders if they ranged up towards the border."

"Slave traders?" repeated Conrad. "You are making your jokes about that, of course, but the camp followers of the revolution is a different thing; —- everywhere they are ranging."

The girl did not answer, and the car sped on to the ranch house while the two horses cantered along after them, but the joyous freedom of the ride had vanished, lost back there on the ranges when the other minds met them in a clash.

"Say," observed Rhodes, "I said nothing about Yaqui slave traders. Where did you get that?"

"I heard Conrad and his man Brehman talking of the profits, —- sixty pesos a head I think it was. I wonder how they knew?"

Singleton was waiting for them at the entrance to the ranch house, great adobe with a patio eighty feet square in the center. In the old old days it had housed all the vaqueros, but now the ranchmen were divided up on different outlying rancherias and the many rooms of Granados were mostly empty. Conrad, his secretary Brehman, and their cook occupied one corner, while Singleton and Billie and Tia Luz with her brood of helpers occupied the other.

Singleton was not equal to the large hospitality of the old days when the owner of a hacienda was a sort of king, dispensing favors and duties to a small army of retainers. A companionable individual he was glad to meet and chat or smoke with, but if the property had been his own he would have sold every acre and spent the proceeds in some city of the East where a gentleman could get something for his money.

Conrad had halted a moment after Singleton climbed out of the car.

"I sent word to Rhodes to come up from La Partida because of the horse shipment," he said looking across the level where the two riders were just entering the palm avenue. "Because of that it would seem he is to be my guest, and I have room."

"Oh, we all have room, more room than anything else," answered Singleton drearily, "but it will be as Billie says. I see Pike's nag here, and she always wants Pike."

The milky blue eyes of Conrad slanted towards Singleton in discreet contempt of the man who allowed a wayward girl to decide the guests or the housing of them. But he turned away.

"The telephone will reach me if there is anything I can do," he said.

Singleton did not reply. He knew Conrad absolutely disapproved of the range boss being accepted as a family guest. Between Billie and Captain Pike, who was a privileged character, he did not quite see how he could prevent it in the case of Rhodes, although he was honestly so glad to see the girl ride home safe that he would have accepted any guest of the range she suggested.

"Papa Phil," she said smiling up into his face teasingly, "I'm on my native heath again, so don't be sulky. And I have a darling new namesake I've been making clothes for for a month, and I'll tell you all about him if you'll give Mr. Rhodes and me a good supper. He is Cap Pike's family, and will have the south corner room; please tell Tia Luz."

And when Billie was like that, and called him "Papa Phil," and looked up at him with limpid childish eyes, there was never much else to be said.

"I'll show Rhodes his quarters myself, and you make haste and get your habit off. Luz has been waiting supper an hour. Today's paper reports a band of bandits running off stock on the Alton ranch, and it is on the Arizona side of the border. That should show you it is no time to ride out of sight of the corrals."

"Now, now! you know the paper raids aren't real raids. They'll have a new one to get excited over tomorrow."

She ran away to be petted and scolded and prayed for by Tia Luz, who had been her nurse, and was now housekeeper and the privileged one to whom Billie turned for help and sympathy.

"You laugh! but the heart was melting in me with the fear," she grumbled as she fastened the yellow sash over the white lawn into which Billie had dashed hurriedly. "It is not a joke to be caught in the raiding of Ramon Rotil, or any of the other accursed! Who could think it was south you were riding? I was the one to send them north in the search, every man of them, and Señor Conrad looks knives at me. That man thinks I am a liar, sure he does! and the saints know I was honest and knew nothing."

"Sure you know nothing, never could and never did, you dear old bag of cotton," and Billie pinched affectionately the fat arm of Tia Luz and tickled her under her fat chin. "Quick Luzita, and fasten me up. Supper waits, and men are always raving wolves."

She caught up a string of amber beads and clasped it about her throat as she ran across the patio, and Kit Rhodes halted a moment in the corridor to watch her.

"White and gold and heavenly lovely," he thought as he rumpled his crisp brown curls meditatively, all forgetful of the earnest attempts he had just made to smooth them decorously with the aid of a damp towel and a pocket comb. "White and gold and a silver spoon, and a back seat for you, Kittie boy!"

Captain Pike emerged from a door at the corner of the patio. He also had damp hair, a shiny face, and a brand-new neckerchief with indigo circles on a white ground.

"Look at this, will you?" he piped gleefully. "Billie's the greatest child ever! Always something stuck under the pillow like you'd hide candy for a kid, and say, —- if any of the outfit would chuck another hombre in my bunk the little lady would raise hell from here to Pinecate, and worse than that there ain't any this side of the European centers of civilization. Come on in, supper's ready."

Rhodes hesitated at the door of the dining room, suddenly conscious of a dusty blouse and a much faded shirt. His spurs clink-clanked as he strode along the tiling of the patio, and in the semi-twilight he felt at home in the ranch house, but one look at the soft glow of the shaded lamps, and the foot deep of Mexican needlework on the table cover, gave him a picture of home such as he had not seen on the ranges.

Singleton was in spotless white linen, the ideal southern ranchman's home garb, while the mistress of all the enticing picture was in white and gold, and flushing pink as she met the grave appreciative gaze of Rhodes.

"H'lo little Santa Claus," chirruped Pike. "It's just the proper caper to set off my manly beauty, so I'm one ahead of Kit who has no one to garnish him for the feast —- and it sure smells like some feast!"

"Venison perhaps a trifle overdone, but we hope it won't disappoint you," remarked Singleton. "Have this seat, Mr. Rhodes. Captain Pike and Miss Bernard always chum together, and have their own side."

"Rather," decided Pike, "and that arrangement reaches back beyond the memory of mere man in this outfit."

"I should say," agreed the girl. "Why, he used to have to toss me over his head a certain number of times before I would agree to be strapped in my high chair."

"Yep, and I carpentered the first one, and it wasn't so bad at that! Now child, if you will pass the lemons, and Kit will pass the decanter of amber, and someone else will rustle some water, I'll manufacture a tonic to take the dust out of your throats."

"Everybody works but father," laughed Billie as the Chinaman sliced and served the venison, and Tia Luz helped supply all plates, and then took her place quietly at the lower end of the table and poured the strong fragrant coffee.

Rhodes spoke to her in Spanish, and her eyes lit up with kindly appreciation.

"Ah, very good!" she commented amicably. "You are not then too much Americano?"

"Well, yes, I'm about as American as you find them aside from the Apache and Pima and the rest of the tribes."

"Maybe so, but not gringo," she persisted. "I am scared of the Apache the same as of El Gavilan, and today my heart was near to stop going at all when we lose señorita and that black horse —- and I say a prayer for you to San Antonio when I see you come fetch her home again."

"Yes, the black horse is valuable," remarked Billie. "Huh! I might as well be in a convent for all I get to see of the ranges these late days. If anyone would grubstake me, I'd break loose with Cap here and go prospecting for adventures into some of the unnamed ranges."

"You see!" said Tia Luz. "Is it a wonder I am cold with the fear when she is away from my eyes? I have lived to see the people who go into the desert for adventure, and whose bare bones are all any man looks on again! Beside the mountain wells of Carrizal my own cousin's husband died; he could not climb to the tank in the hill. There they found him in the moon of Kumaki, which is gray and nothing growing yet."

"Yes, many's the salt outfit in the West played out before they reached Tinajas Altas," said Pike. "I've heard curious tales about that place, and the Carrizals as well. Billie's father nearly cashed in down in the Carrizals, and one of his men did."

"But that is what I am saying. It was Dario Ruiz," stated Tia Luz. "Yes, señor, that was the time, and it was for the nameless ranges they went seeking, and for adventures, treasure too; but —- his soul to God! it was death Dario was finding on that trail. Your father never would speak one word again of the treasure of that old fable, for Dario found death instead of the red gold, and Dario was *compadre* to him."

"The red gold?" and Cap Pike's eyes were alight with interest. "Why, I was telling Kit about that today, the red gold of El Alisal."

"Yes, Señor Capitan, once so rich and so red it was a wonder in Spain when the padres are sending it there from the mission of Soledad, and then witches craft, like a cloud, come down and cover that mountain. So is the vein lost again, and it is nearly one hundred years. So how could Dario think to find it when the padres, with all their prayer, never once found the trail?"

"I never heard it was near a mission," remarked Pike. "Why, if it had a landmark like that there should be no trouble."

"Yet it is so, and much trouble, also deaths," stated Tia Luz. "That is how the saying is that the red gold of El Alisal is gold bewitched, for of Soledad not one adobe is now above ground unless it be in the old walls of the hacienda. All is melted into earth again or covered by the ranch house, and it is said the ranch house is also neglected now, and many of its old walls are going."

"There are still enough left to serve as a very fair fortress," remarked Singleton. "I was down there two years ago when we bought some herds from Perez, and lost quite a number from lack of water before the vaqueros got them to La Partida wells. It is a long way between water holes over in Altar."

"Sure," agreed Pike, "but if the old mine was near a mission, and the mission was near the ranch of Soledad it should not be a great stunt to find it, and there must be water and plenty of it if they do much in cattle."

"They don't these days," said Singleton. "Perez sold a lot rather than risk confiscation, and I heard they did have some raids down there. I thought I had heard most of the lost mine legends of western Sonora, but I never heard of that one, and I never heard that Fred Bernard went looking for it."

The old woman lifted her brows and shrugged her shoulders with the suggestion that Sonora might hold many secrets from the amicable gentleman. But a little later, in an inquiry from Rhodes she explained.

"See you, señor, Dario Ruiz was *compadre* of Señor Alfredo Bernard, Americanos not understanding all in that word, and the grandfather of Dario was major-domo of the rancho of Soledad at that time the Apaches are going down and killing the people there. That is when the mine was lost. On the skin of a sheep it was told in writing all about it, and Dario had that skin. Sure he had! It was old and had been buried in the sand, and holes were eaten in it by wild things, but Don Alfredo did read it, and I was hearing the reading of it to Dario Ruiz, but of what use the reading when that mine bewitched itself into hiding?"

"But the writing? Did that bewitch itself away also?" demanded Billie.

"How could I be asking of that when Dario was dead down there in the desert, and his wife, that was my cousin Anita, was crazy wild against Don Alfredo the father of you! Ai, that was a bad time, and Don Alfredo with black silence on him for very sorrow. And never again in his life did he take the Sonora trail for adventures or old treasure. And it is best that you keep to a mind like his mind, señorita. He grew wise, but Dario died for that wisdom, and in Sonora someone always dies before wisdom is found. First it was two priests went to death for that gold, and since that old day many have been going. It is a witchcraft, and no blessing on it!"

"Well, I reckon I'd be willing to cross my fingers, and take the trail if I could get started right," decided Rhodes. "It certainly sounds alluring."

"I did go in once," confessed Pike, "but we had no luck, struck a *temporale* where a Papago had smallpox, and two dry wells where there should have been water. My working pardner weakened at Paradones and we made tracks for the good old border. That is no trail for a lone white man."

"But the writing, the writing!" persisted Billie. "Tia Luz, you are a gold mine yourself of stories, but this one you never told, and I am crazy about it! You never forget anything, and the writing you *could* not, —- so we know you have the very words of that writing!"

"Yes, that is true too, for the words were not so many, and where some words had been the wild things had eaten holes. The words said that from the mine of El Alisal the mission of Soledad could be seen. And from the door of Soledad it was one look, one only, to the blue cañoncita where the alisal tree was growing, and water from the gold of the rose washed the roots of that tree."

"Good God!" muttered Rhodes staring at the old lady who sat nodding her head in emphasis until her jet and gold earrings were all a-twinkle. "It was as easy as *that*, —- yet no one found it?"

"But señor," —- and it was plain to be seen that Doña Luz was enjoying herself hugely as the center of all attention, "the two padres who made that writing met their death at that place —- and it was said the *barbaros* at last killed also the grandfather of Dario, anyway he did die, and the women were afraid to tell even a new padre of that buried writing for the cause that it must have been accursed when it killed all people. That is how it was, and that mission was forsaken after that time. A Spaniard came up from Sinaloa and hunted gold and built Soledad hacienda where that mission had been in that old time, but no one ever found any more of gold than the chickens always are picking, a little here, a little there with a gravel in the craw. No señor, only once the red gold —- red as flame —- went out of Altar on a mule to the viceroy in Mexico, and the padres never lived to send any more, or see their brothers again. The men who dug that gold dug also their grave. Death goes with it."

"Ugh!" and Billie shivered slightly, and looked at Rhodes, "don't you go digging it!"

His eyes met hers across the table. It was only for an instant, and then Billie got very busy with her coffee which she had forgotten.

"Oh, I'd travel with a mascot to ward off evil," he said. "Would you give me a bead from your string?"

She nodded her head, but did not speak. No one noticed them, for Cap Pike was telling of the old native superstition that the man who first found an ore bed found no good luck for himself, though the next man might make a fortune from it.

"Why," he continued in evidence, "an Indian who finds even a vein of special clay for pottery doesn't blaze a trail to it for anyone else. He uses it if he wants it, because his own special guardian god uncovered it for him, but if it is meant for any other man, that other man's god will lead him to it when the time comes. That is how they reason it out for all the things covered by old Mother Earth. And I reckon the redder the gold the more secret the old *barbaros* would be about it, for gold is their sun-god medicine, or symbol, or something."

"With white priests scattered through Sonora for two centuries one would suppose those old superstitions would be pretty well eradicated," remarked Singleton.

Doña Luz glanced at him as at a child who must be let have his own ideas so long as they were harmless, but Pike laughed.

"Lord love you, Singleton, nothing eradicates superstition from the Indian mind, or any other mind! All the creeds of the earth are built on it, and a lot of the white ones are still alive and going strong! And as for priests, why man, the Indian priests are bred of those tribes, and were here before the white men came from Spain. It's just about like this: If 'Me und Gott' and the U-boats took a notion to come over and put a ball and chain on all of so-called free America, there might be some pacifist mongrels pretend to like it, and just dote on putting gilt on the chain, and kow-towing to that blood-puddin' gang who are raising hell in Belgium. But would the thoroughbreds like it? Not on your life! Well, don't you forget there were a lot of thoroughbreds in the Indian clans even if some of their slaves did breed mongrels! And don't forget that the ships from overseas are dumping more scrub stock on the eastern shores right now than you'll find in any Indian ranchería either here in Pima or over in Sonora. The American isn't to blame for all the seventeen dozen creeds they bring over, —- whether political or religious, and I reckon that's about the way the heads of the red clans feel. They are more polite than we are about it, but don't you think for a moment that the European invasion ever changed religion for the Indian thoroughbred. No sir! He is still close to the earth and the stars, and if he thinks they talk to him —- well, they just *talk to him*, and what they tell him isn't for you or me to hear, —- or to sit in judgment on either, if it comes to that! We are the outsiders."

"Now, Cap," said Billie, "I'm going to take it away. It's too near your elbow, and you have had a double dose for every single one you've been handing out! You can take a rest until the others catch up. Tia Luz, give him a cup of coffee good and strong to help get his politics and religion straightened out."

Pike laughed heartily with the rest of them, and took the coffee.

"All right, dear little Buttercup. Any medicine you hand out is good to me. But say, that dope about hidden ores may not be all Indian at that, for I recollect that mountaineers of Tennessee had the same hunch about coal veins, and an old lead vein where one family went for their ammunition. They could use it and they did, but were mighty sure they'd all be hoodooed if they uncovered it for anyone else, so I reckon that primitive dope does go pretty far back. I'll bet it was old when Tubal Cain first began scratching around the outcroppings by his lonesomes."

Conrad sauntered along the corridor and seated himself, flicking idly some leather thongs he had cut out from a green hide with a curved sheath knife rather fine and foreign looking. Singleton called him to come in and have coffee, but he would not enter, pleading his evil-smelling pipe as a reason.

"It can't beat mine for a downright bachelor equipment," affirmed Pike, "but I've scandalized this outfit enough, or thereabout, and that venison has killed all our appetites until breakfast, so why hang around where ungrateful children swat a man's dearest hobbies?"

"If you think you'll get rid of me that way you had better think again," said Billie. "I don't mind your old smokes, or any other of your evil ways, so long as you and Tia Luz tell us more bewitched mine stories. Say, Cap, wouldn't it be great if that old sheepskin was found again, and we'd all outfit for a Sonora *pasear*, and —- –"

"We would not!" decided the old man patting her hair. "You, my lady, will take a *pasear* to some highbrow finishing school beyond the ranges, and I'll hit the trail for Yuma in a day or two, but at the present moment you can wind up the music box and start it warbling. That supper sure was so perfect nothing but music will do for a finish!"

The men drifted out in the corridor and settled into the built-in seats of the plazita, though Rhodes remained standing in the portal facing inward to the patio where the girl's shimmering white dress fluttered in the moonlight beside the shadowy bulk of Tia Luz.

He lit a cigarette and listened for the music box Pike had suggested, but instead he heard guitar strings, and the little ripple of introduction to the old Spanish serenade *Vengo a tu ventana*, "I come to your window."

He turned and glanced towards the men who were discussing horse shipments, and possibilities of the Prussian sea raiders sinking transports on the way to France, but decided his part of that discussion could wait until morning.

Tia Luz had lit the lamp in the *sala*, and the light streamed across the patio where the night moths fluttered about the white oleanders. He smiled in comical self-derision as he noticed the moths, but tossed away the cigarette and followed the light.

When Captain Pike indulged the following morning in sarcastic comment over Kit's defection, the latter only laughed at him.

"Shirk business? Nothing doing. I was strictly on the job listening to local items on treasure trails instead of powwowing with you all over the latest news reports from the Balkans. Soon as my pocket has a jingle again, I am to get to the French front if little old U. S. won't give me a home uniform, but in the meantime Doña Luz Moreno is some reporter if she is humored, and I mean to camp alongside every chance I get. She has the woman at the *cantina* backed off the map, and my future Spanish lessons will be under the wing of Doña Luz. Me for her!"

"Avaricious young scalawag!" grunted Pike. "You'd study African whistles and clicks and clacks if it blazed trail to that lost gold deposit! Say, I sort of held the others out there in front thinking I would let you get acquainted with little Billie, and you waste the time chinning about death in the desert, and dry camps to that black-and-tan talking machine."

Kit only laughed at him.

"A record breaker of a moon too!" grumbled the old man. "Lord! —- lord! at your age I'd crawled over hell on a rotten rail to just sit alongside a girl like Billie —- and you pass her up for an old hen with a mustache, and a gold trail!"

Kit Rhodes laughed some more as he got into the saddle and headed for the Granados corral, singing:

> Oh —- I'll cut off my long yellow hair
> To dress in men's array,
>
> And go along with you, my dear
> Your waiting man to be!

He droned out the doleful and incongruous love ballad of old lands, and old days, for the absurd reason that the youth of the world in his own land beat in his blood, and because in the night time one of the twinkling stars of heaven had dropped down the sky and become a girl of earth who touched a guitar and taught him the words of a Spanish serenade, —- in case he should find a Mexican sweetheart along the border!

For to neither of the young, care-free things, had come a glimmer of fore-vision of the long tragic days, treasure trails and desert deaths, primitive devotions and ungodly vengeance, in which the threads of their own lives would be entangled before those two ever heard the music of the patio again —- together.

> *If in Holland fields I met a maid*
> *All handsome fond and gay,*
>
> *And I should chance to love her*
> *What would my Mary say?*
>
> *What would I say, dear Willie?*
>
> *That I would love her too,*
>
> *And I would step to the one side*
> *That she might speak with you!*

"Yes, you would —- not!" he stated in practical prose to no one in particular. "Not if you were our girl, would she, Pardner?"

Pardner tossed up his head in recognition of the comradeship in the tone, and Kit Rhodes became silent, and rode on to the corrals, happily smiling at some new thoughts.

CHAPTER III

A VERIFIED PROPHECY OF SEÑORITA BILLIE

That smile was yet with him when he saw the herd and the vaqueros coming up from the water tanks, and noted Conrad and Tomas Herrara talking together beside Conrad's automobile.

The beat of the many hoofs prevented the two men from noting one horse near them, and words of Conrad came to him clearly.

"It has to be that way. You to go instead of Miguel. You have enough English, you can do it."

Tomas Herrara muttered something, evidently reluctance, for again Conrad's words were heard.

"But think of the *dinero*, much of money to you! And that fool swine will not see what is under his nose. You can do it, sure you can! There is no danger. The blame will be to him if it is found; my agent will see to that. Not you but the gringo will be the one to answer the law. You will know nothing."

He spoke in Spanish rapidly, while both men watched the approaching vaqueros.

The smile had gone from Kit's face, and he was puzzled to follow the words, or even trust his own ears.

"*Bueno,*" said Herrara with a nod of consent. "Since Miguel is hurt ——-"

"Whoa, Pardner," sang out Rhodes, back of them as he slid out of the saddle. "Good morning, gentlemen. Do you say Miguel is hurt, Herrara? How comes that?"

The face of Herrara went a curious gray, and his lips blue and apparently stiff for he only murmured, "*Buenas dias*, señor," and gulped and stared at Conrad. But the surprise of Conrad, while apparent, was easily accounted for, and he was too well poised to be startled unduly by any emergency.

"Hah! Is it you, Rhodes, so early? Yes, Miguel is reported hurt over Poso Verde way. Not serious, but for the fact that he was the one to go with you on the horse shipment, and now another must go. Perhaps his brother here."

"Oh ——- ah ——- yes," assented Rhodes thoughtfully. He was not so old as Conrad, and quite aware he was not so clever, and he didn't know their game, so he strove as he could to hold the meaning of what he had heard, and ended rather lamely: "Well, too bad about Miguel, but if you, Tomas, are going instead, you had better get your war togs ready. We start tonight from the Junction, and have three hours to get ready."

"Three hours only!" again Herrara seemed to weaken. To start in three hours a journey into the unknown far East of the Americano was beyond his imaginings. He shrugged his shoulders, tossed his hands outwards in despair, and turned toward the barns.

Conrad looked after him in irritation, and then smiled at Rhodes. He had a rather ingratiating smile, and it the first time he had betrayed it to Kit.

"These explosive Latins," he said derisively. "I think I can make him reasonable, and you go forward with your own preparations."

He followed Herrara, leaving Kit staring after them wondering. His glance then rested on the automobile, and he noted that it had not merely come out of the garage for the usual work of the day. It had been traveling somewhere, for the wheels were crusted with mud ——- mud not there at sunset yesterday. And in that section of Pima there was no water to make mud nearer than Poso Verde, and it was over there Miguel Herrara had been hurt!

He had only three hours, and no time to investigate. There were rumors of smuggling all along the line over there, and strange conferences between Mexican statesmen and sellers of Connecticut hardware of an explosive nature. He recalled having heard that Singleton was from Connecticut, or was it Massachusetts? Anyway, it was over there at the eastern edge of the country somewhere, and it was also where plots and counter plots were pretty thick concerning ammunition; also they were more complicated on the Mexican border. He wondered if Singleton was as simple as he looked, for he certainly was paying wages to a mixed lot. Also it was a cinch to run any desirable contraband from Granados across to La Partida and from there hellwards.

He wondered if Singleton knew? But Singleton had a capable business manager, while he, Rhodes, was only a range boss with the understanding that he adjust himself to any work a white man might qualify for.

The mere fact that once he had sat at the family table might not, in Singleton's eyes, warrant him in criticizing an approved manager, or directing suspicion towards him. He might speak to Pike, but he realized that Pike was not taken very seriously; only welcomed because Billie liked him, and because an American ranch usually had the open door for the old timers of his caliber.

Also Pike had told him plainly that he must not be expected to mix up in the Mexican game for any reason whatsoever.

"I reckon it's up to us, Pardner," he decided, as he called directions to the different men loading the wagons with oats and barley for the stock on the trail. There were three mule teams ready for the railroad junction where the cars were waiting on the siding, or would be by night.

Some of the men were getting the mules straightened out in the harness while others were roping horses in the corral. It would take most of the home outfit to lead and drive them to the railroad, which meant one lonely and brief period of hilarity at the only joint where "bootleg" whiskey could be secured by the knowing, and a "movie" theater could add to other simple entertainments for the gentle Juans of the ranges. Neither Conrad nor Herrara were visible, and he presumed the latter was making arrangements for the sudden and unexpected departure from his family, but he knew he had not attempted to ride home for a farewell greeting, because his horse still stood near Conrad's automobile where he had first overheard that curious conversation between the two men.

After a leisurely breakfast Pike was meandering towards the stock yard on his mule with the intent to trail along to the Junction with the boys. Rhodes, catching sight of him, looked hopefully but unsuccessfully for Singleton. The minutes were slipping by, and no definite instructions had been given him concerning the three car loads of horses. Did Conrad mean to leave every detail until the last moment and make difficulties for the new man? Was that the way he got rid of the Americans he didn't want? He recalled the prophecy of Billie that he would not hold his job. Well, he would show her!

With memories of the white and gold vision of the previous night, and the guitar in the *sala*, and the moonlight touching all to enchantment, he had fully decided that he would not only hold the job, but on some future day he would be business manager. And he'd find that lost mine or know the reason why, and he would —- –

For after all Kit Rhodes was only twenty-three and all of life ahead of him for dreams! He was wondering what he could fetch back from the East that would be acceptable to a witchy elf of a butterfly girl who already had, to his simple estimate, all the requisites of a princess royal.

Juanito came loping past, and Rhodes asked for his father.

"I am myself looking for him," said the boy. "He has there on his horse all the things for Tio Miguel, but Miguel not coming, and I wonder who goes? Maybe it will be me. What you think?" he asked hopefully.

Kit did not answer, for Juanito's mention of the articles for Miguel brought from home by Tomas, and still fastened to the back of the saddle, drew his attention to the articles tied there —- some clothing badly wrapped, a pair of black shoes tied together with brown strings, and under them, yet plainly visible, a canvas water bag.

There was nothing unusual in a water bag or a canteen tied back of any saddle in the dry lands, it was the sensible thing to do, but Kit found himself staring at this particular water bag stupidly, remembering where he had seen it last. It had been only partly full then, but now it was plump and round as if water-filled; yet one glance told him it was not wet, and moreover, he had noted the day before a hole in the side tied up in a hard knot by twine, and there was the knot!

Yet it might be a stock of *pinole*, parched corn, as evidence of Miguel's forethought against privation on the long eastern trail. He could think of several reasonable things to account for an old water bag tied to a Mexican's saddle, but reason did not prevent his glance turning to it again and again.

The fear in Narcisco's eyes came back to him, and his attempt to cover his harmless playthings at the coming of the unexpected American. He wondered —- –

"Say, Bub, I've got ten dollars to invest in some little trinket for Billie boy, and I want you to put it down in your jeans and invest it in whatever it will cover," said Captain Pike at his elbow, clinking the silver coin meditatively. "You'll have time to see plenty attractive things for the money there in the streets of New York, or Baltimore, or whichever of the dock towns you'll be heading for."

Rhodes accepted the coin, absently frowning.

"That's one of the dark secrets not yet divulged by this curious management," he growled. "I'm to go, or so I was told, but have been given no instructions. Where's Singleton?"

"Just rounded up for breakfast."

"Is he coming down here to the corrals?"

"Not that I could notice. Pedro got in from the Junction with last Sunday's papers, and he and Billie have the picture sheets spread around, having a weekly feast."

Kit strode over to his mount, and then halted, glancing towards the house a half mile away, and then at the telephone poles along the wide lane.

"Say, there's a telephone somewhere down here at the works, connecting with the hacienda, isn't there?"

"Sure, in that hallway between the two adobes where the bunk house ends and offices begin."

Kit started briskly towards the long bunk house, and then turned to Pike.

"Do me a favor, Captain. Stay right there till I get back, and don't let anyone take that Herrara horse away, or his load!"

"All right, but load! —- why, the spotted rat hasn't got a load for a jack rabbit, load!" and Pike sniffed disdain at the little knobs of baggage dangling from the rawhide strings. He didn't think the subdued animal needed watching —- still, if Kit said so —- –

At the same time Kit was calling the house, and hearing in reply a soft whistle of the meadow lark, and then a girl's laugh.

"Your music is good to listen to, Lark-child," he called back, "and your ears are perfectly good at telling who's who, but this is a strictly business day, and it is Mr. Singleton I need to speak with."

"Still holding your job, or asking for your time?" came the mocking voice.

"You bet I'm holding my job, also I am on it, and want the boss."

"Well, sometimes you know the boys call me the boss. What can we do for you, Mr. Kit Rhodes?"

"I'll use all three of my Spanish cuss words in a minute, if you don't be reasonable," he thundered.

"Is that a bribe?" came sweetly over the wire, and when he muttered something impatiently, she laughed and told him it was not fair to use another language when he had promised Spanish.

"Listen to me, young lady, if I can't get Singleton on the wire I'll get on a horse and go up there!"

"And you listen to me, young man, it wouldn't do you a bit of good, for just now he is nearly having a fit, and writing telegrams about something more important than the horse corrals."

"There is nothing more important this day and date," insisted Kit.

"Well, if you were as strictly a white dove advocate as Papa Singleton is, and as neutral, and then saw a full page Sunday supplement of your pet picture fraulein, working for your pet charity and sifting poison into hospital bandages and powdered glass in jellies for the soldiers of the Allies, I reckon you would change your mind."

"Powdered glass! —- in *feed*!" repeated Kit, stunned at the words and the sudden thought they suggested. "Great God, girl, you don't have to go to the eastern papers for *that*! You've got the same trick right here in Granados this minute! Why —- damn you!"

The receiver fell from his hand as a crushing blow was dealt him from the door at his back. He heard a girl's scream in the distance as he grappled with Conrad and saved himself a second blow from the automobile wrench in the manager's hands. It fell to the tiles between them, and Rhodes kicked it to one side as he struck and struck again the white, furious face of Conrad.

"The wrench! Tomas, the wrench! Give it to him! The Americano would murder me!" shouted Conrad.

Tomas had other things to think of. He had heard as much as Conrad of the telephone discourse, and was aware of his pinto standing placidly not fifty feet away, with all the damning evidence in the case tied to the back of the saddle!

Juanito, however, ran like a cat at his master's call and caught up the wrench, but halted when Pike closed on his shoulder and pressed a cold little circle of blue steel against his ribs.

"Not this time, *muchacho*!" he shrilled, "drop it! This is a man's game, and you're out."

The men came running, and others attempted to interfere, but the little old man waved the gun at them and ordered them to keep their distance.

"No crowding the mourners!" he admonished them gleefully. "I've a hunch your man started it, and my man will finish it. I don't know what it's about, Kit, but give him hell on suspicion! Go to it, boy, —- do it again! Who-ee! —- that was a sock-dolager! Keep him off you, Kit, he's a gouger, and has the weight. Give it to him standing, and give it to him good! That's it! Ki-yi! Hell's bells and them a-chiming!"

For the finale of that whirl of the two striking, staggering, cursing men, was unexpectedly dramatic. They had surged out into the open, but Conrad, little by little and step by step, or rather stagger by stagger, had given way before the mallet-like precision of the younger man's fists until Kit's final blow seemed actually to lift him off his feet and land him —- standing —- against the adobe wall. An instant he quivered there, and then fell forward, glassy eyed and limp.

Singleton's car came whirling down the lane. Billie leaped from it before it stopped, and ran in horror to the prone figure. One of the older Mexicans tried to ward her off from the sight.

"No good, señorita, it is the death of him," he said gently. "One stroke like that on the heart and it is —- *adios*!"

"What in the name of God —- " began Singleton, and Kit wiped the blood from his eyes and faced him, staggering and breathless.

"Get him water! Get busy!" he ordered. "I don't think he's done for, not unless he has some mighty weak spot he should have had labelled before he waded into this."

The blood was still trickling from the cut in his head made by the wrench, and he presented an unholy appearance as they stared at him.

"I'll explain, Singleton, for I reckon you are white. I'll —- after while —- –"

"You'll explain nothing to me!" retorted Singleton "If the man dies you'll explain to a jury and a judge; otherwise you'd better take yourself out of this country."

Kit blinked at those who were lifting Conrad and listening to his heart, which evidently had not stopped permanently.

"But give me a chance, man!" persisted Rhodes. "I need some mending done on this head of mine, —- then I'll clear it up. Why, the evidence is right here —- powdered glass for the stock at the far end of the trail —- Herrara knows —- Conrad's game —- and —- –"

He did not know why words were difficult and the faces moved in circles about him. The blood soaking his shirt and blouse, and dripping off his sleeve was cause enough, but he did not even know that.

"Take him away, Captain Pike," said Singleton coldly. "He is not wanted any longer on either of the ranches. It's the last man I hire, Conrad can do it in future."

"Conrad, eh?" grunted Kit weakly, "you're a nice easy mark for the frankfurter game, —- you and your pacifist bunch of near-traitors! Why man —- –"

But Singleton waved him away, and followed the men who were carrying Conrad to the bunk house.

"All right, *all* right! But take care you don't meet with a nastier accident than that before you are done with this game!" he said shaking his fist warningly after Singleton, and then he staggered to his horse where Pike was waiting for him.

He got in the saddle, and reeled there a moment, conscious of hostile, watchful eyes, —— and one girl's face all alone in the blur.

"Say," he said, "I heard you scream. You thought it was you I swore at. You're wrong there. But you are some little prophetess, —— *you* are! The job's gone, and Herrara's got away with the evidence, and the jig's up! But it wasn't you I cussed at —- not —- at —- all! Come on, Pike. This new ventilator in my head is playing hell its own way. Come on —- let's go by-bye!"

"There ain't no such animal," decided Kit Rhodes seated on the edge of the bed in Pedro Vigil's adobe. His head was bandaged, his face a trifle pale and the odor of medicaments in the shadowy room of the one deep-barred window. "No, Captain, no man, free, white and twenty-one *could* be such a fool. Can't Singleton see that if Conrad's story was true he'd have the constable after me for assault with intent to kill? He's that sort!"

"Well, Singleton thinks Conrad would be justified in having you prosecuted, and jailed, and fined, and a few other things, but for the reputation of Granados they let you down easy. You know it's *the* dovery for the Pass-up-the-fists of this section, and what the Arizona papers would do would be comic if they ever got hold of the fact that Singleton picked a new bird for the dove cage, and the dratted thing changed before their eyes to a fractious game rooster swinging a right like the hind leg of a mule! No, Bub, we're orderly, peaceable folks around here, so for the sake of our reputation Singleton has prevailed on his manager to be merciful to you, and Conrad has in true pacifist spirit let himself be prevailed upon."

"Which means," grinned Kit, "that I'm to be put off my guard, and done for nicely and quietly some moonless night when I take the trail! And he reports me either drunk or temporarily insane, does he? Well, when the next time comes I'll change that gentleman's mind."

"Shucks, Bub! Thank a fool's luck that your skull was only scratched, and don't go planning future wars. I tell you we are peace doves around here, and you are a stray broncho kicking up an undesirable dust in our front yard. Here is your coin. Singleton turned it over to me and I receipted for it, and we have enough between us to hit the Sonora trail, and there's not a bit of use in your hanging around here. You have no evidence. You are a stranger who ambled in, heard a sensational newspaper report of anti-ally criminal intent, and on the spot accused the highly respectable Granados rancho of indulging in that same variety of hellishness! Now there is your case in a nutshell, Bub, and you wouldn't get the authorities to believe you in a thousand years!"

"What about you?"

"Oh, I have just little enough sense to believe your hunch is right, but that won't get you anywhere. They think I'm loco too! I've an idea there is a lot more and rottener activities down south of the line with which our Teutonic peace arbitrator is mixed up. But he's been on this job five years, all the trails are his, and an outsider can't get a look-in! Now Miguel Herrara has been doing gun-running across the border for someone, and Miguel was not only arrested by the customs officer, but Miguel was killed two nights ago —- shot with his own gun so that it looks like suicide. Suicide nothing! His chief, whoever he is, was afraid Miguel would blunder or weaken under government persuasion, so Miguel was let out of the game. That case is closed, and no evidence against anyone. I reckon everyone knows that the guns and ammunition sneaked over is headed for Rancho Soledad. The owner of Soledad, José Perez, is the valued friend of our nice little Conrad, and it happens that Conrad left Granados this morning for that direction, ostensibly to negotiate with the political powers of Sonora concerning a military guard for La Partida in case revolutionary stragglers should ride north for fresh saddle-horses. All appeals to the neutral chair warmers at Washington wins us no protection from that source; —- they only have guns and men enough to guard some cherished spots in Texas."

"Well, if the Teuton is able for a trail I reckon he got nothing worse in the scrap than I, even if he did look like a job for the undertaker. That fellow travels on the strength of his belly and not the strength of his heart."

"So you say," observed Pike, grinning, "but then again there are others of us who travel on nerve and gall and never get any further! Just put this in your pipe, Bub, and don't forget it: Conrad is *organised* for whatever deviltry he is up to! There is no 'happen so' in his schemes. He is a cog in some political wheel, and it's a fifty-fifty gamble as to whether the wheel is German or Mexican, but it is no little thing, and is not to be despised."

"But I can't see how Singleton, if Singleton is square even——-"

"Singleton is a narrow gauge disciple of Universal Peace by decree——which, translated, means plain damn fool. Lord, boy, if a pack of prairie wolves had a man surrounded, would he fold his hands with the hope that his peaceful attitude would appeal to their better instincts or would he reach for a gun and give them protective pills? The man of sense never goes without his gun in wolf land, but Singleton——well, in peace times he could have lived a long lifetime, and no one ever guessed what a weak sister he was, but he's sure out of place on the border."

"I'm tired wearing this halo," observed Rhodes, referring to the white handkerchief around his head. "Also some of the dope you gave me seems to be evaporating from my system, and I feel like hitting the Piman breeze. Can we strike trail tomorrow?"

"We cannot. Doña Luz has been dosing out the dope for you——Mexican women are natural doctors with their own sort of herbs——and she says three days before you go in the sun. I've a notion she sort of let the Mexicans think that you were likely to cash in, and you bled so like a stuck pig that it was easy enough to believe the worst."

"Perhaps that's why Conrad felt safe in leaving me outside of jail. With Doña Luz as doctor, and a non-professional like you as assistant, I reckon he thought my chance of surviving that monkey wrench assault was slim, mighty slim!"

"Y——yes," agreed Pike, "under ordinary conditions he might have been justified in such surmise, but that would be figuring on the normal thickness of the normal civilized skull, but yours——why, Bub, all I'm puzzling over now is how it happens that the monkey wrench was only twisted a mite, not broke at all!"

"You scandalous old varmint!" grinned Kit. "Go on with your weak-minded amusements, taking advantage of a poor lone cripple,——refused by the army, and a victim of the latest German atrocity! I suppose——I suppose,"——he continued darkly, "everyone on and around Granados agrees that I was the villain in the assault?"

"I couldn't say as to that," returned Pike judicially. "Doña Luz would dose you, and plaster you, just the same if you had killed a half dozen instead of knocking the wind out of one. She's pretty fine and all woman, but naturally since they regard you as my *companero* they are shy about expressing themselves when I'm around——all except Singleton——and you heard him."

"Good and plenty," agreed Kit. "Say, I'm going to catch up on sleep while I've a chance, and you rustle along and get any tag ends of things needed for the trail. I'm going to strike for Mesa Blanca, as that will take us up into the country of that Alisal mine. If we go broke there is Mesa Blanca ranch work to fall back on for a grub stake, but from what I hear we can dry wash enough to buy corn and flour, and the hills are full of burro meat. We'll browse around until we either strike it rich, or get fed up with trying. Anyway, *Companero*, we will be in a quiet, peaceful pastoral land, close to nature, and out of reach of Teuton guile and monkey wrenches. *Buenas noches*, señor. I'm asleep!"

Pike closed the door, and went from the semi-dark of the adobe out into the brilliant sunshine where Billie, with a basket, was waiting under the *ramada* with Merced, and Merced looked gloomy lest Pedro should be blamed by Señor Singleton for practically turning his family out of the adobe that it might be given over to the loco Americano.

"Tomorrow, can he go?" she asked hopefully. "Me, I have a fear. Not before is the adobe here watched by hidden men at night, and that is very bad! Because that he is friend to you I say to everybody that I think the Americano is dying in our house, but today he talks, also he is laughing. No more sick?"

"No more sick, sure not, but it will be one more day. A man does not bleed like a gored bull and ride the next day under a sky hot enough to fry eggs. The tea of Doña Luz drove off the fever, and he only sleeps and talks, and sleeps again, but sick? Not a bit!"

"Nor——nor sorry, I reckon?" ventured Billie.

"Why, no child, not that I could notice. That scalawag doesn't seem to have much conscience concerning his behavior."

"Or his language!" she added.

"Sure, that was some invocation he offered up! But just between pals, Billie, you ought to have been in hearing."

"I —- I don't suppose he even remembers that I was," she remarked, and then after a silence, "or —- or even mentioned —- us?"

"Why, no, Billie. You made the right guess when you sized him up and thought he couldn't hold the job. He certainly doesn't belong, Billie, for this ranch is the homing nest of the peace doves, and he's just an ungainly young game rooster starting out with a dare against the world, and only himself for a backer. Honest, —- if that misguided youth had been landed in jail, I don't reckon there's anyone in Arizona with little enough sense to bail him out."

"Likely not," said Billie. "Well, there's the basket from Tia Luz, and I might as well go home."

CHAPTER V
AN "ADIOS" —- AND AFTER

Two days later in the blue clear air of the Arizona morning a sage hen slipped with her young through the coarse grass by the irrigation ditch, and a flock of quail raised and fluttered before the quick rhythmic beat of a loping horse along the trail in the mesquite thicket.

The slender gallant figure of his rider leaned forward looking, listening at every turn, and at the forks of the trail where a clump of squat mesquite and giant sahuarro made a screen, she checked the horse, and held her breath.

"Good Pat, good horse!" she whispered. "They've got nothing that can run away from us. We'll show them!"

Then a man's quavering old voice came to her through the winding trail of the arroya. It was lifted tunefully insistent in an old-time song of the mining camps:

> Oh, Mexico! we're coming, Mexico!
> Our six mule team,
> Will soon be seen,
> On the trail to Mexico!

"We made it, Pat!" confided the girl grimly. "We made it. Quiet now —- quiet!"

She peered out through the green mesquite as Captain Pike emerged from the west arroya on a gray burro, herding two other pack animals ahead of him into the south trail.

He rode jauntily, his old sombrero at a rakish angle, his eyes bright with enthusiasm supplied by that which he designated as a morning "bracer," and his long gray locks bobbed in the breeze as he swayed in the saddle and droned his cheerful epic of the trail:

> A —- and when we've been there long enough,
> And back we wish to go,
> We'll fill our pockets with the shining dust
> And then leave Mexico!
> Oh —- Mexico!
> Good-bye my Mexico!
> Our six mule team will then be seen
> On the trail from Mexico.

"Hi there! you Balaam —- get into the road and keep a-going, you ornery little rat-tailed son-of-a-gun! Pick up your feet and travel, or I'll yank out your back bone and make a quirt out of it! For —- –"

> My name was Captain Kidd as I sailed
> As I sailed,
>
> My name was Captain Kidd,
> As I sailed!
>
> My name was Captain Kidd
> And most wickedly I di-i-id
> All holy laws forbid
> As I sailed!

The confessor of superlative wickedness droned his avowal in diminishing volume as the burros pattered along the white dust of the valley road, then the curve to the west hid them, and all was silence but for the rustle of the wind in the mesquite and the far bay of Singleton's hounds circling a coyote.

But Pat pricked up his ears, and lifted his head as if feeling rather than hearing the growing thud of coming hoofs. The girl waited until they were within fifty feet, when she pursed up her lips and whistled the call of the meadow lark. It sounded like a fairy bugle call across the morning, and the roan was halted quickly at the forks of the road.

"Howdy, señorita?" he called softly. "I can't see you, but your song beats the birds. Got a flag of truce? Willing to parley with the enemy?"

Then she emerged, eyeing him sulkily.

"You were going without seeing me!" she stated with directness, and without notice of the quizzical smile of comradeship.

"Certainly was," he agreed. "When I got through the scrap with your disciple of *kultur*, my mug didn't strike me as the right decoration for a maiden's bower. I rode out of the scrap with my scratches, taking joy and comfort in the fact that he had to be carried."

"There was no reason for your being so —- so brutal!" she decided austerely.

"Lord love you, child, I didn't need a reason —- I only wanted an excuse. Give me credit! I got away for fear I'd go loco and smash Singleton for interfering."

"Papa Phil only did his duty, standing for peace."

"Huh, let the Neutral League do it! The trouble with Singleton is he hasn't brains enough to lubricate a balance wheel, —- he can't savvy a situation unless he has it printed in a large-type tract. Conrad was scared for fear I'd stumbled on a crooked trail of his and would tell the boss, so he beat me to it with the lurid report that I made an assault on him! This looks like it —- not!" and he showed the slashes in his sombrero to make room for the blue banda around his head. "Suppose you tell that Hun of yours to carry a gun like a real hombre instead of the tools of a second-story man. The neighbors could hear a gun, and run to my rescue."

The girl regarded his flippancy with disapproval.

"He isn't my Hun," she retorted. "I could worry along without him on our map, —- but after all, I don't know a single definite thing against him. Anyway, it's decided I've got to go away somewhere to school and be out of the ranch squabbles. Papa Phil thinks I get in bad company out here."

"Meaning me?"

"Well, he *said* Captain Pike was demoralizing to the youthful mind. He didn't mention you. And Cap certainly did go the limit yesterday!"

"How so?"

"Well, he went to the Junction for his outfit stuff —- –"

"Yes, and never showed up at the adobe until the morning star was in the sky!"

"I know," she confessed. "I went with him. We stayed to see a Hart picture at the theater, and had the time of our young lives. At supper I announced that I was going to adopt Cap as a grandfather, —- and then of course he had to go and queer me by filling up on some rank whiskey he had smuggled in with the other food! My stars! —- he was put to bed singing that he'd 'Hang his harp on a willow tree, and be off to the wars again' —- You needn't laugh!"

But he did laugh, his blue eyes twinkling at her recital.

"You poor kid! You have a hard time with the disreputables you pick up. Sure they didn't warn you against speaking to this reprobate?"

"Sure nothing!" was the boyish reply. "I was to be docked a month's spending money if I dared go near Pedro Vijil's adobe again while you were there, which was very foolish of Papa Phil!" she added judicially. "I reckon he forgot they tried that before."

"And what happened?"

"I went down and borrowed double the amount from old Estevan, the trader at the Junction, and gave him an order against the ranch. Then Cap and I sneaked out a couple of three-year-olds and raced them down in the cottonwood flats against some colts brought down by an old Sierra Blanca Apache. We backed our nags with every peso, and that old brown murderer won!

But Cap and I had a wonderful day while our coin lasted, and —- and you were going away without saying good-bye!"

Kit Rhodes, who had blankly stated that he owned his horse and saddle and little beyond, looked at the spoiled plucky heiress of Granados ranches, and the laughter went out of his eyes.

She was beyond reason loveable even in her boyish disdain of restriction, and some day she would come back from the schools a very finished product, and thank the powers that be for having sent her out of knowledge of happy-go-lucky chums of the ranges.

Granados ranches had been originally an old Spanish grant reaching from a branch of the intermittent Rio Altar north into what is now Arizona, and originally was about double the size of Rhode Island. It was roughly divided into the home or hacienda ranch in Arizona, and La Partida, the cattle range portion, reaching far south into Sonora. Even the remnant of the grant, if intelligently managed, would earn an income satisfactory for a most extravagant princess royal such as its present chatelaine seemed to Rhodes.

But he had noted dubiously that the management was neither intelligent nor, he feared, square. The little rancherias scattered over it in the fertile valleys, were worked on the scratch gravel, ineffective Mexic method by the Juans and Pedros whose family could always count on mesquite beans, and *camotes* if the fields failed. There was seed to buy each year instead of raising it. There was money invested in farming machinery, and a bolt taken at will from a thresher to mend a plow or a buggy as temporarily required. The flocks of sheep on the Arizona hills were low grade. The cattle and horse outfits were south in La Partida, and the leakage was beyond reason, even in a danger zone of the border land.

All this Kit had milled around and around many times in the brief while he had ranged La Partida. A new deal was needed and needed badly, else Wilfreda Bernard would have debts instead of revenue if Singleton let things drift much longer. Her impish jest that she was a damsel in distress in need of a valiant knight was nearer to truth than she suspected. He had an idiotic hungry desire to be that knight, but his equipment of one horse, one saddle, and one sore head appeared inadequate for the office.

Thus Kit Rhodes sat his horse and looked at her, and saw things other than the red lips of the girl, and the chiding gray eyes, and the frank regret at his going.

It was more profitable not to see that regret, or let it thrill a man in that sweet warm way, especially not if the man chanced to be a drifting ranger. She was only a gallant little girl with a genius for friendships, and her loyalty to Pike extended to Pike's chum —- that was what Rhodes told himself!

"Yes," he agreed, "I was going without any tooting of horns. No use in Cap Pike and me hanging around, and getting you in bad with your outfit."

"As if I care!" she retorted.

"You might some day," he said quietly. "School may make a lot of difference; that, and changed surroundings for a year or two. But some day you will be your own manager, and if I'm still on the footstool and can be of service —- just whistle, señorita."

"Sure!" she agreed cheerfully. "I'll whistle the lark call, and you'll know I need you, so that's settled, and we'll always be —- be friends, Trail-hunter."

"We'll always be friends, Lark-child."

"I wanted Cap Pike to let me in on this prospecting trip, wanted to put in money," she said rather hesitant, "and he turned me down cold, except for a measly ten dollars, 'smoke money' he called it. I reckon he only took that to get rid of me, which I don't call friendly, do you? And if things should go crooked with him, and he —- well —- sort of needs help to get out, you'll let me know, won't you?"

"Yes, if it seems best," he agreed, "but you won't be here; you'll be shipped to a school, *pronto!*"

"I won't be so far off the map that a letter can't reach me. Cap Pike won't ever write, but I thought maybe you —--"

"Sure," agreed Rhodes easily. "We'll send out a long yell for help whenever we get stuck."

She eyed him darkly and without faith.

"Wish I knew how to make that certain," she confessed. "You're only dodging me with any kind of a promise to keep me quiet, just as Cap did. I know! I'm jealous, too, because you're taking a trail I've always wanted to take with Cap, and they won't let me because I'm a girl."

"Cheer up! When you are boss of the range you can outfit any little *pasear* you want to take, but you and I won't be in the same class then, Lark-child."

"Are you really going it blind, trailing with Cap into the Painted Hills after that fascinating gold legend?" she demanded. "Or have you some inside trail blazed for yourself? Daddy Pike is the best ever, but he always goes broke, and if he isn't broke, he has a jug at his saddle horn, so ——–"

"Oh it's only a little jug this time, and he's had a fare-you-well drink out of it with everyone in sight, so there's only one hilarious evening left in the jug now. Just enough for a gladsome memory of civilization."

"Are you in deep on this prospect plan?" she persisted.

"Well, not that you could notice. That is, I've got a three months' job offered me down at Whitely's; that will serve the captain as headquarters to range from until we add to our stake. Whitely is rounding up stock for the Allies down Mesa Blanca way, and Pike will feel at home there. Don't you worry, I'll keep an eye on Pike. He is hilariously happy to get into that region with a partner."

"I don't like it," she grumbled at him with sulky gray eyes. "Pedro Vijil just came back from the south, and brought his sister's family from San Rafael. They're refugees from the Federals because their men joined Ramon Rotil, the rebel leader, and Merced is crying herself crazy over the tales of war they tell. One of their girls was stolen, and the mother and Tia Luz are both crying over that. So Papa Phil says he's going to send me away where I won't hear such horrors. I wish I was a man, and I'd join the army and get a chance to go over and fight."

"Huh!" grunted Rhodes skeptically, "some more of us had hopes! Our army officers are both praying and cursing to get a chance to do the same thing, but they are not getting it! So you and I, little girl, will wait till some one pitches a bomb into that dovery on the Potomac. Then we'll join the volunteers and swarm over after our people."

"Oh, yes, *you* can! Men can do anything they like. I told you I was jealous."

"Never mind, Lark-child," he returned soothingly. "If I get over with a gun, you can come along and toot a horn. There now, that's a bargain, and you can practice tooting the lark's call until the time comes."

"I reckon I'll have plenty of time to toot myself black in the face before you show up again at Granados," she prophesied ruefully, and he laughed.

"Whistle an' I'll come to you, Lassie," he said with sudden recklessness, "and that's for *adios*, Billie."

He held out his hand.

"That's enough, Rhodes," said a voice back of them, and Singleton walked forward. "When you got your time, you were supposed to leave Granados. Is this what you've been hanging around for during the past week?"

Rhodes flamed red to his hair as he stared down at the elder man.

"I reckon I'll not answer that now, Mr. Singleton," he said quietly. "You may live to see you made a mistake. I hope you do, but you're traveling with a rotten bunch, and they are likely to use a knife or a rope on you any time you've played the goat long enough for them to get their innings. I'm going without any grudge, but if I was an insurance agent, trying to save money for my company, I'd sure pass you by as an unsafe bet! Keep on this side of the line, Singleton, while the revolution is whirling, and whatever you forget, don't forget I said it! *Adios*, señorita, and ——- good luck!"

"Good luck, Kit," she half whispered, "and *adios*!"

She watched him as he rode away, watched him as he halted at the turn of the trail and waved his hand, and Singleton was quietly observing her the while. She frowned as she turned and caught him at it.

"You thought he waited here, or planned to —- to meet me," she flared. "He was too square to tell you the truth, but it was I rode out here to say good-bye, rode out and held him up! But I did not reckon anyone would try to insult him for it!"

Her stepfather regarded her grimly. She was angry, and very near to tears.

"Time you had your breakfast," he observed, "and all signs indicate I should have sent you East last year, and kept you out of the promiscuous mixups along the border. It's the dumping ground for all sorts of stray adventurers, and no place for a girl to ride alone."

"He seemed to think I am as able to look after myself as you," she retorted. "You aren't fair to him because you take the word of Conrad, but Conrad lies, and I'm glad he got thrashed good and plenty! Now I've got that off my mind, I'll go eat a cheerful breakfast."

Singleton walked silent beside her back to where his horse was grazing by the roadside.

"Huh!" grunted the girl with frank scorn. "So you got out of the saddle to spy? Haven't you some black-and-tan around the ranch to do your dirty work?"

"It's just as well to be civil till you know what you are talking about," he reminded her with a sort of trained patience. "I came out without my breakfast just to keep the ranchmen from thinking what Tia Luz thinks. She told me I'd find that fellow waiting for you. I didn't believe it, but I see she is not so far wrong."

He spoke without heat or feeling, and his tone was that of quiet discussion with a man or boy, not at all that of a guardian to a girl. His charge was evidently akin to the horse ranch of Granados as described by the old ranger: Singleton had acquired them, but never understood them.

"Look here," said his protégée with boyish roughness, "that Dutchman sees everything crooked, especially if there's an American in range, and he prejudices you. Why don't you wake up long enough to notice that he's framing some excuse to run off every decent chap who comes on the place? I knew Rhodes was too white to be let stay. I saw that as soon as he landed, and I told him so! What I can't understand is that you won't see it."

"A manager has to have a free hand, Billie, or else be let go," explained Singleton. "Conrad knows horses, he knows the market, and is at home with the Mexicans. Also he costs less than we used to pay, and that is an item in a bad year."

"I'll bet we lose enough cattle to his friends to make up the difference," she persisted. "Rhodes was right when he called them a rotten bunch."

"Let us hope that when you return from school you will have lost the major portion of your unsavory vocabulary," he suggested. "That will be worth a herd of cattle."

"It would be worth another herd to see you wake up and show you had one good fight in you!" she retorted. "Conrad has all of the ranch outfit locoed but me; that's why he passes on this school notion to you. He wants me out of sight."

"I should have been more decided, and insisted that you go last year. Heaven knows you need it badly enough," sighed Singleton, ignoring her disparaging comment on his own shortcomings. And then as they rode under the swaying fronds of the palm drive leading to the ranch house he added, "Those words of your bronco busting friend concerning the life insurance risk sounded like a threat. I wonder what he meant by it?"

The telephone bell on the Granados Junction line was ringing when they entered the patio. Singleton glanced at the clock.

"A night letter probably," he remarked. "Go get your coffee, child, it's a late hour for breakfast."

Billie obeyed, sulkily seating herself opposite Tia Luz —- who was bolt upright behind the coffee urn, with a mien expressing dignified disapproval. She inhaled a deep breath for forceful speech, but Billie was ahead of her.

"So it was you! You were the spy, and sent him after me!"

"*Madre de Dios!* and why not?" demanded the competent Luz. "You stealing your own horse at the dawn to go with the old Captain Pike. I ask of you what kind of a girl is that? Also Mercedes was here last night tearing her hair because of the girls, her sister's daughters, stolen away over there in Sonora. Well! is that not enough? That Señor Kit is also too handsome. I was a fool to send the medicine with you to Pedro's house. He looked a fine caballero but even a fine caballero will take a girl when she follows after. *I* know! And once in Sonora all trails of a girl are lost. I know that too!"

"You are all crazy, and I never saw him at Pedro's house, never!" said the girl reaching for her coffee, and then suddenly she began to laugh. "Did you think, did you make Papa Philip think, that I was eloping like this?" and she glanced down at her denim riding dress.

"And why not? Did I myself not steal out in a shift and petticoat the first time I tried to run away with my Andreas? And beyond that not a thing under God had I on but my coral beads, and the red satin slippers of my sister Dorotea! She pulled my hair wickedly for those slippers, and I got a *reata* on my back from my grandmother for that running away. I was thirteen years old then! But when I was nearly sixteen we did get away, Andreas and I, and after that it was as well for the grandmother to pay a priest for us, and let us alone. Ai-ji! señorita, I am not forgetting what I know! And while I am here in Granados there must be nothing less than a grand marriage, and may the saints send the right man, for a wrong one makes hell in any house!"

Billie forgot her sulkiness in her joy at the elopements of Tia Luz. No wonder she distrusted an American girl who was allowed to ride alone!

But in the midst of her laughter she was reminded that Singleton was still detained at the telephone in the adjoining room, and that his rather high-pitched tones betrayed irritation.

"Well, why can't you give the telegram to me? Addressed to Conrad? Of course if it's a personal message I don't want it, but you say it is a ranch matter —- and important. Horses? What about them?"

Billie, listening, sped from the table to his side, and putting her hand over the telephone, whispered:

"If Brehman, the secretary, was here, they'd give it to him. They always do."

Singleton nodded to her, and grew decided.

"See here, Webster, one of our men was hurt, and Brehman took his place and went East with that horse shipment. Mr. Conrad had to go down in Sonora on business, and I am the only one here to take his place. Just give me the message as you would give it to the secretary. But you'd better type a copy and send by mail that I can put it on file. All right? Yes, go ahead."

Billie had quickly secured paper and pencil, but instead of taking them, Singleton motioned for her to write the message.

> Adolf Conrad, Granados Ranch, Granados Junction, Arizona. Regret to report September shipment horses developed ailment aboard vessel, fifty per cent dead, balance probably of no military use,

Ogden, Burns & Co.

Word by word Singleton took the message and word by word Billie wrote it down, while they stared at each other.

"Developed ailment aboard vessel!" repeated Singleton. "Then there was something wrong on shipboard, for there certainly is not here. We have no sick horses on the ranch, never do have!"

"But these people?" and Billie pointed to the signature.

"Oh, they are the men who buy stock for the Allies, agents for the French. They paid for the horses on delivery. They are safe, substantial people. I can't understand —- –"

But Billie caught his arm with a gasp of horror and enlightenment.

"Papa Phil! Think —- *think* what Kit Rhodes said! *'Ground glass in the feed at the other end of the road! Conrad's game —- Herrara knows!'* Papa Phil, —- Miguel Herrara was killed —- killed! And Conrad tried to kill Kit! Oh he did, he did! None of the Mexicans thought he would get well, but Tia Luz cured him. And Cap Pike never went out of sight of that adobe until Conrad had left the ranch, and I know Kit was right. I know it, I know it! Oh, my horses, my beautiful horses!"

"There, there! Why, child you're hysterical over this, which is —- is too preposterous for belief!"

"Nothing is too preposterous for belief. You know that. Everybody knows it in these days! Is Belgium too preposterous? Is that record of poison and powdered glass in hospital supplies too preposterous? In *hospital* supplies! If they do that to wounded men, why not to cavalry horses? Why Papa Phil —- –"

"Hush —- hush —- hush!" he said pacing the floor, clasping his head in both hands. "It is too terrible! What can we do? What? Who dare we trust to even help investigate?"

"Well, you might wire those agents for particulars, this is rather skimpy," suggested Billie. "Come and get some breakfast and think it over."

"I might wire the office of the Peace Society in New York to —- –"

"Don't you do it!" protested Billie. "They may have furnished the poison for all *you* know! Cap Pike says they are a lot of traitors, and Cap is wise in lots of things. You telegraph, and you tell them that if the sickness is proven to have started in Granados, that we will pay for every dead horse, tell them we have no sick horses here, and ask them to answer, *pronto!*"

"That seems rather reckless, child, to pay for all —- –"

"I *am* reckless! I am crazy mad over those horses, and over Conrad, and over Kit whom he tried to kill!"

"Tut —- tut! The language and behavior of Rhodes was too wicked for anyone to believe him innocent. He was a beastly looking object, and I still believe him entirely in the wrong. This loss of the horses is deplorable, but you will find that no one at Granados is to blame."

"Maybe so, but you just send that telegram and see what we see!"

CHAPTER VI
A DEAD MAN UNDER THE COTTONWOODS

Billie was never out of hearing of the telephone all day, and at two o'clock the reply came.

> PHILIP SINGLETON, Rancho Granados, Arizona.
>
> Kindly wire in detail the source of your information. No message went to Granados from this office. No publicity has been given to the dead horse situation. Your inquiry very important to the Department of Justice.
>
> OGDEN, BURNS & CO.

"Very strange, very!" murmured Singleton. "No matter how hard I think, or from what angle, I can't account for it. Billie, this is too intricate for me. The best thing I can do is to go over to Nogales and talk to an attorney."

"Go ahead and talk," agreed Billie, "but I'd answer that telegram first. This is no township matter, Papa Phil, can't you see that?"

"Certainly, certainly, but simply because of that fact I feel I should have local advice. I have a legal friend in Nogales. If I could get him on the wire ——–"

An hour later when Billie returned from a ride, she realized Singleton had gotten his friend on the wire, for she heard him talking.

"Yes, this is Granados. Is that you, James? Yes, I asked them to have you call me. I need to consult with you concerning a rather serious matter. Yes, so serious I may say it is mysterious, and appalling. It concerns a shipment of horses. Conrad is in Sonora, and this subject can't wait —— no, I can't get in touch with Conrad. He is out of communication when over there —— No, I can't wait his return. I've had a wire from Ogden and Burns, New York —— said Ogden and Burns —— All right, get a pencil; I'll hold the wire."

There was a moment of silence, and if a telephonic camera had been installed at Granados, Mr. Singleton might have caught a very interesting picture at the other end of the wire.

A middle-aged man in rusty black of semi-clerical cut held the receiver, and the effect of the names as given over the wire was, to put it mildly, electrical. His jaw dropped and he stared across the table at a man who was seated there. At the repetition of the name, the other arose, and with the stealthily secretive movement of a coyote near its prey he circled the table, and drew a chair close to the telephone. The pencil and paper was in his hand, not in that of "James." That other was Conrad.

Then the telephone conversation was resumed after Mr. Singleton had been requested to speak a little louder —— there seemed some flaw in the connection.

In the end Singleton appeared much comforted to get the subject off his own shoulders by discussing it with another. But he had been convinced that the right thing to do was to motor over to the Junction and take the telegrams with him for consultation. He would start about eight in the morning, and would reach the railroad by noon. Yes, by taking the light car which he drove himself it would be an easy matter.

Billie heard part of this discourse in an absent-minded way, for she was not at all interested as to what some strange lawyer in Nogales might think of the curious telegrams.

She would have dropped some of that indifference if she had been able to hear the lurid language of Conrad after the receiver was hung up. James listened to him in silence for a bit, and then said:

"It's your move, brother! There are not supposed to be any mistakes in the game, and you have permitted our people to wire you a victory when you were not there to get the wire, and that was a mistake."

"But Brehman always ——–"

"You sent Brehman East and for once forgot what might happen with your office empty. No, —- it is not Singleton's fault; he did the natural thing. It is not the operator's fault; why should he not give a message concerning horses to the proprietor of the horse ranch?"

"But Singleton never before made a move in anything of management, letters never opened, telegrams filed but never answers sent until I am there! And this time! It is that most cursed Rhodes, I know it is that one! They told me he was high in fever and growing worse, and luck with me! So you yourself know the necessity that I go over for the Sonora conference —- there was no other way. It is that Rhodes! Yes, I know it, and they told me he was as good as dead —- God! if again I get him in these hands!"

He paced the floor nervously, and flung out his clenched hands in fury, and the quiet man watched him.

"That is personal, and is for the future," he said, "but Singleton is not a personal matter. If he lives he will be influenced to investigation, and that must not be. It would remove you from Granados, and you are too valuable at that place. You must hold that point as you would hold a fort against the enemy. When Mexico joins with Germany against the damned English and French, this fool mushroom republic will protest, and that is the time our friends will sweep over from Mexico and gather in all these border states —- which were once hers —- and will again be hers through the strong mailed hand of Germany! This is written and will be! When that day comes, we need such points of vantage as Granados and La Partida; we must have them! You have endangered that position, and the mistake won't be wiped out. The next move is yours, Conrad."

The quiet man in the habiliments of shabby gentility in that bare little room with the American flag over the door and portraits of two or three notable advocates of World Peace and the American League of Neutrality on the wall, had all the outward suggestion of the small town disciple of Socialism from the orthodox viewpoint. His manner was carefully restrained, and his low voice was very even, but at his last words Conrad who had dropped into a seat, his head in his hands, suddenly looked up, questioning.

"Singleton can probably do no more harm today," went on the quiet voice. "I warned him it would be a mistake to discuss it until after he had seen me. He starts at eight in the morning, alone, for the railroad but probably will not reach there." He looked at his watch thoughtfully. "The Tucson train leaves in fifty minutes. You can get that. Stop off at the station where Brehman's sister is waitress. She will have his car ready, that will avoid the Junction. It will be rough work, Conrad, but it is your move. It is an order."

And then before that carefully quiet man who had the appearance of a modest country person, Adolf Conrad suddenly came to his feet in military salute.

"Come, we will talk it over," suggested his superior. "It will be rough, yet necessary, and if it could appear suicide, eh? Well, we will see. We —- will —- see!"

At seven in the morning the Granados telephone bell brought Singleton into the patio in his dressing gown and slippers. And Doña Luz who was seeing that his breakfast was served, heard him express surprise and then say:

"Why, certainly. If you are coming this way as far on the road as the Jefferson ranch of course we can meet there, and I only need to go half way. That will be excellent. Yes, and if Judge Jefferson is at home he may be able to help with his advice. Fine! Good-bye."

When Doña Luz was questioned about it later she was quite sure Mr. Singleton mentioned no name, his words were as words to a friend.

But all that day the telephone was out of order on the Granados line, and Singleton did not return that night. There was nothing to cause question in that, as he had probably gone on to Nogales, but when the second day came and the telephone not working, Billie started Pedro Vijil to ride the line to Granados Junction, get the mail, and have a line man sent out for repairs wherever they were needed.

It was puzzling because there had been no storm, nothing of which they knew to account for the silent wire. The line was an independent one from the Junction, and there were only two stations on it, the Jefferson ranch and Granados.

But Vijil forgot about the wire, for he met some sheep men from the hills carrying the body of Singleton. They had found him in the cottonwoods below the road not five miles from the hacienda. His car he had driven off the road back of a clump of thick mesquite. The revolver was still in his hand, and the right temple covered with black blood and flies.

There was nothing better to do than what the herders were doing. The man had been dead a day and must be buried, also it was necessary to send a man to Jefferson's, where there was a telephone, to get in touch with someone in authority and arrange for the funeral.

So the herders walked along with their burden carried in a *serape*, and covered by the carriage robe. Pedro had warned them to halt at his own house, for telephone calls would certainly gather men, who would help to arrange all decently before the body was taken into the *sala* of Granados.

There is not much room for conjecture as to the means of a man's taking off when he is found with a bullet in his right temple, a revolver in his right hand, and only one empty cartridge shell in the revolver. There seemed no mystery about the death, except the cause of suicide.

It was the same evening that Conrad riding in from the south, attempted to speak over the wire with Granados and got from Central information that the Granados wire was broken, and Singleton, the proprietor, a suicide.

The coroner's inquest so pronounced it, after careful investigation of the few visible facts. Conrad was of no value as a witness because he had been absent in Magdalena. He could surmise no reason for such an act, but confessed he knew practically nothing of Singleton's personal affairs. He was guardian of his stepdaughter and her estate, and so far as Conrad knew all his relations with the personnel of the estate were most amicable. Conrad acknowledged when questioned that Singleton did usually carry a revolver when out in the car, he had a horror of snakes, and he had never known him to use a gun for anything else.

Doña Luz Moreno confused matters considerably by her statement that Mr. Singleton was going to meet some man at the Jefferson ranch because the man had called him up before breakfast to arrange it. Later it was learned that no call was made from any station over the wire that morning to Granados. There was in fact several records of failure to get Granados. No one but Doña Luz had heard the call and heard Singleton reply, yet it was not possible that this communication could be a fact over a broken wire, and the wire was found broken between the Jefferson ranch and Granados.

Whereupon word promptly went abroad among the Mexicans that Señor Singleton had been lured to his death by a spirit voice calling over a broken wire as a friend to a friend. For the rest of her life Doña Luz will have that tale to tell as the evidence of her own ears that warnings of death do come from the fearsome spirits of the shadowed unknown land, —- and this in denial of all the padres' godly discourse to the contrary!

A Mr. Frederick James of Nogales, connected with a group of charitable gentlemen working for the alleviating of distress among the many border exiles from Mexico, was the only person who came forward voluntarily to offer help to the coroner regarding the object of the dead man's journey to Nogales. Mr. James had been called on the telephone by Mr. Singleton, who was apparently in great distress of mind concerning mysterious illness and deaths of horses shipped from Granados to France. A telegram had come from New York warning him that the Department of Justice was investigating the matter, and the excitement and nervousness of Mr. Singleton was such that Mr. James readily consented to a meeting in Nogales, with the hope that he might be of service in any investigation they would decide upon after consultation. When Mr. Singleton did not keep the engagement, Mr. James attempted to make inquiries by telephone. He tried again the following morning, but it was only after hearing of the suicide —— he begged pardon —- the death of Mr. Singleton, that he recalled the fact that all of Singleton's discourse over the telephone had been unusual, excitable to a degree, while all acquaintances of the dead man knew him as a quiet, reserved man, really unusually reserved, almost to the point of the secretive. Mr. James was struck by the unusual note of panic in his tones, but as a carload of horses was of considerable financial value, he ascribed the excitement in part to that, feeling confident of course that Mr. Singleton was in no ways accountable for the loss, but — –

Mr. James was asked if the nervousness indicated by Mr. Singleton was a fear of personal consequences following the telegram, but Mr. James preferred not to say. He had regarded Mr. Singleton as a model of most of the virtues, and while Singleton's voice and manner had certainly been unusual, he could not presume to suspect the inner meaning of it.

The telegraph and telephone records bore out the testimony of Mr. James.

The fact that the first telegram was addressed to the manager, Mr. Conrad, had apparently nothing to do with the case, since the telegraph files showed that messages were about evenly divided in the matter of address concerning ranch matters. They were often addressed simply to "Granados Rancho" or "Manager Granados Ranch." This one simply happened to be addressed to the name of the manager.

The coroner decided that the mode of address had no direct bearing on the fact that the man was found dead under the cottonwoods with copies of both telegrams in his pocket, both written in a different hand from his carefully clear script as shown in his address book. Safe in his pocket also was money, a gold watch with a small gold compass, and a handsome seal ring. Nothing was missing, which of course precluded the thought of murder for robbery, and Philip Singleton was too mildly negative to make personal enemies, a constitutional neutral.

Billie, looking very small and very quiet, was brought in by Doña Luz and Mr. Jefferson of the neighboring ranch, fifty miles to the east. She had not been weeping. She was too stunned for tears, and there was a strangely ungirlish tension about her, an alert questioning in her eyes as she looked from face to face, and then returned to the face of the one man who was a stranger, the kindly sympathetic face of Mr. Frederick James.

She told of the telegrams she had copied, and of the distress of Singleton, but that his distress was no more than her own, that she had been crying about the horses, and he had tried to comfort her. She did not believe he had a trouble in the world of his own, and he had never killed himself — never!

When asked if she had any reason to suspect a murderer, she said if they ever found who killed the horses they would find who killed her Papa Phil, but this opinion was evidently not shared by any of the others. The report of horses dead on a transport in the Atlantic ocean, and a man dead under the cottonwoods in Arizona, did not appear to have any definite physical relation to each other, unless of course the loss of the horses had proven too much of a shock to Mr. Singleton and upset his nerves to the extent that moody depression had developed into temporary dementia. His own gun had been the evident agent of death.

One of the Mexicans recalled that Singleton had discharged an American foreman in anger, and that the man had been in a rage about it, and assaulted Mr. Conrad, whereupon Conrad was recalled, and acknowledged the assault with evident intent to kill. Yes, he heard the man Rhodes had threatened Singleton with a nastier accident than his attempt on Conrad. No, he had not heard it personally, as he was unconscious when the threat was made.

"It wasn't a threat!" interrupted Billie, "it was something different, a warning."

"A warning of what?"

Billie was about to quote Kit's opinion concerning Singleton's ranch force, when she was halted by a strange thing — for Billie; it was merely the mild steady gaze of the quiet gentleman of the peaceful league of the neutrals. There was a slight lifting of his brows as she spoke of a warning; and then a slight suggestion of a smile — it might have been a perfectly natural incredulous smile, but Billie felt that it was not. The yellowish brown eyes narrowed until only the pupils were visible, and warm though the day was, Billie felt a swift chill over her, and her words were cautious.

"I can't say, I don't know, but Kit Rhodes had no grudge against Papa Phil. He seemed in some way to be sorry for him."

She noted that Conrad's gaze was on the face of Mr. James instead of on her.

"Sorry for him?"

"Y-yes, sort of. He tried to explain why, but Papa would not listen, and would not make any engagement with him. Sent his money by Captain Pike and wouldn't see him. But Kit Rhodes did not make a threat, he did not!"

Her last denial was directly at Conrad, who merely shrugged his shoulders as if to dispose of that awkward phase of the matter.

"It was told me so, but the Mexican men might not have understood the words of Rhodes —- he was in a rage —- and it may be he did not mean so much as he said."

"But he didn't say it!" insisted Billie.

"Very good, he did not, and it is a mistake of mine," agreed Conrad politely. "For quite awhile I was unconscious after his assault, naturally I know nothing of what was said."

"And where is this man Rhodes to be found?" asked the coroner, and Conrad smiled meaningly.

"Nowhere, —- or so I am told! He and a companion are said to have crossed the line into Sonora twenty-four hours before the death of Mr. Singleton."

"Well, unless there is some evidence that he was seen later on this side, any threat he might or might not have made, has no relation whatever to this case. Is there any evidence that he was seen at, or near, Granados after starting for Sonora?"

No evidence was forthcoming, and the coroner, in summoning up, confessed he was not satisfied to leave certain details of the case a mystery.

That Singleton had discharged Rhodes in anger, and Rhodes had, even by intimation, voiced a threat against Singleton could not be considered as having any bearing on the death of the latter; while the voice of the unknown calling him to a meeting at Jefferson's ranch was equally a matter of mystery, since no one at Jefferson's knew anything of the message, or the speaker, and investigation developed the fact that the telephone wire was broken between the two ranches, and there was no word at Granados Junction Central of any message to Granados after five o'clock the afternoon of the previous day.

And, since Philip Singleton never reached the Jefferson ranch, but turned his car off the road at the cottonwood cañon, and was found with one bullet in his head, and the gun in his own hand, it was not for a coroner's jury to conjecture the impulse leading up to the act, or the business complications by which the act might, or might not, have been hastened. But incomprehensible though it might seem to all concerned there was only one finding on the evidence submitted, and that was suicide.

"Papa Phil never killed himself, never!" declared Billie. "That would be two suicides in a month for Granados, and two is one too many. We never had suicides here before."

"Who was the other?"

"Why, Miguel Herrara who had been arrested for smuggling, was searched and his gun taken, and yet that night found a gun to kill himself with in the adobe where he was locked up! Miguel would not have cared for a year or two in jail; he had lived there before, and hadn't tried any killing. I tell you Granados is getting more than its share."

"It sure looks like it, little lady," agreed the coroner, "but Herrara's death gives us no light or evidence on Singleton's death, and our jurisdiction is limited strictly to the hand that held the gun. The evidence shows it was in the hand of Mr. Singleton when found."

The Jeffersons insisted that Billie go home with them, as the girl appeared absolutely and pathetically alone in the world. She knew of no relatives, and Tia Luz and Captain Pike were the only two whom she had known from babyhood as friends of her father's.

The grandmother of Billie Bernard had been the daughter of a Spanish *haciendado* who was also an officer in the army of Mexico. He met death in battle before he ever learned that his daughter, in the pious work of nursing friend and enemy alike, had nursed one enemy of the hated North until each was captive to the other, and she rode beside him to her father's farthest northern rancho beyond the Mexican deserts, and never went again to the gay circles of Mexico's capital. Late in her life one daughter, Dorotea was born, and when Alfred Bernard came out of the East and looked on her, a blonde Spanish girl as her ancestresses of Valencia had been, the game of love was played again in the old border rancho which was world enough for the lovers. There had been one eastern summer for them the first year of their marriage, and Philip Singleton had seen her there, and never forgot her. After her widowhood he crossed the continent to be near her, and after awhile his devotion, and her need of help in many ways, won the place he coveted, and life at Granados went on serenely until her death. Though he had at times been bored a bit by the changelessness of ranch life, yet he had given his word to guard the child's inheritance until she came of age, and had kept it loyally as he knew how until death met him in the cañon of the cottonwoods.

But the contented isolation of her immediate family left Billie only such guardian as the court might appoint for her property and person, and Andrew Jefferson, Judge Jefferson by courtesy, in the county, would no doubt be choice of the court as well as the girl. Beyond that she could only think of Pike, and —- well Pike was out of reach on some enchanted gold trail of which she must not speak, and she supposed she would have to go to school instead of going in search of him!

Conrad spoke to her kindly as she was led to the Jefferson car, and there was a subtle deference in his manner, indicating his realization that he was speaking —- not to the wilful little maid who could be annoying —- but to the owner of Granados and, despite his five year contract as manager, an owner who could change entirely the activities of the two ranches in another year —- and it was an important year.

He also spoke briefly to Mr. James offering him the hospitality of the ranch for a day of rest before returning to Nogales, but the offer was politely declined. Mr. James intimated that he was at Conrad's service if he could be of any practical use in the mysterious situation. He carefully gave his address and telephone number, and bade the others good day. But as he was entering his little roadster he spoke again to Conrad.

"By the way, it was a mistake to let that man Rhodes get over into Sonora. It should be the task of someone to see that he does not come back. He seems a very dangerous man. See to it!"

The words were those of a kindly person interested in the welfare of the community, and evidently impressed by the evidence referring to the discharged range boss. Two of the men hearing him exchanged glances, for they also thought that rumor of the threats should have been looked into. But the last three words were spoken too softly for any but Conrad to hear.

The following week Billie went to Tucson with the Jeffersons and at her request Judge Jefferson was appointed guardian of her person and estate, after which she and the judge went into a confidential session concerning that broken wire on the Granados line.

"I'm not loco, Judge," she insisted, "but I want you to learn whether that wire was cut on purpose, or just broke itself. Also I want you to take up that horse affair with the secret service people. I don't want Conrad to be sent away —- yet. I'd rather watch him on Granados. I won't go away to school; I'd rather have a teacher at home. We can find one."

"But, do you realize that with two mysterious deaths on Granados lately, you might run some personal risk of living there with only yourself and two women in the house? I'm not sure we can sanction that, my child."

Billie smiled at him a bit wanly, but decided.

"Now Judge, you know I picked you because you would let me do whatever I pleased, and I don't mean to be disappointed with you. Half the men at the inquest think that Kit Rhodes did come back to do that shooting, and you know Conrad and the very smooth rat of the Charities Society are accountable for that opinion. The Mexican who dragged in Kit's name is one of Conrad's men; it all means something! It's a bad muddle, but Kit Rhodes and Cap Pike will wander back here some of these days, and I mean to have every bit of evidence for Kit to start in with. He suspected a lot, and all Granados combined to silence him —- fool Granados!"

"But, just between ourselves, child, are you convinced Rhodes did not make the statement liable to be construed into a threat against Mr. Singleton?"

"Convinced nothing," was the inelegant reply of his new ward. "I heard him say enough to hang him if evidence could be found that he was north of the line that morning, and that's why it's my job to take note of all the evidence on the other side. The horses did not kill themselves. That telegram concerning it did not send itself. Papa Phil did not shoot himself, and that telephone wire did not cut itself! My hunch is that those four things go together, and that's a combination they can't clear up by dragging in the name of a man who never saw the horses, and who was miles south in Sonora with Cap Pike when the other three things happened. Now can they?"

> There was a frog who lived in the spring:
> Sing-song Kitty, can't yo' carry me, oh?
>
> And it was so cold that he could not sing,
> Sing-song Kitty, can't yo' carry me, oh?
>
> Ke-mo! Ki-mo! Dear —- oh my!
>
> To my hi' —- to my ho —- to my —- –

"Oh! For the love of Mike! Bub, can't you give a man a rest instead of piling up the agony? These old joints of mine are creakin' with every move from desert rust and dry camps, and you with no more heart in you than to sing of springs, —- cold springs!"

"They do exist, Cap."

"Uh —- huh, they are as real to us this minute as the red gold that we've trailed until we're at the tag end of our grub stake. I tell you, Bub, they stacked the cards on us with that door of the old Soledad Mission, and the view of the gold cañon from there! Why, Whitely showed us that the mission door never did face the hills, but looked right down the valley towards the Rio del Altar just as the Soledad plaza does today; all the old Mexicans and Indians tell us that."

"Well, we've combed over most of the arroyas leading into the Altar from Rancho Soledad, and all we've found is placer gravel; yet the placers are facts, and the mother lode is somewhere, Cap."

"Worn down to pan dirt, that's what!" grunted Pike. "I tell you these heathen sit around and dream lost mission tales and lost mine lies; dream them by the dozen to delude just such innocent yaps as you and me. They've nothing else to do between crops. We should have stuck to a white man's land, north into Arizona where the Three Hills of Gold are waiting, to say nothing of the Lost Stone Cabin mine, lost not twenty miles from Quartzite, and in plain sight of Castle Dome. Now there is nothing visionary about *that*, Kit! Why, I knew an old-timer who freighted rich ore out of that mine thirty years ago, and even the road to it has been lost for years! We know things once did exist up in that country, Kit, and down here we are all tangled up with Mexican-Indian stories of ghosts and enchantments, and such vagaries. I'm fed up with them to the limit, for everyone of them we listen to is different from the last. We'll head up into the Castle Dome country next time, hear me?"

"Sure, I hear," agreed Kit cheerfully. "Perhaps we do lose, but it's not so bad. Since Whitely sent his family north, he has intimated that Mesa Blanca is a single man's job, and I reckon I can have it when he goes —- as he will. Then in the month we have scouted free of Whitelys, we have dry washed enough dust to put you on velvet till things come our way. Say, what will you bet that a month of comfort around Nogales won't make you hungry for the trail again?"

"A gold trail?" queried the weary and dejected Pike.

"Any old trail to any old place just so we keep ambling on. You can't live contented under cover, and you know it."

"Well," decided Pike after a rod or two of tramping along the shaly, hot bed of a dry arroya. "I won't bet, for you may be among the prophets. But while you are about it, I'd be thankful if you'd prophesy me a wet trail next time instead of skimpy mud holes where springs ought to be. I'm sick of dry camps, and so is Baby Buntin'."

"'*Oh, there was a frog lived in the spring!*'" chanted Kit derisively. "Cheer up, Cap, the worst is yet to come, for I've an idea that the gang of Mexican vaqueros we glimpsed from the butte at noon will just about muss up the water hole in Yaqui cañon until it will be us for a sleep there before the fluid is fit for a water bottle. *'Oh, there was a frog lived in the spring!'* Buntin' Baby, we'll fish the frog out, and let you wallow in it instead, you game little dusty rat! Say, Pike, when we load up with grub again we'll keep further west to the Cerrado Pintado. I'll follow a hunch of my own next trip."

The older man grunted disdain for the hunches of Kit, even while his eyes smiled response to the ever-living call of youth. To Rhodes there was ever a "next time." He was young enough to deal in futures, and had a way with him by which friends were to be found for even unstable venturings with no backing more substantial than a "hunch."

Not that Kit was gifted with any great degree of fatal beauty —- men are not often pretty on the trail, unwashed, unshaven, and unshorn —- added to which their equipment had reached the point where his most pretentious garment was a square of an Indian *serape* with a hole in the middle worn as a poncho, and adopted to save his coat and other shirt on the hard trail.

Cap Pike growled that he looked like a Mexican peon in that raiment, which troubled Kit not at all. He was red bronze from the desert days, and his blue eyes, with the long black lashes of some Celtic ancestor, looked out on the world with direct mild approval. They matched the boyish voice much given to trolling old-time ditties and sentimental foolishness.

He led the dappled roan over the wild dry "wash" where the sand was deep and slippery, and the white crust of alkali over all. Before him swayed the pack mules, and back of him Captain Pike sagged on the little gray burro, named in derision and affection, the Baby Bunting of the outfit.

The jauntiness was temporarily eliminated from the old prospector. Two months of fruitless scratching gravel when he had expected to walk without special delay to the great legendary deposit, had taken the sparkle of hope from the blue eyes, and he glanced perfunctorily at the walls of that which had once been a river bed.

"What in time do you reckon became of all the water that used to fill these dry gullies?" he asked querulously. "Why, it took a thousand years of floods to wash these boulders round, and then leave them high and dry when nicely polished. That's a waste in nature I can't figure out, and this godforsaken territory is full of them."

"Well, you grouch, if we didn't have this dry bed to skip along, we would be bucking the greasewood and cactus on the mesa above. So we get some favors coming our way."

"Skip along, —- me eye!" grunted Pike, as the burro toiled laboriously through the sand, and Kit shifted and stumbled over treacherous, half-buried boulders. "Say, Kit, don't you reckon it's time for Billie to answer my letter? It's over eight weeks now, and mail ought to get in once a month."

Rhodes grunted something about "mail in normal times, but these times were not normal," and did not seem much interested in word from Granados.

He had not the heart, or else had too much, to tell the old man that the letter to Billie never reached her. When Whitely went north he put it in his coat pocket, and then changed his coat! Kit found it a month later and held it, waiting to find someone going out. He had not even mentioned it to Whitely on his return, for Whitely was having his own troubles, and could not spare a man for a four day trip to mail.

Whitely's folks lived north of Naco, and he had gone there direct and returned without touching at Nogales, or hearing of the tragedy at Granados. The latest news of the Mexican revolutions, and the all-absorbing question as to whether the United States would or would not intervene, seemed all the news the worried Whitely had brought back. Even the slaughter of a dozen nations of Europe had no new features to a ranchman of Sonora, —- it remained just slaughter. And one did not need to cross boundaries to learn of killings, for all the world seemed aflame, and every state in Mexico had its own wars, —- little or big.

Then, in the records of the tumultuous days, there was scarce space for the press or people to give thought after the first day or two, to the colorless life going out in mystery under the cottonwoods of Granados, and no word came to tell Rhodes of the suspicion, only half veiled, against himself.

The ranch house of Mesa Blanca was twenty miles from the hacienda of Soledad, and a sharp spur of the Carrizal range divided their grazing lands. Soledad reached a hundred miles south and Mesa Blanca claimed fifty miles to the west, so that the herds seldom mingled, but word filtered to and from between the vaqueros, and Rhodes heard that Perez had come north from Hermosillo and that El Aleman, (the German) had made the two day trip in from the railroad, and had gone on a little *pasear* to the small rancherias with Juan Gonsalvo, the half-breed overseer. The vaqueros talked with each other about that, for there were no more young men among them for soldiers, only boys and old men to tend the cattle, and what did it mean?

The name of Rhodes was not easy for the Mexican tongue, and at Mesa Blanca his identity was promptly lost in the gift of a name with a meaning to them, El Pajarito, (the singer). Capitan Viajo, (the old captain), was accepted by Pike with equal serenity, as both men were only too well pleased to humor the Indian ranch people in any friendly concessions, for back of some of those alert black eyes there were surely inherited records of old pagan days, and old legends of golden veins in the hills.

The fact that they were left practically nameless in a strange territory did not occur to either of them, and would not have disturbed them if it had. They had met no American but Whitely since they first struck Mesa Blanca. One month Kit had conscientiously stuck to the ranch cares while Whitely took his family out, and Pike had made little sallies into the hills alone.

On Whitely's return he had made an errand to Soledad and taken Rhodes and Pike along that they might view the crumbled walls of old Soledad Mission, back of the ranch house. The ancient rooms of the mission padres were now used principally as corrals, harness shop, and storage rooms.

The situation in itself was one of rare beauty; —- those old padres knew!

It was set on a high plain or mesa, facing a wide valley spreading miles away to the south where mother-of-pearl mountains were ranged like strung jewels far against the Mexican sky. At the north, slate-blue foothills lifted their sharp-edged shoulders three miles away, but only blank walls of Soledad faced the hills, all portals of the old mission appeared to have faced south, as did Soledad. The door facing the hills was a myth. And as Rhodes stood north of the old wall, and searched its thirty-mile circle, he could understand how four generations of gold seekers had failed to find even a clue to the wealth those unknown padres had looked on, and sent joyous evidence of to the viceroy of the south. It would take years of systematic search to cover even half the visible range. A man could devote a long lifetime to a fruitless search there, and then some straying burro might uncover it for an Indian herder who would fill his poncho, and make a sensation for a week or two, and never find the trail again!

"It's just luck!" said Kit thinking it all over as he tramped along the arroya bed, "it either belongs to you, or it doesn't. No man on earth can buy it and make it stay, but if it is yours, no man can keep you from it entirely."

"What the devil are you yammering about?" asked Pike grumpily.

"Oh, I was just thinking of how Whitely exploded our little balloon of hopes when he took us over to size up the prospects at Soledad. I wonder if Perez has no white help at all around that place. We did not even see the foreman."

"He's a half-breed, that Juan Gonsalvo. The Indians don't like him. He's from down Hermosillo way, and not like these Piman children of nature. He and Conrad are up to some devilment, but Whitely thinks Juan took the job, deluded as we are, with the notion that a gold mine was sticking up out of the ground at the Soledad corrals, and it was to be his find. You see, Bub, that story has gone the length of Mexico, and even over to Spain. Oh, we are not the only trailers of ghost gold; there are others!"

The slanting sun was sending shadows long on the levels, and the hills were looming to the east in softest tones of gray and amethyst; the whitish green of desert growths lay between, and much of brown desert yet to cross.

"We can't make the foothills tonight even though there is an early moon," decided Kit. "But we can break camp at dawn and make it before the sun is high, and the water will hold out that long."

"It will hold for Buntin' and the mules, but what of Pardner?" asked the older man. "He's not used to this hard pan gravel scratching."

"But he's thoroughbred, and he can stand it twelve hours more if I can, can't you, old pal?" The tall roan with the dot of black between the eyes returned his owner's caress by nosing his bare neck, and the hand held up to smooth the black mane.

"I'll be glad enough to see him safe across the border in old Arizona," observed Pike. "I can't see how the herders saved him for you at Mesa Blanca when their own stock was picked of its best for the various patriots charging through the settlements."

"Some way, Miguel, the Indian vaquero, managed it, or got his girl to hide it out. Whitely confessed that his Indian cattlemen are the most loyal he can find down here."

"But it's not a white man's land —- yet, and I'm downright glad he's shipped his family north. There's always hell enough in Sonora, but it's a dovecote to what it's bound to be before the end comes, and so, it's no place for white men's wives."

"Right you are! Say, what was it Whitely heard down in Sinaloa concerning the Enchanted Cañon mine?"

"Oh, some old priest's tale —- the same dope we got with a different slant to it. The gold nuggets from some shrine place where the water gushed *muy fuerte*, by a sycamore tree. Same old nuggets sent out with the message, and after that the insurrection of the Indians, and the priests who found it never lived to get out. Why, Bub, that is nearly two hundred years ago! Stop and think of the noble Castilians going over Sonora with a fine tooth comb for that trail ever since and then think of the nerve of us!"

"Well, I'm nearer to it anyway than the Dutchman who trekked in from the south last year with copies of the old mission reports as guide, for the Yaquis killed him, and took his records, while they hide my horse for me."

"Huh! yes, and warn you to ride him north!"

"Correct; —- but Pike, it was a warning, not a threat! Oh, I'm coming back all right, all right! That gold by the hidden stream sure has got me roped and hog tied for keeps."

Pike growled good-natured disdain of his confidence, and suggested that the stream, which was probably only a measly mud hole, could have dropped to purgatory in an earthquake tremor since those first old mission days, or filled up with quicksand.

"Right you are, Cap. That's a first-rate idea," agreed Kit the irrepressible. "Next trip we'll start looking for streams that were and are not; we're in the bed of one now for that matter!"

"Somewhere ahead we should come into the trail south from Carracita," observed Pike, "but I reckon you'd just as soon camp with Pard out of sight of the trail."

There was silence for a bit as they plodded on up the wide dry bed of the river, and then Kit turned, glancing at the old man keenly.

"I didn't fool you much when I called that gang 'vaqueros,' did I?" he observed. "Well, they didn't look good to me, and I decided I'd have to fight for my horse if we crossed trails, and —- it wastes a lot of time, fighting does."

"No, you didn't fool me. You'd be seven kinds of an idiot to walk in this gully of purgatory when you could ride safely on the mesa above, so I guessed you had a hunch it was the friendly and acquisitive patriots."

"Pike, they were between us and the Palomitas rancherias of Mesa Blanca or I'd have made a try to get through and warn the Indians there. Those men had no camp women with them, so they were not a detachment of the irregular cavalry, —- that's what puzzles me. And their horses were fresh. It's some new devilment."

"There's nothing new in Sonora, son. Things happen over and over the same."

The shadows lengthened, and the blue range to the east had sharp, black edges against the saffron sky, and the men plodding along over sand and between boulders, fell silent after the little exchange of confidence as to choice of trail. Once Kit left the gully and climbed the steep grade to the mesa alone to view the landscape over, but slid and scrambled down, —- hot, dusty, and vituperative.

"Not a sign of life but some carrion crows moving around in the blue without flop of a wing," he grumbled. "Who started the dope that mankind is the chosen of the Lord? Huh! we have to scratch gravel for all we rake in but the birds of the air have us beat for desert travel all right, all right!"

"Well, Bub, if you saw no one's dust it must be that gang were not headed for Palomitas or Whitely's."

"They could strike Palomitas, and circle over to the east road without striking Whitely's home corrals," said Kit thoughtfully.

"Sure they could, but what's the object? If it's cattle or horses they're after the bigger ranch is the bigger haul?"

"Yes, —- if it's stock they're after," agreed Kit somberly.

"Why, lad, what —- what's got you now?"

"I reckon it's the damned buzzards," acknowledged the younger man. "I don't know what struck me as I sat up there watching them. Maybe it's their blackness, maybe it's their provender, maybe it was just the loco of their endless drifting shadows, but for a minute up there I had an infernal sick feeling. It's a new one on me, and there was nothing I could blame it on but disgust of the buzzards."

"You're goin' too shy on the water, and never knew before that you had nerves," stated Pike sagely. "I've been there; fought with a pardner once, —- Jimmy Dean, till he had to rope me. You take a pull at the water bottle, and take it now."

Kit did so, but shook his head.

"It touches the right spot, but it was not a thirst fancy. It was another thought and —- O Bells of Pluto! Pike, let's talk of something else! What was that you said about the Sinaloa priest story of the red gold? You said something about a new slant on the old dope."

"Uh-huh!" grunted Pike. "At least it was a new slant to me. I've heard over and over about uprising of Indians, and death of the two priests who found their mine, but this Sinaloa legend has it that the Indians did not kill the priests, but that their gods did!"

"Their gods?"

"Yeh, the special gods of that region rose up and smote them. That's why the Indians barred out other mission priests for so long a spell that no white man remembered just where the lost shrine of the red gold was. Of course it's all punk, Bub, just some story of the heathen sheep to hide the barbecuing of their shepherds."

"Maybe so, but I've as much curiosity as a pet coon. What special process did their gods use to put the friars out of commission?"

"Oh, lightning. The original priests' report had it that the red gold was at some holy place of the tribes, a shrine of some sort. Well, you know the usual mission rule —- if they can't wean the Indian from his shrine, they promptly dig foundations and build a church there under heavenly instructions. That's the story of this shrine of El Alisal where the priests started to build a little branch chapel or *visita*, for pious political reasons —- and built it at the gold shrine. It went down in the priests' letter or record as gold of rose, a deep red gold. Well, under protest, the Indians helped build a shack for a church altar under a great aliso tree there, but when lightning struck the priests, killed both and burned the shack, you can see what that manifestation would do to the Indian mind."

Kit halted, panting from the heart-wearying trail, and looked Pike over disgustedly.

"Holy mackerel! Pike, haven't you *any* imagination? You've had this new side to the story for over a month and never even cheeped about it! I heard you and Whitely talking out on the porch, but I didn't hear this!"

"Why, Bub, it's just the same old story, everyone of them have half a dozen different sides to it."

"But this one explains things, this one has logic, this one blazes a trail!" declared the enthusiast. "This one explains good and plenty why no Indian has ever cheeped about it, no money could bribe him to it. Can't you see? Of course that lightning was sent by their wrathy gods, of course it was! But do you note that place of the gold, and place of the shrine where the water rises, is also some point where there is a dyke of iron ore near, a magnet for the lightning? And that is not here in those sandy mesas and rocky barrancas —- it's to the west in the hills, Pike. Can't you see that?"

"Too far from the old north and south trail, Bub. There was nothing to take padres so far west to the hills. The Indians didn't even live there; only strayed up for nuts and hunting in the season."

"Save your breath!" jeered Kit. "It's me to hike back to Mesa Blanca and offer service at fifty dollars per, and live like a miser until we can hit the trail again. I may find a tenderfoot to buy that valley tract of mine up in Yuma, and get cash out of that. Oh, we will get the finances somehow! I'll write a lawyer soon as we get back to Whitely's —- God! what's that?"

They halted, holding breath to listen.

"A coyote," said Pike.

"No, only one animal screams like that —- a wildcat in the timber. But it's no wildcat."

Again the sound came. It was either from a distance or else muffled by the barrier of the hill, a blood-curdling scream of sickening terror.

A cold chill struck the men as they looked at each other.

"The carrion crows knew!" said Kit. "You hold the stock, Pike."

He quickly slipped his rifle from its case, and started up the knoll.

"The stock will stand," said Pike. "I'm with you."

As the two men ran upward to the summit and away from the crunching of their own little outfit in the bed of the dry river, they were struck by the sound of clatter of hoofs and voices.

"Bub, do you know where we are?" asked Pike —- "this draw slants south and has brought us fair into the Palomitas trail where it comes into the old Yaqui trail, and on south to hell."

"To hell it is, if it's the slavers again after women," said Kit. "Come quiet."

They reached the summit where cacti and greasewood served as shield, and slightly below them they saw, against the low purple hills, clouds of dust making the picture like a vision and not a real thing, a line of armed horsemen as outpost guards, and men with roped arms stumbling along on foot slashed at occasionally with a *reata* to hasten their pace. Women and girls were there, cowed and drooping, with torn garments and bare feet. Forty prisoners in all Kit counted of those within range, ere the trail curved around the bend of a hill.

"But that scream?" muttered Kit. "All those women are silent as death, but that scream?" Then he saw.

One girl was in the rear, apart from the rest of the group. A blond-bearded man spurred his horse against her, and a guard lashed at her to keep her behind. Her scream of terror was lest she be separated from that most woeful group of miserables. The horse was across the road, blocking it, as the man with the light beard slid from the saddle and caught her.

Kit's gun was thrown into position as Pike caught his hand.

"*No!*" he said. "Look at her!"

For the Indian girl was quicker far. From the belt of her assailant she grasped a knife and lunged at his face as he held her. His one hand went to his cheek where the blood streamed, and his other to his revolver.

But even there she was before him, for she held the knife in both hands against her breast, and threw herself forward in the haze of dust.

The other guard dismounted and stared at the still figure on the trail, then kicked her over until he could see her face. One look was enough. He jerked the knife from the dead body, wiped it on her *manta*, and turned to tie a handkerchief over the cheek of the wounded horseman.

Kit muttered an oath of horror, and hastily drew the field glass from its case to stare at the man whose beard, a false one, had been torn off in the struggle. It was not easy to re-adjust it so that it would not interfere with the bandage, and thus he had a very fair view of the man's features, and his thoughts were of Billie's words to Conrad concerning slave raids in Sonora. Had Billie really suspected, or had she merely connected his Mexican friends with reports of raids for girls in the little Indian pueblos?

Pike reached for the glass, but by the time he could focus it to fit his eyes, the man had re-mounted, riding south, and there was only the dead girl left there where she fell, an Indian girl they both knew, Anita, daughter of Miguel, the major-domo of Mesa Blanca, whose own little rancheria was with the Pimans at Palomitas.

"Look above, Cap," said Kit.

Above two pair of black wings swept in graceful curves against the saffron sky —- waiting!

Rhodes went back to the outfit for pick and shovel, and when twilight fell they made a grave there in the dusky cañon of the desert.

They camped that night in the barranca, and next morning a thin blue smoke a mile away drew Kit out on the roan even in the face of the heat to be, and the water yet to find. He hoped to discover someone who had been more fortunate in escape.

He found instead an Indian he knew, one whose gray hair was matted with blood and who stood as if dazed by terror at sound of hoofs. It was Miguel, the Pima head man of Mesa Blanca.

"Why, Miguel, don't you know me?" asked Kit.

The eyes of the man had a strange look, and he did not answer. But he did move hesitatingly to the horse and stroked it.

"*Caballo,*" he said. "*Muy bueno, caballo.*"

"Yes," agreed Pardner's rider, "very good always."

"*Si* señor, always."

Kit swung from the saddle, and patted the old man's shoulder. He was plainly dazed from either a hurt, or shock, and would without doubt die if left alone.

"Come, you ride, and we'll go to camp, then find water," suggested Kit. "Camp here no good. Come help me find water."

That appeal penetrated the man's mind more clearly. Miguel had been the well-trusted one of the Indian vaqueros, used to a certain dependence put upon him, and he straightened his shoulders for a task.

"*Si* señor, a good padrone are you, and water it will be found for you." He was about to mount when he halted, bewildered, and looked about him as if in search.

"All —- my people —- " he said brokenly. "My children of me —- my child!"

Kit knew that his most winning child lay newly covered under the sand and stones he had gathered by moonlight to protect the grave from coyotes.

But there was a rustle back of him and a black-eyed elf, little more than a child, was standing close, shaking the sand from her hair.

"I am hearing you speak. I know it is you, and I come," she said.

It was Tula, the younger daughter of Miguel, —- one who had carried them water from the well on her steady head, and played with the babies on the earthen floors at the pueblo of Palomitas.

But the childish humors were gone, and her face wore the Indian mask of any age.

"Tell me," said Kit.

"It is at Palomitas. I was in the willows by the well when they came, Juan Gonsalvo and El Aleman, and strange soldiers. All the women scream and make battle, also the men, and that is when my father is hurt in the head, that is when they are taking my mother, and Anita, my sister. Some are hiding. And El Aleman and Juan Gonsalvo make the count, and sent the men for search. That is how it was."

"Why do you say El Aleman?" asked Rhodes.

"I seeing him other time with Don José, and hearing how he talk. Also Anita knowing him, and scream his name —- 'Don Adolf!' —- when he catch her. Juan Gonsalvo has a scarf tied over the face —- all but the eyes, but the Don Adolf has the face now covered with hairs and I seeing him. They take all the people. My father is hurt, but lives. He tries to follow and is much sick. My mother is there, and Anita, my sister, is there. He thinks it better to find them —- it is his head is sick. He walks far beside me, and does not know me."

"You are hungry?"

She showed him a few grains of parched corn tied up in the corner of her *manta*. "Water I have, and roots of the sand."

"Water," repeated Miguel mechanically. "Yes, I am the one who knows where it comes. I am the one to show you."

The eyes of the girl met Kit's gaze of understanding.

"The hurt is of his head," she stated again. "In the night he made speech of strange old-time things, secret things, and of fear."

"So? Well, it was a bad night for old men and Indian girls in the desert. Let's be moving."

Tula picked up her hidden wicker water bottle and trudged on sandaled feet beside Kit. Miguel went into a heap in the saddle, dazed, muttering disjointed Indian words, only one was repeated often enough to make an impression, —- it was Cajame.

"What is Cajame?" he asked the girl, and she gave him a look of tolerance.

"He was of chiefs the most great. He was killed for his people. He was the father of my father."

Kit tried to recall where he had heard the name, but failed. No one had chanced to mention that Miguel, the peaceful Piman, had any claims on famous antecedents. He had always seemed a grave, silent man, intent only on herding the stock and caring for the family, at the little cluster of adobes by the well of Palomitas. It was about two miles from the ranch house, but out of sight. An ancient river hill terminated in a tall white butte at the junction of two arroyas, and the springs feeding them were the deciding influence regarding location of dwellings. Rhodes could quickly perceive how a raid could be made on Palomitas and, if no shots were fired, not be suspected at the ranch house of Mesa Blanca.

The vague sentences of Miguel were becoming more connected, and Kit, holding him in the saddle, was much puzzled by some of them.

"It is so, and we are yet dying," he muttered as he swayed in the saddle. "We, the Yaqui, are yet dumb as our fathers bade. But it is the end, señor, and the red gold of Alisal is our own, and — - –"

Then his voice dwindled away in mutterings and Rhodes saw that the Indian girl was very alert, but watching him rather than her father as she padded along beside him.

"Where is it —- Alisal?" he asked carelessly, and her velvet-black eyes narrowed.

"I think not anyone is knowing. It is also evil to speak of that place," she said.

"What makes the evil?"

"Maybe so the padres. I no knowing, what you think?"

But they had reached the place of camp where Cap Pike had the packs on the animals, waiting and restless.

"Well, you're a great little collector, Bub," he observed. "You start out on the bare sand and gravel and raise a right pert family. Who's your friend?"

Despite his cynical comment, he was brisk enough with help when Miguel slid to the ground, ashen gray, and senseless.

"Now we are up against trouble, with an old cripple and a petticoat to tote, and water the other side of the range."

But he poured a little of the precious fluid down the throat of the Indian, who recovered, but stared about vacantly.

"Yes, señor," he said nodding his head when his eyes rested on Rhodes, "as you say —- it is for the water —- as you say —- it is the end —- for the Yaqui. Dead is Cajame —- die all we by the Mexican! To you, señor, my child, and El Alisal of the gold of the rose. So it will be, señor. It is the end —- the water is there, señor. It is to you."

"That's funny," remarked Pike, "he's gone loony and talking of old chief Cajame of the Yaquis. He was hanged by the Mexican government for protesting against loot by the officials. A big man he was, nothing trifling about Cajame! That old Indian had eighty thousand in gold in a government bank. Naturally the Christian rulers couldn't stand for that sort of shiftlessness in a heathen! Years ago it was they burned him out, destroyed his house and family; —- the whole thing was hellish."

The girl squatting in the sand, never took her eyes off Pike's face. It was not so much the words, but the tone and expression she gave note to, and then she arose and moved over beside her father.

"No," she said stolidly, "it is his families here, Yaqui me —- no Pima! Hiding he was when young, hiding with Pima men all safe. The padre of me is son to Cajame, —- only to you it is told, you Americano!"

Her eyes were pitiful in their strained eagerness, striving with all her shocked troubled soul to read the faces of the two men, and staking all her hopes of safety in her trust.

"You bet we're Americano, Tula, and so will you be when we get you over the border," stated Rhodes recklessly. "I don't know how we are going to do it, Cap, but I swear I'm not going to let a plucky little girl like that go adrift to be lifted by the next gang of raiders. We need a mascot anyway, and she is going to be it."

"You're a nice sort of seasoned veteran, Bub," admitted Pike dryly, "but in adopting a family it might be as well to begin with a he mascot instead of what you've picked. A young filly like that might turn hoodoo."

"I reckon I'd have halted for a sober second thought if it hadn't been for that other girl under the stones down there," agreed Rhodes. "But shucks! —- with all the refugees we're feeding across the line where's the obstacle to this one?"

The old prospector was busy with the wounded head for the Indian and had no reply ready, but shook his head ominously. Rhodes scowled and began uncoiling a *reata* in case it would be needed to tie Miguel in the saddle.

"We've got to get some hustle to this outfit," he observed glancing at the sun. "It's too far to take them back to Whitely's, and water has to be had. We are really nearer to Soledad!"

The Indian girl came closer to him, speaking in a low, level manner, strange and secretive, yet not a whisper.

"He does know —- and water is there at that place," she said. "In the night I am hearing him speak all what the ancients hide. He no can walk to that place, maybe I no can walk, but go you for the gold in the hidden cañon. You are Americano, —- strong, —- is it not? A brave heart and much of gold of rose would bring safe again the mother of me and my sister! All this I listen to in the night. For them the gold of rose by the hidden water is to be uncovered again. But see, his hands are weak, his head is like the *niño* in the reed basket. A stronger heart must find the way —- it is you."

Lowly, haltingly, she kept on that level-voiced decision. It was evident that the ravings of her father through the long hours of the dreadful night had filled her mind with his one desire: to dare the very gods that the red gold might be uncovered again, and purchase freedom for the Indians on the exile road to the coast.

So low were her words that even Cap Pike, a rod away, only heard the voice, but not the subject. It was further evident that she meant but the one man to hear. Pike had white hair and to her mind was, like her father, to be protected from responsibilities, but Rhodes loomed strong and kind, and braced by youth for any task.

Rhodes looked at her pityingly, and patted her head.

"I reckon we're all a little loco, kid," he observed. "You're so paralyzed with the hell you saw, and his ravings that you think his dope of the gold is all gospel, but it's only a dream, sister, —- a sick man's fancy, though you sure had me going for a minute, plum hypnotized by the picture."

"It is to hide always," she said. "No man must know. No other eyes must see, only you!"

"Sure," he agreed.

"You promising all?"

"Sure again! Just to comfort you I promise that when I find the gold of El Alisal I will use it to help get your people."

"Half," she decided. "Half to you."

"Half it is! You're a great little planner for your size, kid. Too bad it's only a dream."

Cap Pike rose to his feet, and gave a hand to Miguel, who reeled, and then steadied himself gradually.

"Most thanks, señor," he whispered, "and when we reach the water —- –"

They helped him into the saddle, and Rhodes walked beside, holding him as he swayed.

They passed the new-made grave in the sand, and Rhodes turned to the girl. "Sister," he said, "lift two stones and add to that pile there, one for you and one for your father. Also look around and remember this place."

"I am no forgetting it," she said as she lifted a stone and placed it as he told her. "It is here the exile trail. I mark the place where you take for me the Americano road, and not the south road of the lost. So it is, —- these stone make witness."

"I'll be shot if I don't believe you *are* old Cajames stock," said Cap Pike staring at her, and then meeting the gaze of Rhodes in wonder at her clear-cut summing up of the situation. "But he was a handful for the government in his day, Bub, and I'm hornswaggled if I'd pick out his breed for a kindergarten."

The girl heard and understood at least the jocular tenor of his meaning, but no glance in his direction indicated it. She placed the second stone, and then in obedience to Rhodes she looked back the way she had come where the desert growth crisped in the waves of heat. On one side lay the low, cactus-dotted hillocks, and on the other the sage green and dull yellow faded into the blue mists of the eastern range.

"I am no forgetting it, this place ever," she said and then lifted her water bottle and trudged on beside Rhodes. "It is where my trail begins, with you."

Cape Pike grinned at the joke on the boy, for it looked as if the Yaqui girl were adopting *him*!

CHAPTER IX
A MEETING AT YAQUI WELL

Good luck was with them, for the water hole in Yaqui cañon had not been either muddied or exhausted, evidence that the raiders had not ranged that way. The sorry looking quartette fairly staggered into the little cañon, and the animals were frantic with desire to drink their fill.

"I was so near fried that the first gallon fairly sizzled down my gullet," confessed Cap Pike after a long glorious hour of rest under the alamos with saturated handkerchief over his burning eyes. "That last three mile stretch was hell's back yard for me. How you reckon the little trick over there ever stood it?"

The Indian girl was resting near her father, and every little while putting water on his face and hands. When she heard the voice of Pike she sat up, and then started quietly to pick up dry yucca stalks and bits of brushwood for a fire.

"Look at that, would you, Bub," commented Pike, "the minute she sees you commence to open the cook kit she is rustling for firewood. That little devil is made of whalebone for toughness. Why, even the burros are played out, but she is fresh as a daisy after a half hour's rest!"

Rhodes noted that the excitement by which she had been swayed to confidence in the morning had apparently burned out on the trail, for she spoke no more, only served silently as generations of her mothers of the desert had done, and waited, crouched back of her father, while the men ate the slender meal of *carne seco*, *atole*, and coffee.

Cap Pike suggested that she join them, but it was her adopted guardian who protested.

"We won't change their ways of women," he decided. "I notice that when white folks try to they are seldom understood. How do we know whether that attitude is an humble effacement, or whether the rank of that martyred ancester exalts her too greatly to allow equality with white stragglers of the range?"

Cap Pike snorted disdain.

"You'll be making a Pocahontas of her if you keep on that 'noble Injun' strain," he remarked.

"Far be it from me! Pocahontas was a gay little hanger-on of the camps, —- not like this silent owl! Her mind seems older than her years, and just notice her care of him, will you? I reckon he'd have wandered away and died but for her grip on him through the night."

Miguel sank into sleep almost at once after eating, and the girl waved over him an alamo branch as a fan with one hand, and ate with the other, while Rhodes looked over the scant commissary outfit, reckoning mouths to feed and distance to supplies. The moon was at full, and night travel would save the stock considerably. By the following noon they could reach ranches either west or north. He was conscious of the eyes of the girl ever on his face in mute question, and while Pike bathed the backs of the animals, and led each to stand in the oozy drainage of the meager well, she came close to Kit and spoke.

"You say it is a dream, señor, and you laugh, but the red gold of El Alisal is no dream. He, my father has said it, and after that, I, Tula, may show it to you. Even my mother does not know, but I know. I am of the blood to know. You will take him there, for it is a medicine place, much medicine! He has said it to you, señor, and that gift is great. You will come, alone, —- with us, señor?"

Kit smiled at her entreaty, patted her hair, and dug out a worn deck of cards and shuffled them, slowly regarding the sleeping Indian the while.

"What's on your mind?" demanded Cap Pike, returning with his white locks dripping from a skimpy bath. "Our grub stake is about gone, and you've doubled the outfit. What's the next move?"

"I'm playing a game in futures with Miguel," stated Kit, shuffling the cards industriously.

"Sounds loco to me, Bub," observed the veteran. "Present indications are not encouraging as to futures there. Can't you see that he's got a jar from which his mind isn't likely to recover? Not crazy, you know, not a lunatic or dangerous, but just jarred from Pima man back to Yaqui child. That's about the way I reckon it."

"You reckon right, and it's the Yaqui child mind I'm throwing the cards for. Best two out of three wins."

"What the —– –"

"Highest cards for K. Rhodes, and I hike across the border with our outfit; highest cards for Miguel and my trail is blazed for the red gold of Alisal. This is Miguel's hand —– ace high for Miguel!"

Again he shuffled and cut.

"A saucy queen, and red at that! Oh, you charmer!"

"You got to hustle to beat that, Bub. Go on, don't be stingy."

Rhodes cut the third time, then stared and whistled.

"The cards are stacked by the Indian! All three covered with war paint. What's the use in a poor stray white bucking against that?"

He picked out the cards and placed them side by side, ace, king and queen of hearts.

"Three aces could beat them," suggested Pike. "Go on Bub, shuffle them up, don't be a piker."

Rhodes did, and cut ten of clubs.

"Not even the right color," he lamented. "Nothing less than two aces for salvation, and I —– don't —- get —- them!"

A lonely deuce fell on the sand, and Rhodes eyed it sulkily as he rolled a cigarette.

"You poor little runt," he apostrophized the harmless two-spot. "You've kicked me out of the frying pan into the fire, and a good likely blaze at that!"

"Don't reckon I care to go any deeper into trouble than what we've found," decided Pike. "Ordinary Indian scraps are all in the day's work —- same with a Mexican outfit —— but, Bub, this slave-hunting graft game with the state soldiery doing the raiding is too strong a combine for two lone rangers to buck against. Me for the old U. S. border, and get some of this devilish word to the peace advocates at home."

"They wouldn't believe you, and only about two papers along the border would dare print it," observed Rhodes. "Every time a band of sunny Mexicans loot a ranch or steal women, the word goes north that again the bloodthirsty Yaquis are on the warpath! Those poor devils never leave their fields of their own will, and don't know why the Americans have a holy dread of them. Yet the Yaqui is the best worker south of the line."

"If he wasn't the price wouldn't be worth the slave trader's valuable time," commented Pike.

The Indian girl made a quick gesture of warning, just a sweep outward of her hand along the ground. She didn't even look at them, but down the arroya, the trail they had come.

"*Caballos, hombres!*" she muttered in her throat.

"The kid's right, —— hear them!" said Rhodes, and then he looked at him, and made a strange movement of eyes and head to direct the attention back of her in the thicket of cactus and squat greasewood. He did not look at once, but finally with a circular sweep of the locality, he saw the light glint on a gun barrel along the edge of a little mesa above them.

"Nice friendly attention," he observed. "Someone sizing us up. Time to hit the trail anyway, Cap; —— to get through on the grub we have to travel tonight."

He rose and handed the water bottles to the girl to fill, while he tightened cinches.

"It's a long day's trip, Cap," he stated thoughtfully, "a long day out to Carrizal, and a long one back to Mesa Blanca. I'll divide the dust and the grub fifty-fifty, and you get out to some base of supplies. I'd rather you'd take Pardner, and keep on going across the line. The trail is clear from here for you, and enough water holes and settlements for you to get through. I don't think Pardner would last for the back trip, but you can save him by riding at night; the burro and mule are best for us. Here's the dust."

While Pike had been talking of crossing the border, Kit had been rapidly readjusting the provision so that the old chap had enough to carry him to the first settlement, and the gold dust would more than pay for provision the rest of the way.

"Why —- say, Bub!" remonstrated Pike. "You're so sudden! I don't allow to leave you by your lonesomes like this. Why, I had planned —- –"

"There's nothing else to do," decided Rhodes crisply. "If you don't beat it with Pardner, we'll lose him, sure! I'm going to take these Indians back, and you can help most by waiting north of the line till you hear from me. I'll get word to you at Granados. So, if there should be any trouble with these visitors of ours, your trail is clear; —- savvy?"

Two men rode into view in the bend of the arroya. A cartridge belt across each shoulder, and one around each waist, was the most important part of their equipment.

"*Buenos dias*, señors," said one politely, while his little black eyes roved quickly over the group. "Is there still water to be found in the well here? *Dios!* it is the heat of hell down there in the valley."

"At your service, señor, is water fresh drawn," said Rhodes, and turned to the girl, "Oija, Tulita! —- water for the gentlemen. You ride far, señor?"

"From Soledad wells."

"Yes, I know the brand," remarked Rhodes.

"This is a good season in which to avoid too much knowledge, or too good a memory, señor," observed the man who had not spoken. "Many herds will change hands without markets before tranquility is over in Mexico."

"I believe you, señor, and we who have nothing will be the lucky ones," agreed Rhodes, regarding the man with a new interest. He was not handsome, but there was a something quick and untamed in his keen, black eyes, and though the mouth had cruel hard lines, his tone was certainly friendly, yet dominating.

"What have you here?" he asked with a gesture toward Miguel.

"My Indian who tried to save his women from slavers, and was left for dead," stated Rhodes frankly.

"And this?"

He pointed to the girl filling again the water bottles.

"She is mine, señor. We go to our own homes."

"Hum! you should be enlisted in the fights and become capitan, but these would drop by the trail if you left them. Well, another time perhaps, señor! For the water many thanks. *Adios!*" and with wave of the hand they clattered down the arroya.

"Queer," muttered Rhodes, "did you catch that second chap signal to the gun man in the cactus? He craw-fished back over the mesa and faded away."

"They didn't come for water alone —- some scouten' party trailin' every sign found," decided Pike. "I'll bet they had us circled before the two showed themselves. Wonder who they are after?"

"Anyway they didn't think us worth while gathering in, which is a comfort. That second fellow looks like someone I've crossed trails with, but I can't place him."

"They'll place you all right, all right!" prophesied Pike darkly, "you and your interesting family won't need a brand."

Rhodes stared at him a moment and then grinned.

"Right you are, Cap. Wouldn't it be pie for the gossips to slice up for home consumption?"

He kept on grinning as he looked at the poor bit of human flotsam whom he had dubbed "the owl" because of her silence and her eyes. She aroused Miguel without words, watching him keenly for faintest sign of recovery. The food and sleep had refreshed him in body, but the mind was far away. To the girl he gave no notice, and after a long bewildered stare at Rhodes he smiled in a deprecating way.

"Your pardon, Don José, that I outsleep the camp," he muttered haltingly. "It is a much sickness of the head to me."

"For that reason must you ride slowly today," stated Rhodes with quick comprehension of the groping mind, though the "Don José" puzzled him, and at first chance he loitered behind with the girl and questioned her.

"How makes itself that I must know all the people in the world before I was here on earth?" she asked morosely? "Me he does not know, Don José is of Soledad and is of your tallness, so —- –"

"Know you the man who came for water at the cañon well?" he asked, and she looked at him quickly and away.

"The name of the man was not spoke by him, also he said a true word of brands on herds —- these days."

"In these days?" reflected Rhodes, amazed at the ungirlish logic. "You know what he meant when he said that?"

"We try that we know —- all we, for the Deliverer is he named, and by that name only he is spoke in the prayers we make."

Rhodes stared at her, incredulous, yet wondering if the dusty vaquero looking rider of brief words could be the man who was called outlaw, heathen, and bandit by Calendria, and "Deliverer" by these people of bondage.

"You think that is true; —- he will be the deliverer?"

"I not so much think, I am only remembering what the fathers say and the mothers. Their word is that he will be the man, if —- if —- –"

"Well, if what?" he asked as she crossed herself, and dropped her head.

"I am not wanting to say that thing. It is a scare on the heart when it is said."

"I'd rather be prepared for the scare if it strikes me," he announced, and after a thoughtful silence while she padded along beside him, she lowered her voice as though to hide her words from the evil fates.

"Then will I tell it you: —- a knife in the back is what they fear for him, or poison in his cup. He is hated by strong haters, also he makes them know fear. I hearing all that in the patio at Palomitas, and old Tio Polonio is often saying all saviors are crucified. How you think?"

Rhodes replied vaguely as to the wisdom of Tio Polonio, for the girl was giving him the point of view of the peon, longing for freedom, yet fatalistic as the desert born ever are. And she had known the rebel leader, Ramon Rotil, all the time!

He had no doubt but that she was right. Her statement explained the familiar appearance of the man he had not met before, though he had seen pictures in newspapers or magazines. Then he fell to wondering what Ramon Rotil was doing in a territory so far from the troops, and —- –

"Don José is one of the strong men who are hating him much," confided the child. "Also Don José comes not north alone ever anymore, always the soldiers are his guard. Tio Polonio tells things of these soldiers."

"What kind of things?"

"They are killing boys like rabbits in Canannea, —- pacifico boys who could grow to Calendrista soldiers. Such is done by the guard of Don José and all the friends of the Deliverer are killed with a quickness. That is how the men of Don José Perez please him most, and in the south there are great generals who work also with him, and his hand is made strong, also heavy, and that is what Tio Polonio is telling us often."

When they reached the mouth of the little cañon of the Yaqui well where the trails divide, Pike shook hands and climbed into the saddle of Pardner.

"It's the first time I ever took the easy way out, and left the fight alone to a chum, —- but I'll do it, Bub, because you could not make a quick get-away with me tagging along. Things look murkier in this territory every minute. You'll either have the time of your life, or a headstone early in the game. Billie and I will put it up though we won't know where you're planted. I don't like it, but the minutes and water for the trail are both precious. Come out quick as you can. So long!"

Pardner, refreshed by cooling drink and an hour's standing in wet mud of the well drainage, stepped off briskly toward the north, while Rhodes lifted Tula to the back of the pack mule, and Miguel unheeding all plans or changes, drooped with closed eyes on the back of the little burro. The manager of the reorganized gold-search syndicate strode along in the blinding glare of the high sun, herding them ahead of him, and as Pike turned for a last look backward at a bend of the trail, the words of the old darkey chant came to him on the desert air:

Oh, there was a frog lived in the spring!

CHAPTER X
A MEXICAN EAGLET

The silver wheel of the moon was rolling into the west when the Indian girl urged the mule forward, and caught the bridle of the burro.

"What is it, Tula?" asked Rhodes, "we are doing well on the trail to Mesa Blanca; why stop here?"

"Look," she said. "See you anything? Know you this place in the road?"

He looked over the sand dunes and scrubby desert growths stretching far and misty under the moon, and, then to the rugged gray range of the mountain spur rising to the south. They were skirting the very edge of it where it rose abruptly from the plain; a very great gray upthrust of granite wall beside them was like a gray blade slanted out of the plain. He had noticed it as one of the landmarks on the road to Mesa Blanca, and on its face were a few curious scratchings or peckings, one a rude sun symbol, and others of stars and waves of water. He recalled remarking to Pike that it must have been a prayer place for some of the old tribes.

"Yes, I know the place, when we reach this big rock it means that we are nearing the border of the ranch, this rock wall tells me that. We can be at Palomitas before noon."

"No," she said, and got down from the mule, "not to Palomitas now. Here we carry the food, and here we hide the saddles, and the mule go free. The burro we take, nothing else."

"Where is a place to hide saddles here?" and he made gesture toward the great granite plane glistening in the moonlight.

"A place is found," she returned, "it is better we ride off the trail at this place."

She did so, circling back the way they had come until they were opposite a more broken part of the mountain side, then she began deftly to help unsaddle.

"Break no brush and make all tracks like an Apache on the trail," she said.

Miguel sat silent on the burro as if asleep. He had never once roused to give heed to the words or the trail through the long ride. At times where the way was rough he would mutter thanks at the help of Kit and sink again into stupor.

"I can't spare that mule," protested Kit, but she nodded her head as if that had been all thought out.

"He will maybe not go far, there is grass and a very little spring below. Come now, I show you that hidden trail."

She picked up one of the packs and led the burro.

"But we can't pack all this at once," decided Kit, who was beginning to feel like the working partner in a nightmare.

"Two times," said Tula, holding up her fingers, "I show you."

She led the way, nervous, silent and in haste, as though in fear of unseen enemies. Rhodes looked after her irritably. He was fagged and worn out by one of the hardest trails he had ever covered, and was in no condition to solve the curious problems of the Indian mind, but the girl had proven a good soldier of the desert, and was, for the first time, betraying anxiety, so as the burro disappeared in the blue mist, and only the faint patter of his hoofs told the way he had gone, Kit picked up the saddle and followed.

The way was rough and there was no trail, simply stumbling between great jagged slabs hewn and tossed recklessly by some convulsion of nature. Occasionally dwarfed and stunted brush, odorous with the faint dew of night, reached out and touched his face as he followed up and up with ever the forbidding lances of granite sharp edged against the sky. From the plain below there was not even an indication that progress would be possible for any human being over the range of shattered rock, and he was surprised to turn a corner and find Tula helping Miguel from the saddle in a little nook where scant herbage grew.

"No, not in this place we camp," she said. "It is good only to hide saddles and rest for my father. Dawn is on the trail, and the other packs must come."

He would have remonstrated about a return trip, but she held up her hand.

"It must be, if you would live," she said. "The eyes of you have not yet seen what they are to see, it is not to be told. All hiding must be with care, or ——- –"

She made swift pantomime of sighting along a gun barrel at him, and even in the shadows he could fancy the deadly half closing of her ungirlish eyes. Tula did not play gaily.

Tired as he was, Kit grinned.

"You win," he said. "Let's hit what would be the breeze if this fried land could stir one up."

They plodded back without further converse, secured the packs, and this time it was Rhodes who led, as there appeared no possible way but the one they had covered. Only once did he make a wrong turn and a sharp "s-st" from the girl warned him of the mistake.

They found Miguel asleep, and Kit Rhodes would willingly have sunk down beside him and achingly striven for the same forgetfulness, but Tula relentlessly shook Miguel awake, got him on the burro, unerringly designated the food bag in the dark, and started again in the lead.

"I reckon you're some sort of Indian devil," decided Kit, shouldering the bag. "No mere mortal ever made this trail or kept it open."

Several times the towering walls suggested the bottom of a well, and as another and another loomed up ahead, he gloomily prophesied an ultimate wall, and the need of wings.

Then, just as the first faint light began in the eastern heavens, he was aware that the uneven trail was going down and down, zig-zagging into a ravine like a great gray bowl, and the bottom of it filled with shadows of night.

The girl was staggering now with exhaustion though she would not confess it. Once she fell, and he lifted her thinking she was hurt, but she clung to him, shaking from weakness, but whispering, "*Pronto, pronto!*"

"Sure!" he agreed, "all the swiftness the outfit can muster."

Curious odors came to him from the shadowy bowl, not exactly a pleasing fragrance, yet he knew it ——- But his mind refused to work. As the trail grew wider, and earth was under his feet instead of rock slivers and round boulders, he discovered that he was leading the burro, the grub sack over his shoulder, and with the other arm was supporting the girl, who was evidently walking with closed eyes, able to progress but not to guide herself.

Then there was the swish-swish of grasses about their feet and poor Bunting snatched mouthfuls as all three staggered downward. The light began to grow, and somewhere in the shadowy bowl there was the most blest sound known in the desert, the gurgle of running water!

"We hear it ——- but we can't believe it ——- old Buntin'," muttered Kit holding the burro from steady and stubborn attempts to break away, "and you are just loco enough to think you smell it."

Then suddenly their feet struck rock again, not jagged or slippery fragments, but solid paving, and a whiff of faint mist drifted across his face in the gray of the first dawn, and the burro craned his neck forward at the very edge of a black rock basin where warm vapor struck the nostrils like a soporific.

The girl roused herself at a wordless exclamation from Rhodes, and began automatically helping Miguel from the saddle, and stripping him to the breechcloth.

Kit's amazement startled him out of his lethargy of exhaustion. It was light enough now to see that her eyes were bloodshot, and her movements quick with a final desperation.

"There!" she said and motioned towards a shelving place in the rock, "there ——- medicine ——- all quick!"

She half lifted the staggering, unconscious Indian, and Kit, perceiving her intention, helped her with Miguel to the shallow edge of the basin where she rolled him over until he was submerged to the shoulder in the shallow bath, cupping her hands she scooped water and drenched his face.

"Why, ——- it's warm!" muttered Kit.

"Medicine," said Tula, and staggered away.

How Rhodes shed his own garments and slipped into the basin beside Miguel he never knew, only he knew he had found an early substitute for heaven. It was warm sulphur water, ——- tonic, refreshing and infinitely soothing to every sore muscle and every frazzled nerve. He ducked his head in it, tossed some more over the head and shoulders of the sleeping Indian, and then, submerged to his arms, he promptly drifted into slumber himself.

He wakened to the sound of Baby Bunting pawing around the grub pack. Hunger was his next conviction, for the heavenly rest in the medicine bath had taken every vestige of weariness away. He felt lethargic from the sulphur fumes, and more sleep was an enticing thought, yet he put it from him and got into his clothes after the use of a handkerchief as a bath towel. Miguel still slept and Kit bent over him in some concern, for the sleep appeared curiously deep and still, the breath coming lightly, yet he did not waken when lifted out of the water and covered with a poncho in the shade of a great yucca.

"I reckon it's some dope in these hot springs," decided Kit. "I feel top heavy myself, and won't trouble him till I've rustled some grub and have something to offer. Well, Buntin', we are all here but the daughter of the Glen," he said, rescuing the grub sack, "and if she was a dream and you inveigled me here by your own diabolical powers, I've a hunch this is our graveyard; we'll never see the world and its vanities again!"

A bit of the blue and scarlet on a bush above caught his eye. It was the belt of Tula, and he went upwards vaguely disturbed that he had drifted into ease without question of her welfare.

He found her emerging from a smaller rock basin, her one garment dripping a wet trail as she came towards him. There was no smile in her greeting, but a look of content, of achievement.

"My father," she said, "he is —— —"

"Sleeping beyond belief! good medicine sleep, I hope."

She nodded her head comprehendingly, for she had done the impossible and had triumphed. She looked at the sack of food he held.

"There is one place for fire, and other water is there. Come, it is to you."

She struck off across the sun-bathed little grass plot to a jumble of rock where a cool spring emerged, ran only a few rods, and sank again out of sight. The shattered rock was as a sponge, so completely was the water sucked downward again. Marks of burro's hoofs were there.

"Baby Buntin' been prospecting while we wallowed in the dope bath," said Kit.

"Maybe so, maybe not," uttered the Indian child, if such she could be called after the super-woman initiative of that forbidding trail. She was down on her knees peering at the tracks in the one little wet spot below the spring.

"Two," she said enigmatically. "That is good, much good. It will be meat."

Then she saw him pulling dry grasses and breaking branches of scrub growth for a fire, and she stood up and motioned him to follow. They were in a narrow, deep ravine separated from the main one by the miniature plain of lush grass, a green cradle of rest in the heart of the gray hills. She went as directly upward as the broken rock would permit, and suddenly he followed her into a blackened cave formed by a great granite slab thrusting itself upwards and enduring through the ages when the broken rock had shattered down to form an opposite wall. And the cloud bursts of the desert had swept through, and washed the sands clear, leaving a high black roof slanting upwards to the summit.

Tula moved ahead into the far shadows. He could see that beyond her somewhere a ray of light filtered blue, but he halted at the entrance, puzzled at the black roof where all the rock of the mountain was gray and white except where mineral streaks were of reds and russets and moldy greens. Then he put his hand up and touched the roof and understood. Soot from ancient fires was discernible on his hand, flakes of it fell to the floor, dry and black, scaling off under pressure. The scales were thick and very old, like blackened moss. He had seen blackened rock like that in other volcanic regions, but this was different.

"It is here," said Tula, and he followed the voice through a darker shadowed bit of the way, then through the ray of light, and then ——— —

The first thing he saw was the raised hearth of a rather pretentious fireplace, or place of fire, for it resembled not at all the tiny little cooking hearth of desert Indians. A stone hatchet lay beside it, and, what was much more surprising, two iron instruments of white man's manufacturing, a wedge and a long chisel.

He picked up the chisel, weighed it in his hand, and looked at the girl. He was now becoming accustomed to the dim light and could see her eyes following his every movement with curious questioning. There was a tiny frowning wrinkle between her brows as if serious matters were being decided there.

"It is here," she said again. "Maybe someone dies when a white friend is shown the way —- maybe I die, who knows? —- but it is here —- El Alisal of the gold of the rose!"

She made a little gesture and moved aside, and the chisel fell to the stone floor with a clang as Kit shouted and dropped on his knees before an incredible thing in the gray wall.

That upthrust of the rock wall had strange variety of color, and between the granite and the gray limestone there was a ragged rusty band of iron as a note of contrast to the sprinkling of glittering quartz catching the ray of light, but the quartz was sprinkled on a six inch band of yellow —- not the usual quartz formation with dots of color, but a deep definite yellow held together by white crystals.

"The red gold! it's the red gold!" he said feeling the yellow surface instinctively.

"Yes, señor, it is the red gold of El Alisal, and it is to you," but her eyes were watching him hungrily as she spoke. And something of that pathetic fear penetrated his amazed mind, and he remembered.

"No, Tula, only my share to me. I do the work, but the great share is to you, that it may buy back your mother from the slavers of the south."

"Also my sister," said the girl, and for the first time she wept.

"Come, come! This is the time for joy. The danger is gone, and we are at rest beside this —- why, it's a dream come true, the golden dream! Come, help me cook that we may be strong for the work."

She helped silently, fetching water and more sticks for the fire.

There were many things to ask, but he asked no questions, only gazed between bites and sups at the amazing facts facing him.

"I've seen ores and ores in my time, but nothing like this!" he exulted. "Why, I can 'high grade' mule loads of this and take it out without smelting," and then he grinned at his little partner. "We just struck it in time, —- meat is mighty near done."

"Plenty meat!" she said nodding her head wisely. "Burro, big burro, wild burro! I see track."

"Wild burro? Sure, that makes it simple till we rest up. You are one great little commissary sergeant."

He noted that the pitch of the roof towards the face of the mountain carried the smoke in a sort of funnel to be sifted through high unseen crannies of shattered rock above. All was dark in the end of the gallery, but a perceptible draught from the portal bore the smoke upward.

"It's too good to be true," he decided, looking it over. "I'm chewing bacon and it tastes natural, but I'm betting with myself that this is a dream, and I'll wake up in the dope pond with my mouth full of sulphur water."

The girl watched him gravely, and ate sparingly, though parched corn had been her only sustenance through the trail of the dreadful night. Her poor sandals were almost cut from her feet, and even while jesting at the unreality of it all, Kit was making mental note of her needs —- the wild burro would at least provide green hide sandals for her until better could be found, and she had earned the best.

He was amazed at her keenness. She did not seem to think, but instinctively to feel her way to required knowledge, caring for herself in the desert as a fledgling bird tossed by some storm from the home nest. He remembered there were wild burros in the Sonora hills, but that she should have already located one on this most barren of mountains was but another unbelievable touch to the trail of enchantment, and after a century of lost lives and treasure in the search for the Indian mine, to think that this Indian stray, picked up on a desolate trail, should have been the one to know that secret and lead him to it!

"Other times you have been here?" he asked as he poured coffee in a tin for Miguel, and dug out the last box of crackers from the grub pack.

"Once I come, one time, and it was to make prayer here. It is mine to know, but not my mother, not other peoples, only the father of me and me. If I die then he show the trail to other one, not if I live. That is how."

"He surely picked the right member of his honorable family," decided Kit. "Only once over the trail, once?"

"I knowing it long before I see it," she explained gravely. "The father of me make that trail in the sand for my eyes when I am only little. I make the same for him in a game to play. When I make every turn right, and name the place, and never forget —- then he bring me, for it is mine to know."

"Sufferin' cats!" muttered Rhodes, eyeing her in wonder. "The next time I see an Indian kid playing in the sand, I'll linger on the trail and absorb wisdom!"

"Come," she said, "you not seeing the one enchant look, the —- how you say? —- the not believe look."

"Well, take it from me, Cinderella, I'm seeing not believe things this very now," announced Kit, giving a fond look towards that comforting gleam of yellow metal bedding flecks of quartz. "I see it, but will have to sleep, and wake up to find it in the same place before I can believe what I think I see."

With the food and drink for Miguel in his hands he had followed the girl through the shadowed gallery of the slanting smoke-stained roof. His eyes were mainly directed to the rock floor lest he stumble and spill the precious coffee; thus he gave slight thought to the little ravine up which she had led him to the cave which was also a mine.

But as he stepped out into the sunlight she stood looking up into his face with almost a smile, the first he had seen in her wistful tragic eyes. Then she lifted her hand and pointed straight out, and the "enchant look," the "not believe" look was there! He stared as at a mirage for an incredulous moment, and then whispered, "Great God of the Desert!"

For a little space, a few rods only, the mountain dipped steeply, and trickling water from above fell in little cascades to lower levels, where a great jagged wall of impregnable granite arose as a barrier along the foot of the mountain.

But he was above the sharp outline of the huge saw with the jagged granite teeth, and between the serrated edges he could look far across the yellow-gray reaches of sand and desert growths. Far and wide was the "not believe" look, to the blue phantom-like peaks on the horizon, but between the two ranges was a white line with curious dots drifting and whirling like flies along it, and smoke curling up, and —- –

Then it was he uttered the incredulous cry, for he was indeed viewing the thing scarce to be believed.

He was looking across the great Rancho Soledad, and the white line against the sand was the wall of the old mission where the vaqueros were herding a band of horses into the great quadrangle of the one-time patio turned into a corral since the buildings on three sides had melted down again into mother earth.

He remembered riding around these lines of the old arches seeking trace of that door of the legend, —- the door from which the aliso tree of the mine could be seen, —- and there was nowhere a trace of a door.

"Queer that every other part of the prospect developed according to specifications and not the door," he grumbled whimsically. "Cinderella, why have you hid the door in the wall from me?"

She looked around uncertainly, not understanding.

"No portal but it," she said with a movement of her head towards the great slab forming a pointed arch against the mountain and shielding the unbelievable richness there, "also El Alisal, the great tree, is gone. This was the place of it; the old ones tell my father it was as chief of the trees and stand high to be seen. The sky fire took it, and took the padres that time they make an altar in this place."

"Um," assented Kit, noting traces of ancient charcoal where the aliso tree had grown great in the moisture of the spring before lightning had decided its tragic finish, "a great storm it must have been to send sky fire enough to kill them all."

"Yes," said Tula quietly, —- "also there was already another shrine at this place, and the gods near."

He glanced at her quickly and away.

"Sure," he agreed, "sure, that's how it must have been. They destroyed the aliso and there was no other landmark to steer by. White men might find a thousand other dimples in the range but never this one, the saw-tooth range below us has the best of them buffaloed. Come along, Señorita Aladdin, and help me with the guardian of the treasure. We've got to look after Miguel, and then start in where the padres left off. And you might do a prayer stunt or two at the shrine you mentioned. We need all the good medicine help you can evoke."

As they approached the pool where the faintest mist drifted above the water warm from hidden fires of the mountain, Kit halted before he quite reached the still form beside the yucca, and, handing the food and drink to the girl, he went forward alone.

He was puzzled afterward as to why he had done that, for no fold of the garment was disturbed, nothing visible to occasion doubt, yet he bent over and lifted the cover very gently. The face of Miguel was strangely gray and there was no longer sign of breath. The medicine of the sacred pool had given him rest, but not life.

He replaced the blanket and turned to the girl; —- the last of the guardians of the shrine of the red gold.

"Little sister," he said, "Miguel grew tired of the trails of a hard land. He has made his choice to go asleep here in the place where you tell me the gods are near. He does not want us to have sad hearts, for he was very sad and very tired, and he will not need food, Tula."

Her eyes filled with tears, but she made no reply, only unbound her hair as she had seen mourning women do, and seated herself apart, her face hidden in her arms.

"No one is left to mourn but me, and I mourn!" she half chanted. "I say it for the mother of me, and for my sister, that the ghosts may listen. Happily he is going now from hard trails! He has chosen at this place! Happily he has chosen, and only we are sad. No debt is ours to pay at this place; he has chosen —- and a life is paid at El Alisal! Happily he will find the trail of the birds from this place, and the trail of the clouds over the high mountain. No one is left to mourn but me; and I mourn!"

Rhodes understood no word of her lamentations, chanted now loudly, now lowly, at intervals hour after hour that day. He set grimly to work digging a grave in the lower part of the ravine, gathering dry grass for lining as best he could to make clear to the girl that no lack of care or honor was shown the last man of Cajame's stock.

The work took most of the day, for he carried stone and built a wall around the grave and covered it with slatelike slabs gathered from a shattered upheaval of long ago.

Tula watched all this gravely, and with approval, for she drew with her finger the mark of the sun symbol on one of the slabs.

"It is well to make that mark," she said, "for the sons of Cajame were priests of the sun. The sign is on the great rock of the trail, and it is theirs."

With the chisel he carved the symbol as she suggested, glad to do anything for the one mourner for the dead man who had offered the treasure of the desert to him.

"That is how he made choice," she said when it was marked plainly. "Me, I think he was leading us on the night trail to this place —- I think so. He is here to guard the gold of El Alisal for you. That is how it will be. He has made choice."

Kit got away by himself to think over the unexpected situation. The girl climbed to a higher point, seated herself, and continued her chant of mourning. He knew she was following, as best she knew, the traditional formalities of a woman for the death of a chief. He found himself more affected by that brave fatalistic recital, now loud and brave, now weirdly slow and tender, than if she had given way to tempests of tears. A man could comfort and console a weeping stray of the desert, but not a girl who sat with unbound hair under the yucca and called messages to the ghosts until the sun, —- a flaming ball of fire, —- sank beyond the far purple hills.

And that was the first day of many days at the hidden treasure place of the red gold.

CHAPTER XI
GLOOM OF BILLIE

The return of Captain Pike on Kit's horse was a matter of considerable conjecture at Granados, but the old prospector was so fagged that at first he said little, and after listening to the things Billie had to tell him —-- he said less.

"That explains the curious ways of the Mexicans as I reached the border," he decided. "They'd look first at the horse, then at me, but asked no questions, and told me nothing. Queer that no word reached us about Singleton! No, it isn't either. We never crossed trails with any from up here. There's so much devilment of various sorts going on down there that a harmless chap like Singleton wouldn't be remembered."

"Conrad's down at Magdalena now, but we seldom know how far he ranges. Sometimes he stays at the lower ranch a week at a time, and he might go on to Sinaloa for all we know. He seems always busy and is extremely polite, but I gave him the adobe house across the arroya after Papa Phil —-- went. I know he has the Mexicans thinking Kit Rhodes came back for that murder; half of them believe it!"

"Well, I reckon I can prove him an alibi if it's needed. I'll go see the old judge."

"He'll tell you not to travel at night, or alone, if you know anything," she prophesied. "That's what he tells me. To think of old Rancho Granados coming to that pass! We never did have trouble here except a little when Apaches went on the warpath before my time, and now the whole border is simmering and ready to boil over if anyone struck a match to it. The judge hints that Conrad is probably only one cog in the big border wheel, and they are after the engineer who turns that wheel, and do you know you haven't told me one word of Kit Rhodes, or whether he's alive or dead!"

"Nothing to tell! We didn't find it, and he took the back trail with an Indian girl and her daddy, and —-–"

"An —- Indian girl?"

"Yes, a queer little kid who was in a lot of trouble. Her father was wounded in one of the fracases they have down there every little while. Nary one of us could give an address when we took different trails, for we didn't know how far we'd be allowed to travel —-- the warring factions are swarming and troublesome over the line."

"Well, if a girl could stand the trail, it doesn't look dangerous."

"Looks are deceptive, child, —- and this isn't just any old girl! It's a rare bird, it's tougher than whalebone and possessed of a wise little devil. She froze to Kit as a *compadre* at first chance. He headed back to Mesa Blanca. I reckon they'd make it, —-- barring accidents."

"Mesa Blanca? That's the Whitely outfit?"

"Um!" assented Pike, "but I reckon Whitely's hit the trail by now. There's no real profit in raising stock for the warriors down there; each band confiscates what he needs, and gives a promissory note on an empty treasury."

"Well, the attraction must be pretty strong to hold him down there in spite of conditions," said Billie gloomily.

"Attraction? Sure. Kit's gone loco on that attraction," agreed the old prospector, and then with a reminiscent light in his tired old eyes he added, "I reckon there's no other thing so likely to snare a man on a desert trail. You see, Billie-child, it's just as if the great God had hid a treasure in the beginning of the world to stay hid till the right lad ambled along the trail, and lifted the cover, and when a fellow has youth, and health and not a care in the world, the search alone is a great game —-- And when he finds it! —-- why, Billie, the dictionary hasn't words enough to tell the story!"

"No —- I —- I reckon not," said his listener in a small voice, and when he looked around to speak to her again she had disappeared, and across the patio Doña Luz was coming towards him in no good humor.

"How is it that poor little one weeps now when you are returned, and not at other times?" she demanded. "Me, I have my troubles since that day they find the Don Filipe shot dead, —— *Jesusita* give him rest! That child is watching the Sonora trail and waiting since that day, but no tears until you are come. I ask you how is the way of that?"

Captain Pike stared at her reflectively.

"You are a bringer of news, likewise a faithful warden," he observed. "I'm peaceably disposed, and not wise to your lingo. Billie and me were talking as man to man, free and confidential, and no argument. There were no weeps that I noticed. What's the reason why?"

"The saints alone know, and not me!" she returned miserably. "I think she is scared that it was the Señor Rhodes who shooting Don Filipe, the vaqueros thinking that! But she tells no one, and she is unhappy. Also there is reason. That poor little one has the ranchos, but have you hear how the debts are so high all the herds can never pay? That is how they are saying now about Granados and La Partida, and at the last our señorita will have no herds, and no ranchos, and no people but me. *Madre de Dios!* I try to think of her in a little adobe by the river with only *frijoles* in the dinner pot, and I no see it that way. And I not seeing it other way. How you think?"

"I don't, it's too new," confessed Pike. "Who says this?"

"The Señor Henderson. I hear him talk with Señor Conrad, who has much sorrow because the Don Filipe made bad contracts and losing the money little and little, and then the counting comes, and it is big, very big!"

"Ah! the Señor Conrad has much sorrow, has he?" queried Pike, "and Billie is getting her face to the wall and crying? That's queer. Billie always unloaded her troubles on me, and you say there was none of this weeping till I came back?"

"That is so, señor."

"Cause why?"

"*Quien sabe?* She was making a long letter to Señor Rhodes in Sonora, —- that I know. He sends no word, so —- I leave it to you, señor, it takes faith and more faith when a man is silent, and the word of a killing is against him."

"Great Godfrey, woman! He never got a letter, he knows nothing of a killing. How in hell —- " Then the captain checked himself as he saw the uselessness of protesting to Doña Luz. "Where's Billie?"

Billie was perched on a window seat in the *sala*, her eyes were more than a trifle red, and she appeared deeply engrossed in the pages of a week-old country paper.

"I see here that Don José Perez of Hermosillo is to marry Doña Dolores Terain, the daughter of the general," she observed impersonally. "He owns Rancho Soledad, and promises the Sonora people he will drive the rebel Rotil into the sea, and it was but yesterday Tia Luz was telling me of his beautiful wife, Jocasta, who was only a little mountain girl when he rode through her village and saw her first. She is still alive, and it looks to me as if all men are alike!"

"More or less," agreed Pike amicably, "some of us more, some of us less. Doña Dolores probably spells politics, but Doña Jocasta is a wildcat of the sierras, and I can't figure out any harmonious days for a man who picks two like that."

"He doesn't deserve harmony; no man does who isn't true —- isn't true," finished Billie rather lamely.

"Look here, honey child," observed Pike, "you'll turn man hater if you keep on working your imagination. Luz tells me you are cranky against Kit, and that the ranches are tied up in business knots tighter than I had any notion of, so you had better unload the worst you can think of on me; that's what I'm here for. What difference do the Perez favorites make to our young lives? Neither Dolores nor Jocasta will help play the cards in our fortunes."

Wherein Captain Pike was not of the prophets. The wells of Sonora are not so many but that he who pitches his tent near one has a view and greetings of all drifting things of the desert, and the shadowed star of Doña Jocasta of the south was leading her into the Soledad wilderness forsaken of all white men but one.

CHAPTER XII
COVERING THE TRAIL

Each minute of the long days, Rhodes worked steadily and gaily, picking out the high grade ore from the old Indian mine, and every possible night he and the burro and Tula made a trip out to the foot of the range, where they buried their treasure against the happy day when they could go out of the silent desert content for the time with what gold they could carry in secret to the border.

For two days he had watched the Soledad ranch house rather closely through the field glass, for there was more activity there than before; men in groups rode in who were not herding. He wondered if it meant a military occupation, in which case he would need to be doubly cautious when emerging from the hidden trail.

The girl worked as he worked. Twice he had made new sandals for her, and also for himself in order to save his boots so that they might at least be wearable when he got among people. All plans had been thought out and discussed until no words would be needed between them when they separated. She was to appear alone at Palomitas with a tale of escape from the slavers, and he was carefully crushing and mashing enough color to partly fill a buckskin bag to show as the usual fruits of a prospect trip from which he was returning to Mesa Blanca after exhausting grub stake and shoe leather.

The things of the world had stood still for him during that hidden time of feverish work. He scarcely dared try to estimate the value of the ore he had dug as honey from a hollow tree, but it was rich —- rich! There were nuggets of pure gold, assorted as to their various sizes, while he milled and ground the quartz roughly, and cradled it in the water of the brook.

By the innocent aid of Baby Bunting, two wild burros of the sierra had been enticed within reach for slaughter, and, aside from the food values, they furnished green hide which under Kit's direction, Tula deftly made into bags for carrying the gold.

All activities during the day were carefully confined within a certain radius, low enough in the little cañon to run no risk in case any inquisitive resident of Soledad should study the ranges with a field glass, though Kit had not seen one aside from his own since he entered Sonora. And he used his own very carefully every morning and evening on the wide valley of Soledad.

"Something doing down there, sister," he decided, as they were preparing for the last trail out. "Riders who look like cavalry, mules, and some wagons —- mighty queer!"

Tula came over and stood beside him expectantly. He had learned that a look through the magic glasses was the most coveted gift the camp could grant to her, and it had become part of the regular routine that she stood waiting her turn for the wide look, the "enchant look," as she had called it that first morning. It had become a game to try to see more than he, and this time she mentioned as he had, the wagons, and mules, and riders. And then she looked long and uttered a brief Indian word of surprise.

"Beat me again, have you?" queried Kit good humoredly. "What do you find?"

"A woman is there, in that wagon, —- sick maybe. Also one man is a padre; see you!"

Kit took the glasses and saw she was right. A man who looked like a priest was helping a woman from a wagon, she stumbled forward and then was half carried by two men towards the house.

"Not an Indian woman?" asked Kit, and again her unchildlike mind worked quickly.

"A padre does not bow his head to help Indian woman. Caballeros do not lift them up."

"Well I reckon Don José Perez is home on a visit, and brought his family. A queer time! Other ranch folks are getting their women north over the border for safety."

"Don José not bring woman to Soledad —- ever. He take them away. His men take them away."

It was the first reference she had made to the slavers since they had entered the cañon, though she knew that each pile of nuggets was part of the redemption money for those exiles of whom she did not speak.

But she worked tirelessly until Kit would stop her, or suggest some restful task to vary the steady grind of carrying, pounding, or washing the quartz. He had ordered her to make two belts, that each of them might carry some of the gold hidden under their garments. She had a nugget tied in a corner of her *manta*, and other small ones fastened in her girdle, while in the belt next her body she carried all he deemed safe to weight her with, probably five pounds. At any hint of danger she would hide the belt and walk free.

His own belt would carry ten pounds without undue bulkiness. And over three hundred pounds of high grade gold was already safely hidden near the great rock with the symbols of sun and rain marking its weathered surface.

"A fair hundred thousand, and the vein only scratched!" he exulted. "I was sore over losing the job on Billie's ranch, —- but gee! this looks as if I was knocked out in the cold world to reach my good luck!"

In a blue dusk of evening they left the camp behind and started over the trail, after Tula had carefully left fragments of food on the tomb of Miguel, placed there for the ghosts who are drawn to a comrade.

Kit asked no questions concerning any of her tribal customs, since to do so would emphasize the fact that they were peculiar and strange to him, and the Indian mind, wistfully alert, would sense that strangeness and lose its unconsciousness in the presence of an alien. So, when she went, after meals, to offer dregs of the soup kettle or bones of the burro, she often found a bunch of desert blossoms wilting there in the heat, and these tributes left by Kit went far to strengthen her confidence. It was as if Miguel was a live partner in their activities, never forgotten by either. So they left him on guard, and turned their faces toward the outer world of people.

Knowing more than he dare tell the girl his mind was considerably occupied with that woman at Soledad, for military control changed over night in many a province of Mexico in revolutionary days, and the time at the hidden mine might have served for many changes.

Starlight and good luck was on the trail for them, and at earliest streak of dawn they buried their treasure, divided their dried burro meat, and with every precaution to hide the trail where they emerged from the gray sierra, they struck the road to Mesa Blanca.

Until full day came Tula rode the burro, and slipped off at a ravine where she could walk hidden, on the way to Palomitas.

"Buntin'," said Kit, watching her go, "we'll have pardners and pardners in our time, but we'll never find one more of a thoroughbred than that raggedy Indian witch-child of ours."

He took the slanting cattle trail up over the mesa, avoiding the wagon road below, and at the far edge of it halted to look down over the wide spreading leagues of the Mesa Blanca ranch.

It looked very sleepy, drowsing in the silence of the noon sun. An old Indian limped slowly from the corral over to the ranch house, and a child tumbled in the dust with a puppy, but there was no other sign of ranch activity. As he descended the mesa and drew nearer the corrals they had a deserted look, not merely empty but deserted.

The puppy barked him a welcome, but the child gave one frightened look at Kit, and with a howl of fear, raced to the shelter of the portal where he disappeared in the shadows.

"I had a hunch, Babe, that we needed smoothing down with a currycomb before we made social calls," confessed Kit to the burro, "but I didn't reckon on scaring the natives in any such fashion as this."

He was conscious of peering eyes at a barred window, and then the old Indian appeared.

"Hello, Isidro!"

"At your service, señor," mumbled the old man, and then he stared at the burro, and at the bearded and rather desert-worn stranger, and uttered a cry of glad recognition.

"Ai-ji! It is El Pajarito coming again to Mesa Blanca, but coming with dust in your mouth and no song! Enter, señor, and take your rest in your own house. None are left to do you honor but me, —- all gone like that!" and his skinny black hands made a gesture as if wafting the personnel of Mesa Blanca on its way. "The General Rotil has need the cattle, and makes a divide with Señor Whitely and all go, —- all the herds," and he pointed east.

Kit bathed his face in the cool water brought out by Valencia, Isidro's wife, then unloaded the burro of the outfit, and stretched himself in the shade while the women busied themselves preparing food.

"So General Rotil makes a divide of the cattle, —- of Whitely's cattle? How is that?" he asked.

And the old Indian proceeded to tell him that it was true. The Deliverer must feed his army. He needed half, and promised Whitely to furnish a guard for the rest of the herd and help Whitely save them by driving them to Imuris, where the railroad is.

"He said enemy troops would come from the south and take them all in one week or one month. He, Rotil, would pay a price. Thus it was, and Señor Whitely, and enough vaqueros, rode with the herds, and General Rotil took the rest of the ranchmen to be his soldiers. Of course it might be Señor Whitely would some day return, who knows? And he left a letter for the señor of the songs."

The letter corroborated Isidro's statements —- it was the only way to save any of the stock. Whitely thought there was a hundred or two still ranging in the far corners, but time was short, and he was saving what he could. The men were joining the revolutionists and he would be left without help anyway. If Rhodes came back he was to use the place as his own. If he could round up any more horses or cattle on the range and get them to safety Isidro would find some Indians to help him, and Whitely would divide the profits with him.

"Fine! —- divides first with the Deliverer, and next with me! Can't see where that hombre gets off when it comes to staking his own family to a living. But it's a bargain, and this is my headquarters until I can get out. How long has Whitely and his new friends been gone?"

"Four days, señor."

"Seen any stragglers of cattle left behind?"

Isidro's grandson, Clodomiro, had found both horses and cattle and herded them into far cañons; a man might ride in a circle for five miles around the ranch house and see never a fresh track. Clodomiro was a good boy, and of much craft.

Dinner was announced for the señor, and the women showed him welcome by placing before him the most beautiful repast they could arrange quickly, *chile con carne*, *frijoles*, *tortillas*, and a decanter of Sonora wine —- a feast for a king!

After he had eaten, tobacco was brought him from some little hidden store, and Isidro gave him the details of the slave raid of Palomitas, and Sonora affairs in general. Kit was careful to state that he has been prospecting in the mountains and out of touch with ranch people, and it must be understood that all Isidro could tell would be news to a miner from the desert mountains. And he asked if General Rotil also collected stock from the ranch of Soledad.

Whereupon Isidro told him many things, and among them the wonder that Soledad had been left alone —- the saints only knew why! And Juan Gonsalvo, the foreman at Soledad, had helped with the slave raid, and was known in Palomitas where they took girls and women and men as well, even men not young! Miguel, the major-domo, was taken with his wife and two daughters, the other men were young. The curse of God seemed striking Sonora. A new foreman was now at Soledad, Marto Cavayso, a hard man and, —- it was said, a soldier, but he evidently got tired of fighting and was taking his rest by managing the horse herds of Soledad.

"Doesn't look like rest to me," observed Kit. "The Soledad trail looks pretty well kicked into holes, with wagons, mules, and horsemen."

Isidro volunteered his opinion that work of the devil was going forward over there.

"Juan Gonsalvo and El Aleman were stealing women in Sonora, and driving them the south trail for a price," he stated. "But what think you would be the price for a woman of emerald eyes and white skin carried up from the south under chains, and a lock to the chain?"

"I reckon you are dreaming the lock and chain part of it, Isidro," returned Kit. "Only murderers travel like that."

"*Si*, it is so. There at Soledad it is heard. A killing was done in the south and Soledad is her prison. But she is beautiful, and the men are casting lots as to whose she shall be when the guard is gone south again to Don José Perez."

"Ah! they are Don José's men, are they? Then the prisoner is guarded by his orders?"

"Who knows? They tell that she is a lost soul, and fought for a knife to kill herself, and the padre makes prayers and says hell will be hers if she does. Elena, who is cook, heard him say that word, and Elena was once wife to my brother, and she is telling that to Clodomiro who makes an errand to take her deer meat, and hear of the strangers. He saw the woman, her bracelets are gold, and her eyes are green. The padre calls her Doña Jocasta. I go now and give drink to that burro and make him happy."

"Jocasta, eh? Doña Jocasta!" repeated Kit in wondering meditation. "Doesn't seem possible —- but reckon it is, and there are no real surprises in Sonora. Anything could, and does happen here."

He remembered Pike telling the story of Jocasta one morning by their camp fire in the desert. She was called by courtesy Señora Perez. He had not heard her father's name, but he was a Spanish priest and her mother an Indian half-breed girl —- some little village in the sierras. There were two daughters, and the younger was blond as a child of Old Spain, Jocasta was the elder and raven dark of hair, a skin of deep cream, and jewel-green eyes. Kit had heard three men, including Isidro, speak of Doña Jocasta, and each had mentioned the wonderful green eyes —- no one ever seemed to forget them!

Their magnetism had caught the attention of Don José, —- a distinguished and illustrious person in the eyes of the barefoot mountaineers. No one knew what Jocasta thought of the exalted padrone of the wide lands, whose very spurs were of gold, but she knew there was scarce wealth enough in all the village to keep a candle burning on the Virgin's shrine, and her feet had never known a shoe. The padre died suddenly just as Don José was making a bargain with him for the girl, so he swept Jocasta to his saddle with no bargain whatever except that she might send back for Lucita, her little sister, and other men envied Perez his good luck when they looked at Jocasta. For three years she had been mistress of his house in Hermosillo, but never had he taken her into the wilderness of Soledad, —- it was a crude casket for so rich a treasure.

Kit steeped in the luxury of a square meal, fell asleep, thinking of the green-eyed Doña Jocasta whom no man forgot. He would not connect a brilliant bird of the mountain with that drooping figure he and Tula had seen stumbling towards the portal of Soledad. And the statement of Isidro that there had been a killing, and Doña Jocasta was a lost soul, was most puzzling of all. In a queer confused dream the killing was done by Tula, and Billie wore the belt of gold, and had green eyes. And he wakened himself with the apparently hopeless effort of convincing Billie he had never forgotten her despite the feminine witcheries of Sonora.

The shadows were growing long, and some Indian boys were jogging across the far flats. He reached for his field glass and saw that one of them had a deer across his saddle. Isidro explained that the boys were planting corn in a far field, and often brought a deer when they came in for more seed or provisions. They had a hut and *ramada* at the edge of the planted land six miles away. They were good boys, Benito and Mariano Bravo, and seldom both left the fields at the same time. He called to Valencia that there would be deer for supper, then watched the two riders as they approached, and smiled as they perceptibly slowed up their broncos at sight of the bearded stranger on the rawhide cot against the wall.

"See you!" he pointed out to Kit. "These are the days of changes. Each day we looking for another enemy, maybe that army of the south, and the boys they think that way too."

The boys, on being hailed, came to the house with their offering, and bunkered down in the shadow with a certain shy stolidity, until Kit spoke, when they at once beamed recognition, and made jokes of his beard as a blanket.

But they had news to tell, great news, for a child of Miguel had broken away from the slavers and had hidden in the mountains, and at last had found her way back to Palomitas. She was very tired and very poor in raiment, and the people were weeping over her. Miguel, her father, was dead from a wound, and was under the ground, and of the others who went on she could tell nothing, only that Conrad, the German friend of Don José, was the man who covered his face and helped take the women. Her sister Anita had recognized him, calling out his name, and he had struck her with a quirt.

The women left their work to listen to this, and to add the memories of some of their friends who had hidden and luckily escaped.

"That white man should be crucified and left for the vultures," said the boy Benito.

"No," said the soft voice of Valencia, "God was sacrificed, but this man is a white Judas; the death of God is too good for that man. It has been talked about. He will be found some place, —- and the Judas death will be his. The women are making prayers."

"It will soon be Easter," said Isidro.

Kit did not know what was meant by a "Judas" death, though he did know many of the church legends had been turned by the Indians into strange and lurid caricatures. He thought it would be interesting to see how they could enlarge on the drama of Judas, but he made no comment, as a direct question would turn the Indians thoughtful, and silence them.

They all appeared alert for the return of Rotil. No one believed he had retired utterly from the region without demanding tribute from Soledad. It was generally suspected that Perez received and held munitions for use against the revolutionists though no one knew where they were hidden. There were Indian tales of underground tunnels of Soledad Mission for retreat in the old days in case of hostile attacks, and the Soledad ranch house was built over part of that foundation. No one at Soledad knew the entrance except Perez himself, though it was surmised that Juan Gonsalvo had known, and had been the one to store the mule loads and wagon loads of freight shipped over the border before Miguel Herrara was caught at the work from the American side. Perez was a careful man, and not more than one man was trusted at one time. That man seemed marked by the angels for accident, for something had always ended him, and it was no good fortune to be a favorite of Don José —- Doña Jocasta was learning that!

Thus the gossip and surmise went on around Rhodes for his brief hour of rest and readjustment. He encouraged the expression of opinion from every source, for he had the job ahead of him to get three hundred pounds of gold across the border and through a region where every burro was liable to examination by some of the warring factions. It behooved him to consider every tendency of the genus homo with which he came in contact. Also the bonds between them, —- especially the bonds, since the various groups were much of a sameness, and only "good" or "bad" according to their affiliations. Simple Benito and his brother, and soft-voiced motherly Valencia who could conceive a worse death for the German Judas than crucifixion, were typical of the primitive people of desert and sierra.

"How many head of stock think you still ranges Mesa Blanca?" he asked Isidro, who confessed that he no longer rode abroad or kept tally, but Clodomiro would know, and would be in to supper. Benito and Mariano told of one stallion and a dozen mares beyond the hills, and a spring near their fields had been muddied the day before by a bunch of cows and calves, they thought perhaps twenty, and they had seen three mules with the Mesa Blanca brand when they were getting wood.

"Three mules, eh? Well, I may need those mules and the favor will be to me if you keep them in sight," he said addressing the boys. "I am to round up what I can and remove them after Señor Whitely, together with other belongings."

"Others, señor?" asked Isidro.

Rhodes took the letter from his pocket, and perused it as if to refresh his memory.

"The old Spanish chest is to go if possible, and other things of Mrs. Whitely's," he said. "I will speak of these to your wife if the plan can carry, but there is chance of troops from the south and —- who knows? —- we may be caught between the two armies and ground as meal on a *metate*."

He thus avoided all detail as to the loads the pack animals were to carry, and the written word was a safe mystery to the Indian. He was making no definite plans, but was learning all possibilities with a mind prepared to take advantage of the most promising.

Thus the late afternoon wore on in apparent restful idleness after the hard trail. The boys secured their little allowance of beans and salt, and corn for planting, but lingered after the good supper of Valencia, a holiday feast compared with their own sketchy culinary performance in the *jacal* of the far fields. They scanned the trail towards Palomitas, and then the way down the far western valley, evidently loath to leave until their friend Clodomiro should arrive, and Isidro expected him before sunset.

But he came later from towards Soledad, a tall lad with fluttering ribbands of pink and green from his banda and his elbows, and a girdle of yellow fluttering fringed ends to the breeze, —- all the frank insignia of a youth in the market for marriage. He suggested a gay graceful bird as he rode rapidly in the long lope of the range. His boy friends of the planted fields went out to meet him at the corral, and look after his horse while he went in to supper. He halted to greet them, and then walked soberly across the plaza where pepper trees and great white alisos trailed dusk shadows in the early starlight.

"What *reata* held you?" asked Isidro. "Has Soledad grown a place for comradeship?"

"No, señor," said the lad passing into the dining room where two candles gave him light in the old adobe room, "it is comradeship we do not need, but it is coming to us."

He seated himself on the wooden bench and his grandmother helped him from a smoking plate of venison. He looked tired and troubled, and he had not even taken note that a stranger was beside Isidro in the shadows.

"What nettle stings you, boy?" asked his grandfather sarcastically, and at that he looked up and rose to his feet at sight of Rhodes.

"Your pardon, señor, I stumbled past like a bat blind in the light," he muttered, and as he met Kit's eyes and recognized him his face lit up and his white teeth gleamed in a smile.

"The saints are in it that you are here again, señor!" he exclaimed, "and you came on this day when most needed."

"Eat and then tell your meaning," said Isidro, but Clodomiro glanced toward the kitchen, and then listened for the other boys. They were laughing down at the corral. Clodomiro's horse had thrown one of them.

"With your permission, grandfather, talk first," he said and the two men moved to the bench opposite, leaning over towards him as his voice was lowered.

"Today Marto Cavayso sent for me, he is foreman over there, and strange things are going forward. He has heard that General Rotil stripped Mesa Blanca and that all white people are gone from it. He wants this house and will pay us well to open the door. It is for the woman. They have played a game for her, and he has won, but she is a wild woman when he goes near her, and his plan is to steal her out at night and hide her from the others. So he wants this house. He offered me a good gun. He offers us the protection of Don José Perez."

"But —- why —- that is not credible," protested Kit. "He could not count on protection from Perez if he stole the woman whom many call Señora Perez, for that is what they did call Doña Jocasta in Hermosillo."

"Maybe so," assented Clodomiro stolidly, "but now he is to be the *esposo* of a Doña Dolores who is the child of General Terain, so Marto says. Well, this Doña Jocasta has done some killing, and Don José does not give her to prison. He sends her to the desert that she brings him no disgrace; and if another man takes her or sinks her in the quicksands then that man will be helping Don José. That is how it is. Marto says the woman has bewitched him, and he is crazy about her. Some of the other men, will take her, if not him."

Kit exchanged a long look with the old Indian.

"The house is yours, señor," said Isidro. "By the word of Señor Whitely, you are manager of Mesa Blanca."

84

"Many thanks," replied Kit, and sat with his elbows on the table and his hands over his eyes, thinking —- thinking of the task he had set himself in Sonora, and the new turn of the wheel of fortune.

"You say the lady is a prisoner?" he asked.

"Sure," returned Clodomiro promptly. "She broke loose coming through a little pueblo and ran to the church. She found the priest and told him things, so they also take that priest! If they let him go he will talk, and Don José wanting no talk now of this woman. That priest is well cared for, but not let go away. After awhile, maybe so."

"She is bright, and her father was a priest," mused Kit. "So there is three chances out of four that she can read and write, —- a little anyway. Could you get a letter to her?"

"Elena could."

Kit got up, took one of the candles from the table and walked through the rooms surrounding the patio. Some of them had wooden bars in the windows, but others had iron grating, and he examined these carefully.

"There are two rooms fit for perfectly good jails," he decided, "so I vote we give this bewitched Don Marto the open door. How many guns can we muster?"

"He promised to give me one, and ammunition."

"Well, you get it! Get two if you can, but at least get plenty of ammunition. Isidro, will your wife be brave and willing to help?"

The old Indian nodded his head vigorously and smiled. Evidently only a stranger would ask if his Valencia could be brave!

The two brothers came in, and conversation was more guarded until Clodomiro had finished his supper, and gone a little ways home with them to repay them the long wait for comradeship.

When he came back Kit had his plans fairly settled, and had a brief note written to Señora Jocasta Perez, as follows:

> Honored Señora:
> One chance of safety is yours. Let yourself be persuaded to leave Soledad with Marto. You will be rescued from him by
>
> An American.

"I reckon that will do the trick," decided Kit. "I feel like a blooming Robin Hood without the merry men, —- but the Indians will play safe, even if they are not merry. When can you get this to Elena?"

"In time of breakfast," said Clodomiro promptly. "I go tonight, and tomorrow night he steals that woman. Maybe Elena helps."

"You take Elena a present from me to encourage that help," suggested Kit, and he poured a little of the gold from his belt on the paper. "Also there is the same for you when the lady comes safe. It is best that you make willing offer of your service in all ways so that he calls on none of his own men for help."

"As you say, señor," assented Clodomiro, "and that will march well with his desires, for to keep the others from knowing is the principal thing. She has beauty like a lily in the shade."

"He tells you that?" asked Kit quizzically, but the boy shook his head.

"My own eyes looked on her. She is truly of the beauty of the holy pictures of the saints in the chapel, but Marto says she is a witch, and has him enchanted; —- also that evil is very strong in her. I do not know."

"Well, cross your fingers and tackle the job," suggested Kit. "Get what sleep you can, for you may not get much tomorrow night. It is the work of a brave man you are going to do, and your pay will be a man's pay."

The eyes of the Indian boy glowed with pleasure.

"At your service, señor. I will do this thing or I will not see Mesa Blanca again."

Kit looked after Clodomiro and rolled another cigarette before turning in to sleep.

"When all's said and done, I may be the chief goat of this dame adventure," he told himself in derision. "Maybe my own fingers need crossing."

At the first break of dawn, Rhodes was up, and without waiting for breakfast walked over to the rancherias of Palomitas to see Tula.

She was with some little girls and old women carrying water from the well as stolidly as though adventure had never stalked across her path. A whole garment had been given her instead of the tatter of rags in which she had returned to the little Indian pueblo. She replied briefly to his queries regarding her welfare, and when he asked where she was living, she accompanied him to an old adobe where there were two other motherless children —- victims of the raiders.

An old, half-blind woman stirred meal into a kettle of porridge, and to her Kit addressed himself.

"A blessing will be on your house, but you have too many to feed here," he said "and the child of Miguel should go to the ranch house of Mesa Blanca. The wife of Isidro is a good woman and will give her care."

"Yes, señor, she is a good woman," agreed the old Indian. "Also it may be a safe house for a maiden, who knows? Here it is not safe; other raiders may come."

"That is true. Send her after she has eaten."

He then sought out one of the older men to learn who could be counted on to round up the stray cattle of the ranges. After that he went at once back to the ranch house, and did not even speak to Tula again. There was nothing to indicate that she was the principal object of his visit, or that she had acquired a guardian who was taking his job seriously.

Later in the day she was brought to Mesa Blanca by an elderly Indian woman of her mother's clan, and settled in the quiet Indian manner in the new dwelling place. Valencia was full of pity for the girl of few years who had yet known the hard trail, and had mourned alone for her dead.

There was a sort of suppressed bustle about *la casa de Mesa Blanca* that day, dainties of cookery prepared with difficulty from the diminished stores, and the rooms of the iron bars sprinkled and swept, and pillows of wondrous drawnwork decorated the more pretentious bed. To Tula it was more of magnificence than she had ever seen in her brief life, and the many rooms in one dwelling was a wonder. She would stand staring across the patio and into the various doorways through which she hesitated to pass. She for whom the wide silences of the desert held few terrors, hesitated to linger alone in the shadows of the circling walls. Kit noted that when each little task was finished for Valencia, she would go outside in the sunlight where she had the familiar ranges and far blue mountains in sight.

"Here it makes much trouble only to live in a house," she said pointing to the needlework on a table cover. "The bowls of food will make that dirty in one eating, and then what? Women in fine houses are only as mares in time of thrashing the grain —- no end and no beginning to the work, —- they only tread their circle."

"Right you are, sister," agreed Kit, "they do make a lot of whirligig work for themselves, all the same as your grandmothers painting pottery that smash like eggshells. But life here isn't all play at that, and there may be something doing before sleep time tonight. I went after you so I would have a comrade I knew would stick."

She only gazed at him without question.

"You remember, Tula, the woman led by the padre at Soledad?"

She nodded silently.

"It may be that woman is captive to the same men who took your people," he said slowly watching her, "and it may be we can save her."

"May it also be that we can catch the man?" she asked, and her eyes half closed, peered up at him in curious intensity. "Can that be, O friend?"

"Some day it must surely be, Tula."

"One day it must be, —- one day, and prayers are making all the times for that day," she insisted stolidly. "The old women are talking, and for that day they want him."

"What day, Tula?"

"The Judas day."

Kit Rhodes felt a curious creepy sensation of being near an unseen danger, some sleeping serpent basking in the sun, harmless until aroused for attack. He thought of the gentle domestic Valencia, and now this child, both centered on one thought —- to sacrifice a traitor on the day of Judas!

"Little girls should make helpful prayers," he ventured rather lamely, "not vengeance prayers."

"I was the one to make cry of a woman, when my father went under the earth," she said. It was her only expression of the fact that she had borne a woman's share of all their joint toil in the desert, —- and he caught her by the shoulder, as she turned away.

"Why, Kid Cleopatra, it isn't a woman's work you've done at all. It's a man's job you've held down and held level," he declared heartily. "That's why I am counting on you now. I need eyes to watch when I have to be in other places."

"I watch," she agreed, "I watch for you, but maybe I make my own prayers also; —- all the time prayers."

"Make one for a straight trail to the border, and all sentries asleep!" he suggested. "We have a pile of yellow rock to get across, to say nothing of our latest puzzling prospect."

As the day wore on the latest "prospect" presented many complications to the imagination, and he tramped the corridors of Mesa Blanca wondering why he had seen but one side of the question the night before, for in the broad light of day there seemed a dozen, and all leading to trouble! That emerald-eyed daughter of a renegade priest had proven a host in herself when it came to breeding trouble. She certainly had been unlucky.

"Well, it might be worse," he confided to Bunting out in the corral. "Cap Pike might have tagged along to discourse on the general tomfoolery of a partner who picks up a damsel in distress at every fork of the trail. Not that he'd be far wrong at that, Baby. If any hombre wanted to catch me in a bear trap he'd only need to bait it with a skirt."

Baby Bunting nodded sagaciously, and nuzzled after Kit who was cleaning up the best looking saddle horse brought in from the Indian herd. It was a scraggy sorrel with twitchy ears and wicked eyes, but it looked tough as a mountain buck. Kit knew he should need two like that for the northern trail, and had hopes that the bewitched Marto Cavayso, whoever he was, would furnish another.

He went steadily about his preparations for the border trail, just as if the addition of an enchantress with green-jewel eyes was an every day bit of good fortune expected in every out-fit, but as the desert ranges flamed rose and mauve in the lowering sun there was a restless expectancy at the ranch house, bolts and locks and firearms were given final inspection. Even at the best it was a scantily manned fort for defense in case Mario's companions at dice should question his winning and endeavor to capture the stake.

"I shall go part way on the Soledad trail and wait what happens," he told Isidro. "I will remain at a distance unless Clodomiro needs me. There is no telling what tricks this Cavayso may have up his sleeve."

"I was thinking that same thought," said the old Indian. "The men of Perez are not trusted long, even by Perez. When it is a woman, they are not trusted even in sight! Go with God on the trail."

The ugly young sorrel ran tirelessly the first half of the way, just enough to prove his wind. Then they entered a cañon where scrub cottonwoods and greasebush gathered moisture enough for scant growth among the boulders worn out of the cliffs by erosion. It was the safest place to wait, as it was also the most likely place for treachery if any was intended to Clodomiro. At either end of the pass lay open range and brown desert, with only far patches of oasis where a well was found, or a sunken river marked a green pasture in some valley.

When he wrote the note he had not thought of danger to Clodomiro, regarding him only as a fearless messenger, but if the boy should prove an incumbrance to Cavayso after they were free of Soledad, that might prove another matter, and as old Isidro had stated, no one trusted a Perez man when a woman was in question!

He dismounted to listen and seek safe shadow, for the dusk had come, and desert stars swung like brilliant lamps in the night sky, and the white rocks served as clear background for any moving body.

The plan was, if possible, to get the woman out with Clodomiro while the men were at supper. The *manta* of Elena could cover her, and if she could walk with a water jar to the far well as any Indian woman would walk, and a horse hid in the willows there —- –!

It had been well thought out, and if nothing had interfered they should have reached the cañon an hour earlier. If Clodomiro had failed it might be a serious matter, and Kit Rhodes had some anxious moments for the stolen woman while dusk descended on the cañon.

He listened for the beat of horse hoofs, but what he heard first was a shot, and a woman's scream, and then the walls of the cañon echoed the tumult of horses racing towards him in flight.

He recognized Clodomiro by the bare head and banda, and a woman bent low beside him, her *manta* flapping like the wings of a great bird as her horse leaped forward beside the Indian boy.

Back of them galloped a man who slowed up and shot backward at the foremost of a pursuing band.

He missed, and the fire was returned, evidently with some effect, for the first marksman grunted and cursed, and Kit heard the clatter of his gun as it fell from his hand. He leaned forward and spurred his horse to outrun the pursuers. He was evidently Marto.

Kit had a mental vision of fighting Marto alone for the woman at Mesa Blanca, or fighting with the entire band and decided to halt the leader of the pursuers and gain that much time at least for the woman and Clodomiro.

He had mounted at the first sound of the runaways, and crouching low in the saddle, hid back of the thick green of a dwarfed mesquite, and as the leader came into range against the white rock well he aimed low and touched the trigger.

The horse leaped up and the rider slid off as the animal sunk to the ground. Kit guided his mount carefully along shadowed places into the road expecting each instant a shot from the man on the ground.

But it did not come, and he gained the trail before the other pursuers rounded the bend of the cañon. The sound of their hoofs would deafen them to his, and once on the trail he gave the sorrel the rein, and the wild thing went down the gully like an arrow from a bow.

He was more than a little puzzled at the silence back of him. The going down of the one man and horse had evidently checked all pursuit. Relieved though he was at the fact, he realized it was not a natural condition of affairs, and called for explanation.

The other three riders were a half mile ahead and he had no idea of joining them on the trail. It occurred to him there was a possible chance of taking a short cut over the point of the mesa and beating them to the home ranch. There was an even chance that the rougher trail would offer difficulties in the dark, but that was up to the sorrel and was worth the trial.

The bronco took the mesa walls like a cat, climbed and staggered up, slid and tumbled down and crossed the level intervening space to the corral as the first sound of the others came beating across the sands.

A dark little figure arose by the corral bars and reached for the horse as he slipped from the saddle.

"Quickly, Tulita!" he said, stripping saddle and bridle from its back, "one instant only to make ourselves as still as shadows under the walls of the house."

Fast as he ran, she kept pace with him to the corridor where Isidro waited.

"All is well," he said briefly to the old man. "Clodomiro comes safe with the señora, and the man who would steal her was shot and lost his gun. All has gone very well."

"Thanks to God!" said the old Indian. "The stealing of women has ever been a danger near, but luck comes well to you, señor, and it is good to be under the protection of you."

"Open the door and show a light of welcome," said Kit. "Call your wife and let all be as planned by us. I will be in the shadows, and a good gun for safety of the woman if needed, but all will work well, as you will see."

The three riders came up to the portal before dismounting, and Valencia went forward, while Isidro held high a blazing torch, and Clodomiro dismounted quickly, and offered help to the woman.

"My grandmother has all for your comfort, señora," he said, "will it please you to descend?"

The man swung from the saddle, awkwardly nursing his right arm.

"Yes this is a safe place, Doña Jocasta," he declared. "It is all well arranged. With your permission I may assist you."

He offered his left hand, but she looked from him to Valencia, and then to Clodomiro.

"You are young to be a stealer of women; —- the saints send you a whiter road!" she said. "And you may help me, for my shoulder has a hurt from that first shot of the comrade of this man."

"No, señora," stated her captor, "the evil shot came from no comrade of mine. They did not follow us, those bandits —- accursed be their names! They were hid in the cañoncita and jumped our trail. But have no fear, Doña Jocasta, they are left behind, and it will be my pleasure to nurse the wounds they have made."

"Be occupied with your own," she suggested pointing to his hand from which blood still dripped, "and you, mother, can show me the new prison. It can be no worse than the others."

"Better, much better, little dove," said Marto, who followed after the two women, and glanced over their shoulders into the guest chamber of the iron bars, "it is a bird cage of the finest, and a nest for harmonies."

Then to Valencia he turned with authority, "When you have made the señorita comfortable, bring the key of the door to me."

"*Si*, señor," said Valencia bending low, and even as the prisoner entered the room, she changed the key to the outside of the door. Marto nodded his approval and turned away.

"Now this shirt off, and a basin of water and a bandage," he ordered Isidro. "It is not much, and it still bleeds."

"True, it does, señor, and the room ordered for you has already the water and a clean shirt on the pillow. Clodomiro, go you for a bandage, and fetch wine to take dust out of the throat! This way, señor, —- and may you be at home in your own house!"

Unsuspecting, the amorous Marto followed the old man into the room prepared. He grunted contemptuous satisfaction at evidences of comfort extending to lace curtains hanging white and full over the one window.

"It is the time for a shirt of such cleanness," he observed, with a grin. "*Jesusita!* but the sleeve sticks to me! Cut it off, and be quick to make me over into a bridegroom."

The old man did as he was bidden, and when Clodomiro brought in a woven tray covered with a napkin from which a bottle of wine was discernible, Marto grinned at him.

"It is a soft nest you found for me, boy," he said appreciatively, "and when I am capitan I will make you lieutenant."

"Thanks to you, señor, and hasten the day!"

Clodomiro assisted his grandfather, and stood aside at the door respectfully as the old man passed out with his primitive supply of salves and antiseptics, and only when all need of caution was ended the boy smiled at the would-be Lothario, and the smile held a subtle mockery as he murmured, "The saints send you a good night's sleep, señor, and a waking to health —- and clearer sight!"

"Hell and its blazes to you! why do you grin?" demanded the other setting down the bottle from which he had taken a long and grateful drink, but quick as a cat the boy pulled the door shut, and slipped the bolt on the outside, and laughed aloud.

"Not this night will you be bridegroom for another man's wife, señor!" he called. "Also it is better that you put curb on your curses, —- for the lady has a mind for a quiet night of sleep."

Marto rushed to the curtained window only to find iron bars and the glint of a gun barrel. Isidro held the gun, and admonished the storming captive with the gentle fatalism of the Indian.

"It is done under orders of the major-domo, señor. There is no other way. If your words are hard or rough to the ears of the lady, there is a bullet for you, and a hidden place for your grave. This is the only word to you, señor. It is given me to say."

"But —- Gods, saints, and devils —- hearken you to me!" stormed the man. "This is a fool's joke! It can't go on! I must be back at sunrise —- *I must!*"

"You will see many suns rise through these bars if the padrone so pleases," murmured Isidro gently. "That is not for us to decide."

"To hottest hell with your padrone and you! Bring him here to listen to me. This is no affair of a man and a woman, —- curse her witch eyes and their green fires! There is work afoot, —- big work, and I must get back to Soledad. You know what goes over the trail to Soledad, —- every Indian knows! It is the cache of ammunition with which to save the peon and Indian slave, —- you know that! You know the revolutionists must get it to win in Sonora. A trap is set for tomorrow, a big trap! I must be there to help spring it. To you there will be riches and safety all your life for my freedom —- on the cross I will swear that. I —- –"

"Señor, nothing is in my power, and of your traps I know nothing. I am told you set a trap for a lady who is in grief and your own feet were caught in it. That is all I know of traps," said Isidro.

Kit patted the old man on the shoulder for cleverness, even while he wondered at the ravings of the would-be abductor. Then he crept nearer the window where he could see the face of the prisoner clearly, and without the overshadowing hat he had worn on entrance. The face gave him something to think about, for it was that of one of the men who had ridden up to the Yaqui spring the day he had found Tula and Miguel in the desert. How should this rebel who rode on secret trails with Ramon Rotil be head man at Soledad for Rotil's enemy? And what was the trap?

"Look well at that man, Isidro," he whispered, "and tell me if such a man rode here to Mesa Blanca with General Rotil."

"No such man was here, señor, but this man was foreman at Soledad before the Deliverer came over the eastern range to Mesa Blanca. Also the general and Don José Perez are known as enemies; —- the friend of one cannot be the friend of another."

"True enough, Isidro, but that does not help me to understand the trap set. Call your wife and learn if I can see the Doña Jocasta."

Tula had crept up beside them, and touched him on the arm.

"She asks for you, and sadness is with her very much. She watches us in fear, and cannot believe that the door is open for her."

"If that is her only trouble we can clear it away for her, *pronto*," he stated, and they entered the patio.

"It is not her only trouble, but of the other she does not speak. Valencia weeps to look at her."

"Heavens! Is she as bad looking as that?"

"No, it is another reason," stated the girl stolidly. "She is a caged humming bird, and her wings have broken."

Kit Rhodes never forgot that first picture of their kidnaped guest, for he agreed with Clodomiro who saw in her the living representation of old biblical saints.

The likeness was strengthened by the half Moorish drapery over her head, a black mantilla which, at sound of a man's step, she hurriedly drew across the lower part of her face. Her left arm and shoulder was bare, and Valencia bent over her with a strip of old linen for bandage, but the eyes of Doña Jocasta were turned half shrinking, half appraising to the strange Americano. It was plain to her that conquering men were merely the owners of women.

"It is good you come, señor," said Valencia. "Here is a wound and the bullet under the skin. I have waited for Isidro to help but he is slow on the way."

"He is busy otherwise, but I will call him unless my own help will serve here. That is for the señora to say."

The eyes of the girl, —- she was not more, —- never left his face, and above the lace scarf she peered at him as through a mask.

"It is you who sent messenger to save an unhappy one you did not know? You are the Americano of the letter?"

"At your service, señora. May that service begin now?"

"It began when that letter was written, and this room made ready," she said. "And if you can find the bullet it will end the unhappiness of this good woman. She weeps for the little bit of lead. It should have struck a heart instead of a shoulder."

"Ah, señora!" lamented Valencia, "weep like a woman over sorrows. It is a better way than to mock."

"God knows it is not for me to mock!" breathed the soft voice bitterly. "And if the señor will lend you his aid, I will again be in his debt."

Without further words Kit approached, and Valencia drew the cover from the shoulder and indicated where the ball could be felt.

"I cannot hold the shoulder and press the flesh there without making much pain, too much," stated Valencia, "but it must come out, or there will be trouble."

"Sure there will," asserted Kit, "and if you or Tula will hold the arm, and Doña Jocasta will pardon me —- –"

He took the white shoulder in his two hands and gently traced the direction of the bullet. It had struck in the back and slanted along the shoulder blade. It was evidently fired from a distance and little force left. Marto had been much nearer the pursuer, and his was a clean cut wound through the upper arm.

The girl turned chalky white as he began slowly to press the bullet backward along its trail, but she uttered no sound, only a deep intake of breath that was half a sob, and the cold moisture of sickening pain stood in beads on her face.

All of the little barriers with a stranger were forgotten, and the shielding scarf fell away from her face and bosom, and even with the shadowed emerald eyes closed, Kit Rhodes thought her the most perfect thing in beauty he had ever seen.

He hated himself for the pain he was forcing on her as he steadily followed the bullet upward and upward until it lay in his hand.

She did not faint, as he feared she might, but fell back in the chair, while Valencia busied herself with the ointment and bandage, and Tula, at a word from Kit, poured her a cup of wine.

"Drink," he said, "if only a little, señora. Your strength has served you well, but it needs help now."

She swallowed a little of the wine, and drew the scarf about her, and after a little opened her eyes and looked at him. He smiled at her approvingly, and offered her the bullet.

"It may be you will want it to go on some shrine to a patron saint, señora," he suggested, but she did not take it, only looked at him steadily with those wonderful eyes, green with black lashes, shining out of her marble Madonna-like face.

"My patron saint traveled the trail with you, Señor Americano, and the bullet is witness. Let me see it."

He gave it into her open hand where she balanced it thoughtfully.

"So near the mark, yet went aside," she murmured. "Could that mean there is yet any use left in the world for me?"

"Beauty has its own use in the world, señora; that is why rose gardens are planted."

"True, señor, though I belong no more to the gardens; —- no, not to gardens, but to the desert. Neither have I place nor power today, and I may never have, but I give back to you this witness of your great favor. If a day comes when I, Jocasta, can give favor in return, bring or send this witness of the ride tonight. I will redeem it."

"The favor is to me, and calls for no redemption," said Kit awkward at the regal poise of her, and enchanted by the languorous glance and movement of her. Even the reaching out of her hand made him think of Tula's words, 'a humming bird,' if one could imagine such a jewel-winged thing weighted down with black folds of mourning.

"A caged humming bird with broken wings!" and that memory brought another thought, and he fumbled the bullet, and gave the first steady look into those emerald, side-glancing eyes.

"But —- there is a compact I should appreciate if Doña Jocasta will do me the favor, —- and it is that she sets value on the life that is now her very own, and, that she forgets not to cherish it."

"Ah-h!" She looked up at him piteously a moment, and then the long lashes hid her eyes, and her head was bent low. "Sinful and without shame have I been! and they have told you of the knife I tried to use —- here!"

She touched her breast with her slender ring-laden hand, and her voice turned mocking.

"But you see, Señor Americano, even Death will not welcome me, and neither steel nor lead will serve me!"

"Life will serve you better, señora."

"Not yet has it done so, and I am a woman —- old —- old! I am twenty, señor, and refused of Death! Jocasta Benicia they named me. Jocasta Perdida it should have been to fit the soul of me, so why should I promise a man whom I do not know that I will cherish my life when I would not promise a padre? Answer me that, señor whose name has not been told me!"

"But you will promise, señora," insisted Kit, smiling a little, though thrilled by the sadness of life's end at twenty, "and as for names, if you are Doña Perdida I may surely name myself Don Esperenzo, for I have not only hope, but conviction, that life is worth living!"

"To a man, yes, and Mexico is a man's land."

"Ay, it must be yours as well, —- beautiful that thou art!" murmured Valencia adoringly. "You should not give yourself a name of sadness, for this is our Señor El Pajarito, who is both gay and of honesty. He, —- with God, —- is your protection, and harm shall not be yours."

Doña Jocasta reached out and touched kindly the bent head of the Indian woman.

"As you will, mother. With hope and a singer for a shield, even a prison would not be so bad, El Pajarito, eh? Do you make songs —- or sing them, señor?"

"Neither, —- I am only a lucky bluff. My old partner and I used to sing fool things to the mules, and as we could out-bray the burros my Indio friends are kind and call it a singing; —- as easy as that is it to get credit for talent in this beneficent land of yours! But —- the compact, señora?"

Her brows lifted wearily, yet the hint of a smile was in her eyes.

"Yes, since you ask so small a thing, it is yours. Jocasta makes compact with you; give me a wish that the life is worth it."

"Sure I will," said Kit holding out his hand, but she shrunk perceptibly, and her hand crept out of sight in the black draperies.

"You have not, perhaps, ever sent a soul to God without absolution?" she asked in a breathless hushed sort of voice. "No señor, the look of you tells me you have not been so unpardonable. Is it not so?"

"Why, yes," returned Kit, "it hasn't been a habit with me to start anyone on the angels' flight without giving him time to bless himself, but even at that —- –"

"No, no!" as he took a step nearer. "The compact is ours without handclasp. The hand of Jocasta is the hand of the black glove, señor."

He looked from her to the two Indians, the old woman kneeling beside Jocasta and crossing herself, and Tula, erect and slender against the adobe wall, watching him stolidly. There was no light on the subject from either of them.

"Pardon, I'm but a clumsy Americano, not wise to your meanings," he ventured, "and beautiful hands look better without gloves of any color."

"It may be so, yet I have heard that no matter how handsome a headsman may be, he wears a black mask, and hands are not stretched out to touch his."

"Señora!"

"Señor, we arrive at nothing when making speech of me," she said with a little sigh. "Our ride was hard, and rest is best for all of us. Our friend here tells me there is supper, and if you will eat with me, we will know more of how all this has come about. It is strange that you, a lone Americano in this land, should plan this adventure like a bandit, and steal not only the major-domo of Soledad, but the woman he would steal!"

"It was so simple that the matter is not worth words except as concerns Clodomiro, who was the only one in danger."

"Ah! if ever they had suspected him! You have not seen that band of men, they are terrible! Of all the men of José Perez they are the blackest hearts, and if it had not been for the poor padre — —"

"Tell me of him," said Kit who perceived she was willing enough to speak plainly of all things except herself. "He is a good man?"

"A blessing to me, señor!" she asserted earnestly as they were seated at the table so carefully prepared by Valencia. "Look you! I broke away from those animals and in a little mountain village, —- such a one as I was born in, señor! —- I ran to the altar of the little chapel, and that priest was a shield for me. Against all the men he spoke curses if they touched me. Well, after that there was only one task to do, and that was to carry him along. I think they wanted to kill him, and had not the courage. And after all that I came away from Soledad without saving him; —- that was bad of me, very bad! I —- I think I went wild in the head when I saw the men play games of cards, and I to go to the winner! Not even a knife for food would they give me, for they knew — —"

She shuddered, and laid down quickly the knife she had lifted from beside her plate, and glanced away when she found him regarding her.

"It has been long weeks since I was trusted as you are trusting me here," she continued quietly. "See! On my wrists were chains at first."

"And this Marto Cavayso did that?" demanded Kit as she showed her scarred slender wrist over which Valencia had wept.

"No, it was before Cavayso —- he is a new man —- so I think this was when Conrad was first helping to plan me as an insane woman and have me put secretly to prison, but some fear struck José Perez, and that plan would not serve. In the dark of night I was half smothered in wraps and put in an ox-cart of a countryman and hauled north out of the city. Two men rode as guard. They chained me in the day and slept, traveling only in the night until they met Cavayso and his men. After that I remember little, I was so weary of life! One alcalde asked about me and Cavayso said I was his wife who had run away with a gypsy fiddler, and he was taking me home to my children. Of what use to speak? A dozen men would have added their testimony to his, and had sport in making other romance against me. They were sullen because they thought I had jewels hid under my clothes, and Cavayso would not let them search me. It has been hell in these hills of Sonora, Señor Pajarito."

"That is easy to understand," agreed Kit wondering at her endurance, and wondering at the poise and beauty of her after such experience. There was no trace of nervousness, or of tears, or self-pity. It was as if all this of which she told had been a minor affair, dwarfed by some tragic thing to which he had no key.

"So, Conrad was in this plot against you?" he asked, and knew that Tula, standing back of his chair had missed no word. "You mean the German Conrad who is manager of Granados ranches across the border?"

"Señor, I mean the beast whose trail is red with the blood of innocence, and whose poison is sinking into the veins of Mexico like a serpent, striking secretly, now here, now there, until the blood of the land is black with that venom. Ay! I know, señor; —- the earth is acrawl with the German lizards creeping into the shining sun of Mexico! This so excellent Don Adolf Conrad is only one, and José Perez is his target —- I am the one to know that! A year ago, and Don José was a man, with faults perhaps; but who is perfect on this earth? Then came Don

Adolf riding south and is very great gentleman and makes friends. His home in Hermosillo becomes little by little the house of Perez, and little by little Perez goes on crooked paths. That is true! First it was to buy a ship for coast trade, then selling rifles in secret where they should not be sold, then —- shame it is to tell —- men and women were sold and carried on that ship like cattle! Not rebels, señor, not prisoners of battle, —- but herdsmen and ranch people, poor Indian farmers whom only devils would harm! Thus it was, señor, until little by little Don Adolf knew so much that José Perez awoke to find he had a master, and a strong one! It was not one man alone who caught him in the net; it was the German comrades of Don Adolf who never forgot their task, even when he was north in the States. They needed a man of name in Hermosillo, and José Perez is now that man. When the whip of the German cracks, he must jump to serve their will."

"But José Perez is a strong man. Before this day he has wiped many a man from his trail if the man made him trouble," ventured Kit.

"You have right in that, señor, but I am telling you it is a wide net they spread and in that net he is snared. Also his household is no longer his own. The Indian house servants are gone, and outlaw Japanese are there instead. That is true and their dress is the dress of Indians. They are Japanese men of crimes, and German men gave aid that they escape from justice in Japan. It is because they need such men for German work in Mexico, men who have been taught German and dare not turn rebel. Not an hour of the life of José Perez is free from the eyes of a spy who is a man of crimes. And there are other snares. They tell him that he is to be a governor by their help; —- that is a rich bait to float before the eyes of a man! His feet are set on a trail made by Adolph Conrad, —- He is trapped, and there is no going back. Poison and shame and slavery and death have come upon that trail like black mushrooms grown in a night, and what the end of the trail will be is hid in the heart of God."

"But your sympathy is with those women in slavery there in the south, and not with the evil friend of José Perez?" asked Kit.

"Can you doubt, señor? Am I not as truly a victim as they? I have not worked under a whip, but there are other punishments —- for a woman!"

Her voice dropped almost to a whisper, and she rested her chin on her hand, staring out into the shadows of the patio, oblivious of them all. Tula gazed at her as if fascinated, and there was a difference in her regard. That she was linked in hate against Conrad gave the Indian girl common cause with the jewel-eyed woman whose beauty had been the boast of a province. Kit noticed it and was vastly comforted. The absolute stolidity of Tula had left him in doubt as to the outcome if his little partner had disapproved of his fascinating protégée. He knew the thing she wanted to know, and asked it.

"Señora, the last band of Indian slaves from Sonora were driven from the little pueblo of Palomitas at the edge of this ranch. And there are sisters and mothers here with sick hearts over that raid. Can you tell me where those women were sent?"

"Which raid was that, and when?" asked Jocasta arousing herself from some memory in which she had been submerged. "Pardon, señor, I am but a doleful guest at supper, thinking too deeply of that which sent me here. Your question?"

He repeated it, and she strove to remember.

"There were many, and no one was told whence they came. It was supposed they were war prisoners who had to be fed, and were being sent to grow their own maize. If it were the last band then it would be the time Conrad had the wound in the face, here, like a knife thrust, and that —- –"

"That was the time," interrupted Kit eagerly. "If you can tell us where those people were sent you will prove the best of blessings to Mesa Blanca this night."

She smiled sadly at that and looked from him to Tula, whom she evidently noted for the first time.

"It is long since the word of blessing has been given to Jocasta," she said wistfully. "It would be a comfort to earn it in this house. But that band was not sent away, —- not far. Something went wrong with the boat down the coast, I forgot what it was, but there was much trouble, and the Indians were sent to a plantation of the General Terain until the boat was ready. I do not know what plantation, except that Conrad raged about it. He and Don José had a quarrel, very terrible! That wound given to him by a woman made him very difficult; then the quarrel ended by them drinking together too much. And after that many things happened very fast, and —- I was brought north."

"And the Indians?"

"Señor, I do not think anyone thought again of those Indians. They are planting maize or cane somewhere along the Rio Sonora."

Tula sank down weeping against the wall, while Valencia stroked her hair and patted her. Doña Jocasta regarded her curiously.

"To be young enough to weep like that over a sorrow!" she murmured wistfully. "It is to envy her, and not mourn over her."

"But this weeping is of joy," explained Valencia. "It is as the señor says, a blessing has come with you over the hard road. This child was also stolen, and was clever to escape. Her mother and her sister are yet there in that place where the maize is planted. If the boat has not taken them, then they also may get back. It is a hope!"

"Poor little one! and now that I could make good use of power, it is no longer mine," said Jocasta, looking at Kit regretfully. "A young maid with courage to escape has earned the right to be given help."

"She will be given it," he answered quietly, "and since your patience has been great with my questions, I would ask more of this Cavayso we have trapped tonight. He is raging of curious things there across the patio. Isidro holds a gun on him that he subdue his shouts, and his offer is of rich bribes for quick freedom. He is as mad to get back to Soledad as he was to leave it, and he tells of a trap set there for someone. It concerns ammunition for the revolutionists."

"No, not for them, but for trade in the south," said Jocasta promptly. "Yes, Soledad has long been the place for hiding of arms. It was the task of Don Adolf to get them across the border, and then a man of Don José finds a safe trail for them. Sometimes a German officer from Tucson is of much help there in the north. I have heard Don José and Conrad laugh about the so easily deceived Americanos, —- your pardon, señor!"

"Oh, we are used to that," agreed Kit easily, "and it is quite true. We have a whole flock of peace doves up there helping the Hohenzollern game. What was the officer's name?"

"A name difficult and long," she mused, striving to recall it. "But that name was a secret, and another was used. He was known only as a simple advocate —- James, the name; I remember that for they told me it was the English for Diego, which was amusing to me, —- there is no sound alike in them!"

"That's true, there isn't," said Kit, who had no special interest in any advocate named James. "But to get back to the man in the cell over there and the ammunition, may I ask if he confided to you anything of that place of storage? I mean Cavayso?"

"No, señor; and for a reason of the best. He knows nothing, and all his days and nights were spent searching secretly for the entrance to that dungeon, —- if it is a dungeon! He thought I should know, and made threats against me because I would not tell. Myself, I think José Perez tells no one that hiding place, not even Conrad, though Conrad has long wanted it! I told Don José that if he told that he was as good as a dead man, and I believe it. But now," and she shook her head fatefully, "now he is sure to get it!"

"But he swears he must get back to Soledad by sunrise for a trap is set. A trap for whom?" persisted Kit.

Doña Jocasta shook her head uncomprehendingly.

"God forbid he should get free to put those wolves on my track; then indeed I would need a knife, señor! He held them back from me on the trail, but now he would not hold them back."

"But the trap, señora?" repeated the puzzled Kit. "That man was in earnest, —- dead in earnest! He did not know I was listening, his words were only for an Indian, —- for Isidro. Who could he trap? Was he expecting anyone at Soledad?"

Doña Jocasta looked up with a little gasp of remembrance.

"It is true, a courier did come two days ago from the south, and Cavayso told me he meant to take me to the desert and hide me before Don José arrived. Also more mules and wagons came in. And Elena scolded about men who came to eat but not to work. Yes, they smoked, and talked, and talked, and waited! I never thought of them except to have a great fear. Yesterday after the lad brought me that letter I had not one thought, but to count the hours, and watch the sun. But it may be Cavayso told the truth, and that Don José was indeed coming. He told me he had promised Perez to lose me in the Arroya Maldioso if in no other way, and he had to manage that I never be seen again."

"Arroya Maldioso?" repeated Kit, "I don't understand."

"It is the great quicksand of Soledad, green things grow and blossom there but no living thing can cross over. It is beautiful —- that little arroya, and very bad."

"I had heard of it, but forgot," acknowledged Kit, "but that is not the trap of which he is raving now. It is some other thing."

Doña Jocasta did not know. She confessed that her mind was dark and past thinking. The ways of Don José and Conrad were not easy for other men of different lives to understand; —- there was a great net of war and scheming and barter, and Don José was snared in that net, and the end no man could see!

"Have you ever heard that Marto Cavayso was once a lieutenant of General Rotil?" Kit asked.

"The Deliverer!" she gasped, leaning forward and staring at him. A deep flush went over her face and receded, leaving her as deathly pale as when the bullet had been forced from the white shoulder. Her regard was curious, for her brows were contracted and there was domination and command in her eyes. "Why do you say this to me, señor? And why do you think it?"

Kit was astonished at the effect of his words, and quite as much astonished to hear anyone of the Perez household refer to Rotil as "the Deliverer."

"Señora, if you saw him ride side by side with Rotil, drinking from the same cup in the desert, would you not also think it?"

Tula rose to her feet, and moved closer to Kit.

"I too was seeing them together, señora," she said. "It was at the Yaqui well; I drew the water, and they drank it. This man of the loud curses is the man."

Doña Jocasta covered her eyes with her hand, and she seemed shaken. No one else spoke, and the silence was only broken by the muffled tones of Marto in the cell, and the brief bark of Clodomiro's dog at the corral.

"God knows what may be moving forward," she said at last, "but there is some terrible thing afoot. Take me to this man."

"It may not be a pleasant thing to do," advised Kit. "This is a man's game, señora, and his words might offend, for his rage is very great against you."

"Words!" she said with a note of disdain, and arose to her feet. She swayed slightly, and Valencia steadied her, and begged her to wait until morning, for her strength was gone and the night was late.

"Peace, woman! Who of us is sure of a morning? This minute is all the time that is ours, and —- I must know."

She leaned on Valencia as they crossed the patio, and Tula moved a seat outside the door of Marto's room. Kit fastened a torch in the holder of the brick pillar and opened the door without being seen, and stood watching the prisoner.

Marto Cavayso, who had been pleading with Isidro, whirled only to find the barrel of another gun thrust through the carved grill in the top of the door.

"Isidro," said Kit, "this man is to answer questions of the señora. If he is uncivil you can singe him with a bullet at your own will."

"Many thanks, señor," returned Isidro promptly. "That is a pleasant work to think of, for the talk of this shameless gentleman is poison to the air."

"You!" burst out Marto, pointing a hand at Jocasta in the corridor. "You put witchcraft of hell on me, and wall me in here with an old lunatic for guard, and now ——–"

Bing! A bullet from Isidro's rifle whistled past Marto's ear and buried itself in the adobe, scattering plaster and causing the prisoner to crouch back in the corner.

Jocasta regarded him as if waiting further speech, but none came.

"That is better," she said. "No one wishes to do you harm, but you need a lesson very badly. Now Marto Cavayso, —– if that be your name! —– why did you carry me away? Was it your own doing, or were you under orders of your General Rotil?"

"I should have let the men have you," he muttered. "I was a bewitched man, or you never would have traveled alive to see Soledad. Rotil? Do not the handsome women everywhere offer him love and comradeship? Would he risk a good man to steal a woman of whom José Perez is tired?"

"You are not the one to give judgment," said a strange voice outside the barred window. —– "That I did not send you to steal women is very true, and the task I did send you for has been better done by other men in your absence."

Cavayso swore, and sat on the bed, his head in his hands. Outside the window there were voices in friendly speech, that of Clodomiro very clear as he told his grandfather the dogs did not bark but once, because some of the Mesa Blanca boys were with the general, who was wounded.

Kit closed and bolted again the door of Cavayso, feeling that the guardianship of beauty in Sonora involved a man in many awkward and entangling situations. If it was indeed Rotil —– –

But a curious choking moan in the corridor caused him to turn quickly, but not quickly enough.

Doña Jocasta, who had been as a reed of steel against other dangers, had risen to her feet as if for flight at sound of the voice, and she crumpled down on the floor and lay, white as a dead woman, in a faint so deep that even her heartbeat seemed stilled.

Kit gathered her up, limp as a branch of willow, and preceded by Tula with the torch, bore her back to the chamber prepared for her. Valencia swept back the covers of the bed, and with many mutterings of fear and ejaculations to the saints, proceeded to the work of resuscitation.

"To think that she came over that black road and held fast to a heart of bravery, —– and now at a word from the Deliverer, she falls dead in fear! So it is with many who hear his name; yet he is not bad to his friends. Every Indian in Sonora is knowing that," stated Valencia.

CHAPTER XIV
THE HAWK OF THE SIERRAS

"That is what we get, Tula, by gathering beauty in distress into our outfit," sighed Kit. "She seems good foundation for a civil war here. Helen of Troy, —- a lady of an eastern clan! —- started a war on less, and the cards are stacked against us if they start scrapping. When Mexican gentry begin hostilities, the innocent bystander gets the worst of it, —- especially the Americano. So it is just as well the latest Richard in the field does not know whose bullet hit him in the leg, and brought his horse down."

Tula, who since their entrance to the civilized surroundings of Mesa Blanca, had apparently dropped all initiative, and was simply a little Indian girl under orders, listened impassively to this curious monologue. She evidently thought white people use many words for a little meaning.

"The Deliverer says will you graciously come?" she stated for the second time.

"Neither graciously, gracefully or gratefully, but I'll arrive," he conceded. "His politeness sounds ominous. It is puzzling why I, a mere trifle of an American ranch hand, should be given audience instead of his distinguished lieutenant."

"Isidro and Clodomiro are talking much with him, and the man Marto is silent, needing no guard," said Tula.

"Sure, —- Rotil has the whole show buffaloed. Well, let's hope, child, that he is not a mind reader, for we have need of all the ore we brought out, and can't spare any for revolutionary subscriptions."

Kit followed Tula into the *sala* where a rawhide cot had been placed, and stretched on it was the man of Yaqui Spring.

One leg of his trousers was ripped up, and there was the odor of a greasewood unguent in the room. Isidro was beside him, winding a bandage below the knee. A yellow silk banda around the head of Rotil was stained with red.

But he had evidently been made comfortable, for he was rolling a cigarette and was calling Isidro "doctor." Two former vaqueros of Mesa Blanca were there, and they nodded recognition to Kit. Rotil regarded him with a puzzled frown, and then remembered, and waved his hand in salute.

"Good day, señor, we meet again!" he said. "I am told that you are my host and the friend of Señor Whitely. What is it you do here? Is it now a prison, or a hospital for unfortunates?"

"Only a hospital for you, General, and I trust a serviceable one," Kit hastened to assure him. "More of comfort might have been yours had you sent a courier to permit of preparation."

"The service is of the best," and Rotil pointed to Isidro. "I've a mind to take him along, old as he is! The boys told me he was the best medico this side the range, and I believe it. As to courier," and he grinned, "I think you had one, if you had read the message right."

"The surprises of the night were confusing, and a simple man could not dare prophesy what might follow," said Kit, who had drawn up a chair and easily fell into Rotil's manner of jest. "But I fancy if that courier had known who would follow after, he would have spent the night by preference at Soledad."

"Sure he would, —- hell's fire shrivel him! That shot of his scraped a bone for me, and put my horse out of business. For that reason we came on quietly, and these good fellows listened at the window of Marto before they carried me in. It is a good joke on me. My men rounded up Perez and his German slaver at Soledad today —- yesterday now! —- and when we rode up the little cañon to be in at the finish what did we see but an escape with a woman? Some word had come my way of a Perez woman there, and only one thought was with me, that the woman had helped Perez out of the trap as quickly as he had ridden into it! After that there was nothing to do but catch them again. No thought came to me that Marto might be stealing a woman for himself, the fool! Perez made better time than we figured on, and is a day ahead. Marto meant to hide the woman and get back in time. It's a great joke that an Americano took the woman from him. I hope she is worth the trouble," and he smiled, lifting his brows questioningly.

"So that was the 'trap' that Marto raved and stormed to get back to?" remarked Kit. "I am still in the dark, though there are some glimmers of light coming. If Marto knew of that trap it explains —- –"

"There were three others of my men on the Soledad rancho, drawing pay from Perez. It is the first time that fox came in when we could spread the net tight. To get him at another place would not serve so well, for if Soledad was the casket of our treasure, at Soledad we make a three strike, —- the cattle, the ammunition, and Perez there to show the hiding place! It is the finish of four months' trailing, and is worth the time, and but for Marto running loco over a girl, there would have been a beautiful quiet finish at Soledad ranch house last night."

"But, if your men have Perez —- –"

"Like that!" and Rotil stretched out his open hand, and closed it significantly, with a cruel smile in his black, swift-glancing eyes. "This time there is no mistake. For over a week men and stout mules have been going in; —- it is a *conducta* and it is to take the ammunition. Well, señor, it is all well managed for me; also we have much need of that ammunition for our own lads."

"And it was done without a fight?" asked Kit. "I have heard that the men picked for Soledad were not the gentlest band Señor Perez could gather."

"We had their number," said Rotil placidly. "Good men enough, but with their cartridges doctored what could they do? I sent in two machine guns, and they were not needed. A signal smoke went up to show me all was well, and in another minute I heard the horses of Marto and his girl. He must have started an hour before Perez arrived. It is a trick of Don José's that no one can count on his engagements, but this time every hill had its sentinels for his trail, not anything was left to chance."

"And your accident?" asked Kit politely.

"Oh, I was setting my own guards at every pass when the runaway woman and men caught my ear and we took a short cut down the little cañon to head them off. I knew they would make for here, and that houses were not plenty —- " he smiled as if well satisfied with the knowledge. "So, as this was a friendly house it would be a safe bet to keep on coming." He blew rings of smoke from the cigarette, and chuckled.

"The boys will think a quicksand has swallowed us, and no one will be sleeping there at Soledad."

"Is there anything I can do to be of service," asked Kit. "I have a good room and a bed —- –"
But the chuckling of Rotil broke into a frank laugh.

"No, señor!" he said with humorous decision, watching Kit as he spoke, "already I have been told of your great kindness in the giving of beds and rooms of comfort. Why, with a house big enough, you could jail all the district of Altar! Not my head for a noose!"

Kit laughed awkwardly at the jest which was based on fact, but he met the keen eyes of Rotil very squarely.

"The Indians no doubt told you the reason the jail was needed?" he said. "If a girl picks a man to take a trail with, that is her own affair and not mine, but if a girl with chains on her wrists has to watch men throwing dice for her, and is forced to go with the winner —- well —- the man who would not help set her free needs a dose of lead. That is our American way, and no doubt is yours, señor."

"Sure! Let a woman pick her own, if she can find him!" agreed Rotil, and then he grinned again as he looked at Kit. "And, señor, it is a safe bet that this time she'll find him! —- you are a good big mark, not easily hidden."

The other men smiled and nodded at the humor of their chief, and regarded Kit with appreciative sympathy. It was most natural of course for them to suppose that if he took a woman from Marto, he meant to win her for himself.

Kit smiled back at them, and shook his head.

"No such luck for a poor vaquero," he confessed. "The lady is in mourning, and much grief. She is like some saint of sorrows in a priest's tale, and —- –"

"The priests are liars, and invented hell," stated Rotil.

"That may be, but sometimes we see sad women of prayers who look like the saints the priests tell about, —- and to have such women sold by a gambler is not good to hear of."

No one spoke for a little. The eyes of Rotil closed in a curious, contemptuous smile.

"You are young, boy," he said at last, "and even we who are not so young are often fooled by women. Trust any woman of the camp rather than the devout saints of the shrines. All are for market, —- but you pay most for the saint, and sorrow longest for her. And you never forget that the shrine is empty!"

His tone was mocking and harsh, but Kit preferred to ignore the sudden change of manner for which there seemed no cause.

"Thanks for the warning, General, and no saints for me!" he said good naturedly. "Now, is there any practical thing I can do to add to your comfort here? Any plans for tomorrow?"

"A man of mine is already on the way to Soledad, and we will sleep before other plans are made. Not even Marto will I see tonight, knowing well that you have seen to his comfort!" and he chuckled again at the thought of Marto in his luxurious trap. "My lads will do guard duty in turn, and we sleep as we are."

"Then, if I can be of no service — – "

"Tomorrow perhaps, not tonight, señor. Some sleep will do us no harm."

"Then good night, and good rest to you, General."

"Many thanks, and good night, Don Pajarito."

Kit laughed at that sally, and took himself out of the presence. It was plain that the Deliverer had obtained only the most favorable account of Kit as the friend of Whitely. And as an American lad who sang songs, and protected even women he did not know, he could not appear formidable to Rotil's band, and certainly not in need of watching.

He looked back at them as the general turned on his side to sleep, and one of his men blew out the two candles, and stationed themselves outside the door. As he noted the care they took in guarding him, and glanced at the heavy doors and barred windows, he had an uncomfortable thrill at the conviction that it would serve as a very efficient prison for himself if his new friends, the revolutionists, ever suspected he held the secret of the red gold of El Alisal. It was a bit curious that the famous lost mine of the old mission had never really been "lost" at all!

Isidro, looking very tired, had preceded him from the *sala*, as Kit supposed to go to bed. The day and night had been trying to the old man, and already it was the small hours of a new day.

There was a dim light in the room of Doña Jocasta, but no sound. Tula was curled up on a blanket outside her door like a young puppy on guard. He stooped and touched her shoulder.

"The señora?" he whispered.

"Asleep, after tears, and a sad heart!" she replied. "Valencia thanks the saints that at last she weeps, —- the beautiful sad one!"

"That is well; go you also to sleep. Your friends keep guard tonight."

She made no reply, and he passed on along the corridor to his own rooms. The door was open, and he was about to strike a light when a hand touched his arm. He drew back, reaching for his gun.

"What the devil — – "

"Señor," whispered Isidro, "make no light, and make your words in whispers."

"All right. What's on your mind?"

"The señora and the Deliverer. Know you not, señor, that she is sick with shame? It is so. No man has told him who the woman is he calls yours. All are afraid, señor. It is said that once Ramon Rotil was content to be a simple man with a wife of his own choosing, but luck was not his. It was the daughter of a priest in the hills, and José Perez took her!"

"Ah-h!" breathed Kit. "If it should be this one — – "

"It is so, —- she went like a dead woman at his voice, but he does not know. How should he, when Don José has women beyond count? Señor, my Valencia promised Doña Jocasta you would save her from meeting the general. That promise was better than a sleeping drink of herbs to her. Now that the promise is made, how will you make it good?"

"Holy smoke —- also incense —- also the pipe!" muttered Kit in the dark. "If I live to get out of this muddle I'll swear off all entangling alliances forevermore! Come into the kitchen where we can have a fire's light. I can't think in this blackness."

They made their way to the kitchen, and started a blaze with mesquite bark. The old Indian cut off some strips of burro *jerke* and threw them on the coals.

"That is better, it's an occupation anyway," conceded Kit chewing with much relish. "Now, Isidro, man, you must go on. You know the land best. How is one to hide a woman of beauty from desert men?"

"She may have a plan," suggested Isidro.

"Where is Clodomiro?" asked Kit, suddenly recalling that the boy had disappeared. The old man did not answer; he was very busy with the fire, and when the question was repeated he shook his head.

"I do not know who went. If Tula did not go, then Clodomiro was the one. They were talking about it."

"Talking, —- about what?"

"About the German. He is caught at Soledad, and must not be let go, or let die. All the Indians of Palomitas will be asking the Deliverer for that man."

"Isidro, what is it they want to do with him?" asked Kit, and the old Indian ceased fussing around with a stick in the ashes, and looked up, sinister and reproving.

"That, señor, is a question a man does not ask. If my woman tells me the women want a man for Judas, I —- get that man! I ask nothing."

"Good God! And that child, Tula —- " began Kit in consternation, and old Isidro nodded his head.

"It is Tula who asked. She is proving she is a woman; Clodomiro goes for her because that is his work. Your white way would be a different way, —- of an alcalde and the word of many witness. Our women have their own way, and no mistake is made."

"But Rotil, the general, —- he will not permit —- –"

"Señor, for either mother or grandmother the general had an Indian woman. He has the knowing of these things. I think Tula gets the man they ask for. She is wise, that child! A good woman will be chosen to have speech with the Deliverer —- when they come."

"There is a thought in that," mused Kit, glancing sharply at the old man. "Do they make choice of some wise woman, to be speaker for the others? And they come here?"

"That is how it is, señor."

"Then, what better way to hide Doña Jocasta than to place her among Indian women who come in a band for that task? Many women veil and shroud their heads in black as she does. The music of her voice was dulled when she spoke to Marto, and General Rotil had no memory of having ever heard it. Think, —- is there to be found an old dress of your wife? Can it be done and trust no one? Doña Jocasta is clever when her fear is gone. With Tula away from that door the rest is easy. The dawn is not so far off."

"Dawn is the time the women of Palomitas will take the road," decided Isidro, "for by the rising time of the sun the Deliverer has said that his rest here is ended, and he goes on to Soledad where José Perez will have a trembling heart of waiting."

"Will they tell him whose trap he is caught in?"

"Who knows? The Deliverer has plans of his own making. It was not for idleness he was out of sight when the trap was sprung. He sleeps little, does Ramon Rotil!"

In a mesquite tree by the cook house chickens began to crow a desultory warning. And Isidro proceeded to subtract stealthily a skirt and shawl from wooden pegs set in the adobe wall where Valencia slept. She startled him by stirring, and making weary inquiry as to whether it was the time.

"Not yet, my treasure, that fighting cock of Clodomiro crows only because of a temper, and not for day. It is I will make the fire and set Maria to the grinding. Go you to your sleep."

Which Valencia was glad to do, while her holiday wardrobe, a purple skirt bordered with green, and a deeply fringed black shawl, was confiscated for the stranger within their gates.

Thrusting the bundle back of an olla in the corridor he touched Tula on the shoulder.

"The señor waits you in the kitchen," he muttered in the Indian tongue, and she arose without a word, and went silent as a snake along the shadowy way.

It took courage for Isidro to enter alone the room of Doña Jocasta, as that was the business of a woman. But Kit had planned that, if discovered, the girl should apparently have no accomplices. This would protect Tula and Valencia should Rotil suspect treachery if an occupant of the house should disappear. It would seem most natural that a stolen woman would seek to escape homeward when not guarded, and that was to serve as a reasonable theory.

She slept with occasional shuddering sighs, as a child after sobbing itself to sleep. That sad little sound gave the old Indian confidence in his errand. It might mean trouble, but she had dared trouble ere now. And there could not be continual sorrow for one so beautiful, and this might be the way out!

She woke with a startled cry as he shook her bed, but it was quickly smothered as he whispered her name.

"It is best you go to pray in the chapel room, and meet there the women of Palomitas. Others will go to pray for a Judas; among many you may be hidden."

She patted his arm, and arose in the dark, slipping on her clothes. He gave her the skirt and she donned that over her own dress. Her teeth were chattering with nervous excitement, and when she had covered herself with the great shawl, her hand went out gropingly to him to lead her.

As they did not pass the door of the *sala*, no notice was given them by Rotil's guard. Mexican women were ever at early prayers, or at the *metate* grinding meal for breakfast, and that last possibility was ever welcome to men on a trail.

In the kitchen Kit Rhodes was seeking information concerning Clodomiro from Tula, asking if it was true he would fetch the women of Palomitas to petition Rotil.

"Maybe so," she conceded, "but that work is not for a mind of a white man. Thus I am not telling you Clodomiro is the one to go; his father was what you call a priest, —- but not of the church," she said hastily, "no, of other things."

Looking at her elfin young face in the flickering light of the hearth fire, he had a realization of vast vistas of "other things" leading backward in her inherited tendencies, the things known by his young comrade but not for the mind of a white man, —- not even for the man whom Miguel had trusted with the secret of El Alisal. Gold might occasionally belong to a very sacred shrine, but even sacred gold was not held so close in sanctuary as certain ceremonies dear to the Indian thought. Without further words Kit Rhodes knew that there were locked chambers in the brain of his young partner, and to no white man would be granted the key.

"Well, since he has gone for them, there is nothing to say, though the general may be ill pleased at visitors," hazarded Kit. "Also you and I know why we should keep all the good will coming our way, and risk none of it on experiments. Go you back to your rest since there is not anything to be done. Clodomiro is at Palomitas by now, and you may as well sleep while the dawn is coming."

She took the strip of roasted meat he offered her, and went back to her blanket on the tiles at the door of the now empty room.

CHAPTER XV
THE "JUDAS" PRAYER AT MESA BLANCA

Isidro was right when he said Ramon Rotil slept but little, for the very edge of the dawn was scarce showing in the east when he opened his eyes, moved his wounded leg stiffly, and then lay there peering between half-shut eyelids at the first tint of yellow in the sky.

"Chappo," he said curtly, "look beyond through that window. Is it a band of horses coming down the mesa trail, or is it men?"

"Neither, my General, it is the women who are left of the rancherias of Palomitas. They come to do a prayer service at an old altar here. Once Mesa Blanca was a great hacienda with a chapel for the peons, and they like to come. It is a custom."

"What saint's day is this?"

"I am not wise enough, General, to remember all; —- our women tell us."

"Um! —- saint's day unknown, and all a pueblo on a trail to honor it! Call Fidelio."

There was a whistle, a quick tread, and one of the men of Palomitas stood in the door.

"Take two men and search every woman coming for prayers —- guns have been carried under *serapes*."

"But, General —- –"

"Search every woman, —- even though your own mother be of them!"

"General, my own mother is already here, and on her knees beyond there in the altar room. They pray for heart to ask of you their rights in Soledad."

"That is some joke, and it is too early in the morning for jokes with me. I'm too empty. What have Palomitas women to do with rights in Soledad?"

"I have not been told," said Fidelio evasively. "It is a woman matter. But as to breakfast, it is making, and the *tortillas* already baking for you."

"Order all ready, and a long stirrup for that leg," said the general, moving it about experimentally. "It is not so bad, but Marto can ride fasting to Soledad for giving it to me."

"But, my General, he asks —- –"

"Who is he to ask? After yesterday, silence is best for him. Take him along. I will decide later if he is of further use —- I may —- need —- a —- man!"

There was something deliberately threatening in his slow speech, and the guards exchanged glances. Without doubt there would be executions at Soledad!

Rotil got off the cot awkwardly, but disdaining help from the guards hopped to a chair against the wall between the two windows.

Isidro came in with a bowl of water, and a much embroidered towel for the use of the distinguished guest, followed by a vaquero with smoking *tortillas*, and Tula with coffee.

The general eyed the ornate drawnwork of the linen with its cobweb fingers, and grinned.

"I am not a bridegroom this morning, *muchachita*, and need no necktie of such fineness for my beauty. Bring a plainer thing, or none."

Tula's eyes lit up with her brief smile of approval.

"I am telling them you are a man and want no child things, my General," she stated firmly, "and now it proves itself! On the instant the right thing comes."

She darted out the door, bumping into Rhodes, and without even the customary "with your permission" ran past him along the corridor, and, suddenly cautious, yet bold, she lifted the latch of the guest room where she had seen what looked to her like wealth of towels, —- and felt sure Doña Jocasta would not miss one of the plainest.

Stealthy as a cat she circled the bed, scarce daring to glance at it lest the lady wake and look reproach on her.

But she stepped on some hard substance on the rug by the wooden bench where the towels hung, and stooping, she picked it up, a little wooden crucifix, once broken, and then banded with silver to hold it solid. The silver was beautifully wrought and very delicate, surely the possession of a lady, and not a thing let fall by chance from the pocket of Valencia.

Tula turned to lay it carefully on the pillow beside the señora, and then stared at the vacant bed.

Only an instant she halted and thrust her hand under the cover.

"Cold, —- long time cold!" she muttered, and with towel and crucifix she sped back to the *sala* where Rotil was joking concerning the compliment she paid him.

"Don't make dandies of yourselves if you would make good with a woman," he said. "Even that little crane of a *muchacha* has brain, —- and maybe heart for a man! She has boy sense."

Kit, seeing her dart into the guest room, stood in his tracks watching for her to emerge. She gave him one searching curious look as she sped past, and he realized in a flash that his glance should have been elsewhere, or at least more casual.

She delivered the towel and retired, abashed and silent at the jests of the man she regarded with awe as the god-sent deliverer of her people. Once in the corridor she looked into Valencia's room, then in the kitchen where Valencia and Maria and other women were hastening breakfast, and last she sought Clodomiro at the corral.

"Where did you take her, and how?" she demanded, and the youth, tired with the endless rides and tasks of two days and nights, was surly, and looked his impatience. "She, and she, and she! Always women!" he grumbled. "Have I not herded all of them from over the mesa at your order? Is one making a slow trail, and must I go herding again?"

She did not answer, but looked past him at the horses.

"Which did the señora ride from Soledad?" she inquired, and Clodomiro pointed out a mare of shining black, and also a dark bay ridden by Marto.

"Trust him to take the best of the saddle herd," he remarked. "Why have you come about it? Is the señora wanting that black?"

"Maybe so; I was not told," she answered evasively. "But there is early breakfast, and it is best to get your share before some quick task is set, —- and this day there are many tasks."

The women were entering the portal at the rear, because the chapel of the old hacienda was at the corner. There was considerable commotion as Fidelio enforced the order to search for arms; —- if the Deliverer suspected treachery, how could they hope for the sympathy they came to beg for?

"Tell him there is nothing hidden under our rags but hearts of sorrow," said the mother of Fidelio. "Ask that he come here where we kneel to give God thanks that El Aleman is now in the power of the Deliverer."

"General Rotil does not walk, and there is no room for a horse in this door. Someone of you must speak for the others, and go where he is."

The kneeling women looked at each other with troubled dark eyes.

"Valencia will be the best one," said an old woman. "She lost no one by the pale beast, but she knows us every one. Marta, who was wife of Miguel, was always mother and spoke for us to the padre, or anyone, but Marta —- –"

She paused and shook her head; some women wept. All knew Marta was one who cried to them for vengeance.

"That is true," said Valencia. "Marta was the best, but the child of Marta is here, and knows more than we. She has done much, —- more than many women. I think the daughter can speak best for the mother, and that the Deliverer will listen."

Tula had knelt like the others, facing a little shelf on the wall where a carven saint was dimly illuminated by the light of a candle. All the room was very dark, for the dawn was yet but as a gray cloak over the world, and no window let in light.

The girl stood up and turned toward Valencia.

"I will go," she said, "because it is my work to go when you speak, but the Deliverer will ask for older tongues and I will come back to tell you that."

Without hesitation she walked out of the door, and the others bent their heads and there was the little click-click of rosary beads, slipping through their fingers in the dusk. Among the many black-shawled huddled figures kneeling on the hard tiles, none noticed the one girl

in the corner where shadows were deepest, and whose soft slender hands were muffled in Valencia's fringes.

Kit stood until he noted that the searching for arms did not include her, and then crossed
the patio with Fidelio on his way to the corrals. If the black mare of Doña Jocasta could be
gotten to the rear portal, together with the few burros of the older women, she might follow
after unnoticed. The adobe wall at the back was over ten feet high and would serve as a shield,
and the entire cavalcade would be a half mile away ere they came in range from the plaza.

He planned to manage that the mare be there without asking help of any Indian, and he
thought he could do it while the guard was having breakfast. It would be easy for them to
suppose that the black was his own. Thus scheming for beauty astray in the desert, he chatted
with Fidelio concerning the pilgrimage of the Palomitas women, and the possibility of Rotil's
patience with them, when Tula crossed the patio hurriedly and entered the door of the *sala*.

The general was finishing his breakfast, while Isidro was crouched beside him rewinding the
bandage after a satisfactory inspection of the wound. The swelling was not great, and Rotil,
eating cheerfully, was congratulating himself on having made a straight trail to the physician
of Mesa Blanca; it was worth a lost day to have the healing started right.

He was in that complacent mood when Tula sped on silent bare feet through the *sala* portal,
and halted just inside, erect against the wall, gazing at him.

"Hola! *Niña* who has the measure of a man! The coffee was of the best. What errand is
now yours?"

"Excellency, it is the errand too big for me, yet I am the one sent with it. They send me
because the mother of me, and Anita, my sister, were in the slave drive south, and the German
and the Perez men carried whips and beat the women on that trail."

Her brave young heart seemed to creep up in her throat and choke her at thought of those
whips and the women who were driven, for her voice trembled into silence, and she stood there
swallowing, her head bent, and her hands crossed over her breast, and clasped firmly there was
the crucifix she had found in the guest room. Little pagan that she was, she regarded it entirely
as a fetish of much potency with white people, and surely she needed help of all gods when she
spoke for the whole pueblo to this man who had power over many lives.

Rotil stared at her, frowning and bewildered.

"What the devil, —- " he began, but Isidro looked up at him and nodded assent.

"It is a truth she is telling, Excellency. Her father was Miguel, once major-domo of this
rancho. He died from their fight, and his women were taken."

"Oh, yes, that! —- it happens in many states. But this German —- who says the German
and Perez were the men to do it?"

"I, Tula, child of Miguel, say it," stated the girl. "With my eyes I saw him, —- with my ears
I heard the sister call out his name. The name was Don Adolf. Over his face was tied a long
beard, so! But it was the man, —- the friend of Don José Perez of Soledad; all are knowing
that. He is now your man, and the women ask for him."

"What women?"

"All the women of Palomitas. On their knees in the chapel they make prayers. Excellency,
it robs you of nothing that you give them a Judas for Holy Week. I am sent to ask that of
the Deliverer."

She slid down to her knees on the tiles, and looked up at him.

He stared at her, frowning and eyeing her intently, then chuckled, and grinned at the others.

"Did I not tell you she had the heart of a boy? And now you see it! Get up off your knees,
chiquita. Why should you want a Judas? It is a sweetheart I must find for you instead."

"I am not getting up," said Tula stolidly. "I am kneeling before you, my General. See! I
pray to you on the tiles for that Judas. All the women are praying. Also the old women have
made medicine to send El Aleman once more on this trail, and see you, —- it has come to pass!
You have him in your trap, but he is ours. Excellency, come once and see all the women on

their knees before the saint as I am here by you. We make prayers for one thing: —- the Judas for our holy day!"

"You young devil!" he grinned. "I wish you were a boy. Here, you men help me, or get me a crutch. I will see these women on their knees, and if you don't lie —- –"

With the help of Fidelio and a cane, he started very well, and nodded to Kit.

"You pick well, amigo," he observed. "She is a wildcat, and of interest. Come you and see. *Por Dios!* I've seen a crucifixion of the Penitentes and helped dig the hidden grave. Also I have heard of the 'Judas' death on Holy Friday, but never before this has so young a woman creature picked a man for it, —- a man alive! Courage of the devil!"

Tula arose, and went before them across the plaza to the door of the chapel. Kit knew this was the right moment for him to disappear and get the black mare back of the wall, but Rotil kept chuckling to him over the ungirlish request, and so pointedly included him in the party that there seemed no excuse available for absenting himself.

A flush of rose swept upward to the zenith heralding the sun, but in the adobe room, with its door to the west, no light came, except by dim reflection, and as Tula entered and the men stood at the threshold, they blocked the doorway of even that reflection, and the candle at the saint's shrine shone dimly over the bent heads of the kneeling women.

Rotil stood looking about questioningly; he had not expected to see so many. Then at the sound of the click of the prayer beads, some recollection of some past caused him to automatically remove his wide-brimmed hat.

"Mothers," said Tula quietly, "the Deliverer has come."

There was a half-frightened gasp, and dark faces turned toward the door.

"He comes as I told you, because I am no one by myself, and he could not know I was sent by you. I am not anyone among people, and he does not believe. Only people of importance should speak with a soldier who is a general."

"No, *por Dios*, my boy, you speak well!" said Rotil, clapping his hand on her shoulder, "but your years are not many and it cannot be you know the thing you ask for."

"I know it," asserted Tula with finality.

An old woman got up stiffly, and came towards him. "We are very poor, yet even our children are robbed from us —- that is why we pray. Don Ramon, your mother was simple as we, and had heart for the poor. Our lives are wasted for the masters, and our women children are stolen for the sons of masters. That is done, and we wish they may find ways to kill themselves on the trail. But the man who drove them with whips is now your man —- and we mothers ask him of you."

The wizened old creature trembled as she spoke, and scarce lifted her eyes. She made effort to speak further, but words failed, and she slipped to her knees and the beads slid from her nervous fingers to the tiles. She was very old, and she had come fasting across the mesa in the chill before the dawn; her two grandchildren had been driven south with the slaves —- one had been a bride but a month —- and they killed her man as they took her.

Valencia came to her and wiped the tears from her cheeks, patting her on the back as one would soothe a child, and then she looked at Rotil, nodding her head meaningly, and spoke.

"It is all true as Tia Tomasa is saying, señor. Her children are gone, and this child of Capitan Miguel knows well what she asks for. The days of the sorrows of Jesus are coming soon, and the Judas we want for that day of the days will not be made of straw to be bound on the wild bull's back, and hung when the ride is over. No, señor, we know the Judas asked of you by this daughter of Miguel; —- it is the pale beast called El Aleman. For many, many days have we made prayers like this, before every shrine, that the saints would send him again to our valley. You, señor, have brought answer to that prayer. You have him trapped, but he belongs only to us women. The saints listened to us, and you are in it. Men often are in prayers like that, and have no knowing of it, señor."

Kit listened in amazement to this account of prayers to Mexican saints for a Judas to hang on Good Friday! After four centuries of foreign priesthood, and foreign saints on the shrines, the mental effect on the aborigines had not risen above crucifixion occasionally on some proxy for their supreme earthly god, or mad orgies of vengeance on a proxy for Judas. The great drama of Calvary had taught them only new forms of torture and the certainty that vengeance was a debt to be paid. Conrad was to them the pale beast whipping women into slavery, —- and as supreme traitor to human things must be given a Judas death!

He shivered as he listened, and looked at the eyes of women staring out of the dusk for the answer to their prayers.

"*Por Dios!*" muttered Rotil, half turning to Kit, yet losing nothing of the pleading strained faces. "Does your head catch all of that, señor? Can't women beat hell? And women breed us all! What's the answer?"

"In this case it's up to you, General," replied Kit. "I'm glad the responsibility is not mine. Even as it is, women who look like these are likely to walk through my dreams for many a night!"

Rotil gloomed at them, puzzled, frowning, and at times the flicker of a doubtful smile would change his face without lighting it. No one moved or spoke.

"Here!" he said at last, "this child and two women have spoken, but there are over twenty of you here. Three out of twenty is no vote —- hold up your hands. Come, don't hang back, or you won't get Judas! There are no priests here, and no spies for priests, and there have been words enough. Show your hands!"

Kit looked back into the darkest corner, wondering what the vote of Jocasta would be; her mother was said to be Indian, or half Indian, and her hatred of the German would help her understand these darker tribal sisters.

But in the many lifted hands her own could not be seen and he felt curiously relieved, though it was no affair of his, and one vote either way would weigh nothing.

Rotil looked at the lifted hands, and grunted.

"You win, *muchacha*," he said to Tula. "I think you're the devil, and it's you made the women talk. You can come along to Soledad and fetch their Judas back to them."

"My thanks to you, and my service, Excellency," said Tula. "I will go and be glad that I go for that. But I swear by the Body and Blood, and I swear on this, that I only pay the debt of my people to El Aleman."

She was helping old Tia Tomasa to her feet with one hand, and held up the little crucifix to him with the other. She had noted that white people make oath on a cross when they want to be believed, and she wished with all her pagan heart to be believed by this man who had been a sort of legendary hero to her many months before she had seen his face, or dared hope he would ever grant favor to her —- Tula!

But whatever effect she hoped to secure by emphasizing her oath on the Christian symbol, she was not prepared for the rough grasp on her arm, or the harsh command of his voice.

"Holy God!" he growled, "why do you thrust that in my face, —- you?"

"Excellency —- I —- " began Tula, but he shook her as a cat would shake a mouse.

"Answer me! How comes it in your hands?"

"I found it, señor —- and did no harm."

"When? Where?"

"Why —- I —- I —- –"

A note of warning flashed from some wireless across the girl's mind, for it was no little thing by which Ramon Rotil had suddenly become a growling tiger with his hand near her throat.

"Where?" he repeated.

"On a trail, señor."

"When?"

"Three days ago."

"Where?"

"At the place where the Soledad trail leaves that of Mesa Blanca."

Rotil stared at her, and then turned to Kit.

"Do you know of this thing?"

"No, General, I don't," he said honestly enough, "but these women have many such —- –"

"No," contradicted Rotil, "they haven't, —- there's a difference."

He had seized the crucifix and held it, while he scanned the faces, and then brought his gaze back to Tula.

"You will show me that place, and prove yourself, *muchacha*," he said grimly. "There's something —- something —- Do you know, you damned young crane, that I can have my men shoot you against the wall out there if you lie to me?"

"Yes, my General, but it is better to give lead to enemies —- and not friends. Also a knife is cheaper."

"Silence! or you may get both!" he growled. "Here, look well —- you —- all of you! Have any of you but this creature seen it?"

He held it out, and Valencia, who was nearest, caught sight of it.

"Ai! Tula!" she said in reproof, "you to take that when the poor —- –"

Tula flashed one killing look at her, and Valencia stopped dead, and turned an ashen gray, and Rotil watching!

"Ah —- ha! I thought it!" he jeered. "Now whose trick is it to make me a fool? Come, sift this thing! You," to Valencia, "have looked on this before. Whose is it?"

"Señor —- I —- –"

"So!" he said with a sort of growl in the voice, "something chokes you? Look at me, not at the others! Also listen: —- if a lie is told to me, every liar here will go before a firing squad. Whose is this crucifix?"

Valencia's eyes looked sorrow on Tula, still under his hand, and then on the wood and silver thing held up before her. The sun was just rolling hot and red above the mountains, and Rotil's shaggy head was outlined in a sort of curious radiance as the light struck the white wall across the patio at his back. Even the silver of the crucifix caught a glimmer of it, and to Valencia he looked like the warrior padres of whom her grandmother used to tell, who would thunder hell's terrors on the frightened neophytes until the bravest would grovel in the dust and do penances unbelievable.

That commanding picture came between her and Rotil, —- the outlaw and soldier and patriot. She stumbled forward with a pleading gesture towards Tula.

"Excellency, the child does no harm. She is a stranger in the house. She has picked it up perhaps when lost by the señora, and —- –"

"What señora?"

"She who is most sorrowful guest here, Excellency, and her arms still bruised from the iron chains of El Aleman."

"And her name?"

"Excellency, it is the woman saved from your man by the Americano señor here beside you. And, —- she asked to be nameless while sheltered at Mesa Blanca."

"But not to me! So this is a game between you two —- " and he looked from Tula to Kit with sinister threat in his eyes, "it is then *your* woman who —- –"

"Ramon —- no!" said a voice from the far shadows, and the black shawled figure stood erect and cast off the muffling disguise. Her pale face shone like a star above all the kneeling Indians.

"God of heaven!" he muttered, and his hand fell from the shoulder of Tula. "You —- *you* are one of the women who knelt here for vengeance?"

"For justice," she said, "but I was here for a reason different; —- it was a place to hide. No one helped me, let the child go! Give these women what they ask or deny them, but send them away. To them I am nameless and unknown. You can see that even my presence is a thing of fear to them, —- let them go!"

He stared at her across those frightened dark faces. It was true they drew away from her in terror; her sudden uprising was as if she had materialized from the cold tiles of the chapel floor. Kit noted that their startled eyes were wide with awe, and knew that they also felt they were gazing on a beauty akin to that of the pictured saints. Even the glimmer of the candle touching her perfect cheek and brow added to the unearthly appearance there in the shadows.

But Ramon Rotil gazed at her across a wider space than that marked by the kneeling Indian women! Four years were bridged by that look, and where the others saw a pale Madonna, he saw a barefooted child weaving flowers of the mountain for a shrine where poverty prevented a candle.

He had sold maize to buy candles, and shoes for her feet, and she had given him the little brown wooden crucifix.

Once in the height of her reign of beauty in the hacienda of Perez, a ragged brown boy from the hills had lain in wait for her under the oleanders, and thrust a tightly bound package of corn husks into her hand, and her maid regarded with amazement the broken fragments of a wooden cross so poor and cheap that even the most poverty stricken of the peons could own one, and her wonder was great that her mistress wept over the broken pieces and strove to fit them together again.

And now it lay in his hand, bound and framed in silver wires delicately wrought.

He had traveled farther than she during the years between, and the memento of the past made him know it.

"Ramon, let them go!" she repeated with gentle appeal.

"Yes," he said, taking a deep breath as if rousing from a trance, "that is best. Child —- see to it, and have your way. Señor, will you arrange that the señora has what comfort there is here? Our horses wait, and work waits —- –"

He saw Valencia go with protecting, outstretched hands to Jocasta, and turned away.

Jocasta never moved. To save her friends from his rage she had spoken, and to her the big moment of humiliation dreamed of and feared had come and been lived through. He had seen her on her knees among all that brown herd made up of such women as his mother and her mother had been. From mistress of a palace on an estate large as many European kingdoms she had become an outcast with marks of fetters on her arms, while he was knelt to as a god by the simple people of the ranges, and held power of life and death over a wide land!

Kit could not even guess at all the tempestuous background of the drama enacted there in the chill of the chapel at sunrise, but the clash of those two outlaw souls suddenly on guard before each other, thrilled him by the unexpected. Rotil, profane, ruthless, and jeering, had suddenly grown still before the face of a woman from whom he turned away.

"Late! An hour late!" he grumbled, hobbling back to the plaza. "What did I tell you? Hell of women! Well, your damned little crane got what she started after —- huh! Why did she lie?"

"Well, you know, General," said Kit doubtfully, "that the enmity between you and José Perez is no secret. Even the children talk of it, and wish success to you —- I've heard that one do it! Doña Jocasta is of a Perez household, so it was supposed you would make prisoner anyone of their group. And Tula —- well, I reckon Tula listened last night to some rather hard things the señora has lived through at Soledad, and knew she would rather die here than go back there."

Kit realized he was on delicate ground when trying to explain any of the actions of any of the black and tan group to each other, but he sought the safest way out, and drew a breath of relief at his success, for Rotil listened closely, nodding assent, yet frowning in some perplexity.

"Um! what does that mean, —- rather die than go back?" he demanded. "No one has told me why the lady has come to Mesa Blanca, or what she is doing here. I don't see —- What the devil ails you?"

For Kit stared at him incredulous, and whistled softly.

"Haven't you got it *yet?*" he asked. "Last night you joked about a girl Marto stole, and we stole from him again. Don't you realize now who that girl is?"

"*Jocasta!*"

It was the first time he had uttered her name and there was a low terrible note in his voice, half choked by smothered rage.

"But how could Marto, —- or why should —- " he began and then halted, checked by various conflicting facts, and stared frowningly at Rhodes who again strove to explain that of which he had little knowledge.

"General, I reckon Marto was square to your interests about everything but the woman Perez and Conrad sent north into the desert, and it was Marto's job to see that she never left it alive. Evidently he did not report that extra task to you, for he meant to save the woman for himself. But even at that, General, you've got to give him credit. He says she bewitched him, and he couldn't kill her, and he wouldn't let the others have her. Also he risked a whale of a beating up, and some lead souvenirs, in trying to save her, even if it was for himself. So you see, Marto was only extra human, and is a good man. His heart's about broke to think he failed you, and I'll bet he wouldn't fail you again in a thousand years!"

"Yes, you have the right of that," agreed Rotil. "I did not know; I don't know yet what this means about Perez and —- and —- –"

"None of us do, General," stated Kit. "I heard Valencia say it must be something only a confessor could know, —- but it must be rather awful at that! She was started north like an insane criminal, hidden and in chains. She explains nothing, but General, you have now the two men at Soledad who made the plan, and you have here Marto who was their tool —- and perhaps —- at Soledad —- " he paused questioning.

"Sure! that is what will be done," decided Rotil. "See to it, you, after we are gone. Bring Doña Jocasta to Soledad with as much show of respect as can be mustered in a poor land, your girl and Isidro's wife to go along, and any comforts you can find. Yes, that is the best! Some way we will get to the bottom of this well. She must know a lot if they did not dare let her live, and Marto —- well, you make a good talk for him, straight too —- Marto will go with me. Tell no one anything. Make your own plans. By sunset I will have time for this mystery of the chains of Doña Jocasta. Be there at Soledad by sunset."

"At your command, General."

Then Chappo and Fidelio helped their leader into the saddle. Marto, crestfallen and silently anticipating the worst, was led out next; a *reata* passed around the saddle horn and circling his waist was fastened back of the saddle. His hands were free to guide his horse, but Chappo, with a wicked looking gun and three full cartridge belts, rode a few paces back of him to see that he made no forbidden use of them.

Kit watched them ride east while the long line of women of Palomitas took up the trail over the mesa to the north. Their high notes of a song came back to him, —- one of those wailing chants of a score of verses dear to the Mexican heart. In any other place he would have deemed it a funeral dirge with variations, but with Indian women at sunrise it meant tuneful content.

Kit listened with a shiver. Because of his own vagrant airs they had called him "El Pajarito" when he first drifted south over Mexican trails, —- but happy erratic tunefulness was smothered for him temporarily. Over the vast land of riches, smiling in the sun, there brooded the threats of Indian gods chained, inarticulate, reaching out in unexpected ways for expression through the dusky devotees at hidden shrines. The fact that occasionally they found expression through some perverted fragment from an imported cult was a gruesome joke on the importers. But under the eagle of Mexico, whose wide wings were used as shield by the German vultures across seas, jokes were not popular. German educators and foreign priests with Austrian affiliations, saw to that. The spiritual harvest in Mexico was not always what the planters anticipated, —- for curious crops sprung up in wild corners of the land, as Indian grains wrapped in a mummy's robe spring to life under methods of alien culturists.

Vague drifting thoughts like this followed Kit's shiver of repulsion at that Indian joy song over the promise of a veritable live Judas. On him they could wreak a personal vengeance, and go honestly to confession in some future day, with the conviction that they had, by the sufferings they could individually and collectively invent for Judas, in some vague but laudable manner mitigated the sufferings of a white god far away whose tribulations were dwelt upon much by the foreign priesthood.

He sensed this without analysis, for his was not the analytical mind. What brain Kit had was fairly well occupied by the fact that his own devoted partner was the moving spirit of that damnable pagan *Come, all ye* —- drifting back to him from the glorified mesa, flushed golden now by the full sun.

Clodomiro came wearily up from the corral. The boy had gone without sleep or rest until his eyes were heavy and his movements listless. Like the women of Palomitas he also had worked overtime at the call of Tula, and Kit wondered at the concerted activity —- no one had held back or blundered.

"Clodomiro," he said passing the lad a cigarette and rolling one for himself from good new tobacco secured from Fidelio, "how comes it that even the women of years come in the night for prayers when you ride for them? Do they give heed to any boy who calls?"

Clodomiro gave thanks for the cigarette, but was too well bred to light it in the presence of an elder or a superior. He smelled it with pleasure, thrust it over his ear and regarded Rhodes with perfectly friendly and apparently sleepy black eyes.

"Not always, señor, but when Tula sends the call of Miguel, all are surely coming, and also making the prayer."

"The call of Miguel? Why —- Miguel is dead."

"That is true, señor, but he was head man, and he had words of power, also the old Indians listened. Now Tula has the words, and as you see, —- the words are still alive! I am not knowing what they mean, —- the words, —- but when Tula tells me, I take them."

"*O Tippecanoe, and Tyler too!*" hummed Kit studying the boy. "What's in a word? Do you mean that you take a trail to carry words you don't understand, because a girl younger than you tells you to?"

The boy nodded indifferently.

"Yes, señor, it is my work when it is words of old prayer, and Tula is sending them. It would be bad not to go, a quicksand would surely catch my horse, or I might die from the bite of a *sorrilla rabioso*, or evil ghosts might lure me into wide *medanos* where I would seek trails forever, and find only my own! Words can do that on a man! and Tula has the words now."

"Indeed! That's a comfortable chum to have around —- not! And have you no fear?"

"Not so much. I am very good," stated Clodomiro virtuously. "Some day maybe I take her for my woman; —- her clan talks about it now. She has almost enough age, and —- you see!"

He directed the attention of Rhodes to the strips of red and green and pink calico banding his arms, their fluttering ends very decorative when he moved swiftly.

"Oh, yes, I've been admiring them. Very pretty," said Kit amicably, not knowing the significance of it, but conscious of the wide range one might cover in a few minutes of simple Sonora ranch life. From the tragic and weird to the childishly inane was but a step.

Clodomiro passed on to the kitchen, and Kit smoked his cigarette and paced the outer corridor, striving for plans to move forward with his own interests, and employ the same time and the same trail for the task set by Ramon Rotil.

Rotil had stated that the escort of Doña Jocasta must be as complete as could be arranged. This meant a dueña and a maid at least, and as he had bidden Tula have her way with her "Judas," it surely meant that Tula must go to Soledad. Very well so far, and as Rotil would certainly not question the extent of the outfit taken along, why not include any trifles Tula and he chanced to care for? He remembered also that there were some scattered belongings of the Whitely's left behind in the haste of departure. Well, a few mule loads would be a neighborly gift to take north when he crossed the border, and Soledad was nearer the border!

It arranged itself very well indeed, and as Tula emerged from the patio smoothing out an old newspaper fragment discarded by Fidelio, and chewing *chica* given her by Clodomiro, he hailed her with joy.

"Blessed Indian Angel," he remarked appreciatively, "you greased the toboggan for several kinds of hell for us this day of our salvation, but your jinx was on the job, and turned the trick our way! Do you know you are the greatest little mascot ever held in captivity?"

But Tula didn't know what "mascot" meant, and was very much occupied with the advertisement of a suit and cloak house in the old Nogales paper in which some trader at the railroad had wrapped Fidelio's tobacco. It had the picture of an alluring lady in a dress of much material slipping from the shoulders and dragging around the feet. To the aboriginal mind that seemed a very great waste, for woven material was hard to come by in the desert.

She attempted an inquiry concerning that wastefulness of Americanas, but got no satisfactory reply. Kit took the tattered old paper from her hand, and turned it over because of the face of Singleton staring at him from the other side of the page. It was the account of the inquest, and in the endeavor to add interest the local reporters had written up a column concerning Singleton's quarrel with the range boss, Rhodes, —- and the mysterious disappearance of the latter across the border!

There was sympathetic mention made of Miss Wilfreda Bernard, heiress of Granados, and appreciative mention of the efficient manager, Conrad, who had offered all possible assistance to the authorities in the sad affair. The general expression of the article was regret that the present situation along the border prevented further investigation concerning Rhodes. The said Rhodes appeared to be a stranger in the locality, and had been engaged by the victim of the crime despite the objections of Manager Conrad.

There followed the usual praise and list of virtues of the dead man, together with reference to the illustrious Spanish pioneer family from whom his wife had been descended. It was the first time Kit had been aware of the importance of Billie's genealogy, and remembering the generally accepted estimates of Spanish pride, he muttered something about a "rose leaf princess, and a Tennessee hill-billy!"

"It's some jolt, two of them!" he conceded.

> Twinkle, twinkle little star,
> How I wonder what you are!

"They say bunches of stars and planets get on a jamboree and cross each other's trail at times, and that our days are rough or smooth according to their tantrums. Wish I knew the name of the luminary raising hell for me this morning! It must be doing a highland fling with a full moon, and I'm being plunked by every scattered spark!"

CHAPTER XVI
THE SECRET OF SOLEDAD CHAPEL

It took considerable persuasion to prevail upon Doña Jocasta that a return to Soledad would be of any advantage to anybody. To her it was a place fearful and accursed.

"But, señora, a padre who sought to be of service to you is still there, a prisoner. In the warring of those wild men who will speak for him? The men of Soledad would have killed him but for their superstitions, and Rotil is notorious for his dislike of priests."

"I know," she murmured sadly. "There are some good ones, but he will never believe. In his scales the bad ones weigh them down."

"But this one at Soledad?"

"Ah, yes, señor, he spoke for me, —- Padre Andreas."

"And a prisoner because of you?"

"That is true. You do well to remind me of that. My own sorrows sink me in selfishness, and it is a good friend who shows me my duty. Yes, we will go. God only knows what is in the heart of Ramon Rotil that he wishes it, but that which he says is law today wherever his men ride, and I want no more sorrow in the world because of me. We will go."

Valencia had gone placidly about preparations for the journey from the moment Kit had expressed the will of the Deliverer. To hesitate when he spoke seemed a foolish thing, for in the end he always did the thing he willed, and to form part of the escort for Doña Jocasta filled her with pride. She approved promptly the suggestion that certain bed and table furnishings go to Soledad for use of the señora, and later be carried north to Mrs. Whitely, whose property they were.

As capitan of the outfit, Kit bade her lay out all such additions to their state and comfort, and he would personally make all packs and decide what animals, chests, or provisions could be taken.

This was easier managed than he dared hope. Clodomiro rode after mules and returned with Benito and Mariano at his heels, both joyously content to leave the planting of fields and offer their young lives to the army of the Deliverer. Isidro was busy with the duties of the ranch stock, and there was only Tula to see bags of nuggets distributed where they would be least noticed among the linen, Indian rugs, baskets and such family possessions easiest carried to their owner.

He marked the packs to be opened, and Tula, watching, did not need to be told.

The emotions of the night and the uncertainty of what lay ahead left Rhodes and Doña Jocasta rather silent as they took the trail to the gruesome old hacienda called by Doña Jocasta so fearful and accursed. Many miles went by with only an occasional word of warning between them where the way was bad, or a word of command for the animals following.

"In the night I rode without fear where I dare not look in the sunlight," said Jocasta drawing back from a narrow ledge where stones slipped under the hoofs of the horses to fall a hundred feet below in a dry cañon.

"Yes, señora, the night was kind to all of us," returned Kit politely. "Even the accidents worked for good except for the pain to you."

"That is but little, and my shoulder of no use to anyone. General Rotil is very different, —- a wound to a soldier means loss of time. It is well that shot found him among friends for it is said that when a wolf has wounds the pack unites to tear him to pieces, and there are many, —- many pesos offered to the traitor who will trap Rotil by any lucky accident."

"Yet he took no special care at Mesa Blanca."

"Who knows? He brought with him only men of the district as guard. Be sure they knew every hidden trail, and every family. Ramon Rotil is a coyote for the knowing of traps."

She spoke as all Altar spoke, with a certain pride in the ability of the man she had known as a burro driver of the sierras. For three years he had been an outlaw with a price on his head, and as a rebel general the price had doubled many times.

"With so many poor, how comes it that no informer has been found? The reward would be riches untold to a poor *paisano*."

"It might be to his widow," said Doña Jocasta, "but no sons of his, and no brothers would be left alive."

"True. I reckon the friends of Rotil would see to that! Faithful hearts are the ones he picks for comrades. I heard an old-timer say the Deliverer has that gift."

She looked at him quickly, and away again, and went silent. He wondered if it was true that there had been love between these two, and she had been unfaithful. Love and Doña Jocasta were fruitful themes for the imagination of any man.

Valencia was having the great adventure of her life in her journey to Soledad, and she chattered to Tula as a maiden going to a marriage. Three people illustrious in her small world were at once to be centered on the stage of war before her eyes. She told Tula it was a thing to make songs of, —- the two men and the most beautiful woman!

When they emerged from the cañon into the wide spreading plain, with the sierras looming high and blue beyond, the eyes of Kit and Tula met, and then turned toward their own little camp in the lap of the mother range. All was flat blue against the sky there, and no indications of cañon or gulch or pocket discernible. Even as they drew nearer to the hacienda, and Kit surreptitiously used the precious field glasses, thus far concealed from all new friends of the desert, he found difficulty in locating their hill of the treasure, and realized that their fears of discovery in the little cañon had been groundless. In the far-away time when the giant aliso had flourished there by the cañon stream, its height might have served to mark the special ravine where it grew, but the lightning sent by pagan gods had annihilated that landmark forever, and there was no other.

The glint of tears shone in the eyes of Tula, and she rode with downcast eyes, crooning a vagrant Indian air in which there were bird calls, and a whimpering long-drawn tremulo of a baby coyote caught in a trap, a weird ungodly improvisation to hear even with the shining sun warming the world.

Kit concluded she was sending her brand of harmony to Miguel and the ghosts on guard over the hidden trail. —- And he rather wished she would stop it!

Even the chatter of Valencia grew silent under the spell of the girl's gruesome intonings, —- ill music for her entrance to a new portal of adventure.

"It sounds of death," murmured Doña Jocasta, and made the sign of the cross. "The saints send that the soul to go next has made peace with God! See, señor, we are truly crossing a place of death as she sings. That beautiful valley of the green border is the *sumidero*, —- the quicksands from hidden springs somewhere above," and she pointed to the blue sierras. "I think that is the grave José meant for me at Soledad."

"Nice cheerful end of the trail —- not!" gloomed Kit strictly to himself. "That little imp is whining of trouble like some be-deviled prophetess."

Afterwards he remembered that thought, and wished he could forget!

Blue shadows stretched eastward across the wide zacatan meadows, and the hacienda on the far mesa, with its white and cream adobe walls, shone opal-like in the lavender haze of the setting sun.

Kit Rhodes had timed the trip well and according to instruction of the general, but was a bit surprised to find that his little cavalcade was merely part of a more elaborate plan arranged for sunset at Soledad.

A double line of horsemen rode out from the hacienda to meet them, a rather formidable reception committee as they filed in soldier-like formation over the three miles of yellow and green of the spring growths, and halted where the glint of water shone in a dam filled from wells above.

Their officer saluted and rode forward, his hat in his hand as he bowed before Doña Jocasta.

"General Rotil presents to you his compliments, Señora Perez, and sends his guard as a mark of respect when you are pleased to ride once more across your own lands."

"My thanks are without words, señor. I appreciate the honor shown to me. My generalissimo will answer for me."

She indicated Kit with a wan smile, and her moment of hesitation over, his title reminded him that no name but El Pajarito had been given him by his Indian friends. That, and the office of manager of Mesa Blanca, was all that served as his introduction to her, and to Rotil. With the old newspaper in his pocket indicating that Kit Rhodes was the only name connected with the murder at Granados, he concluded it was just as well.

The guard drew to either side, and the officer and Kit, with Doña Jocasta between them, rode between the two lines, followed by Tula and Valencia. Then the guard fell in back of them, leaving Clodomiro with the pack animals and the Indian boys to follow after in the dust.

Doña Jocasta was pale, and her eyes sought Kit's in troubled question, but she held her head very erect, and the shrouding lace veil hid all but her eyes from the strangers.

"Señor Pajarito," she murmured doubtfully. "The sun is still shining, and there are no chains on my wrists, —- otherwise this guard gives much likeness to my first arrival at the hacienda of Soledad!"

"I have a strong belief that no harm is meant to you by the general commanding," he answered, "else I would have sought another trail, and these men look friendly."

"God send they be so!"

"They have all the earmarks, —- and look!"

They were near enough the hacienda to see men emerge from the portal, and one who limped and leaned on a cane, moved ahead of the others and stood waiting.

"It is an honor that I may bid you welcome to your own estate, Doña Jocasta," he said grimly. "We have only fare of soldiers to offer you at first, but a few days and good couriers can remedy that."

"I beg that you accept my thanks, *Commandante*," she murmured lowly. "The trail was not of my choosing, and it is an ill time for women to come journeying."

"The time is a good time," he said bluntly, "for there is a limit to my hours here. And in one of them I may do service for you."

His men stood at either side watching. There were wild tales told of Ramon Rotil and women who crossed or followed his trail, but here was the most beautiful of all women riding to his door and he gave her no smile, —- merely motioned to the Americano that he assist her from the saddle.

"The supper is ready, and your woman and the priest will see that care is given for your comfort," he continued. "Afterwards, in the *sala* —- –"

She bent her head, and with Kit beside her passed on to the inner portal. There a dark priest met her and reached out his hand.

"No welcome is due me, Padre Andreas," she said brokenly. "I turned coward and tried to save myself."

"Daughter," he returned with a wry smile at Kit, and a touch of cynic humor, "you had right in going. The lieutenant would have had no pleasure in adding me to his elopement, and, as we hear, —- your stolen trail carried you to good friends."

Kit left them there and gave his attention to space for the packs and outfit, but learned that the general had allotted to him the small corral used in happier days for the saddle horses of the family. There was a gate to it and a lock to the gate. Chappo had been given charge, and when all was safely bestowed, he gave the key to the American.

The brief twilight crept over the world, and candles were lit when Kit returned to the corridor. Rotil was seated, giving orders to men who rode in and dismounted, and others who came out from supper, mounted and rode away. It was the guard from a wide-flung arc bringing report of sentinels stationed at every pass and water hole.

Padre Andreas was there presenting some appeal, and to judge by his manner he was not hopeful of success. Yet spoke as a duty of his office and said so.

"What is your office to me?" asked Rotil coldly. "Do your duty and confess him when the time comes if that is his wish. It is more than he would have given to her or the foreman who stored the ammunition. Him he had killed as the German had Miguel Herrara killed on the border, —- and Herrara had been faithful to that gun running for months. When man or woman is faithful to José Perez long enough to learn secrets, he rewards them with death. A dose of his own brew will be fit medicine."

"But the woman, —- she is safe. She is —- –"

"Yes, very safe!" agreed Rotil, sneering. "Shall I tell you, pious Father, how safe she is? The cholo who took food to Perez and that German dog has brought me a message. See, it is on paper, and is clear for any to read. You —- no not you, but Don Pajarito here shall read it. He is a neutral, and not a padre scheming to save the soul of a man who never had a soul!"

Kit held it to the light, read it, and returned it to Rotil.

"I agree with you, General. He offers her to you in exchange for his own freedom."

"Yes, and to pay for that writing I had him chained where he could see her enter the plaza as a queen, if we had queens in Mexico! You had an unseen audience for your arrival. The guard reports that the German friend of Perez seems to love you, Don Pajarito, very much indeed."

"Sure he does. Here is the mark of one of his little love pats with a monkey wrench," and Kit parted his hair to show the scar of the Granados assault. "I got that for interfering when he was trying to kill his employer's herds with ground glass in their feed."

"So? no wonder if he goes in a rage to see you riding as a lady's caballero while he feels the weight of chains in a prison. This world is but a little place!"

"That is true," said Padre Andreas, regarding Kit, for the story of the horses was told to me by Doña Jocasta here in Soledad!"

"How could that be?" demanded Rotil. "Is it not true you met the lady first at Mesa Blanca?"

"As you say," said Kit, alert at the note of suspicion, "if the lady knows aught of Granados, it is a mystery to me, and is of interest."

"Not so much a mystery," said the priest. "Conrad boasted much when glasses were emptied with Perez on the Hermosillo rancho, and Doña Jocasta heard. He told the number of cavalry horses killed by his men, also the owner of that ranch of Granados who had to be silenced for the cause."

"Thanks for those kind words, Padre," said Kit. "If Doña Jocasta has a clear memory of that boasting, she may save a life for me."

"So?" said Rotil speculatively. "We seem finding new trails at Soledad. Whose life?"

"The partner of a chum of mine," stated Kit lightly, as he did some quick thinking concerning the complications likely to arise if he was regarded as a possible murderer hiding from the law. "My own hunch is that Conrad himself did it."

"Have you any idea of a trap for him?"

"N-no, General, unless he was led to believe that I was under guard here. He might express his sentiments more freely if he thought I would never get back across the border alive."

"Good enough! This offer from Perez is to go into the keeping of Doña Jocasta. You've the duty of taking it to her. We have not yet found that ammunition."

"Well, it did cross the border, and somebody got it."

"He says it was moved to Hermosillo before Juan Gonsalvo, the overseer, died."

"Was shot, you mean, after it was cached."

"Maybe so, but he offers to trade part of it for his liberty, and deliver the goods north of Querobabi."

"Yes, General, —- into the bodies of your men if you trust him."

Rotil chuckled. "You are not so young as you look, Don Pajarito, and need no warning. It is the room next the *sala* where I will have Perez and Conrad brought. The señora can easily overhear what is said. It may be she will have the mind to help when she sees that offer he made."

"It would seem so, yet — women are strange! They go like the padre, to prayers when a life is at stake."

"Some women, and some priests, boy," said the dark priest. "It may be that you do not know Doña Jocasta well."

This remark appeared to amuse Rotil, for he smiled grimly and with a gesture indicated that they were to join Doña Jocasta.

She was rested and refreshed by a good supper. Valencia and Elena, the cook, had waited upon her and the latter waxed eloquent over the stupendous changes at Soledad from the time of Doña Jocasta's supper the previous day. Many of the angry men had been ready to start after Marto who had cheated them, when a courier rode in with the word that Don José and Señor Conrad were close behind. Then the surprise of all when Don José was captured, and it was seen that Elena had been cooking these many days, not for simple vaqueros, but for some soldiers of the revolution by which peace and plenty was to come to all the land! It was a beautiful dream, and the Deliverer was to make it come true!

Tula sat in the shadow against the wall, like some slender Indian carving, mute and expressionless while the eyes of the woman rolled as the two old friends exchanged their wonder tales of the night and day! Elena made definite engagement to be with the "Judas" trailers on the dark Friday, and both breathed blessings on Rotil who had promised them the right man for the hanging.

It was this cheerful topic Kit entered upon with the written note from Perez to the general. He had no liking for his task, as his eyes rested on Doña Jocasta, beautiful, resigned and detached from the scene about her. He remembered what Rotil had said scoffingly of saints lifted from shrines — a man never forgot that shrine was empty!

"Mine is a thankless task, señora, but the general decided you are the best keeper of this," and he gave to her the scribbled page torn from a note book.

She took it and held it unread, looking at him with dark tragic eyes.

"I have fear of written words, señor, and would rather hear them spoken. So many changes have come that I dread new changes. No matter where my cage is moved, it is still a cage to me," she said wistfully.

"I've a hunch, Doña Jocasta, that the bars of that cage are going to be broken for you," ventured Kit, taking the seat she indicated, "and this note may be one of the weapons to do it. Evidently Señor Perez has had some mistaken information concerning the stealing of you from here; — he thought it was by the general's order. So mistaken was he that he thought you were the object of Rotil's raid on Soledad, and for his own freedom he has offered to give you, and half his stock of ammunition, to General Ramon Rotil, and agree to a truce between their factions."

"Ah! he offers to make gift of me to the man he hates," she said after a long silence. "And the guns and ammunition, — he also surrenders them?"

"He offers — but it is written here! Since the guns, however, have been taken south, he cannot give them; he can only promise them, until such time — —"

"Ho!" she said scornfully. "Is that the tale he tells? It is true there are guns in the south, but guns are also elsewhere! He forgets, does José Perez, — or else he plays for time. This offer," and she referred to the note, "it is not written since we arrived — no. It was written earlier, when he thought I was held by that renegade far in the desert."

"I reckon that is true, señora, for after receiving it, Rotil had him chained in a room fronting the plaza that he might see you enter Soledad with honors."

"Ramon Rotil did that?" she mused, looking at the note thoughtfully, "and he gives to me the evidence against José? Señor, in the Perez lands we hear only evil things and very different things about Rotil. They would say this paper was for sale, but not for a gift. And — he gives it to me!"

Kit also remembered different things and evil things told of Rotil, but they were not for discussion with a lady. He had wondered a bit that it was not the padre who was given the message to transmit, yet suddenly he realized that even the padre might have tried to make it a question of barter, for the padre wanted help for his priestly office in the saving of Perez' soul, and incidentally of his life.

"Yes, señora, it seems a free-will offering, and he said to tell you it would be in the room adjoining this that Perez would be questioned as to the war material. Rotil's men have searched, and his officers have questioned, but Perez evidently thinks Rotil will not execute him, as a ransom will pay much better."

"That is true, death pays no one —- no one!"

Her voice was weighted with sadness, and Kit wondered what the cloud was under which she lived. The padre evidently knew, but none of Rotil's men. It could not be the mere irregularity of her life with Perez, for to the peon mind she was the great lady of a great hacienda, and wife of the padrone. No, —- he realized that the sin of Doña Jocasta had been a different thing, and that the shadow of it enveloped her as a dark cloak of silence.

"It is true, señora, that death pays no one, except that the death of one man may save other lives more valuable. That often happens," remarked Kit, with the idea of distracting her from her own woe, whatever it was. "It might have seemed a crime if one of his nurses had chucked a double dose of laudanum into Bill Hohenzollern's baby feed, but that nurse would have saved the lives of hundreds of thousands of innocents, so you never can tell whether a murderer is a devil, or a man doing work of the angels."

"Bill?" Evidently the name was a new one to Doña Jocasta.

"That's the name of the Prussian pirate of the Huns across the water. Your friend Conrad belongs to them."

"My friend! My *friend*, señor!" and Doña Jocasta was on her feet, white and furious, her eyes flaming hatred. Kit Rhodes was appalled at the spirit he had carelessly wakened. He remembered the statement of the priest that he evidently did not know the lady well, and realized in a flash that he certainly did not, also that he would feel more comfortable elsewhere.

"Señora, I beg a thousand pardons for my foolishness," he implored. "My —- my faulty Spanish caused me to speak the wrong word. Will you not forgive me such a stupid blunder? Everyone knows the German brute could not be a friend of yours, and that you could have only hatred of his kind."

She regarded him steadily with the ever ready suspicion against an Americano showing in her eyes, but his regret was so evident, and his devotion to her interests so sincere, that the tension relaxed, and she sank back in her chair, her hand trembling as she covered her eyes for a moment.

"It is I who am wrong, señor. You cannot know how the name of that man is a poison, and why absolution is refused me because I will not forgive, —- and will not say I forgive! I will not lie, and because of the hate of him my feet will tread the fires of hell. The padre is telling me that, so what use to pray? Of what use, I ask you?"

Kit could see no special use if she had accepted the threat of the priest that hell was her portion anyway.

"Oh, I would not take that gabble of a priest seriously if I were you," he suggested. "No one can beat me in detesting the German and what he stands for, but I have no plans of going to hell for it —- not on your life! To hate Conrad, or to kill him would be like killing a rattlesnake, or stamping a tarantula into the sand. He has been let live to sting too many, and Padre Andreas tells me you heard him boast of an American killing at Granados!"

"That is true, señor, and it was so clever too! It was pleasure for him to tell of that because of clever tricks in it. They climbed poles to the wires and called the man to a town, then they waited on that road and shot him before he reached the town. The alcalde of that place decided the man had killed himself, and Conrad laughed with José Perez on account of that, because they were so clever!"

"They?" queried Kit trying to prevent his eagerness from showing in his voice. "Who helped him? Not Perez?"

"No, señor, in that sin José had no part. It was a very important man who did not appear important; —- quite the other way, and like a man of piety. His name, I am remembering it well, for it is Diego, —- but said in the American way, which is James."

"Diego, said in the American way?" repeated Kit thoughtfully. "Is he then an American?"

"Not at all, señor! He is Aleman *commandante* for the border. His word is an order for life or death, and José Perez is of his circle. The guns buried by Perez are bought with the German money; it is for war of Sonora against Arizona when that day comes."

"Shucks! that day isn't coming unless the Huns put more of a force down here than is yet in sight," declared Kit, "but that 'Diego' bothers me. I know many James', —- several at Granados, but not the sort you tell of, señora. Will you speak of that murder again, and let it be put on paper for me? I have friends at Granados who may be troubled about it, and your help would be as —- as the word of an angel at the right hour."

"A sad angel, señor," she said with a sigh, "but why should I not help you to your wish since you have guarded me well? It is a little thing you ask."

The Indian women at the far end of the *sala* had lowered their voices, but their gossip in murmurs and expressive gestures flowed on, and only Tula gave heed to the talk at the table of wars and guns, and secrets of murder, and that was no new thing in Sonora.

One door of the *sala* opened from the patio, and another into a room used as a chapel after the old adobe walls of the mission church had melted utterly back into the earth. Rotil had selected it merely because its only window was very high, an architectural variation caused by a wing of the mission rooms still standing when Soledad hacienda was built. A new wall had been built against the older and lower one which still remained, with old sleeping cells of the neophytes used as tool sheds, and an unsightly litter of propped or tumbling walls back of the ranch house.

The door from the *sala* was slightly ajar, and the voice of Fidelio was heard there. He asked someone for another candle, and another chair. And there was the movement of feet, and rearrangement of furniture.

Rotil entered the *sala* from the patio, and stood just inside, looking about him.

With a brief word and gesture he indicated that Elena and Valencia vacate. At Tula he glanced, but did not bid her follow. He noted the folded paper in the hand of Doña Jocasta, but did not address her; it was to Kit he spoke.

"The door will be left open. I learn that Conrad distrusts Perez because he paid German money, and shipped the guns across the border, but Perez never uncovered one for him. They are badly scared and ready to cut each other's throats if they had knives. Doña Jocasta may overhear what she pleases, and furnish the knives as well if she so decides."

But Doña Jocasta with a shudder put up her hand in protest.

"No knife, no knife!" she murmured, and Rotil shrugged his shoulders and looked at Kit.

"That little crane in the corner would walk barefoot over embers of hell to get a knife and get at Conrad," he said. "You have taste in your favorites, señor."

He seemed to get a certain amusement in the contemplation of Kit and Tula; he had seen no other American with quite that sort of addition to his outfit. Kit was content to let him think his worst, as to tell the truth would no doubt lose them a friend. It tickled the general's fancy to think the thin moody Indian girl, immature and childlike, was an American's idea of a sweetheart!

Voices and the clank of chains were heard in the patio, and then in the next room.

"Why bring us here when your questions were given answer as well in another place?" demanded a man's voice, and at that Doña Jocasta looked at Rotil.

"Yes, why do you?" she whispered.

He stared at her, frowning and puzzled.

"Did I not tell you? I did it that you might hear him repeat his offer. What else?"

"I —- see," she said, bending her head, but as Rotil went to the door, Kit noted that the eyes of Doña Jocasta followed him curiously. He concluded that the unseen man of the voice was José Perez.

Then the voice of Conrad was heard cursing at a chain too heavy. Rotil laughed, and walked into the chapel.

"I can tell you something, you German Judas!" he said coldly. "You will live to see the day when these chains, and this safe old chapel, will be as a paradise you once lived in. You will beg to crawl on your knees to be again comfortably inside this door."

"Is that some Mexican joke?" asked Conrad, and Rotil laughed again.

"Sure it is, and it will be on you! They tell me you collect girls in Sonora for a price. Well, they have grown fond of you, —- the Indian women of Sonora! They say you must end your days here with them. I have not heard of a ransom price they would listen to, —- though you might think of what you have to offer."

"Offer?" growled Conrad. "How is there anything to offer in Sonora when Perez here has sent the guns south?"

"True, the matter of ransom seems to rest with Señor Perez who is saving of words."

"I put the words on paper, and sent it by your man," said Perez. "What else is there to say?"

"Oh, that?" returned Rotil. "My boys play tricks, and make jokes with me like happy children. Yes, Chappo did bring words on paper, —- foolish words he might have written himself. I take no account of such things. You are asked for the guns, and I get foolish words on paper of a woman you would trade to me, and guns you would send me."

"Well?"

"Who gives you right to trade the woman, señor?"

"Who has a better right? She belongs to me."

"Very good! And her name?"

"You know the name."

"Perhaps, but I like my bargains with witness, and they must witness the name."

"Jocasta —- " There was a slight hesitation, and Rotil interrupted.

"She has been known as Señora Jocasta Perez, is it not so?"

"Well —- yes," came the slow reply, "but that was foolishness of the peons on my estates. They called her that."

"Very good! One woman called Jocasta Perez is offered to me in trade with the guns. José Perez, have you not seen that the Doña Jocasta Perez is even now mistress of Soledad, and that my men and I are as her servants?"

Jocasta on the other side of the door strangled a half sob as she heard him, and crept nearer the door.

"Oh, you are a good one at a bargain, Ramon Rotil! You try to pretend the woman cannot count in this trade, but women always count, —- women like Jocasta!"

"So? Then we will certainly take count of the woman —- one woman! Now to guns and ammunition. How many, and where?"

"At Hermosillo, and it will take a week."

"I have no week to waste, and I do not mean the guns at Hermosillo. You have five minutes, José Perez. Also those playful boys are building a nice warm fire for the branding irons. And you will both get a smell of your own burning hides if I wait longer for an answer."

"Holy God!" shouted Conrad. "Why burn me for his work? From me the guns have been hid as well as from you; —- all I got was promises! They are my guns, —- my money paid, but he is not straight! Here at Soledad he was to show me this time, but I think now it was a trick to murder me as he murdered Juan Gonsalvo, the foreman who stored them away for him."

"Animal!" growled Perez. "You have lost your head to talk of murders to me! Two murders at Granados are waiting for you, and it is not far to ship you back to the border! Walk with care, señor!"

"You are each wasting time with your truth telling," stated Rotil. "This is no time to count your dead men. It is the count of the guns I want. And a sight of the ammunition."

"Give me a guide to Hermosillo, and the price of guns can be got for you."

"It is not the *price* of guns I asked you for, it is guns, —- the guns Conrad and Herrara got over the border for you. Your time is going fast, José Perez."

"They are not to be had this side of Hermosillo, send me south if you want them. But it is well to remember that if an accident happens to me you never could get them, —- never! I alone know their hiding place."

"For that reason have I waited for your visit to Soledad, —- you and your carts and your pack mules," stated Rotil. "Do not forget that Marto Cavayso and other men of mine have been for weeks with your ranchmen. Your pack train comes here empty, and means one thing only —- they came for the American guns! Your minutes are going, señor, and the branding irons are getting heat from the fire. One more minute!"

"Write the figures of the ransom, and grant me a messenger to Hermosillo. You have the whip hand, you can make your price."

"But me? What of *my* ransom?" demanded Conrad. "My money, and my time paid for those guns —- I have not seen one of them this side of the border! If no guns are paid for me, money must be paid."

"No price is asked for you. I told you the women have named no ransom."

"Women? That is foolishness. It is not women for whom you hold me! He has turned traitor, has Perez! He wants me sent back across the border without that price of the guns for his mushroom government! He has told his own tales of Herrara, and of Singleton, and they are lies —- all lies!"

"But what of the tale of Diego, said in the American way?" asked Kit stepping inside the room.

"Diego! Diego!" repeated Conrad and made a leap at Perez. "You have sold me out to the Americans, you scum! James warned me you were scum of the gutters, and now —- –"

The guard caught him, and he stood there shaking with fury in the dim light. Perez drew away with a curse.

"To hell with you and James and your crew on the border," he growled. "I care nothing as to how soon the damned gringos swing you both. When you Germans want to use us we are your 'dear brothers.' When we out-trick you, we are only scum, eh? You can tell your *commandante* James that I won the game from him, and all the guns!"

"My thanks to you, General Rotil, that I have been allowed to hear this," said Kit, "also that I have witness. I'd do as much for you if the chance comes. Two men were killed on the border by Conrad under order of this James. Herrara was murdered in prison for fear he would turn informer about the guns. Singleton was murdered to prevent him investigating the German poisoning of cavalry horses. The German swine meant to control Granados rancho a few months longer for their own purposes."

"*Meant* to?" sneered Conrad. "You raw cub! —- you are playing with dynamite and due for a fall. So is your fool country! Though Perez here has lost his nerve and turned traitor to our deal, that is only a little puff of wind against the bulwarks of the Fatherland! We will hold Granados; we will hold the border; and with Mexico (not this crook of the west, but *real* Mexico) we will win and hold every border state and every Pacific coast state! You, —- poor fool! —- will never reach Granados alive to tell this. You are but one American in the Indian wilderness, and you are sure to go under, but you go knowing that though James and I die, and though a thousand more of us die, there will be ten thousand secret German workers in America to carry on our plan until all the world will be under the power of the Prussian eagle! You, —- who think you know so much, can add *that* to finish your education in Sonora, and carry it to hell with you!"

His voice, coldly contemptuous at first, had risen to a wrathful shriek as he faced the American and hurled at him the exultance of the Teuton dream.

"I certainly am in great luck to be your one American confessor," grinned Kit, "but I'll postpone that trip as long as possible. I reckon General Rotil will let the padre help me make note of this education you are handing out to me. A lot of Americans need it! Have I your permission, General?"

"Go as far as you like," snapped Rotil. "They have used up their time limit in scolding like old women. Perez, I wait for the guns."

"Send me to Hermosillo and I will recover enough for a ransom," said Perez.

Rotil regarded him a moment through half-closed, sinister eyes.

"That was your last chance, and you threw it away. Chappo, strip him; Fidelio, fetch the branding irons."

Perez shrank back, staring at Rotil as if fascinated. He was striving to measure the lengths to which the "Hawk of the Sierras" would go, and a sudden gleam of hope came into his eyes as Padre Andreas held up a crucifix before Chappo, waving him aside.

"No, Rotil, —- torture is a thing for animals, not men! Hell waits for the sinner who —- –"

"Hell won't wait for you one holy minute!" snapped Rotil. "Get back with the women where you belong; there is men's work to do here."

He caught the priest by the arm in an iron grip and whirled him towards the *sala*. The man would have fallen but for Kit who caught him, but could not save the crash of his head against the door. Blood streamed from a cut in his forehead, and thus he staggered into the room where Doña Jocasta stood, horror-stricken and poised for flight.

But the sight of the blood-stained priest, and the sound of a strange, half animal cry from the other room, turned her feet that way.

"No, Ramon! No-*no*!" she cried and sped through the door to fling herself between him and his victims.

Her arms were stretched wide and she halted, almost touching him, with her back to the chained man towards whom she had not glanced, but she could not help seeing the charcoal brazier with the red-hot branding irons held by Fidelio. The gasping cry had come from Conrad by whom the brazier was set.

Ramon Rotil stared at her, frowning as if he would fling her from his path as he had the priest.

"No, Ramon!" she said again, still with that supplicating look and gesture, "send them out of here, —- both these men. I would smother and die in a room with that German beast. You will not be sorry, Ramon Rotil, I promise you that, —- I promise you by the God I dare not face!"

"Ho!" snarled Perez. "Is the priest also her lover that she —- –"

"Send the German out, and let José Perez stay to see that I keep my promise," she said letting her arms fall at her side, but facing Rotil with an addition of hauteur in her poise and glance. "The price he will pay for the words he has spoken here will be a heavy price, —- one he has risked life to hold! Send that pale snake and your men outside, Ramon."

Perez was leaning forward, his face strained and white, watching her. He could not see her face, but the glimpse of hope came again into his eyes —- a woman might succeed with Rotil where a priest would fail!

Rotil, still frowning at her, waved his hand to Chappo and Fidelio.

"Take him away," he said, "and wait beyond."

The shuffling movement and clank of chains was heard, but she did not turn her head. Instead she moved past Rotil, lifted a candle, and went towards the shrine at the end of the room.

A table was there with a scarf across it, and back of the table three steps leading up to a little platform on which were ranged two or three mediocre statues of saints, once brilliant with blue and scarlet and tinsel, but tarnished and dim from the years.

In the center was a painting, also dark and dim in which only a halo was still discernible in the light of the candle, but the features of the saint pictured there were shadowed and elusive.

For a moment she knelt on the lower step and bent her head because of those remnants of a faith which was all she knew of earthly hope, —- and then she started to mount the steps.

"The curse of God shrivel you!" muttered Perez in cold fury —- "come down from there!"

Without heed to the threat, she moved the little statues to right or left, and then lifted her hand, resting it on the wooden frame of the painting.

"Call the Americano," she said without turning. "You will need a man, but not a man of Altar. Another day may come when you, Ramon, may have need of this house for hiding!"

Rotil strode to the door and motioned Kit to enter, then he closed both doors and gave no heed to Perez, crouched there like a chained coyote in a trap.

"Come down!" he said again. "You are in league with hell to know of that. I never gave it to you! Come down! I meant to tell after he had finished with Conrad —- I mean to tell!"

"He waited too long, and spoke too much," she said to Rotil. "Keep watch on him, and let the Americano give help here."

Kit mounted the step beside her, and at her gesture took hold of the frame on one side. She found a wedge of wood at the other side and drew it out. The loosened frame was lifted out by Kit and carried down the three steps; it was a panel a little over two feet in width and four in height.

"Set it aside, and watch José Perez while General Rotil looks within," she said evenly.

Rotil glanced at Perez scowling black hate at her, and then turned to Jocasta who held out the candle.

"It is for you to see, —- you and no other," she said. "You have saved a woman he would have traded as a slave, and I give you more than a slave's ransom."

He took the candle and his eyes suddenly flamed with exultation as her meaning came to him.

"*Jocasta!*" he muttered as if scarce believing, and then he mounted the step, halted an instant in the panel of shadow, and, holding the candle over his head, he leaned forward and descended on the other side of the wall.

"You damned she-wolf of the hills!" growled Perez with the concentrated hate of utter failure in his voice. "I fed you, and my money covered your nakedness, and now you put a knife in my neck and go back to cattle of the range for a mate! You, —- without shame or soul!"

"That is true," she said coldly. "You killed a soul in the *casita* of the oleanders, José Perez, and it was a dead woman you and the German chained to be buried in the desert. But even the dead come back to help friends who are faithful, José, —- and I am as the dead who walk."

She did not look at him as she spoke, but sank on her knees before the dark canvas where only the faint golden halo gave evidence of some incarnated holiness portrayed there. Her voice was low and even, and the sadness of it thrilled Kit. He thought of music of sweet chords, and a broken string vibrating, for the hopelessness in her voice held a certain fateful finality, and her delicate dark loveliness —- –

Rotil emerged from the doorway of the shrine and stood there, a curious substitute for the holy picture, looking down on her with a wonderful light in his face.

"Your ransom wins for you all you wish of me, —- except the life of one man," he said, and with a gesture indicated that Kit help her to her feet. He did so, and saw that she was very white and trembling.

Rotil looked at Perez over her head, and Perez scowled back, with all the venom of black hate.

"You win! —- but a curse walks where she walks. Ask her? Ask Marto of the men she put under witchcraft! Ask Conrad who had good luck till she hated him! If you have a love, or a child, or anything dear, let her not look hate on them, for her knife follows that look! Ask her of the knife she set in the heart of a child for jealousy of Conrad! Ai, general though you are, your whole army is not strong enough to guard you from the ill luck you will take with the gift *she* gives! She is a woman under a curse. Ha! Look at her as I say it, for you hear the truth. Ask the padre!"

Kit realized that Perez was launching against her the direst weight of evil the Mexican or Indian mind has to face. Though saints and heaven and hell might be denied by certain daring souls, the potency of witchcraft was seldom doubted. Men or women accused of it were shunned as pariahs, and there had been known persons who weakened and dwindled into death after accusation had been put against them.

He thought of it as she cowered under each separate count of the curse launched against her. She bent like a slender reed under the strokes of a flail, lower and lower against his arm, but when the deadly voice flung the final taunt at her, she straightened slowly and looked at Rotil.

"Yes, ask the padre —- or ask me!" she said in that velvet soft voice of utter despair. "That I sent an innocent soul to death is too true. To my great sorrow I did it; —- I would do it again! For that my life is indeed a curse to me, —- but his every other word a lie!"

Then she took a step forward, faltered, and fell back into the outstretched arm of Kit.

"Take Señora Perez to the women, and come back," said Rotil. Kit noted that even though he moved close, and bent over the white unconscious face, he did not touch her.

"Señora Perez!" repeated Perez contemptuously. "You are generous with other men's names for your women! Her name is the Indian mother's name."

"Half Indian," corrected Rotil, "and her naming I will decide another time."

Kit returned, and without words proceeded to help replace the holy picture in its niche. In the struggle with the padre, a chunk of adobe had been knocked from the wall near the door, and he picked it up, crumbling it to a soft powder and sprinkled it lightly over the steps where foot prints were traceable in the dust.

Rotil who had gone to the door to recall the guard, halted and watched him closely.

"Good!" he said. "You also give me a thought concerning this animal; he will bark if he has listeners, and even the German should not hear —- one never knows! I need a cage for a few hours. You have been a friend, and know secret things. Will you lock him in your own room and hold the key to yourself?"

"Surest thing you know," answered Kit though with the uncomfortable certainty that the knowledge of too many secret things in Mexico was not conducive to long life for the knower. "I may also assure you that Marto is keen on giving you honest service that his one fault may be atoned for."

"He will get service," stated Rotil. "You saved me a good man there, amigo."

He flung open the door of the corridor and whistled for the guard.

"Remove this man and take your orders from Capitan —- –" He halted, and his eyes narrowed quizzically.

"It seems we never were introduced, amigo, and we know only your joy name of the singer, but there must be another."

"Oh, yes, there's another, all right," returned Kit, knowing that Conrad would enlighten Rotil if he did not. "I'm the hombre suspected of that Granados murder committed by Conrad, —- and the name is Rhodes."

"So? Then the scolding of these two comrades gives to you your freedom from suspicion, eh? That is good, but —- " He looked at Kit, frowning. "See here, I comprehend badly. You told me it was the friend of your *compadre* who was the suspected one!"

"Sure! I've a dandy partner across the border. He's the old man you saw at Yaqui Spring, and I reckon I'm a fairly good friend of his. He'd say so!"

Rotil's face relaxed in a grin.

"That is clever, a trick and no harm in it, but —- have a care to yourself! It is easy to be too clever, and on a trail of war no one has time to learn if tricks are of harm or not. Take the warning of a friend, Capitan Rhodes!"

"You have the right of it, General. I have much to learn," agreed Kit. "But no man goes abroad to shout the crimes he is accused of at home, —- and the story of this one is very new to me. This morning I learned I was thought guilty, and tonight I learn who is the criminal, and how the job was done. This is quick work, and I owe the luck of it to you."

"May the good luck hold!" said Rotil. "And see that the men leave you alone as the guard of Perez. I want no listeners there."

CHAPTER XVII
THE STORY OF DOÑA JOCASTA

Ramon Rotil stood a long minute after the clank of chains ceased along the corridor; then he bolted the outer door of the chapel, and after casting a grim satisfied smile at the screen of the faded canvas, he opened the door of the *sala* and went in.

Valencia was kneeling beside Doña Jocasta and forcing brandy between the white lips, while Elena bustled around the padre whose head she had been bathing. A basin of water, ruby red, was evidence of the fact that Padre Andreas was not in immediate need of the services of a leech. He sat with his bandaged head held in his hands, and shrank perceptibly when the general entered the room.

Doña Jocasta swallowed some of the brandy, half strangled over it, and sat up, gasping and white. It was Tula who offered her a cup of water, while Valencia, with fervent expressions of gratitude to the saints, got to her feet, eyeing Rotil with a look of fear. After the wounded priest and the fainting Jocasta emerged from the chapel door, the two women were filled with terror of the controlling spirit there.

He halted on the threshold, his eyes roving from face to face, including Tula, who stood, back against the wall, regarding him as usual with much admiration. One thing more he must know.

"Go you without," he said with a gesture towards the two women and the priest. "I will speak with this lady alone."

They all moved to the door, and after a moment of hesitation Tula was about to follow when he stopped her.

"You stay, girl. The Doña Jocasta may want a maid, but take yourself over there."

So Tula slipped silently back into the niche of the window seat where the shadows were deepest, and Rotil moved towards the center table dragging a chair. On the other side of the table was the couch on which Jocasta sat, white and startled at the dismissal of the woman and priest.

"Be composed," he said gentling his tone as one would to soothe a child. "There are some things to be said between us here, and too many ears are of no advantage."

She did not reply; only inclined her head slightly and drew herself upright against the wall, gathering the lace *rebosa* across her bosom where Valencia had unfastened her garments and forgotten them in her fear.

"First is the matter of my debt to you. Do you know in your own mind how great that is?"

"I —- count it as nothing, señor," she murmured.

"That is because you do not know the great need, and have not made count of the cases of rifles and ammunition."

"It is true, I never looked at them. Juan Gonsalvo in dying blamed José Perez for the shot. It was fired by another hand, —- but God alone knows! So Juan sent for me, and José never knew. The secret of Soledad was given to me then, but I never thought to use it, until —- –"

She ceased, shuddering, and he knew she was thinking of the blood-stained priest whirled into her presence. Fallen though the state of the priesthood might be in Mexico, there were yet women of Jocasta's training to whom an assault on the clergy was little less than a mortal sin. He knew that, and smiled grimly at the remembrance of her own priestly father who had refused her in honest marriage to a man of her mother's class, and was busily engaged haggling over the gift price of her with José Perez when death caught him. The bewildered girl was swept to the estate of Perez without either marriage or gift, unless one choose to consider as gift the shelter and food given to a younger sister and brother.

All this went through his mind as she shrank and sighed because he had tossed a priest from his way with as slight regard as he would the poorest peon. She did not even know how surely the destiny of her mother and her own destiny had been formed by a priest's craft. She would never know, because her mind would refuse to accept it. There were thousands like her because of their shadowed inheritance. Revolution for the men grew out of that bondage of women, and Rotil had isolated moments when he dreamed of a vast and blessed freedom of the land —- schools, and schools, and more schools until knowledge would belong to the people instead of to the priests!

But he knew it was no use to tell thoughts like that to women; they were afraid to let go their little wooden saints and the jargon of prayers they did not understand. The mystery of it held them!

Thus brooded Rotil, unlearned driver of burros and general of an army of the people!

"We will forget all but the ammunition," he said. "It is as food to my men, and some of them are starving there to the east; with ammunition food can be commandeered. I knew the guns were on Soledad land, but even a golden dream of angels would not have let me hope for as much as you have given me. It is packed, —- that room, from floor to roof tiles. In the morning I take the trail, and there is much to be done before I go. You; —- I must think of first. Will you let me be your confessor, and tell me any wish of your heart I may help you to?"

"My heart has no wish left alive in it," she said. "There have been days when I had wish for the hut under the palms where my mother lived. A childish wish, —- but other wishes are dead!"

"There is no going back," he said, staring at the tiles, and not looking at her. "It is of future things we must think. He said things —- Perez did, and you —- –"

"Yes!" she half whispered. "There is no way but to tell of it, but —- I would ask that the child wait outside. The story is not a story for a girl child, Ramon."

He motioned to Tula.

"Outside the door, but in call," he said, and without a word or look Tula went softly out.

There was silence for a bit between them, her hands were clasped at full length, and she leaned forward painfully tense, looking not at him, but past him.

"It is not easy, but you will comprehend better than many," she said at last. "There were three of us. There was my little brother Palemon, who ran away last year to be a soldier —- he was only fourteen. José would not let me send searchers for him, and he may be dead. Then there was only —- only Lucita and me. You maybe remember Lucita?"

Her question was wistful as if it would help her to even know he remembered. He nodded his head in affirmation.

"A golden child," he said. "I have seen pictured saints and angels in great churches since the days in the hills, but never once so fair a child as little Lucita."

"Yes, white and gold, and an angel of innocence," she said musingly. "Always she was that, always! And there was a sweetheart, Mariano Avila, a good lad, and the wedding was to be. She was embroidering the wedding shirt for Mariano when —- God! God!"

She got up suddenly and paced the floor, her arms hugging her shoulders tight as if to keep from sobbing. He rose and stood watching, but uttered no word.

After a little she returned to the couch, and began to speak in a more even tone.

"There is so much to tell. Much happened. Conrad was driving José to do many things not at first in their plans. Also there was more drinking, —- much more! It was Conrad made plans for the slave raids. He no longer asked José's permission for anything; he gave command to the men and José had to listen. Only one secret thing was yet hidden from him, the hiding place of the guns from the north. José said if that was uncovered he might as well give up his ranchos. In his heart he could not trust Conrad. Each had a watch set on the other! Juan got his death because he made rendezvous with the German.

"That is how it was when the slave raid was made north of here, and the most beautiful Indian girl killed herself somewhere in this desert when there was no other way to escape the man; —- the scar on the face of Conrad was from her knife. It was a bad cut, and after that there was trouble, and much drink and mad quarrels. Also it was that time Juan Gonsalvo was shot and died from it. Juana, his sister, came in secret for me while he could yet speak, and that was when —- –"

She halted, closing her eyes as if to shut out some horror. He thought she shrank from remembrance of how the secret of Soledad was given to her, for Juan must have been practically a dead man when he gave it up. After a moment she went on in the sad tone of the utterly hopeless.

"I speak of the mad quarrels of those two men, Ramon, but it was never of that I had fear. The fear came each time the quarrel was done, and they again swore to be friends, for in the new 'friend hours' of drinking, strange things happened, strange wagers and strange gifts."

Again she paused, and this time she lifted her eyes to Rotil.

"Always I hated the German. I never carried a blade until after his eyes followed me! He tried to play the prince, the great gentleman, with me —- a girl of the hills! Only once he touched my hand, and I scoured it with sand afterwards while José laughed. But the German did not laugh, —- he only watched me! Once when José was in a rage with me Conrad said he could make of me a great lady in his own land if I would listen. Instead of listening I showed him my knife. After that God only knows what he told against me, but José became bitter —- bitter, and jealous, and spies always at my back!

"So Lucita and Mariano and I made plans. They were to marry, and we three would steal away in secret and cross the border. That was happiness to plan, for my life —- my life was hell, so I thought! But I had not yet learned what hell could be," she confessed drearily.

"Tell me," he said very gently. Those who thought they knew "El Gavilan," the merciless, would not have recognized his voice at that moment.

"No, I had not learned," she went on drearily. "I thought that to carry a knife for myself made all safe —- I did not know! I told you Juana Gonsalvo came for me very secretly to hear the last words of Juan. But I did not tell you we lived in the *casita*, little Lucita and I. It is across a garden from the hacienda, and was once a priest's house; that was in the days of the mother of José. It is very sweet there under the rose vines, and it was sanctuary for us. When José and the German had their nights of carouse we went there and locked ourselves in. There were iron bars on the high windows, and shutters of wood inside, so we were never afraid. I heard Conrad tell José he was a fool not to blow it up with dynamite some day of fiesta. It was the night after their great quarrel, and it was a terrible time. They were pledging friendship once more in much wine. Officers from the town were at the hacienda with women who were —- well, I would not go in, and José was wild. He came to the *casita* and called threats at me. I thought the German was with him, for he said Conrad was right, and the house would be blown up with the first dynamite he could spare, —- but threats were no new thing to us! I tried to soothe little Lucita by talk of the wedding, and all the pretty bride things were taken out of the chest and spread on the bed; one *rebosa* of white I put over her shoulders, and the child was dancing to show me she was no longer afraid —- –!

"That was when Juana came to the window. I knew her voice and opened the door. I did not want Lucita frightened again, so I did not let her know a man was dying —- only that a sick person wanted me for a little —- little minute, and I would be back.

"I knew Juan Gonsalvo had been killed because he had been trusted far enough, —- I knew it! That thought struck me very hard, for I —- I might be the next, and I wanted first to send those two children happily out of reach of sorrow. Strange it is that because she was first, the very first in my heart, I went out that door in the night and for the first time left her alone! But that is how it was; we had to be so quick —- and so silent —- and it was her hand closed the door after us, her hand on the bolt!

"Juan Gonsalvo had only fought for life until he could see me, and then the breath went. No one but I heard his whispers of the door of the picture here in Soledad. He told me his death was murder, and his last word was against Perez. It was only minutes, little minutes I was there, and the way was not far, but when I went back through the garden the door of the *casita* stood wide and light streamed out! I do not know how I was sure it was empty, but I was, and I seemed to go dead inside, though I started to run.

"To cross that garden was like struggling in a dream with bands about my feet. I wake with that dream many nights —- many! —- I heard her before I could reach the path. Her screams were not in the *casita*, but in the hacienda. They were —- they were —- terrible! I tried to go —- and then I knew she had broken away —- I could see her like a white spirit fly back towards the light in the open door. The man following her tripped in some way and fell, and I leaped over him to follow her. We got inside and drew the bolt.

"Then —- But there are things not to be told —- they belong to the dead!

"Perez came there to the door and made demands for Conrad's woman, —- that is how he said it! He said she had gone to Conrad's apartment of her own will and must go back. Lucita knelt at my feet in her torn bridal garment and told how a woman had come as Juana had come, and said that I wanted her. The child had no doubt, she followed, and —- and it was indeed to that drunken beast they took her!

"José was also drunk, crazy drunk. He told me to stand away from that door for they were coming in, also that he had made gift of Lucita to his friend, and she must be given up. Then they began to fire guns in the lock! It seemed a long, long time she held to me there and begged me to save her, but it could not have been.... The lock gave way, and only the bolt held. I clasped her close to me and whispered telling her to pray, but I never took my eyes off the door. When I saw it shaking, I made the sign of the cross over her, and the knife I had carried for myself found her heart quickly! That is how I took on me the shadow of murder, and that is why the priest threatens me with the fires of hell if I do not repent —- and I am not repenting, Ramon."

"By God, no!" he muttered, staring into her defiant eyes. "That was a fine thing, and your mother gave good blood to her children, Jocasta. And then —- –?"

"I laid her on the bed among her bridal laces, all white —- white! Over her breast I folded her still hands, and set a candle at her head, though I dared not pray! The door was giving way.

"I pushed back the bolt, also I spoke, but it did not seem me! That is strange, but of a truth I did not know the voice I heard say: 'Enter, her body is yours —- and she no longer flees from you.'

"'Ha! That is good sense at last!' said José, and Conrad laughed and praised himself as a lover.

"'I told you so!' he grunted. 'The little dear one knows that a nice white German is not so bad!'

"And again I heard the voice strange to me say, 'She knows nothing, José —- and she knows all!'

"José stumbled in smiling, but Conrad, though drunk, stopped at the door when he saw my hand with the knife. I thought my skirt covered it as I waited for him —- for the child had told me enough —- I —- I failed, Ramon! His oath was a curious choked scream as I tried to reach him. I do not know if it was the knife, or the dead girl on the bed made him scream like that, but I knew then the German was at heart a coward.

"José was too strong for me, and the knife could not do its work. I was struck, and my head muffled in a *serape*. After that I knew nothing.

"Days and nights went by in a locked room. I never got out of it until I was chained hand and foot and sent north in a peon's ox-cart. Men guarded me until Marto with other men waited for me on the trail. José Perez could have had me killed, yes. Or he could have had me before the judges for murder, but silence was the thing he most wanted —- for there is Doña Dolores Terain yet to be won. He has sent me north that the General Terain, her father, will think me out of his life. One of the guards told an alcalde I was his wife, he was sure that story would be repeated back to Hermosillo! These are days in Sonora when no one troubles about one woman or one child who is out of sight, and we may be sure he and Conrad had a well-made story to tell. He knows it is now all over with me, that I have a hate of which he is afraid, so he does not have me shot; —- he only sends me to Soledad in the wilderness where fighting bands of the revolution cross all trails, and his men have orders that I am not to go out of the desert alive."

"I see!" said Rotil thoughtfully, "and —- it is all gone now —- the love of him?"

"All the love in the world is gone, amigo," she said, looking away from him through the barred window where the night sky was growing bright from the rising moon. "I was a child enchanted by the glory of the world and his love words. Out of all that false glitter of life I have walked, a blackened soul with a murderer's hand. How could love be again with me?"

He looked at her steadily, the slender thing of creamy skin and Madonna eyes that had been the Dream of Youth to him, the one devotee at an altar in whom he had believed —- nothing in the humanity of the world would ever have faith of his again!

"That is so, Jocasta," he said at last, "you are a woman, and in the shadow. The little golden singing one is gone out of your life, and the new music must be different! I will think about that for you. Go now to your sleep, for there is work of men to be done, and the night scarce long enough for it."

He opened the door for her and stood with bent head as she passed. His men lounging in the patio could see that manner of deference, and exchanged looks and comments. To the victor belong the spoils in Mexico, and here was a sweeping victory, —- yet the general looked the other way!

"Child, accompany the señora," he said kindly to Tula at the door. "Chappo, bring Marto to see me. The new American capitan said he was a man of value, and the lad was right. Work of importance waits for him tonight."

CHAPTER XVIII
RAMON ROTIL DECIDES

Whatever the labors of Marto Cavayso for the night they appeared to have been happy ones, for ere the dawn he came to Kit's door in great good humor.

"Amigo," he said jovially, "you played me a trick and took the woman, but what the devil is that to hold a grudge for? My general has made it all right, and we need help. You are to come."

"Glad to," agreed Kit, "but what of this guard duty?"

"Lock the door —- there is but one key. Also the other men are not sleeping inside the portal. It is by order of General Rotil."

Perez awoke to glare at his false major-domo, but uttered no words. He had not even attempted conversation with Kit since the evening before when he stated that no Americano could fool him, and added his conviction that the said Americano was a secret service man of the states after the guns, and that Rotil was a fool!

Kit found Rotil resting in the chapel, looking fagged and spent.

"Marto is hell for work, and I had to stay by," he grumbled with a grin. "Almost I sent for you. No other man knows, and behold!"

Stacked on either side were packing cases of rifles and ammunition, dozens and dozens of them. The dusty canvas was back in its place and no sign to indicate where the cases had come from.

"It is a great treasure chest, that," stated Rotil, "and we have here as much as the mules can carry, for the wagons can't go with us. But I want every case of this outside the portal before dawn comes, and it comes quick! It means work and there are only three of us, and this limp of mine's a trouble."

"Well," said Kit, stripping off his coat, "if the two of you got them up a ladder inside, and down the steps to this point I reckon three of us can get them across that little level on record time. Say, your crew will think it magic when guns and ammunition are let fall for you by angels outside of the gate."

"The thought will do no harm," said Rotil. "Also I am not sure but that you speak true, and the magic was much needed when it came."

They worked fast, and ere the first hint of dawn the cases were stacked in imposing array on the plaza. And no sign by which they could be traced. Rotil looked at them, and chuckled at the wonder the men would feel.

"It is time they were called, for it is a long trail, go you, Capitan, and waken them, tell them to get ready the pack mules and get a move."

"All right, but if they ask questions?"

"Look wise and say nothing! When they see the cases they will think you either the devil or San Antonio to find what was lost in the desert. It is a favor I am doing you, señor."

"Sure you are! If the Indians ever get the idea that I can win guns from out the air by hokus-pokus, I will be a big medicine chief, and wax fat under honors in Sonora. Head me to them!"

Rotil had seen to it that though sentinels stood guard at Soledad, none were near enough the plaza to interfere with work of the night, and Kit found their main camp down by the *acquia* a quarter of a mile away. He gave orders as directed for the pack animals and cook wagon over which a son of the Orient presided. That stolid genius was already slicing deer meat for broiling, and making coffee, of which he donated a bowl to Kit, also a cart wheel of a *tortilla* dipped in gravy. Both were joyously accepted, and after seeing that the men were aroused from the blankets, he returned to the hacienda full of conjecture as to the developments to be anticipated from the night's work. That reserve stock of ammunition might mean salvation to the revolutionists.

Rain had fallen somewhere to the east in the night time, and as the stars faded there were lines of palest silver and palest gold in the grays of dawn on the mountains. As he walked leisurely up the slight natural terrace to the plaza, he halted a moment and laughed aloud boyishly at a discovery of his, for he had solved the century-old riddle of the view of El Alisal seen from the "portal" of Soledad. The portal was not anyone of the visible doors or gateways of the old mission, it was the hidden portal of the picture, —- once leading to a little balcony under which the neophytes had gathered for the morning blessing and daily commands of their superiors!

That explained its height from the floor. The door had at some later period been sealed, and a room built against it from the side towards the mountain. In the building of the ranch house that old strong walled section of the mission had been incorporated as the private chapel of some pious ranchero. It was also very, very simple after one knew of that high portal masked by the picture, and after one traced the line of vision from the outside and realized all that was hidden by the old harness room and the fragmentary old walls about it. He chuckled to think of how he would astonish Cap Pike with the story when he got back. He also recalled that Conrad had unburdened his heart to him with completeness because he was so confident an American never *could* get back!

He was speculating on that ever-present problem when he noted that light shone yellow in the dawn from the plaza windows, and on entering the patio it took but a glance to see that some new thing was afoot.

Padre Andreas, with his head upholstered in strips of the table linen, was pacing the patio reciting in a murmuring undertone, some prayer from a small open volume, though there was not yet light enough to read. Valencia was bustling into the room of Doña Jocasta with an olla of warm water, while Tula bore a copper tray with fruit and coffee.

"This is of a quickness, but who dare say it is not an act for the blessing of God?" the padre said replying in an absent-minded manner to the greeting of Kit.

"True, Padre, who can say?" agreed the latter politely, without the slightest idea of what was meant.

But Marto, who fairly radiated happiness since his reinstatement, approached with the word that General Rotil would have him at breakfast, for which time was short.

"It is my regret that you do not ride with me, señor," said Rotil as he motioned him to a seat. "But there is work to be done at Soledad for which I shall give you the word. I am hearing that you would help recover some of the poor ones driven south from Palomitas, if they be left alive!"

"I am pledged to that, General," stated Kit simply.

"Who has your pledge?"

"A dead man who cannot free me from it."

"By God!" remarked Rotil in a surprised tone. "By God, Don Pajarito, that is good! And it may be when that pledge is kept, you may be free to join my children in the fight? I make you a capitan at once, señor."

"Perhaps, after —- –"

"Sure, —- after," agreed Rotil chuckling. "For I tell you there is work of importance here, and when I am gone the thinking will be up to you! What message did you give the muleteers?"

"To bring the animals to the plaza, and pack for the trail all the provisions found there."

"Provisions is good! They will burn with curiosity. There could be fun in that if we had time to laugh and watch them, but there is no time. Marto!"

Marto, on guard at the door, came forward.

"Has the Señor Don José Perez received my message for conference?"

"Yes, my General. Except that he wished your messenger in hell, he will be happy to join you according to order."

"Good!" grinned Rotil, "it is well to conduct these matters with grace and ceremony where a lady is concerned. Take him to the *sala*; it is illuminated in his honor. Come, señor, I want for witness an Americano who is free from Sonora influence."

"Am I?" queried Kit dubiously. "I'm not so sure! I seem all tangled up with Sonora influences of all shades and varieties."

Rotil's jocularity disappeared as he entered the sala where quill pen and ink and some blank sheets from an old account book gave a business-like look to the table where four candles made a radiance.

Perez was there, plainly nervous by reason of the mocking civility of Marto. His eyes followed Rotil, —- questioning, fearful!

The latter passed him without notice and seated himself at the table.

"Call the padre," he said to Marto. But that was scarce needed as the padre was hovering near the door waiting for the word. He seated himself by the table at a motion from Rotil.

The latter turned for the first time to Perez, and bestowed on him a long, curious look.

"They tell me, señor, that you were about to take as bride a lovely lady?"

Perez frowned in perplexity. Evidently this was the last subject he had expected to hear touched upon.

"Perhaps so," he said at last, "but if this is a question of ransom we will not trouble the lady. I will arrange your figures for that."

"This is not a matter of figures, Señor Perez. It is a marriage we are interested in, and it is all well arranged for you. The padre here will draw up the contract of marriage in the old form; it is better than the manner of today. You will give him your name, the names of your parents, the name of your parish and abode."

"I will see you damned first!"

"And, Padre," continued Rotil, giving no heed to that heartfelt remark, "use less than one-third of the page, for there must be space for the record of the bride, and below that the contract between the happy two with all witnesses added."

"If you think — " began Perez furiously.

"I do not think; I know, señor! Later you also will know," Rotil promised with grim certainty. "This marriage is of interest to me, and has been too long delayed. It is now for you to say if you will be a bridegroom in chains, or if it please you to have the irons off."

"This cannot be! I tell you a marriage is not legal if —- –"

"Oh, señor! Your experience is less than I thought," interrupted Rotil, "and you are much mistaken, —- much! We are all witnesses here. Señor Rhodes will be pleased to unfasten those heavy chains to oblige the lady. The chains might not be a pleasant memory to her. Women have curious prejudices about such things! But it must be understood that you stand quiet for the ceremony. If not, this gun of mine will manage it that you stay quiet forever."

Perez stood up, baffled and beaten, but threatening.

"Take them off, you!" he snarled, "though it is a hell of a ransom, —- and that woman will pay. Let no one forget that her pay will be heavy!"

"That paying is for afterwards!" decided Rotil airily, "but here and now we men would see a wedding before we leave Soledad. Capitan Rhodes, will you bring in Doña Jocasta?"

Kit, in some wonder, went on the errand, and found the women eager to deck her with blossoms and give some joyous note to the wedding of the dawn, but she sat cold and white with the flowers of the desert springtime about her, and forbade them.

"He terrifies me much in sending that word to wake me with this morning," she protested. "I tell you I will kill myself before I live one more day of life with José Perez! I told him all my heart in the *sala* last night, and it means not anything to Ramon Rotil; —- he would tie me in slavery to that man I hate!"

"Señora, I do not know what the general means, but I know it is not that. His work is for your service, even though appearance is otherwise."

"You think that?"

"I almost know it."

"Then I go," she decided. "I think I would have to go anyway, but the heart would be more heavy, *Santa Maria*! —- but this place of Soledad is strange in its ways."

It was the first time he had seen her frightened, but her mouth trembled, and her eyes sought the floor.

He reached out and took her hand; it was terribly cold.

"Courage, and trust Rotil," he said reassuringly. "When you sift out the whole situation that is about all left to any of us here in the desert."

He led her along the corridor, the women following. Men with pack animals were gathering in wonder around the cases in the plaza, and through the portal they saw the impromptu bridal procession, and fell silent. The Americano appeared to have a hand in every game, —- and that was a matter of wonder.

As they entered, Padre Andreas was reading aloud the brief history of Jocasta Benicia Sandoval, eldest daughter of Teresa Sandoval and Ignatius Sanchez of Santa Ysobel in the Sierras. Padre Andreas had balked at writing the paternity of children of Teresa Sandoval, but a revolver in Rotil's hand was the final persuader.

"This is to be all an honest record for which there are witnesses in plenty," he stated. "Teresa Sandoval had only one lover, —- even though Padre Ignatius Sanchez did call her daughters nieces of his! But the marriage record of Señora Jocasta Sandoval shall have only truth." Jocasta wrote her name to the statement as directed, and noted that José had already signed.

She did not look at him, but moved nearer to Rotil and kept her eyes on the table. He noted her shrinking and turned to the priest.

"Señor," he said, "these two people will write their names together on the contract, but this is a marriage without kisses or clasping of hands. It is a civil contract bound by word of mouth, and written promise, under witness of the church. Read the service."

There was a slight hesitation on the part of Perez when asked if he would take Jocasta Sandoval as wife, but the gun of Rotil hastened his decision, and his voice was defiantly loud. Jocasta followed quietly, and then in a benediction which was emptiest mockery, José Perez and Jocasta Sandoval were pronounced man and wife.

"May I now go?" she murmured, but the contract was signed by all present before Rotil nodded to Kit.

"You will have the honor of conducting the Doña Jocasta Perez to breakfast," he said. "The rest of us have other business here. Señora, will you do us the favor to outline to this gentleman the special tasks you would like attention given at once. There are some Indian slaves in the south for whom the Palomitas people ask help. You are now in a position to be of service there, and it would be a good act with which to establish a new rule at Soledad."

"Thanks, General Rotil," she answered, rather bewildered by the swiftness with which he turned over to her the duties devolving upon her newly acquired position. "I am not wise in law, but what I can I will do."

"And that will be nothing!" volunteered Perez. "A woman of my name will not make herself common in the markets or law courts, —- to have her Indian ancestry cast in my teeth!"

"As to that," said Rotil humorously, "there is not so much! The father of Teresa Sandoval was the priestly son of a marquise of Spain! only one drop of Indian to three of the church in the veins of Señora Perez, so you perceive she has done honor to your house. You will leave your name in good hands when God calls you to judgment."

Kit noted the sudden tension of Perez at the last sentence, and a look of furtive, fearful questioning in his eyes as he looked at Rotil, who was folding the marriage contract carefully, wrapping it in a sheet of paper for lack of an envelope.

But, as squire of dames, Kit was too much occupied to give further heed to business in the *sala*. Doña Jocasta expressed silently a desire to get away from there as soon as might be; she looked white and worn, and cast at Rotil a frightened imploring glance as she clung to Kit's arm. He thought he would have to carry her before they crossed the patio.

"When Ramon laughs like that —- " she began and then went silent, shuddering. Kit, remembering the look in the eyes of Perez, did not care to ask questions.

The older women went back to the kitchen to finish breakfast and gossip over the amazing morning, but Tula remained near Doña Jocasta, —- seeing all and her ears ever open.

Padre Andreas followed, under orders from Rotil, who told him to do any writing required of him by the Señora Perez, and arrange for safe couriers south when she had messages ready. His knowledge of villages and rancheros was more dependable than that of the vaqueros; he would know the names of safe men.

Doña Jocasta sighed, and looked from one to the other appealingly.

"It is much, very much to plan for before the sun is showing," she murmured. "Is there not some little time to think and consider?"

"Even now the men of Ramon Rotil are packing the beasts for the trail," said the priest, "and he wants all your plans and desires stated before he goes east."

"*My* desires!" and her smile held bitterness as she turned to Kit. "You, señor, have never seen the extent of the Perez holdings in Sonora. They are so vast that one simple woman like me would be lost in any plans of change there. José Perez meant what he said; —- no woman can take control while he lives."

"Still, there are some things a woman could do best," ventured Kit, "the things of mercy;" and he mentioned the Palomitas slaves —- –

"That is true. Also I am in debt for much friendship, and this child of Palomitas must have the thing she asks. Tell me the best way."

"Learn from Perez which ranch of General Estaban Terain shelters the political prisoners taken from the district of Altar," suggested Kit. "Either Perez or Conrad can tell."

Doña Jocasta looked at the priest.

"José Perez will hate you for this marriage, and we must seek safety for you in some other place," she said kindly, "but you are the one most able to learn this thing. Will it please you to try?"

Padre Andreas went out without a word. In his heart he resented the manner of the marriage ceremony, and scarce hoped Perez would be acquiescent or disposed to further converse, and he personally had no inclination to ask help of the General Rotil.

He was surprised as he crossed the patio to see Perez, still free from chains, walking through the portal to the plaza with Marto Cavayso beside him. He was led past the ammunition cases, and the men in their jubilant work of packing the mules. Far out up the valley to the north a cloud of dust caught the red glow of sunrise, and the priest knew the vaqueros with the Soledad cattle were already on the trail for the main body of revolutionists in the field.

Saddle horses were held a little apart in the plaza, and Padre Andreas hastened his steps lest they mount and be gone, but Marto spoke to him sharply.

"Walk in front to do your talking," he suggested. "This gentleman is not inviting company for his *pasear*."

José Perez turned a startled, piercing look on the priest.

"Did Rotil send you?" he demanded.

"No, señor, I came back to ask a simple thing concerning the Altar people who went south for Yucatan. Can you give me the name of the ranch where they are held?"

"I can, —- but I give nothing for nothing!" he said bitterly. "Already I am caught in a trap by that marriage, and I will see that the archbishop hears of your share in it. Nothing for nothing!"

"Yet there may be some service I can give, or send south, for you," said the priest.

Perez regarded him doubtfully.

"Yes —- you might get a message to General Terain that I am a prisoner, on my own estate —- if Rotil does not have you killed on the road!"

"I could try," agreed the priest. "I —- I might secure permission."

"Permission?"

"It is true, señor. I could not attempt it without the word of General Rotil," announced Padre Andreas. "Of what use to risk the life of a courier for no purpose? But I make a bargain: if you will tell which ranch the Altar Indians were driven to I will undertake to get word for you to a friend. Of course I can get the information from the German if you say no."

"Damn the German!" swore Perez.

"Good Father," said Marto, "you halt us on the way to join the advance, and we have no mind to take all the dust of the mule train. Make your talk of fewer words."

"Shall I go to the German?" repeated the priest.

"No, —- let him rot alone! The plantation is Linda Vista, and Conrad lied to General Terain to get them housed there. He thought they were rebels who raided ranches in Altar, —- political prisoners. Take General Terain word that I am a prisoner of the revolutionists, and —- –"

"Señor, the sun is too high for idle talk," said Marto briefly, "and your saddle waits."

The priest held the stirrup for José Perez, who took the courtesy as a matter of course, turning in the saddle and casting a bitter look at the sun-flooded walls of Soledad.

"To marry a mistress and set her up as the love of another lover —- *two* other lovers! —- is not the game of a man," he growled moodily. "If it was to do over, I —- –"

"Take other thoughts with you," said Padre Andreas sadly, "and my son, go with God!"

He lifted his hand in blessing, and stood thus after they had turned away. Perez uttered neither thanks nor farewell.

The men, busy with the final packing, stared after him with much curiosity, and accosted the priest as he paced thoughtfully back to the portal.

"Padre, is this ammunition a gift of Don José, or is it magic from the old monks who hid the red gold of El Alisal and come back here to guard it and haunt Soledad?" inquired one of the boldest.

"There are no hauntings, and that red gold has led enough men astray in the desert. It is best forgotten."

"But strange things do come about," insisted another man. "Marto Cavayso swore he had witchcraft put on him by the green, jewel eyes of Doña Jocasta, and you see that since she follows our general he has the good luck, and this ammunition comes to him from God knows where!"

"It may be the Americano knows," hazarded the first speaker. "He took her from Marto, and rides ever beside her. Who proves which is the enchanter?"

"It is ill work to put the name of 'enchantment' against any mortal," chided the priest.

"That may be," conceded the soldier, "but we have had speech of this thing, and look you! —- Doña Jocasta rode in chains until the Americano crossed her trail, and Don Ramon, and all of us, searched in vain for the American guns, until the Americano rode to Soledad! Enchantment or not, he has luck for his friends!"

"As you please!" conceded the priest with more indifference than he felt. The Americano certainly did not belong to Soledad, and the wonder was that Ramon Rotil gave him charge of so beauteous a lady. Padre Andreas could easily perceive how the followers of Rotil thought it enchantment, or any other thing of the devil.

Instinctively he disapproved of Rhodes' position in the group; his care-free, happy smile ill fitted the situation at Soledad. Before the stealing away of Doña Jocasta she had been as a dead woman who walked; her sense of overwhelming sin was gratifying in that it gave every hope of leading to repentance, but on her return the manner of her behavior was different. She rode like a queen, and even the marriage was accepted as a justice! Padre Andreas secretly credited the heretic Americano with the change, and Mexican girls put no such dependence on a man outside of her own family, —- unless that man was a lover!

He saw his own influence set aside by the stranger and the rebel leader, and with Doña Jocasta as a firebrand he feared dread and awful things now that Rotil had given her power.

He found her with bright eyes and a faint flush in her cheeks over the letter Kit was writing to the south. It was her first act as the wife of José Perez, and it was being written to the girl whom Perez had hoped to marry!

Kit got considerable joy in framing her request as follows:

> To Señorita Dolores Terain,
> Linda Vista Rancho, Sonora,
> Honored Señorita:

As a woman who desires to secure justice and mercy for some poor peons of our district of Altar, I venture to address you, to whom womanly compassion must belong as does beauty and graciousness.

This is a work for the charity of women, rather than debates in law courts by men.

I send with this the names of those poor people who were herded south for slavery by Adolf Conrad, a German who calls himself American. To your father, the illustrious General Terain, this man Conrad represented these poor people as rebels and raiders of this region. It is not true. They were simple peaceful workers on little ranches.

They were given shelter at your rancho of Linda Vista to work for their food until they could be deported, but I send with this a payment of gold with which to repay any care they have been, or any debts incurred. If it is not enough, I pledge myself to the amount you will regard as justice.

Dear Señorita, my husband, Don José, warns me that women cannot manage such affairs, but we can at least try. Parents wait here for sons and daughters, and little children wait for their parents. Will you aid in the Christian task of bringing them together quickly?

At your service with all respect,
Jocasta Benicia Perez,

Soledad Rancho, Sonora.

"But you write here of gold sent by messenger, señor! —– I have no gold, only words can I send," protested Doña Jocasta helplessly.

"Ah, but the words are more precious than all," Kit assured her. "It is the right word we have waited for, and you alone could give it, señora. These people have held the gold ransom while waiting that word, and this child can bring it when the time is right."

Doña Jocasta regarded Tula doubtfully; she certainly gave no appearance of holding wealth to redeem a pueblo.

"You, —– the little one to whom even the Deliverer listens?" she said kindly. "But the wealth of a little Indian ranch would not seem riches to this illustrious lady, the Doña Dolores Terain."

"Yet will I bring riches to her or to you, Excellencia, if only my mother and my sister are coming again to Palomitas," said Tula earnestly.

"But whence comes wealth to you in a land where there is no longer wealth for anyone?"

Kit listened with little liking for the conversation after the padre entered. It was a direct question, and to be answered with directness, and he watched Tula anxiously lest she say the wrong thing. But she told the straight truth in a way to admit of no question.

"Long ago my father got gold for sacred prayer reasons; he hid it until he was old; when he died he made gift of it to me that my mother and sister buy freedom. That is all, Excellencia, but the gold is good gold."

She slipped her hand under her skirt and unfastened the leather strings of the burro-skin belt, —– it fell heavily on the tile floor. She untied the end of it and poured a handful on the table.

"You see, señora, there is riches enough to go with your words, but never enough to pay for them."

"*Santa Maria!*" cried the amazed priest. "That is *red* gold! In what place was it found?"

Tula laid her hand over the nuggets and faced him.

"That secret was the secret of Miguel who is dead."

"But —– some old Indian must know —– –"

Tula shook her head with absolute finality.

137

"No old Indian in all the world knows that!" she said. "This was a secret of the youth of Miguel, and only when old and dying did he give it for his people. This I, ––- Tula, child of Miguel tell you."

Padre Andreas looked from the girl to Kit and back again, knowing that the death of Miguel was a recent thing since it had occurred after the stealing of the women.

"Where did your father die?" he asked.

"In the hills of the desert."

"And ––- who had absolving and burial of him?"

"Absolving I do not know, but this man, his friend, had the making of the grave," she said, indicating Kit, and the eyes of the priest rested again on Kit with a most curious searching regard. Evidently even this little Indian stray of the desert arrived at good fortune under the friendship of the American stranger, ––- and it was another added to the list of enchantings!

"Ah," he murmured meaningly, "then this strange señor also has the knowing of this Indian gold? Is it truly gold of the earth, or witches' gold of red clay?" and he went nearer, reaching his hand to touch it.

"Why all this question when the child offers it for a good Christian use?" demanded Doña Jocasta. "See, here is a piece of it heavy enough to weigh down many lumps of clay, and north or south it will prove welcome ransom. It is a miracle sent by the saints at this time."

"Would the saints send the red gold of El Alisal to a heretic instead of a son of the church?" he asked. "And this is that gold for which the padres of Soledad paid with their lives long ago. There was never such red gold found in Sonora as that, and the church had its own claim on it; ––- it is mission gold!"

"No, not now," said Tula, addressing Doña Jocasta, ––- "truly not now! They claimed it long ago, but the holding of it was a thing not for them. Fire came out of the clouds to kill them there, and no one saw them alive anymore, and no other priest ever found the gold. This much is found by Miguel, for a dead man's promise!"

"The girl speaks straight, señora," ventured Kit. "I have already told General Rotil of the promise, but no good will come of much talk over the quality of gold for that ransom. To carry that message south and bring back the women is a task for council, but outside these walls, no tongue must speak of the gold, else there would be no safety for this maid."

"Yet a priest may ask how an Americano comes far from his home to guard gold and a maid in Sonora?" retorted Padre Andreas. "Strange affairs move these days in Altar ––- guns, ammunition, and the gold of dead men! In all these things you have a say, señor, yet you are but young in years, and ––- –"

"Padre," interrupted Doña Jocasta with a note of command, "he was old enough to save this child from starvation in the desert, and he was old enough to save me when even you could no longer save me, so why object because he has guarded wealth, and means to use it in a way of mercy? Heretic he may be, but he has the trust of Ramon Rotil, and of me. Also it is forbidden to mention this belt or what it covers. I have given my word, and this is no time to halt the task we have set. It would better serve those lost people if you help us find a messenger who is safe."

It was the first time the new Señora Perez assumed a tone of authority at Soledad, and Kit Rhodes thanked his lucky stars that she was arrayed with him instead of against him, for her eyes glowed green lightning on the priest whose curiosity had gotten him into trouble. Kit could not really blame him, for there was neither priest nor peon of the land who had not had visions of conquest if only the red gold of the Alisal should be conveniently stumbled upon!

And Tula listened to the words of Doña Jocasta as she would have listened to a god.

"I go," she said eagerly. "The trail it is strange to me, but I will find that way. I think I find in the dark that trail on which the mother of me was going!"

Doña Jocasta patted the hand of the girl, but looked at Kit. "That trail is not for a maid," she said meaningly. "I came over it, and know."

"I think it is for me," he answered. "The promise was mine. I know none of the people, but the names are written. It is eighty miles."

"Three days."

"More, double that," he said thoughtfully, and the eyes of Tula met his in disapproval. It was the merest hint of a frown, but it served. She could do the errand better than she could guard the rest of the gold. If her little belt was lost it was little, but if his store should be found it would be enough to start a new revolution in Sonora; —- the men of Rotil and the suspicious padre would unite on the treasure trail. It was the padre who gave him most uneasiness, because the padre was guessing correctly! The dream of a mighty church of the desert to commemorate all the ruined missions of the wilderness, was a great dream for the priest of a little pueblo, and the eyes of the Padre Andreas were alight with keen, —- too keen, anticipation.

"I go," stated Tula again. "No other one is knowing my people."

"That is a true word," decided Padre Andreas, "a major-domo of evil mind at Linda Vista could take the gold and send north whatever unruly vagabonds he had wished to be free from. Let the maid go, and I can arrange to see her there safe."

This kind offer did not receive the approval deserved. Kit wished no man on the trail with Tula who knew of the gold, and Tula herself was not eager to journey into unknown regions with a man of religion, who had already learned from Valencia of the elaborate ceremony planned for a "Judas day!" Little though Tula knew of churchly observances, she had an instinctive fear that she would be detained in the south too long to officiate in this special ceremony on which she had set her heart.

"Not with a priest will I go," she announced. "He would shut me in a school, and in that place I would die. Clodomiro can go, or Isidro, who is so good and knowing all our people."

"That is a good thought," agreed Doña Jocasta, who had no desire that Padre Andreas meet the family of Terain and recount details of the Perez marriage, —- not at least until she had worn her official title a little longer and tested the authority it gave her. "That is a good thought, for I have no wish that my house be left without a priest. Señor Rhodes, which man is best?"

But before Kit could answer Ramon Rotil stood in the door, and his eyes went to the papers on the table. Tula had recovered her belt, and fastened it under the *manta* she wore.

"So! you are working in council, eh?" he asked. "And have arrived at plans? First your own safety, señora?"

"No, señor, —- first the bringing back of the people driven off by the slavers. The letter is written; this child is to take it because the people are her people, but a safe man is wanted, and these two I cannot let go. You know José Perez, and his wife must not be without a man of religion as guard, yet he alone would not save me from others, hence the American señor —- –"

"Sure, that is a safe thought," and he took the seat offered by Kit. But he shook his head after listening to their suggestions.

"No. Isidro is too old, and Clodomiro with his flying ribbands of a would-be lover, is too young for that trail. You want —- you want —- –"

He paused as his mind evidently went searching among his men for one dependable. Then he smiled at Kit.

"You saved me the right man, señor! Who would be better than the foreman of Soledad? Would it not be expected that Señora Perez would send the most important of the ranchmen? Very well then. Marto is safe, he will go."

"But Marto —- " began Padre Andreas, when Rotil faced about, staring him into silence.

"Marto will return here to Soledad today," he said, and the face of the priest went pale. It was as if he had said that the task of Marto on the east trail would be ended.

"Yes, Marto Cavayso has been at Hermosillo," assented Doña Jocasta. "He will know all the ways to arrive quickly."

"That will be attended to. Will you, señor, see to it that horse and provision are made ready for the trail? And you, señora? Soledad in the wilderness is no good place for a lady. When this matter of the slaves is arranged, will it please you to ride south, or north? Troops of the south will be coming this way; —- it will be a land of soldiers and foraging."

"How shall I answer that?" murmured Doña Jocasta miserably. "In the south José Perez may make life a not possible thing for me, —- and in the north I would be a stranger."

"José Perez will not make trouble; yet trouble might be made, —- at first," said Rotil avoiding her eyes, and turning again to Kit. "Señor, by the time Marto gets back from the south, the pack mules will be here again. Until they are gone from Soledad I trust you in charge of Señora Perez. She must have a manager, and there is none so near as you."

"At her service," said Kit promptly, "but this place —- –"

"Ai, that is it," agreed Rotil. "North is the safer place for women alone, and you —- did you not say that on Granados there were friends?"

"Why, yes, General," replied Kit. "My friend, Captain Pike, is somewhere near, and the owner of Granados is a lady, and among us we'll do our best. But it's a hard trip, and I've only one gun."

"You will take your choice of guns, horses, or men," decided Rotil. "That is your work. Also you will take with you the evidence of Señora Perez on that matter of the murder. The padre can also come in on that, —- so it will be service all around."

Chappo came to the door to report that all was ready for the trail, and Rotil stood up, and handed to Doña Jocasta the marriage contract.

"Consider the best way of protecting this until you reach an alcalde and have a copy made and witnessed," he said warningly. "It protects your future. The fortunes of war may take all the rest of us, but the wife of Perez needs the record of our names; see to it!"

She looked up at him as if to speak, but no words came. He gazed curiously at her bent head, and the slender hands over the papers. In his life of turmoil and bloodshed he had halted to secure for her the right to a principality. In setting his face to the east, and the battle line, he knew the chance was faint that he would ever see her again, and his smile had in it a touch of self-derision at the thought, —- for after all he was nothing to her!

"So —- that is all," he said, turning away. "You come with me a little ways, señor, and to you, señora, *adios*!"

"Go with God, Ramon Rotil," she murmured, "and if ever a friend is of need to you, remember the woman to whom you gave justice and a name!"

"*Adios*," he repeated, and his spurs tinkled as he strode through the patio to the portal where the saddle horses were waiting. The pack mules were already below the mesa, and reached in a long line over the range towards the cañon of the eastern trail.

"You have your work cut out," he said to Kit. "For one thing, Marto Cavayso will carry out orders, but you must not have him enter a room where Doña Jocasta may be. It would be to offend her and frighten him. He swears to the saints that he was bewitched. That is as may be, but it is an easy way out! When the pack mules come back, and Marto is here, it is for you two to do again the thing we did last night. I may need Soledad on another day, and would keep all its secrets. After you have loaded the last of the guns it is best for you to go quickly. Here is a permit in case you cross any land held by our men; —- it is for you, your family, and all your baggage without molestation. Señora Perez has the same. This means you can take over the border any of the furnishings of Soledad required by the lady for a home elsewhere. The wagons sent north by Perez will serve well for that, and they are hers."

"But if he should send men of his own to interfere —- –"

"He won't," stated Rotil. "You are capitan, and Soledad is under military rule. There is only one soul here over which your word is not law. I have given the German Judas to your girl, and the women can have their way with him. He is as a dead man; call her."

There was no need, for Tula had followed at a discreet distance, and from beside a pillar gazed regretfully after her hero, the Deliverer, whom she felt every man should follow.

"*Oija, muchacha!*" he said as Kit beckoned her forward, "go to Fidelio. He is over there filling the cantins at the well. Tell him to give you the key to the quarters of El Aleman, and hearken you! —- I wash my hands of him from this day. If you keep him, well, but if he escapes, the loss is to you. I go, and not again will Ramon Rotil trap a Judas for your hellishness."

Tula sped to Fidelio, secured the key and was back to hold the stirrup of Rotil as he was helped to the saddle.

"If God had made me a man instead of a maid, I would ride the world as your soldier, my General," she said, holding the key to her breast as an amulet.

"Send your lovers instead," he said, and laughed, "for you will have them when you get more beef on your bones. *Adios*, soldier girl!"

She peered up at him under her mane of black hair.

"Myself, —- I think that is true," she stated gravely, "also my lovers, when they come, must follow you! When I see my own people safe in Palomitas it may be that I, Tula, will also follow you, —- and the help of the child of Miguel may not be a little help, my General."

Kit Rhodes alone knew what she meant. Her intense admiration for the rebel leader of the wilderness had brought the glimmer of a dream to her; —- the need of gold was great as the need of guns, and for the deliverer of the tribes what gift too great?

But the others of the guard laughed at the crazy saying of the brown wisp of a girl. They had seen women of beauty give him smiles, and more than one girl follow his trail for his lightest word, but to none of them did it occur that this one called by him the young crane, or the possessor of many devils, could bring more power to his hand than a regiment of the women who were comrades of a light hour.

But her solemnity amused Rotil, and he swept off his hat with exaggerated courtesy.

"I await the day, Tulita. Sure, bring your lovers, —- and later your sons to the fight! While you wait for them tell Marto Cavayso he is to have a care of you as if you were the only child of Ramon Rotil! I too will have a word with him of that. See to it, Capitan of the roads, and *adios!*"

He grinned at the play upon the name of Rhodes, and whirled his horse, joining his men, who sat their mounts and watched at a little distance.

Within the portal was gathered all those left of the household of Soledad to whom the coming and the going of the revolutionary leader was the great event of their lives, and all took note of the title of "Capitan" and the fact that the Americano and the Indian girl had his last spoken words.

They had gone scarce a mile when Fidelio spurred his horse back and with Mexican dash drew him back on his haunches as Kit emerged from the corridor.

"General Rotil's compliments," he said with a grin, "and Marto will report to you any event requiring written record, —- and silence!"

"Say that again and say it slow," suggested Kit.

"That is the word as he said it, Capitan, 'requiring the writing of records, and —- silence!'"

"I get you," said Kit, and with a flourish and a clatter, Fidelio was soon lost in the dust.

Kit was by no means certain that he did "get" him. He felt that he had quite enough trouble without addition of records and secrecy for acts of the Deliverer.

The sentinel palms of Soledad were sending long lines of shadows toward the blue range of the Sierras, and gnarled old orange trees in the ancient mission garden drenched the air with fragrance from many petals.

There had been a sand storm the day before, followed by rain, and all the land was refreshed and sparkling. The pepper trees swung tassels of bloom and the flaming coral of the occotilla glowed like tropic birds poised on wide-reaching wands of green. Meadow larks echoed each other in the tender calls of nesting time, and from the jagged peaks on the east, to far low hills rising out of a golden haze in the west, there was a great quiet and peace brooding over the old mission grounds of the wilderness.

Doña Jocasta paced the outer corridor, watched somberly by Padre Andreas on whom the beauty of the hour was lost.

"Is your heart turned stone that you lift no hand, or speak no word for the soul of a mortal?" he demanded. "Already the terrible women of Palomitas are coming to wait for their Judas, and this is the morning of the day!"

"It is no work of mine, Padre," she answered wearily. "I am sick, —- here! —- that the beast has been all these days and nights under a roof near me. I know how the women feel, though I think I would not wait, as they have waited, —- for Good Friday."

"It is murder in your heart to harbor such wickedness of thought," he insisted. "Your soul is in jeopardy that you do not contemplate forgiveness. Even though a man be a heretic, a priest must do his office when it comes to a sentence of death. After all —- he is a human."

"I do not know that," replied Doña Jocasta thoughtfully, and she sank into a rawhide chair in the shade of a pillar. "Listen, Padre. I am not learned in books, but I have had new thoughts with me these days. Don Pajarito is telling me of los Alemanos all over the world; —- souls they have not, and serpents and toads are their mothers! Here in Mexico we have our flag from old Indian days with the eagle and the snake. Once I heard scholars in Hermosillo talk about that; they said it was from ancient times of sky worship, and the bird was a bird of stars, —- also the serpent."

Padre Andreas lifted his brows in derision at the childishness of Indian astrology.

"Myself, I think the Indian sky knowers had the prophet sight," went on Doña Jocasta. "They make their eagle on the standard and they put the serpent there of the reason that some day a thing of poison would crawl to the nest of the eagle of Mexico to comrade there. It has crawled over the seas for that, Padre, and the beak and claws and wing of the eagle must all do battle to kill the head and the heart of it; —- for the heart of a serpent dies hard, and they breed and hatch their eggs everywhere in the soil of Mexico. Señor Padre, the Indian women of Palomitas are right! —- the girl Tula is a child of the eagle, and her stroke at the heart of the German snake will be a true stroke. I will not be one to give the weak word for mercy."

Her gaze, through half-closed lids, was directed towards the far trail of the cañon where moving dots of dark marked the coming of the Palomitas women. A ray of reflected light touched the jewel green of her eyes like shadowed emeralds in their dusky casket, and the priest, constantly proclaiming the probable loss of her soul, could not but bring his glance again and again to the wondrous beauty of her. She had bloomed like a royal rose in the days of serene rest at Soledad.

"If the heretic Americano gives you these thoughts which are not Christian, it will be a day of good luck when you see the last of him," was his cold statement as he watched her. "My mind is not well satisfied as to his knowledge of secret things here in Sonora. The Indians say he is an enchanter or Ramon Rotil would never have left him here as capitan with you, —- and that belt of gold —- -"

"But it was not the belt of the Americano!"

"No, but he *knows*! I tell you that gold is of the gold lost before we were born, —- the red gold of the padres' mine!"

"But the old women are telling me that the gold was Indian gold long before Spanish priests saw the land! Does the Indian girl then not have first right?"

"None has right ahead of the church, since all those pagans are under the rule of church! They are benighted heathen who must come under instruction and authority, else are they as beasts of the field."

"Still, —- if the girl makes use of her little heritage for a pious purpose —- –"

"Her intent has nothing to do with that secret knowledge of the Americano!" he insisted. "Has he bewitched you also that you have so little interest in a mine of gold in anyone of the arroyas of your land?"

She smiled at that without turning her head.

"If a mountain of gold should be uncovered at Soledad, of what difference to me? Would he let a woman make traffic with it? Surely not."

"He?"

"José Perez, —- who else?"

Padre Andreas closed his eyes a moment and arose, but did not answer. He paced the length of the corridor and back before he spoke.

"It is for you to ask the Americano that the prisoner be given a priest if he wants prayer," he said returning to their original subject of communication. "It is a duty that I tell you this; it is your own house."

"Señor Rhodes is capitan," she returned indifferently. "It is his task to give me rest here to prepare for that long north journey. I do not rest in my mind or my soul when you talk to me of the German snake, so I will ask that you speak with Capitan Rhodes. He has the knowing of Spanish."

"Too much for safety of us," commented the priest darkly. "Who is to say how he uses it with the Indians? It is well known that the American government would win all this land, and work with the Indians that they help win it."

"So everyone is saying in Hermosillo," agreed Doña Jocasta, "but the American capitan has not told me lies of any other thing, and he is saying that is a lie made by foreign people. Also —- " and she looked at him doubtfully, "the man Conrad cursed your name yesterday as a damned Austrian whose country had cost his country much."

"My mother was not Austrian!" retorted Padre Andreas, "and all my childhood was in Mexico. But how did Conrad know?"

"He told Elena it was his business to know such things. The Germans help send many Mexican priests north over the border. He had the thought that you are to go with me for some reason political of which I knew nothing!"

"I? Did *I* come in willingness to this wilderness? From the beginning to the end I am as a prisoner here; —- as much a prisoner as is El Aleman behind the bars! No horse is mine; —- if I walk abroad for my own health a vaquero ever is after me that I ride back with no fatigue to myself! It is the work of the heretic Americano who will have his own curse for it!"

He fumed nervously over the unexpected thrust of Austrian ancestry, and the beautiful eyes of Doña Jocasta regarded him with awakened interest. She had never thought of his politics, or possible affiliations, but after all it was true that he had been stationed at a pueblo where everything on wheels must pass coming north towards the border, also that was a very small pueblo to support a padre, and perhaps —- –

"Padre," she said after a moment, "but for the Americano you would be a dead man. Think you what Ramon would have done to a priest who let a vaquero carry me to the ranges! Also I came back to Soledad because the Americano told me it was only duty and justice that I come for your sake as Ramon has no liking for priests. You see, señor, our American capitan of Soledad is not so bad; —- he had a care of you."

"Too much a care of me!" retorted the priest. "Know you not that the door of my sleeping room is bolted each night, and unbolted at dawn? He laughs with a light heart, and sings foolishly, ——- your new Americano; but under that cloak of the simple his plotting is not idle!"

"As to that, I think his light heart is not so light these days," said Doña Jocasta. "Two days now the Indian girl and Marto Cavayso could have been back in Soledad, and he is looking, looking ever over that empty trail. Before the sun was above the sierra today he was far there coming across the mesa."

"A man does not go in the dark to look for a trail," said Padre Andreas meaningly. "He unbolted my door on his return, and to me he looked as a man who has done work that was heavy. What work is there for him to do alone in the hills?"

"Who knows? A horse herd is somewhere in a cañon beyond. There are colts, and the storm of yesterday might make trouble. The old father of Elena says that storm has not gone far and will come back! And while the Americano rides to learn of colts, and strays, he also picks the best mules for our journey to the border."

"Does he find the best mules with packs already on their backs in the cañons?" demanded the padre skeptically. "From my window I saw them return."

"I also," confessed Doña Jocasta amused at the persistence of suspicion, "and the load was the water bags and *serape*! Does any but a fool go into the wilderness without water?"

"You cover him well, señora, but I think it was not horses he went in the night to count," said the priest sarcastically. "Gold in the land is to him who finds it, ——- and I tell you the church will hear of that red gold belt from me! Also there will be a new search for it! If it is here the church will see that it does not go with American renegades across the border!"

"Padre, all the land speaks peace today, yet you are as a threatening cloud over Soledad!"

"I speak in warning, not threat, ——- and I am not the only cloud in the sky. The women of vengeance are coming beyond there where the willows are green."

Doña Jocasta looked the way he pointed, and stood up with an exclamation of alarm.

"Clodomiro! Call Clodomiro!" she said hurriedly, and as the priest only stared at her, she sped past him to the portal and called the boy who came running from the patio.

She pointed as the priest had pointed.

"They are strangers, they do not know," she said. "Kill a horse, but meet them!"

His horse was in the plaza, and he was in the saddle before she finished speaking, digging in his heels and yelling as though leading a charge while the frightened animal ran like a wild thing.

Doña Jocasta stood gazing after him intently, shading her eyes with her hand. Women came running out of the patio and Padre Andreas stared at her.

"What new thing has given you fear?" he asked in wonder.

"No new thing, ——- a very old thing of which Elena told me! That green strip of willow is the edge of a quicksand where no one knows the depth. The women are thinking to make a short path across, and the one who leads will surely go down."

The priest stared incredulous.

"How a quicksand and no water?" he asked doubtfully.

"There *is* water, ——- hidden water! It comes under the ground from the hills. In the old, old days it was a wide well boiling like a kettle over a fire, also it was warm! Then sand storms filled that valley and filled the well. It is crusted over, but the boiling goes on far below. Elena said not even a coyote will touch that cañoncita though the dogs are on his trail. The Indians say an evil spirit lives under there, but the women of Mesa Blanca and Palomitas do not know the place."

"It should have a fence, ——- a place like that."

"It had, but the wind took it, and, as you see, Soledad is a forgotten place."

They watched Clodomiro circle over the mesa trail and follow the women down the slope of the little valley. It was fully three miles away, yet the women could be seen running in fear to the top of the mesa where they cast themselves on the ground resting from fright and exertion.

Quite enjoying his spectacular dash of rescue, Clodomiro cantered back along the trail, and when he reached the highest point, turned looking to the southeast where, beyond the range, the old Yaqui trail led to the land of despair.

He halted there, throwing up his hand as if in answer to some signal, and then darted away, straight across the mesa instead of toward the buildings.

"Tula has come!" said Doña Jocasta in a hushed voice of dread. "She has come, and Señor Rhodes is needed here. That coming of Tula may bring an end to quiet days, —- like this!"

She sighed as she spoke, for the week had been as a space of restful paradise after the mental and physical horrors she had lived through.

In a half hour Clodomiro came in sight again just as Kit rode in from the west.

"Get horses out of the corrals," he called, "all of them. That trail has been long even from the railroad."

It was done quickly, and the vaqueros rode out as Clodomiro reached the plaza.

"*Tula?*" asked Kit.

"Tula is as the living whose mind is with the dead," said the boy. "Many are sick, some are dead, —- the mother of Tula died on the trail last night."

"Good God!" whispered Kit. "After all that hell of a trail, to save no one for herself! Where is Marto?"

"Marto walks, and sick ones are on his horse. I go back now that Tula has this horse."

"No, I will go. Stay you here to give help to the women. Bring out beds in every corridor. Bring straw and blankets when the beds are done."

Doña Jocasta put out her hand as he was about to mount.

"And I? What task is mine to help?" she asked, and Kit looked down at her gravely.

"Señora, you have only to be yourself, gracious and kind of heart. Also remember this is the first chance in the lands of Soledad to show the natives they have not alone a padrona, but a protecting friend. In days to come it may be a memory of comfort to you."

Then he mounted, and led the string of horses out to meet the exiles. While she looked after him murmuring, "In days to come?"

And to the padre she said, "I had ceased to think of days to come, for the days of my life had reached the end of all I could see or think. He gives hope even in the midst of sadness, —- does the Americano."

Kit met the band where the trail forked to Palomitas and Mesa Blanca. Some wanted to go direct to their own homes and people, while Marto argued that food and rest and a priest awaited them at Soledad, and because of their dead, they should have prayers.

Tula said nothing. She sat on the sand, and caressed a knife with a slightly curved blade, —- a knife not Mexican, yet familiar to Kit, and like a flash he recalled seeing one like it in the hand of Conrad at Granados.

She did not even look up when he halted beside her though the others welcomed with joy the sight of the horses for the rest of the trail.

"Tula!" he said bending over her, "Tula, we come to welcome you, —- my horse is for your riding."

She looked up when he touched her.

"Friend of me," she murmured wistfully, "you made me put a mark at that place after we met in the first dawn, —- so I was knowing it well. Also my mother was knowing, —- and it was where she died last night under the moon. See, this is the knife on which Anita died in that place. It is ended for us —- the people of Miguel, and the people of Cajame!"

"Tula, you have done wonderful things, many deeds to make the spirit of Miguel proud. Is that not so, my friends?" and he turned to the others, travel-stained, sick and weary, yet one in their cries of the gratitude they owed to Tula and to him, by which he perceived that Tula had, for her own reasons, credited him with the plan of ransom.

They tried brokenly to tell of their long fear and despair in the strangers' land, —- and of sickness and deaths there. Then the miracle of Tula walking by the exalted excellencia of that great place, and naming one by one the Palomitas names, forgetting none; —- until all who lived were led out from that great planting place of sugar cane and maize, and their feet set on the northern way.

When they reached this joyous part of the recital words failed, and they wept as they smiled at him and touched the head of Tula tenderly. Even a gorgeous and strange *manta* she now wore was pressed to the lips of women who were soon to see their children or their desolate mothers.

His eyes grew misty as they thronged about her, —- the slender dark child of the breed of a leader. The new *manta* was of yellow wool and cotton, bordered with dull green and little squares of flaming scarlet woven in it by patient Indian hands of the far south coast. It made her look a bit royal in the midst of the drab-colored, weary band.

She seemed scarcely to hear their praise, or their sobs and prayers. Her face was still and her gaze far off and brooding as her fingers stroked the curved blade over and over.

"An Indian stole that knife from the German after his face was cut with it by her sister," said Marto Cavayso quietly while the vaqueros were helping the weaker refugees to mount, two to each animal. "That man gives it to her at the place where Marta, her mother, died in the night. So after that she does not sleep or eat or talk. It is as you see."

"I see! Take you the others, and Tula will ride on my saddle," said Kit in the same tone. Then he pointed to the beautifully worked *manta*, "Did she squander wealth of hers on that?"

Marto regarded him with an impatient frown —- it seemed to him an ill moment for the American joke.

"Tula had no wealth," he stated, "we lived as we could on the fine gold you gave to me for myself."

"Oh yes, I had forgotten that," declared Kit in some wonder at this information, "but *mantas* like that do not grow on trees in Sonora."

"That is a gift from the very grand daughter of the General Terain," said Marto. "Also if you had seen affairs as they moved there at Linda Vista you would have said as does Ramon Rotil, that this one is daughter of the devil! I was there, and with my eyes I saw it, but if I had not, —- an angel from heaven would not make me believe!"

"What happened?"

"The Virgin alone knows! for women are in her care, and no man could see. As ordered, I went to the gates of that hacienda very grand. *Sangre de Christo!* if they had known they would have strung me to a tree and filled me with lead! But I was the very responsible vaquero of Rancho Soledad in Altar —- and the lizards of guards at the gate had no moment of suspicion. I told them the Indian girl carried a letter for the eyes of their mistress and the sender was Doña Jocasta Perez. At that they sent some messenger on the run, for they say the Doña Dolores is fire and a sword to any servant of theirs who is slow in her tasks."

"I heard she was a wonder of pride and beauty," said Kit. "Did you see her?"

"That came later. She sent for Tula who would give the letter to no one, —- not even to me. The guard divided their dinner with me while I waited; if they were doing work for their general I was doing work for mine and learned many things in that hour! At last Tula came walking down that great stair made from one garden to another where laurel trees grow, and with her walked a woman out of the sun. There is no other word, señor, for that woman! Truly she is of gold and rose; her mother's family were of old Spain and she is a glory to any day!"

"Did you feel yourself under witchcraft —- once more?" queried Kit.

"*Sangre de Christo!* Never again! But José Perez had a good eye for making choice of women, —- that is a true word! So Doña Dolores walked down to the drive with that *manta* over her arm, also a belt in her hand, —- a belt of gold, señor, see!"

To the astonished gaze of Kit Rhodes he drew from under his coat the burro-skin belt he had directed the making of up there in the hidden cañon of El Alisal. Marto balanced it in his hand appreciatively.

"And there was more of it than this!" he exulted, "for the way on the railroad was paid out of it for all the Indians. That is why we lost two days, —- our car was put on a side track, and for the sick it was worse than to walk the desert."

"Yes; well?"

"Doña Dolores got in a fine carriage there. *Madre de Dios!* what horses! White as snow on the sierras, and gold on all the harness! Me, I am dreaming of them since that hour! They got in, Tula also in her poor dress, and a guard told me to follow the carriage. It was as if San Gabriel made me invitation to enter heaven! Twenty miles we went through that plantation, a deep sea of cane, señor, and maize of a tree size, —- the richness there is riches of a king. Guards were everywhere and peons rode ahead to inform the major-domo, and he came riding like devils to meet Doña Dolores Terain. I am not a clever man, señor, but even I could see that never before had the lady of Linda Vista made herself fatigue by a plantation ride there, and I think myself he had a scare that she see too much! At the first when Doña Dolores had speech with him, it was easy to see he blamed me, and his eyes looked once as if to scorch me with fire. Then she pointed to the child beside her, and gave some orders, and he sent a guard with Tula through another gate into a great corral where men and women were packed like cattle. Señor, I have been in battles, but I never heard screams of wounded like the screams of joy I heard in that corral! Some of these Indians dropped like dead and were carried out of the gate that way as Tula stood inside and named the names.

"When it was over that woman of white beauty told that manager to have them all well fed, and given meat for the journey, for he would answer to the general if any stroke of harm came to anyone of them on the plantation of Linda Vista. Then she gave to my hand the belt of gold to care for the poor people on the trail; —- also she said the people were a free gift to Doña Jocasta Perez, and there was no ransom to pay. Myself I think the Doña Dolores had happiness to tell the general, her father, that José Perez had a wife, for that plan of marriage was but for politics. *Sangre de Christo!* what a woman! When all was done she held out the *manta* to Tula, and her smile was as honey of the mesquite, and she said, "In my house you would not take the gift I offered you, but now that you have your mother, and your friends safe, will you yet be so proud?" and Tula with her arms around her mother, stood up and let the thing be put over her head as you see, and that, Señor Capitan, is the way of the strange *manta* of Tula."

"And that?" queried Kit, indicating the belt. Marto smiled a bit sheepishly and lowered his voice because the last of the horses were being loaded with the homesick human freight, and the chatter, and clatter of hoofs had ceased about them.

"Maybe it is the *manta*, and maybe I am a fool," he confessed, "but she told me to spend not one ounce beyond what was needed, for it was to use only for these sick and poor people of hers. There was a good game going on in that train, —- and fools playing! I could have won every peso if I had put up only a little handful of the nuggets. That is why I think my general knew when he said she was the devil, for she stood up in that straight rich garment of honor and looked at me —- only looked, not one spoken word, señor! —- and on my soul and the soul of my mother, the wish to play in that game went away from me in that minute, and did not come back! How does a man account for a thing like that; I ask you?"

Kit thought of that first night on the treasure trail in the mountain above them, and smiled.

"I can't account for it, though I do recognize the fact," he answered. "It is not the first time Tula has ruled an outfit, and it is not the *manta*!"

Then he walked over and lifted her from the ground as he would lift a child, she weighed so little more!

"Little sister," he said kindly, "now that you are rested, you will ride my horse to Soledad. Your big work is done for your people. All is finished."

"No, señor, —- not yet is the finish," she said shaking her head, "not yet!"

Kit felt uncomfortably the weight in his pocket of the key of Conrad's room. He had made most solemn promise it would be guarded till she came. He had studied up some logical arguments to present to her attention for herding the German across the border as a murderer the United States government would deal justice to, but after the report of Marto concerning her long trail, and the death of her mother in the desert, he did not feel so much like either airing ideas or asking questions. He was rather overwhelmed by the knowledge that she had not allowed even Marto to guess that the bag of gold was her very own!

He took her on the saddle in front of him because she drooped so wearily there alone, and her head sank against his shoulder as if momentarily she was glad to be thus supported.

"Poor little eaglet!" he said affectionately, "I will take you north to Cap Pike, and someone else who will love you when she hears all this; and in other years, quieter years, we will ride again into Sonora, and —— –"

She shook her head against his shoulder, and he stopped short.

"Why, Tula!" he began in remonstrance, but she lifted her hand with a curious gesture of finality.

"Friend of me," she said in a small voice with an undertone of sad fatefulness, "words do not come today. They told you I am not sleeping on this home trail, and it is true. I kept my mother alive long after the death birds of the night were calling for her —— it is so! Also today at the dawn the same birds called above me, ——- above *me*! and look!"

They had reached the summit of the valley's wall and for a half mile ahead the others were to be seen on the trail to Soledad, but it was not there she pointed, but to the northeast where a dark cloud hung over the mountains. Its darkness was cleft by one lance of lightning, but it was too far away for sound of thunder to reach them.

"See you not that the cloud in the sky is like a bird, ——- a dark angry bird? Also it is over the trail to the north, but it is not for you, ——- *I* am the one first to see it! Señor, I will tell you, but I telling no other ——- I think my people are calling me all the time, in every way I look now. I no knowing how I go to them, but ——- I think I go!"

CHAPTER XX
EAGLE AND SERPENT

Marto Cavayso gave to Kit Rhodes the burro-skin belt and a letter from Doña Dolores Terain to the wife of José Perez.

"My work is ended at the hacienda until the mules come back for more guns, and I will take myself to the adobe beyond the corrals for what rest there may be. You are capitan under my general, so this goes to you for the people of the girl he had a heart for. Myself, —- I like little their coyote whines and yells. It may be a giving of thanks, or it may be a mourning for dead, —- but it sounds to me like an anthem made in hell."

He referred to the greeting songs of the returned exiles, and the wails for the dead left behind on the trail. The women newly come from Palomitas sat circled on the plaza, and as food or drink was offered each, a portion was poured on the sand as a libation to the ghosts of the lately dead, and the name of each departed was included in the wailing chant sung over and over.

It was a weird, hypnotic thing, made more so by the curious light, yellow and green in the sky, preceding that dark cloud coming slowly with sound of cannonading from the north. Though the sun had not set, half the sky was dark over the eastern sierras.

"The combination is enough to give even a sober man the jim-jams," agreed Kit. "Doña Jocasta is sick with fear of them, and has gone in to pray as far from the sound as possible. The letter will go to her, and the belt will go to Tula who may thank you another day. This day of the coming back she is not herself."

"Mother of God! that is a true word. No girl or woman is like that!"

The priest, who had talked with the sick and weary, and listened to their sobs of the degradation of the slave trail, had striven to speak with Tula, who with head slightly drooped looked at him under her straight brows as though listening to childish things.

"See you!" muttered Marto. "That *manta* must have been garb of some king's daughter, and no common maid. It makes her a different thing. Would you not think the padre some underling, and she a ruler giving laws?"

For, seated as she was, in a chair with arms, her robe of honor reached straight from her chin to her feet, giving her appearance of greater height than she was possessed of, and the slender banda holding her hair was of the same scarlet of the broideries. Kit remembered calling her a young Cleopatra even in her rags, and now he knew she looked it!

He was not near enough to hear the words of the priest, but with all his energy he was striving to win her to some view of his. She listened in long silence until he ceased.

Then her hand went under her *manta* and drew out the curved knife.

She spoke one brief sentence, and lifted the blade over her head. It caught the light of the hovering sun, and the Indians near enough to hear her words set up a scream of such unearthly emotion that the priest turned ashen, and made the sign to ward off evil.

It was merely coincidence that a near flash of lightning flamed from the heavens as she lifted the knife, —- but it inspired every Indian to a crashing cry of exultation.

And it did not end there, for a Palomitas woman had carried across the desert a small drum of dried skin stretched over a hollow log, and at the words of Tula she began a soft tum-tum-tum-tum on the hidden instrument. The sound was at first as a far echo of the thunder back of the dark cloud, and the voices of the women shrilled their emphasis as the drum beat louder, or the thunder came nearer.

Kit Rhodes decided Marto was entirely correct as to the inspiration back of that anthem.

"*Sangre de Christo!* look at that!" muttered Marto, who meant to turn his back on the entire group, yet was held by the fascination of the unexpected.

Four Indian youths with a huge and furious bull came charging down the mesa towards the corral. A *reata* fastened to each horn and hind foot of the animal was about the saddle horn of a boy, and the raging bellowing creature was held thus at safe distance from all. The boys, shouting with their joy of victory, galloped past the plaza to where four great stakes had already been driven deep in the hard ground. To those stakes the bull would be tied until the burden was ready for his back —- and his burden would be what was left of "Judas" when the women of the slave trail got through with him!

"God the father knows I am a man of no white virtues," muttered Marto eyeing the red-eyed maddened brute, "but here is my vow to covet no comradeship of aught in the shape of woman in the district of Altar —- bred of the devil are they!"

He followed after to the corral to watch the tying of the creature, around which the Indian men were gathered at a respectful distance.

But Rhodes, after one glance at the bellowing assistant of Indian vengeance, found himself turning again to Tula and the padre. That wild wail and the undertone of the drum was getting horribly on his nerves, —- yet he could not desert, as had Marto.

Tula sat as before, but with the knife held in her open hand on the arm of the chair. She followed with a grim smile the careering of the bull, then nodded her head curtly to the priest and turned her gaze slowly round the corridor until she saw Rhodes, and tilted back her head in a little gesture of summons.

"Well, little sister," he said, "what's on your mind?"

"The padre asks to pray with El Aleman. I say yes, for the padre has good thoughts in his heart, —- maybe so! You have the key?"

"Sure I have the key, but I fetch it back to you when visitors start going in, and —- oh yes —- there's your belt for your people."

"No; you be the one to give," she said with a glance of sorrow towards a girl who was youngest of the slaves brought back. "You, amigo, keep all but the key."

"As you say," he agreed. "Come along, padre, you are to get the privilege you've been begging for, and I don't envy you the task."

Padre Andreas made no reply. In his heart he blamed Rhodes that the prisoner had not been let escape during the absence of the girl, and also resented the offhand manner of the young American concerning the duty of a priest.

The sun was at the very edge of the world, and all shadows spreading for the night when they went to the door of Conrad's quarters. Kit unlocked the door and looked in before opening wide. The one window faced the corral, and Conrad turned from it in shaking horror.

"What is it they say out there?" he shouted in fury. "They call words of blasphemy, that the bull is Germany, and 'Judas' will ride it to the death! They are wild barbarians, they are —- —"

"Never mind what they are," suggested Kit, "here is a priest who thinks you may have a soul worth praying for, and the Indians have let him come —- once!"

Then he let the priest in and locked the door, going back to Tula with the key. She sat where he had left her, and was crooning again the weird tuneless dirge at which Marto had been appalled.

But she handed him a letter.

"Marto forgot. It was with the Chinaman trader at the railroad," she said and went placidly on fondling the key as she had fondled the knife, and pitching her voice in that curious falsetto dear to Indian ceremonial.

He could scarce credit the letter as intended for himself, as it was addressed in a straggling hand filling all the envelope, to Capitan Christofero Rhodes, Manager of Rancho Soledad, District of Altar, Sonora, Mexico, and in one corner was written, "By courtesy of Señor Fidelio Lopez," and the date within a week. He opened it, and walked out to the western end of the corridor where the light was yet good, though through the barred windows he could see candles already lit in the shadowy *sala*.

The letter was from Cap Pike, and in the midst of all the accumulated horror about him, Kit was conscious of a great homesick leap of the heart as he skimmed the page and found her name —- "Billie is all right!"

> How are you, Capitan? (began the letter). That fellow Fidelio rode into the *cantina*
> here at La Partida today. He asked a hell's slew of questions about you, and Billie

and me nearly had fits, for we thought you were sure dead or held for ransom, and I give it to you straight, Kit, there isn't a peso left on the two ranches to ransom even Baby Buntin' if the little rat is still alive, and that ain't all Kit: it don't seem possible that Conrad and Singleton mortgaged both ranches clear up to the hilt, but it sure has happened, every acre is plastered with ten per cent paper and the compound interest strips it from Billie just as sure as if it was droppin' through to China. When Conrad was on the job he had it all blanketed, but now saltpeter can't save it without cash. Billie is all right, but some peaked with worry. So am I. But you cheer up, for I got plans for a hike up into Pinal County for us three on a search for the Lost Dutchman Mine, lost fifty years and I have a hunch we can find it, got the dope from an old half breed who knew the Dutchman. So don't you worry about trailing home broke. The Fidelio hombre said to look for you in six days after Easter, and meet you with water at the Rio Seco, so we'll do that. He called you capitan and said the Deliverer had made you an officer; how about it? He let loose a line of talk about your two women in the outfit, but I sort of stalled him on that, so Billie wouldn't get it, for I reckon that's a greaser lie, Kit, and you ain't hitched up to no gay Juanita down there. I had a monkey and parrot time to explain even that Tula squaw to Billie, for she didn't savvy —- not a copper cent's worth! She is right here now instructin' me, but I won't let her read this, so don't you worry. She says to tell you it looks at last like our old eagle bird will have a chance to flop its wings in France. The pair of us is near about cross-eyed from watchin' the south trail into Altar, and the east trail where the troops will go! She says even if we are broke there is an adobe for you at Vijil's, and a range for Buntin' and Pardner. Billie rides Pardner now instead of Pat.

I reckon that's all Kit, and I've worked up a cramp on this anyway. I figured that maybe you laid low down there till the Singleton murder was cleared up, but I can alibi you on that O. K., when Johnny comes marchin' home! So don't you worry.

Yours truly,

Pike.

He read it over twice, seeking out the lines with *her* name and dwelling on them. So Billie was riding Pardner, —- and Billie had a camp ready for him, —- and Billie couldn't savvy even a little Indian girl in his outfit —- *say!*

He was smiling at that with a very warm glow in his heart for the resentment of Billie. He could just imagine Pike's monkey and parrot time trying to make Billie understand accidents of the trail in Sonora. He would make that all clear when he got back to God's country! And the little heiress of Granados ranches was only an owner of debt-laden acres, —- couldn't raise a peso to ransom even the little burro! Well, he was glad she rode Pardner instead of another horse; that showed —- –

Then he smiled again, and drifted into dreams. He would let Bunting travel light to the Rio Seco, and then load him for her as no burro ever was loaded to cross the border! He wondered if she'd tell him again he couldn't hold a foreman's job? He wondered —- –

And then he felt a light touch on his arm, and turned to see the starlike beauty of Doña Jocasta beside him. Truly the companionship of Doña Jocasta might be a more difficult thing to explain than that of the Indian girl of a slave raid!

Her face was blanched with fear, and her touch brought him back from his vision of God's country to the tom-tom, and the weird chant, and the thunder of storm coming nearer and nearer in the twilight.

"Señor!" she breathed in terror, "even on my knees in prayer it is not for anyone to shut out this music of demons. Look! Yesterday she was a child of courage and right, but what is she today?"

She pointed to Tula and clung to him, for in all the wild chorus Tula was the leader, —-
she who had the words of ancient days from the dead Miguel. She sat there as one enthroned
draped in that gorgeous thing, fit, as Marto said, for a king's daughter, while the others sat in
the plaza or rested on straw and blankets in the corridor looking up at her and shrilling savage
echoes to the words she chanted.

"And that animal, —- I saw it!" moaned Doña Jocasta. "Mother of God! that I should deny
a priest who would only offer prayers for that wicked one who is to be tortured on it! Señor,
for the love of God give me a horse and let me go into the desert to that storm, any place, —-
any place out of sight and sound of this most desolate house! The merciful God himself has
forsaken Soledad!"

As she spoke he realized that time had passed while he read and re-read and dreamed a dream
because of the letter. The sun was far out of sight, only low hues of yellow and blue melting
into green to show the illumined path it had taken. By refraction rays of copper light reached
the zenith and gave momentarily an unearthly glow to the mesa and far desert, but it was only
as a belated flash, for the dusk of night touched the edge of it.

And the priest locked in with Conrad had been forgotten by him! At any moment that girl
with the key might give some signal for the ceremony, whatever it was, of the death of the
German beast!

"Sure, señora, I promise you," he said soothingly, patting her hand clinging to him. "There
is my horse in the plaza, and there is Marto's. We will get the padre, and both of you can ride
to the little adobe down the valley where Elena's old father lives. He is Mexican, not Indian.
It is better even to kneel in prayer there all the night than to try to rest in Soledad while this
lasts. At the dawn I will surely go for you. Come, —- we will ask for the key."

Together they approached Tula, whose eyes stared straight out seeing none of the dark faces
lifted to hers, she seemed not to see Kit who stopped beside her.

"Little sister," he said, touching her shoulder, "the padre waits to be let out of the room of
El Aleman, and the key is needed."

She nodded her head, and held up the key.

"Let me be the one," begged Doña Jocasta, —- "I should do penance! I was not gentle in
my words to the padre, yet he is a man of God, and devoted. Let me be the one!"

The Indian girl looked up at that, and drew back the key. Then some memory, perhaps
that kneeling of Doña Jocasta with the women of Palomitas, influenced her to trust, and after
a glance at Kit she nodded her head and put the key in her hand.

"You, señor, have the horses," implored Doña Jocasta, "and I will at once come with Padre
Andreas."

"*Pronto!*" agreed Kit, "but I must get you a *serape*. Rain may fall from that cloud."

She seemed scarcely to hear him as she sped along the patio towards the locked door. Kit
entered his own room for a blanket just as she fitted the key in the lock, and spoke the padre's
name.

The next instant he heard her screams, and a door slam shut, and as he came out with the
blanket, he saw the priest dash toward the portal leading from the patio to the plaza.

He ran to her, lifting her from the tiles where she had been thrown.

"Conrad!" she cried pointing after the flying figure. "There! Quickly, señor, quickly!"

He jerked open the door and looked within, a still figure with the face hidden, crouched by
a bench against the wall. In two strides Kit crossed from the door and grasped the shoulder,
and the figure propped there fell back on the tiles. It was the dead priest dressed in the clothes
of Conrad, and the horror of that which had been a face showed he had died by strangulation
under the hands of the man for whom he had gone to pray.

Doña Jocasta ran wildly screaming through the patio, but the Indian voices and the drum
prevented her from being heard until she burst among them just as Conrad leaped to the back
of the nearest horse.

"El Aleman! El Aleman!" she screamed pointing to him in horror. "He has murdered the padre and taken his robe. It is El Aleman! Your Judas has killed your priest!"

Kit ran for his own horse, but with the quickness of a cat Tula was before him in the saddle, and whirling the animal, leaning low, and her gorgeous *manta* streaming behind like a banner she sped after the German screaming, "Judas! Judas! Judas of Palomitas!"

And, as in the other chants led by her, the Indian women took up this one in frenzied yells of rage.

The men of the corral heard and leaped to saddles to follow the flying figures, but Kit was ahead, —- not much, but enough to be nearest the girl.

Straight as an arrow the fugitive headed for Mesa Blanca, the nearest ranch where a fresh horse could be found, and Doña Jocasta and some of the women without horses stood in the plaza peering after that wild race in the gray of the coming night.

A flash of lightning outlined the three ahead, and a wail of utter terror went up from them all.

"Mother of God, the cañon of the quicksand!" cried Doña Jocasta.

"Tula! Tula! Tula!" shrilled the Indian women.

Tula was steadily gaining on the German, and Kit was only a few rods behind as they dashed down the slight incline to that too green belt in the floor of the brown desert.

He heard someone, Marto he thought, shouting his name and calling *"Sumidero! Sumidero!"* He did not understand, and kept right on. Others were shouting at Tula with as little result, the clatter of the horses and the rumble of the breaking storm made all a formless chaos of sound.

The frenzied scream of a horse came to him, and another lightning flash showed Conrad, ghastly and staring, leap from the saddle —- in the middle of the little valley —- and Tula ride down on top of him!

Then a rope fell around Kit's shoulders, pinioning his arms and he was jerked from the horse with a thud that for a space stunned him into semi-unconsciousness, but through it he heard again the pitiful scream of a dumb animal, and shouts of Marto to the frenzied Indians.

"Ha! Clodomiro, the *reata*! Wait for the lightning, then over her shoulders! Only the horse is caught; —- steady and a true hand, boy! Ai-yi! You are master, and the Mother of God is your help! Run your horse back, —- run, curse you! or she will sink as he sinks! *Sangre de Christo!* she cuts the *reata*!"

Kit struggled out of the rope, and got to his feet in time to see the flash of her knife as she whirled to her victim. Again and again it descended as the man, now submerged to the waist, caught her. His screams of fear were curdling to the blood, but high above the German voice of fear sounded the Indian voice of triumph, and from the vengeful cry of "Judas! Judas! Judas of the world!" her voice turned sharply to the high clear chant Kit had heard in the hidden cañon of the red gold. It was as she said —- there would be none of her caste and clan to sing her death song to the waiting ghosts, and she was singing it.

As those weird triumphant calls went out from the place of death every Indian answered them with shouts as of fealty, and in the darkness Kit felt as if among a circle of wolves giving tongue in some signal not to be understood by men.

He could hear the sobs of men and boys about him, but not a measure of that wild wail failed to bring the ever recurring response from the brown throats.

Marto, wet and trembling, cursed and prayed at the horror of it, and moved close to Kit in the darkness.

"Jesus, Maria, and José!" he muttered in a choked whisper, "one would think the fathers of these devils had never been christened! *Sangre de Christo!* look at that!"

For in a vivid sheet of lightning they saw a terrible thing.

Tula, on the shoulders of the man, stood up for one wavering instant and with both hands raised high, she flung something far out from her where the sands were firm for all but things of weight. Then her high triumphant call ended sharply in the darkness as she cast herself forward. She died as her sister had died, and on the same knife.

Doña Jocasta stumbled from a horse, and clung to Kit in terror. "Mother of God!" she sobbed. "It is as I said! She is the Eagle of Mexico, and she died clean —-- with the Serpent under her feet!"

In a dawn all silver and gold and rose after the storm, there was only a trace at the edge of the sand where two horses had carried riders to the treacherous smiling arroya over which a coyote would not cross.

And one of the Indian women of Palomitas tied a *reata* around the body of her baby son, and sent him to creep out as a turtle creeps to that thing cast by Tula to the women cheated of their Judas.

The slender naked boy went gleefully to the task as to a new game, and spit in the dead face as he dragged it with him to his mother who had pride in him.

It was kicked before the women back over the desert to Soledad, and the boys used it for football that day, and tied what was left of it between the horns of the roped wild bull at the corral. The bellowing of the bull when cut loose came as music to the again placid Indian women of Palomitas. They were ready for the home trail with their exiles. It had been a good ending, and their great holiday at Soledad was over.

CHAPTER XXI
EACH TO HIS OWN

A straggling train of pack mules followed by a six-mule wagon, trailed past Yaqui Springs ten days later, and was met there by the faithful Chappo and two villainous looking comrades, who had cleaned out the water holes and stood guard over them until arrival of the ammunition train.

"For beyond is a dry hell for us, and on the other side the Deliverer is circled by enemy fighters who would trap him in his own land. He lies hid like a fox in the hills waiting for this you bring. Water must not fail, and mules must not fail; for that am I here to give the word for haste."

"But even forty mule loads will not serve him long," said Kit doubtfully.

"Like a fox in the hills I tell you, Señor Capitan, ——- and only one way into the den! Beyond the enemy he has other supplies safe ——- this is to fight his way to it. After that he will go like a blaze through dry meadows of zacatan."

Kit would have made camp there for the night, but Chappo protested.

"No, señor! Every drop in the sand here is for the mules of the army. It is not my word, it is the word of my general. Four hours north you will find Little Coyote well. One day more and at the crossing of Rio Seco, water will be waiting from the cold wells of La Partida. It is so arrange, señor, and the safe trail is made for you and for excellencia, the señora. In God's name, take all your own, and go in peace!"

"But the señora is weary to death, and ——-"

"That is true, Capitan," spoke Doña Jocasta, who drooped in the saddle like a wilted flower. "But the señora will not die, and if she does it is not so much loss as the smallest of the soldiers of El Gavilan. We will go on, and go quickly, see! ——- there is yet water in the cantin, and four hours of trail is soon over."

Ugly Chappo came shyly forward and, uncovered, touched the hem of her skirt to his lips.

"The high heart of the excellencia gives life to the men who fight," he said and thrust his hand in a pocket fastened to his belt. "This is to you from the Deliverer, señora. His message is that it brought to him the lucky trail, and he would wish the same to the Doña Jocasta Perez."

It was the little cross, once sent back to her by a peon in bitterness of soul, and now sent by a general of Mexico with the blessing of a soldier.

"Tell him Jocasta takes it as a gift of God, and his name is in her prayers," she said and turned away.

Clodomiro pushed forward, ——- a very different Clodomiro, for the fluttering bands of color were gone from his arms and his hair ——- the heart of the would-be bridegroom was no longer his. He was stripped as for the trail or for war, and fastened to his saddle was the gun and ammunition he had won from Cavayso who had gone quickly onward with his detachment of the pack.

But Clodomiro halted beside Chappo, regardless of need for haste on the trail, and asked him things in that subdued Indian tone without light, shade, or accent, in which the brown brothers of the desert veil their intimate discourse.

"There, beyond!" said Chappo, "two looks on the trail," and he pointed west. "Two looks and one water hole, and if wind moves the sand no one can find the way where we go. It is not a trail for boys."

"I am not now a boy," said Clodomiro, "and when the safety trail of the señora is over ——-"

But Chappo waved him onward, for the wagon and the pack mules, and even little gray Bunting had turned reluctant feet north.

Clodomiro had come from Soledad because Elena, ——- who never had been out of sight of the old adobe walls, ——- sat on the ground wailing at thought of leaving her old sick father and going to war, for despite all the persuasions of Doña Jocasta, Elena knew what she knew, and did not at all believe that any of them would see the lands of the Americano, ——- not with pack mules of Ramon Rotil laden with guns!

"If Tula had lived, no other would have been asked," Rhodes had stated. "But one is needed to make camp for the señora on the trail, —- and to me the work of the packs and the animals."

"That I can do," Clodomiro offered. "My thought was to go where Tula said lovers of hers must go, and that was to El Gavilan. But this different thing can also be my work to the safe wells of the American. That far I go."

Thus the three turned north from the war trail, and Clodomiro followed, after making a prayer that the desert wind would hear, and be very still, and fill no track made by the mules with the ammunition.

This slight discussion at the parting of the ways concerning two definite things, —- need of haste, and conserving of water, —- left no moment for thought or query of the packs of furnishings deemed of use to Señora Perez in her removal to the north.

Doña Jocasta herself had asked no question and taken no interest in them. Stripped of all sign of wealth and in chains, she had ridden into Soledad, and in comfort and much courtesy she was being conducted elsewhere. How long it might endure she did not know, and no power of hers could change the fact that she had been made wife of José Perez; —- and at any turn of any road luck might again be with his wishes, and her estate fall to any level he choose to enforce.

At dusk they reached the Little Coyote well, and had joy to find water for night and morning, and greasewood and dead mesquite wood for a fire. The night had turned chill and Clodomiro spread the *serape* of Doña Jocasta over a heap of flowering greasewood branches. It was very quiet compared with the other camps on the trail, and had a restful air of comfort, and of that Jocasta spoke.

"Always the fear is here, señor," she said touching her breast. "All the men and guns of Ramon Rotil did not make that fear go quiet. Every cañon we crossed I was holding my breath for fear of hidden men of José Perez! You did not see him in the land where he is strong; but men of power are bound to him there in the south, and —- against one woman —- –"

"Señora, I do not think you have read the papers given to you by Padre Andreas to put with the others given by General Rotil," was Kit's quiet comment. He glanced toward the well where the boy was dipping water into a wicker bottle. "Have you?"

"No, señor, it is my permit to be passed safely by all the men of Ramon Rotil," she said. "That I have not had need of. Also there is the record that the American murder at Granados was the crime of Conrad."

"But, señora, there is one other paper among them. —- I would have told you yesterday if I had known your fear. I meant to wait until the trail was ended, but —- –"

"Señor!" she breathed leaning toward him, her great eyes glowing with dreadful question, "*Señor!*"

"I know the paper, for I signed it," said Kit staring in the leaping blaze. "So did the padre. It is the certificate of the burial of José Perez."

"Señor! *Madre de Dios!*" she whispered.

"Death reached him on his own land, señora. We passed the grave the first day of the trail."

Her face went very white as she made the sign of the cross.

"Then he —- Ramon —- –?"

"No, —- the general did not see Perez on the trail. He tried to escape from Cavayso and the man sent a bullet to stop him. It was the end."

She shuddered and covered her eyes.

Kit got up and walked away. He looked back from where he tethered the mules for the night, but she had not moved. The little crucifix was in her hand, he thought she was praying. There were no more words to be said, and he did not go near her again that night. He sent Clodomiro with her *serape* and pillow, and when the fire died down to glowing ash, she arose and went to the couch prepared. She went without glance to right or left —- the great fear had taken itself away!

Clodomiro rolled himself in a *serape* not far from her place of rest, but Kit Rhodes slept with the packs and with two guns beside him. From the start on the trail no man had touched his outfit but himself. He grinned sometimes at thought of the favorable report the men of Rotil would deliver to their chief, —- for the Americano had taken all personal care of the packs and chests of Doña Jocasta! He was as an owl and had no human need of sleep, and let no man help him.

The trail to the cañon of the Rio Seco was a hard trail, and a long day, and night caught them ere they reached the rim of the dry wash where, at long intervals, rain from the hills swept down its age-old channel for a brief hour.

Doña Jocasta, for the first time, had left the saddle and crept to the rude couch afforded by the piled-up blankets in the wagon; Clodomiro drove; and Kit, with the mules, led the way.

A little water still swished about in their water bottles, but not enough for the mules. He was more anxious than he dared betray, for it was twenty miles to the lower well of La Partida, and if by any stroke of fortune Cap Pike had failed to make good —- Cap was old, and liable to —- –

Then through the dusk of night he heard, quite near in the trail ahead, a curious thing, the call of a bird —- and not a night bird!

It was a tremulous little call, and sent a thrill of such wild joy through his heart that he drew back the mule with a sharp cruel jerk, and held his breath to listen. Was he going *loco* from lack of sleep, —- lack of water, —- and dreams of —- –

It came again, and he answered it as he plunged forward down a barranca and up the other side where a girl sat on a roan horse under the stars: —- his horse! also his girl!

If he had entertained any doubts concerning the last —- but he knew now he never had; a rather surprising fact considering that no word had ever been spoken of such ownership! —- they would have been dispelled by the way she slipped from the saddle into his arms.

"Oh, and you didn't forget! you didn't forget!" she whimpered with her head hidden against his breast. "I —- I'm mighty glad of that. Neither did I!"

"Why, Lark-child, you've been right alongside wherever I heard that call ever since I rode away," he said patting her head and holding her close. He had a horrible suspicion that she was crying, —- girls were mysterious! "Now, now, now," he went on with a comforting pat to each word, "don't worry about anything. I'm back safe, though in big need of a drink, —- and luck will come your way, and —- –"

She tilted her cantin to him, and began to laugh.

"But it has come my way!" she exulted. "O Kit, I can't keep it a minute, Kit —- we did find that sheepskin!"

"What? A sheepskin?" He had no recollection of a lost sheepskin.

"Yes, Cap Pike and I! In the bottom of an old chest of daddy's! We're all but crazy because it came just when we were planning to give up the ranch if we had to, and now that you are here —- !" her sentence ended in a happy sigh of utter content.

"Sure, now that I'm here," he assented amicably, "we'll stop all that moving business —- *pronto*. That is if we live to get to water. What do you know about any?"

"Two barrels waiting for you, and Cap rustling firewood, but I heard the wagon, and —- –"

"Sure," he assented again. "Into the saddle with you and we'll get there. The folks are all right, but the cayuses —- –"

A light began to blaze on the level above, and the mules, smelling water, broke into a momentary trot and were herded ahead of the two who followed more slowly, and very close together.

Cap Pike left the fire to stand guard over the water barrels and shoo the mules away.

"Look who's here?" he called waving his hat in salute. "The patriots of Sonora have nothing on you when it comes to making collections on their native heath! I left you a poor devil with a runt of a burro, a cripple, and an Indian kid, and you've bloomed out into a bloated aristocrat with a batch of high-class army mules. And say, you're just in time, and you don't know it! We're in at last, by Je-rusalem, we're *in*!"

Kit grinned at him appreciatively, but was too busy getting water to ask questions. The wagon was rattling through the dry river bed and would arrive in a few minutes, and the first mules had to be got out of the way.

"You don't get it," said Billie alongside of him. "He means war. We're in!"

"With Mexico? *Again?*" smiled Kit skeptically.

"No —- something real —- helping France!"

"No!" he protested with radiant eyes. "Me for it! Say, children, this is some homecoming!"

The three shook hands, all talking at once, and Kit and Billie forgot to let go.

"Of course you know Cap swore an alibi for you against that suspicion Conrad tried to head your way," she stated a bit anxiously. "You stayed away so long!"

"Yes, yes, Lark-child," he said reassuringly, "I know all that, and a lot more. I've brought letters of introduction for the government to some of Conrad's useful pacifist friends along the border. Don't you fret, Billie boy; the spoke we put in their wheel will overturn their applecart! The only thing worrying me just now, —- beautifullest! —- is whether you'll wait for me till I enlist, get to France, do my stunt to help clean out the brown rats of the world, and come back home to marry you."

"Yip-pee!" shrilled Pike who was slicing bacon into a skillet. "I'm getting a line now on how you made your other collections!"

Billie laughed and looked up at him a bit shyly.

"I waited for you before without asking, and I reckon I can do it again! I'm —- I'm wonderfully happy —- for I didn't want you to worry over coming home broke —- and —- –"

"Whisper, Lark-child. *I'm not!*"

"What?"

"Whisper, I said," and he put one hand over her mouth and led her over to the little gray burro. "Now, not even to Pike until we get home, Billie, —- but I've come out alive with the goods, while every other soul who knew went 'over the range'! Buntin' carries your share. I knew you were sure to find the sheepskin map sooner or later," he lied glibly, "but luck didn't favor me hanging around for it. I had to get it while the getting was good, but we three are partners for keeps, Buntin' is yours, and I'll divide with Pike out of the rest."

Billie touched the pack, tried to lift it, and stared.

"You're crazy, Kit Rhodes!"

"Too bad you've picked a crazy man to marry!" he laughed, and took off the pack. "Seventy-five pounds in that. I've over three hundred. Lark-child, if you remember the worth of gold per ounce, I reckon you'll see that there won't need to be any delay in clearing off the ranch debts, —- not such as you would notice! and maybe I might qualify as a ranch hand when I come back, —- even if I couldn't hold the job the first time."

"O Kit! O Cap! O me!" she whispered chantingly. "Don't you dare wake me up, for I'm having the dream of my life!"

But he caught her, drew her close and kissed her hair rumpled in the desert wind.

And as the wagon drew into the circle of light, that was the picture Doña Jocasta saw from the shadows of the covered wagon: —- young love, radiant and unashamed!

She stared at them a moment strangely in a sudden mist of tears, as Clodomiro jumped down and arranged for her to alight. Cap Pike looking up, all but dropped the coffeepot.

"Some little collector —- that boy!" he muttered, and then aloud, "You *Kit!*"

Kit turned and came forward leading Billie, who suddenly developed panic at vision of the most beautiful, tragic face she had ever seen.

"Some collector!" murmured Cap Pike forgetting culinary operations to stare. "Shades of Sheba's queen!"

But Kit, whose days and nights of Mesa Blanca and Soledad had rather unfitted him for hasty adjustments to conventions, or standardized suspicion regarding the predatory male, held the little hand of Billie very tightly, and did not notice her gasp of amazement. He went forward to assist Doña Jocasta, whose hesitating half glance about her only enhanced the wonder of jewel-green eyes whose beauty had been theme of many a Mexic ballad.

For these were the first Americanos she had ever met, and it was said in the south that Americanos might be wild barbaros, —- though the señor of the songs —- –

The señor of the songs reached his hand and made his best bow as he noted her sudden shrinking.

"Here, Doña Jocasta, are friends of good heart. We are now on the edge of the lands of La Partida, and this little lady is its padrona waiting to give you welcome at the border. Folks, this is Señora Perez who has escaped from hell by help of the guns of El Gavilan."

"Doña Jocasta!" repeated Cap Pike standing in amazed incredulity with the forgotten skillet at an awkward angle dripping grease into the camp fire, but his amazement regarding personality did not at all change his mental attitude as to the probable social situation. "Some collector, Brother, but hell in Sonora isn't the only hell you can blaze the trail to with the wrong combination!"

Kit turned a silencing frown on the philosopher of the skillet, but Billie went toward the guest with outstretching hands.

"Doña Jocasta, oh!" she breathed as if one of her fairy tales of beauty had come true, and then in Spanish she added the sweet gracious old Castillian welcome, "Be at home with us on your own estate, Señora Perez."

Jocasta laid her hands on the shoulder of the girl, and looked in the clear gray eyes.

"You are Spanish, Señorita?"

"My grandmother was."

"Thanks to the Mother of God that you are not a strange Americana!" sighed Jocasta in sudden relief. Then she turned to her American courier and guard and salvation over the desert trails.

"I saw," she said briefly. "She is as the young sister of me who —- who is gone to God! Make yourself her guard forever, Don Pajarito. May you sing many songs together, and have no sorrows."

After the substantial supper, Kit heard at first hand all the veiled suspicion against himself as voiced in the fragment of old newspaper wrapped around Fidelio's tobacco, and he and Doña Jocasta spread out the records written by the padre, and signed by Jocasta and the others, as witness of how Philip Singleton met death in the arroya of the cottonwoods.

"It is all here in this paper," said Jocasta, "and that is best. I can tell the alcalde, yes, but if an —- an accident had come to me on the trail, the words on the paper would be the safer thing."

"But fear on the trail is gone for you now," said Kit smiling at her across the camp fire. Neither of them had said any word of life at Mesa Blanca or Soledad, or of the work of Tula at the death.

The German had strangled a priest, and escaped, and in ignorance of trails had ridden into a quicksand, and that was all the outer world need know of his end!

The fascinated eyes of Billie dwelt on Jocasta with endless wonder.

"And you came north with the guns and soldiers of Ramon Rotil, —- how wonderful!" she breathed. "And if the newspapers tell the truth I reckon he needs the guns all right! Cap dear, where is that one José Ortego rode in with from the railroad as we were leaving La Partida?"

"In my coat, Honey. You go get it —- you are younger than this old-timer."

Jocasta followed Billie with her eyes, though she had not understood the English words between them. It was not until the paper was unfolded with an old and very bad photograph of Ramon Rotil staring from the front page that she whispered a prayer and reached out her hand. The headline to the article was only three words in heavy type across the page: "Trapped at last!"

But the words escaped her, and that picture of him in the old days with the sombrero of a peon on his head and his audacious eyes smiling at the world held her. No picture of him had ever before come her way; strange that it should be waiting for her there at the border!

The Indian boy at sight of it, stepped nearer, and stood a few paces from her, looking down.

"It calls," he said.

It was the first time he had spoken except to make reply since entering the American camp. Doña Jocasta frowned at him and he moved a little apart, leaning, —- a slender dark, semi-nude figure, against the green and yellow mist of a palo verde tree, —- listening with downcast eyes.

Doña Jocasta looked from the pictured face to the big black letters above.

"Is it a victorious battle, for him?" she asked and Kit hesitated to make reply, but Billie, not knowing reason for silence, blurted out the truth even while her eyes were occupied by another column.

"Not exactly, señora. But here is something of real interest to you, something of Soledad — oh, I *am* sorry!"

"What does it say, —- Soledad?"

"See! —- I forgot you don't know the English!"

Troops from the south to rescue Don José Perez from El Gavilan at Soledad turn guns on that survival of old mission days, and level it to the ground. Soledad was suspected as an ammunition magazine for the bandit chief, and it is feared Señor Perez is held in the mountains for ransom, as no trace of him has been found.

"Now you've done it," remarked Kit, and Billie turned beseeching eyes on the owner of Soledad, and repeated miserably —- "I *am* so sorry!"

But Doña Jocasta only lifted her head with a certain disdain, and veiled the emerald eyes slightly.

"So!" she murmured with a shrug of the shoulder. "It is then a bandit he is called in the words of the American newspaper?"

Cap Pike not comprehending the rapid musical Spanish, leaned forward fishing for a coal to light his pipe, noting her voice and watching her eyes.

"There you have it already!" he muttered to Kit. "All velvet, and mad as hell!"

Billie, much bewildered, turned to Kit as for help, but the slender hand of Doña Jocasta reached out pointing to the headlines.

"And —- this?" she said coldly. "It is, you say, not victorious for Ramon Rotil, that —- bandit?"

"It says, señora," hesitated Billie, "that he is hid in the hills, and —- –"

"That we know," stated Doña Jocasta, "what other thing?"

"'He has a wound and was carried by his men to one of his retreats, a hidden place,'" read Billie slowly, translating into Spanish as she went on. "That is all except that the Federals had to retreat temporarily because a storm caused trouble and washed out a bridge over which their ammunition train has to go. The place of the accident is very bad. Timber and construction engineers are being rushed to service there, but for a few days luck is with the Hawk."

"So! —- For a few days!" repeated Doña Jocasta in the cool sweet voice. "In a few days Ramon Rotil could cross Mexico. He is El Gavilan!"

Things were coming too fast for Billie. She regarded the serenity of Doña Jocasta with amazement, and tried to imagine how she would feel if enemy guns battered down the old walls of Granados, or —- thought of terror —- if Kit should be held in the hills and tortured for ransom!

"Speaking of floods," remarked Pike in amiable desire to bridge over an awkward pause, "we've used half the water we brought, and need to make a bright and early start tomorrow. Rio Seco is no garden spot to get caught in short of water. Our La Partida mules are fresh as daisies right off a month of range, but yours sure look as if they had made the trip."

"What does he say, —- the old señor?" asked Doña Jocasta.

Billie translated for her, whereupon she arose and summoned Clodomiro by a gesture.

"My bed," she said briefly, "over there," and she indicated a thicket of greasewood the wagon had passed on their arrival. "Also this first night of safety you will be the sentinel to keep guard that Señor Rhodes may at last have sleep. All the danger trail he had none."

Cap Pike protested that he do guard duty, but the smile of Doña Jocasta won her way.

"He is younger and not weary, señor. It is good for him, and it pleases me," she said.

"The camp is yours," he agreed weakly, and against his better judgment. He did not like Indians who were like "sulky slim brown dumb snakes"; that was what he muttered when he looked at Clodomiro. In his irritation at the Indian's silence it didn't even occur to him that he never had known any snakes but dumb ones.

But if the voice of Clodomiro was uncannily silent, his eyes spoke for him as they followed Doña Jocasta. Kit could only think of a lost, homesick dog begging for the scent of the trail to his own kennel. He said so to Billie as he made her bed in the camp wagon.

"Cap and I will be right here at the hind wheels," he promised. "Yes, —- sure, I'll let the Indian ride herd for the night. Doña Jocasta is right, it's his turn, and we seem to have passed the danger line."

"Knock wood!" cautioned Billie.

So he rapped his head with his knuckles, and they laughed together as young happy things do at trifles. Then he stretched himself for sleep under the stars and almost within arm's reach of the girl —- the girl who had ridden to meet him in the night, the wonderful girl who had promised to wait until he came back from France … of course he could get into the army *now*! They would need men too badly to turn him down again. If there was a trifle of discrepancy in sight of his eyes —- which he didn't at all believe —- he had the dust now, also the nuggets, to buy any and all treatment to adjust *that* little matter. He had nearly four hundred pounds, aside from giving all he dared give at once as Tula's gift to those women of the slave raid. After the war was over he would find ways of again crossing over to the great treasure chest in the hidden cañon. The little information Pike had managed to convey to him about that sheepskin map told him that the most important indications had been destroyed during those years it had been buried for safe-keeping. The only true map in existence was the one in his own memory, —- no use to tell Pike and Billie that! He could leave them in comfort and content, and when he got back from France —- He wondered how long it would last —- the war. Hadn't the greatest of Americans tried three years ago to hammer the fact into the alleged brain pans of the practical politicians that the sooner the little old United States made guns, and ships, and flying machines for *herself*, the sooner she could help end that upheaval of hell in Europe?… and they wouldn't listen! Listen? —- They brought every ounce of influence they could round up to silence those facts, —- the eternally condemned ostriches sticking their own heads in the sand to blind the world to the situation! Now they were in, and he wondered if they had even ten rounds of ammunition for the cartridge belts of the few trained soldiers in service? They had not had even three rounds for the showy grand review attempted in Texas not long since; also the transportation had been a joke, some of the National Guards started, but never did arrive —- and France was a longer trail than Texas. God! they should be ready to fight as the French were ready, in twelve hours —- and it would have to be months —- a long unequal hell for a time over there, but only one finish, and the brown rats driven back to their den! After that the most wonderful girl would —- would —- would —- –

Then all the sleep due him on the sleepless trail settled over him like a net weighted, yet very caressing, and the world war and the wonderful girl drifted far away!

Beyond, on the other side of the fire, and out of the circle of light, Clodomiro bore the *serape* of Doña Jocasta, and made clear the place for her couch. She had returned to the light of the fire and was scanning again the annoying paper of the Americanos. Especially that remembered face of the audacious eyes. They were different eyes in these latter days, level and cynical, and sometimes cruel.

"He calls," said Clodomiro again beside her. She had not heard him, and turned in anger that he dare startle her.

"Who does he call?" she asked irritably tossing aside the paper.

"All Mexico, I think. All Mexico's heart," and he touched his breast. "Me, I do not sleep. I do your work and when the end of the trail is yours, I ask, Excellencia, that you send me back that I find him again, —- the Deliverer!"

"What did Ramon Rotil ever do for you that you fret like a chained coyote because his enemies are strong?"

"Not anything, Excellencia. Me, he would not know if I told him my name, but —- he is the Deliverer who will help the clans. Also, *she* would go, —- Tula. *Sangre de Christo!* there would be no chain strong enough to hold her back if his wounds cried for help."

"If—- his wounds cried for help!" repeated Doña Jocasta mechanically.

"It is true, Excellencia, El Gavilan was giving help to many people in the lands he crossed. Now the many will forget, and like a hawk with the weight of an arrow in his breast he will fly alone to a high nest of the hills. Death will nest with him there some night or some day, Excellencia. And the many will forget."

"Quiet you!" ordered Doña Jocasta angrily.

Abashed, Clodomiro went silent, and with a murmured apology took himself into the shadows.

She lifted the pictured face barely discernible now in the diminished light.

"And —- the many will forget!" she repeated irritably. "The boy has the truth of it, but if *she* had lived, so terribly wicked, —- so lost of God, I wonder if—- –"

She lifted her face looking up at the still stars as if for light on a thought, then flung her hands out despairingly and turned away to the couch by the green bush of fragrant yellow bloom.

But not to sleep. Long after the Americanos were wrapped in slumber a little blaze sent glimmer of light through the undergrowth, and she saw Clodomiro stretched beside the fire. He had tossed a bit of greasewood on the coals that he might again study the face of El Gavilan.

She had heard him say that if no desert wind lifted the sand he could follow to that hidden nest of the Hawk. It was very dark now except for glimmer of stars through lacy, slow-drifting clouds, —- there was no wind. Later there would be a waning moon! Much of every waking life is a dream, and her dreams were of the No Man's Land of the desert, —- the waterless trail from which she had been rescued for peace!

Twice during the night Kit roused from the depths sufficiently to realize that sleep is one of the greatest gifts to man. Once Clodomiro was stretched by the little fire inspecting the paper he could not read, the second time he thought Baby Bunting was nosing around trying to get close to human things. Both times he reached out his hands to the precious packs beside which he slept on the trail. All were safe, and he drifted again into a great ocean of slumber.

He was wakened at dawn by the voice of Cap Pike, keyed high for an ultra display of profanity.

"By the jumping Je-hosophat, I knew it!" he shrilled. "That's your latest collection, begod! I hoped he wouldn't, and knew he would! The all-firedest finest pair of mules on Granados, and every water bag in the outfit! Can you beat it?"

At the first shout Kit jumped to his feet, his eyes running rapidly over his pack saddle outfit. All was safe there, and as Billie lifted her head and looked at him drowsily over the edge of the wagon bed he realized that in the vital things of life all was well with his world.

"Let Sheba run your camp, and run it to hell, will you?" went on Cap Pike accusingly. He was thrashing around among the growth back of the Soledad outfit wagon where the mules had been tethered. "Two —- four —- six, and Baby Buntin' —- yes sir! Lit out by the dark of the moon, and left neither hide nor hair, —- "

"Oh, be reasonable, Cap!" protested Kit. "Buntin' isn't gone —- she's right alongside here, waiting for breakfast."

"You're shoutin' she's here; so is every dragged-to-death skate you hit camp with! It's Billie's crackerjack mules, the pick of the ranch, that the bare-legged greasy heathen hit the trail with! And every water bag!"

"Well," decided Kit, verifying the water statement by a glance at the barrels, "no one is to blame. The boy didn't want to come this trail. He stuck until we were over the rough of it, and then he cut loose. A pair of mules isn't so bad."

"Now, of course not!" agreed Cap sarcastically. "A mere A-number-one pair of mules belonging to another fellow is only a flea bite to offer a visitor for supper! Well, all *I* got to say —- –"

"Don't say it, Cap dear," suggested Billie. "The Indian was here because of Doña Jocasta, and *she* can't help it! As she doesn't understand English, she'll probably think you're murdering some of us over here. Whist now, and put your muzzle on! We'll get home without the two mules. I'll go and tell her that the hysterics is your way of offering morning prayers!"

She slipped away, laughing at his protests, but when a little past the fire place she halted, standing very still, peering beyond at something on the ground under the greasewood where the *serape* of Doña Jocasta had been spread. No *serape* or sleeper was there!

Kit noted her startled pause, and in a few strides was beside her; then, without a word, the two went forward together and he picked up the package of papers laid carefully under the greasewood. He knew without opening them what they were, —- the records made for her safety, and for his, in Soledad, place of tragedies.

"They are the papers I was to put on record for her in case —- Well, I'll do it, and you'll take care of the copies for her, Billie, and —- and do your best for the girl if a chance ever comes. We owe her a lot more than she will ever guess, —- our gold come out of Mexico under the guard arranged for her, and when I come back —- –"

"But Kit," protested Billie, "to think of her alone with that thieving Indian! He took flour and bacon too! And if she hopes to find her husband —- –"

"She doesn't," concluded Kit thoughtfully turning over the certificate signed by the padre and him, of the husband's safe burial in the sands of Soledad. He glanced at Billie in doubt. One never knew how safe it was to tell things, —- some things, —- to a woman; also Billie was so enchanted by Jocasta's sad beauty, and —- –

"No, I reckon she doesn't hope much along that line. She has probably gone back to the wilderness for another reason, —- one I never suspected until last night. And Lark-child, we won't talk about that, not at least till I return from the 'back of beyond' over there," and he pointed eastward where shafts of copper light touched the gray veil of the morning.

After his first explosion of amazement Cap Pike regarded the elopement, as he called it, very philosophically, considering his disgust over lost mules and flour and bacon.

"What did I tell you right here last night?" he demanded of Kit. "Soft as velvet and hard as hell, —- that's what I said! She looks to me like a cross between a saint in a picture frame and a love bird in a tree, and her eyes! Yet after all no man can reckon on that blood, —- she is only a girl of the hills down there, and the next we hear of her she'll likely be leaden' a little revolution of her own."

The young chap made no reply, but busied himself hastening a scant breakfast in order that the worn mules be got to water before the worst heat of a dry day. Also the losses to the culinary outfit did make problems for the trip.

Cap eyed him askance for a space, and then with a chuckle wilfully misconstrued his silence and lowered his tone.

"I don't blame you for feeling downhearted on your luck, Bub, for she sure was a looker! But it's all in a lifetime, and as you ramble along in years, you'll find that most any hombre can steal them, and take them home, but when it comes to getting a permanent clinch on the female affections —- –"

Billie, who was giving a short ration of water to the burro, called across to ask what Kit was laughing at in that hilarious way. She also stated that she did not think it a morning for hilarity, not at all! That wonderful, beautiful, mystery woman might be going to her death!

After the packs were all on, Cap Pike swung the mules of the first wagon into the home trail and passed over the mesa singing rakishly.

> Oh-h! Biddy McGee has been after me,
> Since I've been in the army!

And Billie turned in the saddle to take a last look over the trail where the woman of the emerald eyes had passed in the night.

"All my life I have looked, and looked into the beautiful mirages of the south desert wondering what would come out of it —- and *she* was the answer," she said, smiling at Kit. "Tomorrow I'll feel as if it was all a dream, all but the wonderful red gold, and you! Some fine day we'll take a little *pasear* down there, I'll follow that dream trail, and —- –"

"You will not!" decided the chosen of her heart with rude certainty. "The dreams of that land of mirages are likely to breed nightmares. You are on the right side of the border for women to stay. Our old American eagle is a pretty safe bird to roost with."

"Well," debated the only girl, "if it comes to that, Mexico also has the eagle, and had it first!"

"Yes, contrary child," he conceded, herding the mules into line, "so it has, —- but the eagle of Mexico is still philandering with a helmeted serpent. Wise gamblers reserve their bets on that game, we can only hope that the eagle fights its way free!"